TOKYO VANILLA

Thomas Boggs

Tokyo Vanilla

THE GAY MEN'S PRESS

First published 1998 by GMP Publishers Ltd,
P O Box 247, Swaffham PE37 8PA, England

A CIP catalogue record for this book is available
from the British Library

ISBN 0 85449 255 0

Distributed in Europe by Central Books,
99 Wallis Rd, London E9 5LN

Distributed in North America by InBook/LPC Group,
1436 West Randolph, Chicago, IL 60607

Distributed in Australia by Bulldog Books,
P O Box 300, Beaconsfield, NSW 2014

Printed and bound in the EU by The Cromwell Press,
Trowbridge, Wilts, England

For Ake

Book One: Secrets of the Rose

1

WHEN HE thought about it much later, Fumio was amazed that a tiny peephole — no more than a centimeter in diameter — had given him access to a whole new world, a whole new vision. For it was through this opening, in a manner of speaking, that he first encountered Tatsuya, the boy who was to loom so large in his life, and who would ultimately become his destroyer and his savior.

It had been a hot sultry evening in July, shortly after he'd first come up to Tokyo. At the time, Fumio was living in a small wooden two-story apartment house in Koenji, three stops on the Chuo Line from his university in Yotsuya. With the rainy season just over, the heat had begun in earnest, and the humidity still in the air and ground had turned the city into a dank, miserable hothouse. As it was Sunday, he'd stayed home all day reading comic books, trying to cool off by lying in the shade provided by the drawn curtains. But his window faced south, and by mid afternoon, the heat inside the apartment had become unbearable. Impatiently, he got up and stepped over to the tiny veranda to take in the futon he'd left out to air in the sun. The only view he had from his window was of the building next door. It was so close that he'd felt claustrophobic when he first moved in. Buildings in Tokyo stood so promiscuously near each other that true privacy was virtually nonexistent. But he'd learned to cope with it. It was part of living in the metropolis.

In any case, there was enough space on the veranda to hang up his washing on sunny days. And if he leaned out far enough, he could even get a narrow glimpse of the street below. Just now, he could see transparent, feverish ripples shimmering over the asphalt without the slightest breeze to cool them. The city appeared deserted. In this heat, no one who didn't have business outside had ventured out of their air-conditioned homes. Normally, these streets were filled with people. Fumio recalled how his first sight of the crowded masses of commuters, shoppers, and idlers in Shinjuku and Shibuya had almost panicked him. Back home, such numbers of people could only be seen at festival time. Indeed, during his first few weeks in Tokyo, every day had felt like festival.

As he took down his futon from the bamboo pole, he noted with displeasure that the people in the building opposite had their air conditioner on full, and it was blowing warm moist air straight up into his room. A trickle of sweat slid down his back. His tiny, six-mat room had only the barest necessities for survival, and naturally, this didn't include an air conditioner. He could only envy those college students who could afford to live in rooms with air conditioners and private baths. His family wasn't rich, and he had no relatives in Tokyo with whom he could board. His father had died when Fumio was only eight years old, and his mother had taken over the bicycle shop the family had run for two generations. She'd managed to raise Fumio and his older brother by the living eked out from the sale and repair of bicycles. They had barely managed to scrape together enough money to send Fumio to college. He couldn't afford many luxuries; the money he made from his part-time job as a tutor went mostly for food and necessities. Still, he'd managed to save up enough to buy the second-hand stereo, television set, and video-cassette player which took up most of the space of the room he lived in. There was a refrigerator in the kitchen, just in front of the water-closet next to the sink, and a two-burner gas range on which he cooked his meals. Otherwise, the only furnishing in his apartment was a bookshelf crammed with comic books, with an unplayed guitar leaning against it.

After putting away the futon in the closet, he went back to the window and whisked the curtains shut, keeping the window open for any breeze which might come. The sound of someone's television set came wafting up to him from downstairs. He pulled off his t-shirt and wiped his chest with it, then lay down on the tatami in only his shorts. What he missed most of all on hot summer afternoons like this was a breeze. Back in Nagano prefecture, in his hometown near the foot of the Central Japan Alps, he'd yearned to escape to the big city, and Tokyo had seemed the answer to all his dreams. He had been one of the top scholars in his high school and all his teachers had taken it for granted that he would go on to the capital for further education. When his mother and brother had come to the station to see him off, Fumio had confessed, half proud, half embarrassed, that Tokyo was where he planned to spend the rest of his life. But it was only now, after he'd come here, that he could look back at his own hometown with an objectivity which revealed to him how much he'd taken for granted back then: the clean air, the open spaces, the friendly townspeople. Above all, he missed the mountains. They'd always been there somewhere in the background, a solace for his restlessness.

He'd loved to lie on the floor of his room with all the windows open, and a view of the cool mountaintops towering in the west, cutting off the whole sky. The sound of cicadas crying in the nearby woods, accompanying the soft rustle of the bamboo blinds, had evoked a coolness which was deeper than all memory. The tinkle of the melting ice in the glass of cool barley tea his mother had brought up... Here the only breeze was the exhaust from the infernal air conditioner next door.

He thought of the research paper he still had to write for his economics class, and of the spoiled, pampered city children he tutored in the evenings. Sometimes his feelings of loneliness and boredom became overwhelming. The fast pace of Tokyo and the anonymous, cold cruelty of life in the big city was just too different from the easy-going lifestyle back in his own hometown, with the familiar faces and names he'd known all his life. Here, he knew no one but a handful of fellow students from Nagano. There was another month to go until the O-bon holidays, when he could take the train back west...

Suddenly the whole apartment began to shudder and tremble, and a hollow booming sound made the air reverberate. It was not an earthquake, but someone coming up the steps outside. Fumio listened carefully to the steps — a pair of them — walk past his apartment door and halt outside the room next door. He knew it was his neighbor,Tatsuya, bringing a girl back to his apartment. Stealthily, Fumio drew nearer to the wall, his heart beginning to quicken. Tatsuya, like himself, was a student at J University. Also like himself, Tatsuya was from the provinces, though in his case it was Ibaraki prefecture, a rice-growing region to the north of Tokyo. His family, too, was probably poor, as he had to live in the same cheap apartment building. Tatsuya had introduced himself to Fumio when he'd first moved in, but since then, though they greeted each other whenever they met, they hadn't become close friends. They should have been drawn to one another because they were two country bumpkins in the big city, but it hadn't happened. They were just too different.

Unlike Fumio, Tatsuya had taken to Tokyo like a fish to water, completely in his element, confident about his eventual success. He was an attractive, outgoing extrovert who seemed to have no trouble picking up girls. Yet, despite his seemingly effortless success rate (or, indeed, because of it), Tatsuya remained indefatigable in his pursuit of new conquests. He brought back a different girl to his room almost every weekend — Fumio knew so because the girls all made distinctive sounds when making love. Some whimpered softly through the whole act, others moaned in seemingly complaining tones, while others actually began sobbing as their pleasure became intense; still others cried out as if being beaten with a stick. Though it was torture to listen to all this while he himself was so starved for intimacy, Fumio had unwittingly become a connoisseur of these amatory soundtracks. In fact, he'd grown to depend on them for his own pleasure — the sordid pleasure of a listening addict. Knowing that Tatsuya always checked to see if Fumio's lights were out before making love, Fumio had often sat in his darkened room for hours on end, waiting for his neighbor to return. Whenever the lovemaking in the next room began, he could never resist joining in as a secret participant. The wall between the two rooms was so thin that he really couldn't help but hear quite clearly what was going on; furthermore, Tatsuya's bed was located flush against the wall, so that the plywood-thin layer acted almost as a sound board to amplify each creak and groan. Fumio had sometimes been wakened from a sound sleep by his neighbor's lovemaking.

Despite the pleasure he got out of it, though, this eavesdropping only made things worse for him. The so obvious evidence of his neighbor's promiscuous success only served to increase his own frustration and jealousy, sometimes to the point where it was this very jealousy which seemed to be the focus of his stimulation. Perhaps it was because he was still a virgin. Though already nineteen years old, an age when most Japanese boys nowadays had long lost their virginity, he could only imagine what it must be like to gratify a sensual longing which seemed to grow stronger by the day. Sometimes it became so overwhelming that he felt he was turning into a hopeless erotomaniac. The wastepaper basket in his room was always filled with balled-up tissues. It had gotten to the point where he felt ashamed to buy boxes of tissues at the Seven-Eleven, especially if there was a young girl behind the counter. He could understand the wry jokes of his friends — virgin, too, like himself — about getting blisters on the palms of their hands....

His almost constant sexual yearning could, he felt, easily be converted into an urge to commit a crime or some similar outrage against society. It was as if there was a deep well within himself which was a hollow, aching need for sex. He woke up every morning feeling he couldn't go another day without doing something about it. So this morning, after Tatsuya had left his room, Fumio had taken down the picture he normally kept hanging on the wall and drilled a tiny hole in that spot. He knew that Tatsuya's bed was just below this peephole, so he probably wouldn't be able to see very much, but when he put his eye to the hole, he'd discovered that a large mirror atop a dresser on the opposite side of the room gave him a fairly good view of the bed. And now he was sitting here, his skin sticky from sweat, listening for his chance to add an ocular thrill to his auditory one.

For a long time, the couple next door talked in low tones, with an occasional laugh from Tatsuya. The television was turned on, adding a barely audible background murmur of intermittent studio laughter, cut into at intervals by commercial jingles. The girl seemed to have gotten up to go to the kitchen. There was the sound of a faucet being turned on. Perhaps she was going to prepare something to eat. Fumio lay back to wait. It could take hours before anything started to happen. He tried to picture how the girl looked. Was she one of those sophisticated, distant beauties that could be seen on the trains dressed in Chanel suits and clutching their Louis Vuitton bags? Or was she like many of the girl students in his school who were supremely, arrogantly confident that they were at the very peak of their beauty, and desired by all men, young and old? A boy with Tatsuya's looks would have no hesitation about striking up a conversation with such a girl and inviting her to a meal, and then back to his apartment, despite the fact that he was a poor, penniless student. Any girl would gladly welcome a chance to become intimate with such an attractive boy.

Fumio wondered what went through a girl's mind when she accepted an invitation to a boy's apartment. She obviously knew what it implied, and what it would lead to, but did she allow herself the pleasure of anticipation, or did she pretend to herself that she had accepted it in all innocence? How enviable an attractive girl's life must be. All she had to do was make herself look as beautiful as possible, and wait for a boy to come along and flirt with her. She had the luxury of choosing whether to accept or decline an invitation: to give the shy nod or to dip into her repertory of rejections.

Suddenly Fumio became aware that the only sound coming from the next room was the television. Quietly, he got to his feet and lifted the picture off its nail. He put his eye to the hole. The curtains in the next room had been drawn, creating an eerie underwater atmosphere. The television screen emitted a flickering glow into the gloom, turning everything a pale blue. In the mirror on the opposite wall Fumio could see two pairs of legs, one pair muscular and hairy, the other smooth and slim, doing a strange dance. As he watched, one of the girl's knees came up slowly, very slowly, until it couldn't rise any higher, then descended again with the same somnolent motion. Fumio actually began shivering with excitement, an excitement which surpassed anything he'd ever felt before. Rather than being sexual, though, it was more akin to the thrill of doing something illicit, like shoplifting or theft. He glued his eye to the hole, but he could see nothing more than the girl's smooth legs twining themselves like snakes around the other pair, then slowly unravelling, their toes — painted scarlet — straining, clenching, then unclenching in a spasmodic manner. The random, stealthy creaking of the bed beneath them gradually assumed a regular rhythm. Fumio listened carefully in the enforced silence for the moments when the girl's attempts at suppression became more and more strained, until the silence had modulated, almost unnoticed, into the tiniest germs of sound. Barely noticeable at first, soft, gentle moans gradually fluctuated in pitch, and steadily increased in volume, until the initial brave resistance had given way to a surrender more and more complete. Inevitably, as always, the point was eventually reached when any attempt at resisting was abandoned.

This one was a whimperer. Fumio felt so dizzy he was afraid he might faint. For about five minutes, there was an eerie, lamenting sound which, if one didn't know better, might well have been a little girl crying over a lost doll, or a tiny kitten mewling after its mother. Then the whimpering began to die down, after which there was silence for a long while, broken only by the noise from the television.

The blood pounding in Fumio's ears was like a roar. There was a loud creak, and Fumio caught a brief glimpse of the girl as she flashed past. She remained out of view for some time. In the meanwhile, Tatsuya was apparently lying on the bed smoking a cigarette, for blue smoke had begun curling up into Fumio's vision. Then the bed made another loud creak, and Fumio saw that Tatsuya had gotten up with the ashtray in his hand. He walked over to the dresser on the other side of the room and placed the ashtray atop it, stubbing out the cigarette he'd been smoking. In that spot he was almost completely visible from the peephole. He was still nude. Unaware that he was being watched, he gazed at himself in the mirror, pushing back his hair with both hands and turning his body slightly to the side. It was obvious that he was admiring his own body in the way that only attractive people can. In the mirror's reflection, Fumio noted how his full chest tapered down to his slim hips. From behind, the broadness of the shoulders only emphasized the narrowness of the waist and hips. A shallow groove ran down the smoothly tapered back. The whole body was tanned so deeply that the white outline of the tiny swimsuit Tatsuya had worn to the beach this summer was clearly visible, a phantom bikini clinging so tightly to the skin that it made actual nudity even more erotic.

Fumio's whole body felt electrified, as if charged with a mysterious secret energy. Deep in his belly, a sudden churning sensation made him feel almost nauseous. With a dawning sense of wonder, he recalled another time when he'd felt something similar; back in high school, he and his friends had come across a picture book in the art room which showed classic works of Western art. Many of the paintings had depicted male nudes, and Fumio still remembered the distinct feeling of embarrassment he'd felt then. And that embarrassment had been accompanied, like a treacherous counterpoint, by the discovery of a secret melody whose music he knew he would never be able to reveal to his classmates. He'd always admired and envied boys who were more attractive than himself, but it was only now that he suddenly realized how he'd always been hoping for a chance like this to gaze at another boy's body to his heart's content without the need to feel self-conscious about it.

Almost as if Tatsuya secretly knew he was being watched, he flexed his shoulders and back, lightly rubbed his hand over his chest and started to turn around, perhaps to admire the view of his own backside. Fumio held his breath with all the sensation of someone about to dive deep underwater. He caught himself hoping for a glimpse of the other boy's genitals. A fierce shame swept over him, making the surface of his skin flush, prickling the nape of his neck. His heart began to pound and he felt his breath come short. He was almost relieved when the girl came back and began dressing. Tatsuya, too, began to dress. Fumio, afraid his eye might be noticed gleaming in the tiny hole, silently hung the picture back on its nail. Then, shakily, he sank down cross-legged onto the tatami. His heart continued to pound hard for quite some time after the couple in the next room had resumed their normal conversation. Mixed with the lingering excitement of having trespassed into forbidden territory was an indescribable shame. Yet somehow, this very shame only seemed to enhance the value of the unspeakable act he'd just committed.

2

AT FUMIO'S university, there was a small, informal network of boys from Nagano. Their leader was an older boy in the judo club who had organized some get-togethers and drinking parties in the early weeks of April to welcome the freshmen, but because he was too busy lately to see them very much, the boys had taken it on themselves to keep up the network, getting together sometimes at one or another of their apartments, or — like tonight — meeting in Shinjuku for a drinking party. Fumio felt most comfortable around these boys. Though they all hailed from different towns and high schools in Nagano, here in Tokyo they felt drawn to one another by a mutual sense of loneliness and estrangement. In their various attempts to adjust to life in the metropolis, they had experienced a feeling of bonding which they would never have done back home.

One of the things which brought them together was a shared anxiety over their perception that people in Tokyo looked down on anyone who wasn't from the city. Like his friends, Fumio, even after living here for five months, still couldn't shake his complex about being a small-town boy. Perhaps he was a little too sensitive to slights, for it seemed to him that Tokyoites never let him forget that he was a provincial. So he really only felt relaxed around friends like Harada, Mori, and Kurita; with them he never had to put up his guard or be wary of accidentally letting a provincial expression slip out in his speech.

The plaza outside the east exit of Shinjuku station was unusually crowded tonight. No doubt it was due to the continued sultriness of the evenings; the weather forecasters had lately taken to dubbing these nights when the temperature stayed above 20 degrees, 'tropical nights'. When he arrived at the designated rendezvous point —the sidewalk before the Alta building — Fumio saw that Mori, as usual, had arrived early. "Hi, what's up?"

Mori returned the greeting with a shy nod. He was a quiet boy, a little overweight, whose expressionless face behind his thick glasses seemed to hide numerous secrets from the world. His father was a doctor in Nagano City, and could afford to send his son a generous allowance each month. And though Mori was modest and unassuming about it, the spacious apartment he lived in was the envy of his friends. Fumio wiped his forehead with the back of his hand. "I don't know about you, but I sure could use a drink tonight."

"Why? Did you have a hard day?"

Fumio nodded. The pupil he'd tutored this afternoon had been a particularly loathsome nine-year-old who'd acted the complete spoiled brat, refusing to listen to him, pretending not to understand the simplest instructions. Several times he'd been on the verge of slapping her. There were some parents who actually encouraged a tutor to use force if necessary, but Fumio didn't want to hit the child. He only wished her parents would discipline her more. The mother was a very kind woman — perhaps a little too kind — and Fumio was fond of her. She never failed to serve him the choicest cakes when she brought in the tea at the four o'clock break. "If it wasn't for her mother, I'd quit."

"And a good tutor like you would be hard to replace, too."

"That's not true. If anything, it's the opposite: a good position is hard to replace." Like many students attending good universities, Fumio worked part-time as a private tutor for elementary and junior high-school children. It was the easiest work to be found, and paid quite well — three to four thousand yen an hour. He had to travel to the students' homes, of course, but he didn't mind. Travel expenses were paid, and the home visits helped him find his way around Tokyo. Thanks to them, he was gradually learning the map of Tokyo. Names which he had known only through books and television had now become familiar, real landmarks to him.

"I wonder what's taking Kurita and Harada?"

"Surely they haven't lost their way? Shinjuku is practically their second home now." They'd naturally reverted to Nagano dialect, which they strictly avoided with anyone outside their circle for fear of being ridiculed. Of course they'd both mastered Tokyo — or 'standard' — speech. But somehow, Fumio felt most comfortable hearing the assuring sounds of Nagano.

"I think I see them now." In the jostling crowd of people emerging from an underground passageway, they spotted their two friends walking together. Kurita, a tall, slender boy with large eyes and a sensitive-looking face, was the most attractive of the four, while Harada, a chunky sportsman type who'd played catcher for his high-school baseball team, was the acknowledged leader and comedian of the group.

"Sorry. Did we keep you waiting? We were about to be picked up by a couple of office ladies, and —"

"Sure, sure."

"Well, shall we go?" They proceeded without any further comment to their usual spot, a pub in the Shinjuku Kabukicho area called Gauchos, located on the second floor of a game center. It usually remained open till two o'clock on weekday nights. When they got there, it was smoke-filled and lively. Most of the customers were students — some of them suspiciously like high-school students. The music was current and the waiters young and loud-voiced — they had to be, for their shouted orders to the kitchen had to compete with the loud rock music blasting out of speakers.

The boys all ordered beers. As Fumio took his first refreshing drink, he felt an elbow prod him in the ribs. "Look," Harada said. He nodded to a group of girls sitting two tables away. "What do you say? After we have a couple of drinks to work up our courage, how about if we go over and ask them to join us?"

"I don't know..." Though he'd had numerous crushes on girls all through junior high and high school, Fumio had never been brave enough to talk to anyone he really cared about. It had gotten to the point where he felt that an unconfessed one-sided love was all he could ever hope for. He knew the main reason for his shyness: he wasn't attractive enough to have a girl reciprocate his feelings. And because of this, he lacked the confidence to make small talk with girls. Though it was said that some boys succeeded merely by their ability to keep girls laughing, Fumio had learned that his talent for comedy was limited also. So he could easily imagine how girls viewed him — a quiet, somewhat dull boy, not worth the effort to get to know. If he were a girl, he would quite agree with this assessment of him. Perhaps that was why he was so envious of attractive boys. They seemed to have an inborn confidence which bred success in anything they tried. No doubt his next-door neighbor, Tatsuya, had the looks and confidence to pick up a girl in a place like this, but such things just didn't happen to people like Fumio. It was a depressing thought.

"Wait till we've had a few more beers," said Kurita to Harada. "Then maybe he'll agree."

"Right."

"I only hope none of the other guys here get the same idea before then." Kurita peered around at the various tables of young men boisterously shouting each other down, challenging each other to drinking contests. "Because I would hate for them to snatch a possible treat from under our noses."

Harada laughed. "You sound almost desperate, Kurita."

"I am. Listen, I'm telling you if I don't have a woman soon, I might end up doing something strange."

"Something strange?" Mori peered at Kurita with a curious expression.

"Yes. I get strange thoughts in my head."

"Such as — ?"

"Listen, you guys," interrupted Harada. "If that's the way you feel, I know just the thing for you."

"What?" They all turned to him.

"You know I work part-time as a furniture mover..." Harada began telling them about how his co-workers had taken him along to visit a 'fashion health' parlor recently. The others listened in excitedly, especially Mori, who kept asking for more details about the experience. Fumio, looking at his usually taciturn friend, was surprised at the extent of his interest. He found it hard to believe that Mori had harbored such sensual cravings. His eyes actually seemed to glow in the reflected light from the imitation chandelier over their table.

Finally Mori couldn't take it anymore. "Why don't we all go tonight?" he stammered, looking around at the others for support. Fumio seconded it, surprising himself with his own enthusiasm. He was just drunk enough to brave it, provided the others went along, too. "How about it?"

Harada laughed. "If you guys are so willing, I'm the last person in the world to be a party-pooper."

After having a few more beers to ensure that their initial resolve wouldn't wither, they let Harada lead them to the place he'd visited with his co-workers. It was called Petit Doll and was located in the step-down basement of a nearby building. As they reached the bottom of the steps a kindly-looking man greeted them smiling, looking at each of them in turn.

"Is this the first time for you gentlemen?"

The boys murmured a vague reply but the man quickly put them at their ease, explaining in a business-like way that a short time would cost 10,000 yen. Fumio thought it a little expensive but well worth it — as the price for exorcising his demons.

After each boy had paid the man, they were led along a corridor lined with doors. Each door had a round window in it about shoulder high, some of them covered with a towel from the inside. The man passed by the covered ones but stopped at the first one which wasn't. He knocked on the door before inviting them to peer inside. One by one the boys stepped up to the window. Inside, they saw a small room with a single bed, on which a girl in a bathrobe reclined, reading a magazine. At the sound of the knock she'd looked up and was now smiling and waving. She was about their age or younger, and very pretty. There was nothing about her to suggest she worked in the sex industry; she could have passed for a college girl, one of their classmates.

"This is Kaori," said the man.

"She's beautiful," murmured Kurita.

The boys could barely contain their excitement as they were led to the next uncovered window where the introduction was repeated. This girl, too, was quite attractive — the very image of a popular starlet on a TV commercial for Shiseido cosmetics.

After they'd inspected about nine of the girls, their guide said, "Take your pick." The boys looked at each other with delight; the girls were so much younger and prettier than they'd expected. They stated their choices and were led off to their rooms one by one. On an impulse, Fumio had picked the one called Mariko, though he had no idea why. When the time had come to make his choice, his mind had gone blank, and he'd merely nodded at the door in front of which he was standing.

As her door was opened, she got up from her bed with a look of welcome. "Please come in." Nervously Fumio stepped in. Mariko seemed to be quite at ease, not self-conscious at all about the sort of work she was doing. Smilingly, she introduced herself with a cute bow and asked him his name.

"Are you a student?"

"Do I look it?"

She smiled. "We get many students. Here, let me help you." Before he knew it, Fumio was allowing himself to be undressed by her. It all went so smoothly that he was soon standing naked before her as she hung up his jeans and shirt and neatly folded his underpants and placed them atop a chair. As she slipped a towel around his middle, she said, "Right this way, please."

To his surprise, he was led outside, then down the corridor to a large shower room at the far end. There, other girls were helping their clients get cleaned up. Fumio tried not to look at the others. Mariko had him sit on a small plastic bath seat shaped curiously like a throne, then soaped him up and rinsed him clean with a hand-held shower. After briskly drying him off with a towel she led him back to the room. There, she casually hung the towel over the round window and took off her bathrobe without the slightest hesitation. She was naked underneath. Fumio tried not to stare. They got on the bed.

"Is this your first time?" asked Mariko. His pride wounded, Fumio said nothing, but she only smiled and made him lie back. With a quick glance at his face, she ran her hand over his chest and then downward, past his belly. Quite boldly, she began touching him with an intimacy which had hitherto been his own prerogative. Fumio closed his eyes and willed himself to relax. His body felt all tensed up. After a while, Mariko whispered, "You're a little tired tonight, perhaps?" Wordlessly Fumio nodded. "Would you like to kiss, then?" He opened his eyes and brought his face to hers but she pulled away.

"I'm sorry, not the mouth." She half-sat up and leaned her body over his face. This was what he'd dreamed of so often back in his lonely apartment, but strangely enough, now that he was finally doing it, he felt a little detached from it all. It turned out that having sex with a girl was not the wild erotic thrill he'd thought it would be. Perhaps it had all been built up too much... by his friends, by society, by the media. He even felt a little silly being here like this. And he suspected that Mariko, despite her solicitude, had her mind on something else. Perhaps on someone like Tatsuya.

"At last," she whispered. She became so intent on what she was doing that Fumio, with some detachment, was able to study the look of concentration on her face. But soon — all too soon — his thoughts became centered on the rapidly approaching culmination. He closed his eyes as he heard her gasp: "Oh, my. So much!" His first thought was: Is this all there is? 10,000 yen just for this, gone in a flash. His next thought was: It's so much better doing it by myself. But he didn't let his disappointment show.

"Thank you," he said awkwardly. "You're really nice." She cleaned him up as efficiently as she'd done everything else. When he was dressed again, she showed him back to the waiting room where he sat down on the tiny sofa to wait for the others. He'd been the first one to finish, but a few moments later Harada returned, followed by Kurita. Both of them looked a little sheepish, and all three boys avoided looking at one another. When Mori still hadn't shown up after five more minutes they began to joke about it.

"Boy, I wish I could have taken as long."

"He's making sure he's getting his money's worth."

"Good for him."

Finally Mori came back, accompanied by his girl. As if this were the signal, the other girls (who must have been waiting in the corridor) also came out to the waiting-room to thank the boys for coming to Petit Doll. Then they lined up and bowed their goodbyes, for all the world like maids at an inn, or the uniformed female clerks at a department store. The man who'd been their guide was standing just outside the entrance holding several cheap clear-vinyl umbrellas. "It's beginning to rain outside. Perhaps you'll need these. They're a service of the house."

"Thank you."

He bowed. "Thank you. Please come again."

Outside it had indeed begun to drizzle. Putting up their umbrellas, the boys laughingly teased Mori about taking so long to finish, but he kept a serious expression, refusing to be drawn into their banter. At Shinjuku station the party split up, Harada and Kurita for the Keio Line, and Mori for the Odakyu Line. Fumio refused Mori's invitation to have a few more drinks before heading home, and went straight to the Chuo Line platform. As it was past midnight, the usual platform was closed for the night. Fumio had to go all the way to where the Sobu Line usually stopped. It was quite crowded; as the time for the last train neared, everyone seemed slightly tipsy, and disheveled salarymen were wobbling slightly as they waited. After about three minutes, the train came in, right on schedule.

Fumio stepped in and found a spot in the aisle where he could get a good grip on a strap. After a seemingly interminable wait, the train finally started up with a lurch, as if even the driver were drunk, and the slow, monotonous clacking of the rails commenced. Hanging onto his strap, Fumio swayed with the motions of the train, allowing himself to be buffeted about by the passengers on either side of him. He didn't care. His eyes were fixed on the myriad lights of the city glittering beyond the train windows, cold, heartless and eternal. He felt depressed. Tonight's experience was supposed to be the turning point in his life, the big step he'd been waiting for. He'd assumed that once he slept with a girl all his demons would be vanquished, all his doubts put to rest. He would become a man, as the saying went. But in fact he didn't feel as if he'd accomplished anything at all — only verified his own inadequacy.

When he compared his miserable experience tonight with what he so often overheard in his neighbor's apartment, he felt ashamed. Tatsuya was such a skilled lover that Fumio's adventure couldn't even be put in the same category. And Tatsuya got it for free, as often as he liked, from any girl he wanted, whereas Fumio had to pay a professional who was only doing a job, doing him the favor of being nice for several minutes. Even Mori, with his plain-looking face and his soft, flabby body had apparently gotten more out of the experience.

The railroad car swayed slightly and he caught at the strap. A screeching sound came from the wheels below as the train took the curve just before Higashi Nakano. By the time he'd gotten off at

Koenji station and stepped out the south exit, the drizzle had let up and the air felt refreshingly clean. Fumio grimly twirled the cheap umbrella around his finger as he walked home through the empty streets. Tokyo at night, with all the store shutters closed and all the windows dark, was a different world. There was a thrilling sense of mystery in the air, a promise of all the endless possibilities awaiting a young man from the provinces. This was the magical city of his dreams, the one which appealed mutely to him whenever he was in an expansive mood.

He tried to imagine all the lives being lived in all these sleeping houses. Not a sound stirred the night. It was as if the sodden air had deadened every echo. His footsteps sounded loud as he walked down the street. He imagined someone lying awake in one of the houses and listening to him pass. He himself had often listened from his futon at night to homeward bound steps and occasional snatches of drunken singing.

In front of a closed pachinko parlor he found a vending machine which sold hot coffee. He slipped a hundred-yen coin into the slot and selected a can of Georgia. It clattered down to the receptacle with a clunking sound. He reached down, popped open its tab and took a sip. The taste was sickly sweet, coming after all the beers he'd had tonight, but somehow it seemed to brace him up. The sky above was a deep indigo which seemed to hover there like a suspended weight.

Suddenly the night was shattered by the noisy revving of a car engine. With a squealing of tires, a bright red convertible sports car came careening around the corner, its canvas top down. In it were two people, a young man and a woman, the latter in the driver's seat. As it flashed past, Fumio had just enough time to note the man waving at him. It was Tatsuya, with a wild, reckless look in his eyes. The woman with him seemed older and richer than the usual girls he brought back to his room. She had a Chanel scarf around her neck. The slam of the car door sounded faintly from the direction of the apartment building, and the car's engine revved once more, noisily, then roared away in the other direction.

All was silent in the streets once more. It was as if a pall had been briefly lifted, then allowed to descend again, deadening everything. Fumio finished drinking his coffee and tossed the empty can into the cardboard box sitting beside the vending machine. He took a few steps homeward then stopped. Suddenly he reached into his back pocket and pulled out his wallet. He'd just remembered the business card Mariko had given him as he'd left her room. It had Petit Doll's logo on it and guaranteed a 1,000 yen discount the next time he went. On it Mariko had written in pen, "I'll be waiting for you." He stared at it, recalling her expert, professional caresses. With a wretched feeling he tore the card up into tiny pieces and scattered them like snowflakes over the damp pavement.

3

THE THING he liked most about Tokyo was its atmosphere of freedom. Living on his own for the first time in his life was — after the initial homesickness had worn off — a heady introduction to independent adulthood. For one thing, it meant that there was no one to supervise his reading material. There was a little-frequented bookstore north of the station which he'd discovered quite by accident one evening after a tutoring lesson. He'd been wandering around just killing time when he'd spotted the shop in an alley leading off from one of the main thoroughfares. Located next to a dismal-looking bar, the tiny bookstore was the old-fashioned kind which still had sliding glass doors and always looked a little dark and empty. Though put off by its gloominess at first, he decided to see what it had to offer. The usual comic books and weeklies were displayed in the front area, but when he stepped around to the back, behind a concealing rack he saw an array of men's magazines designed to appeal to all sexual tastes.

It was too good to believe. Back home he'd had to sneak to the next town for such thrills, at a bookstore where no one knew who he was. Or he'd buy one from the vending machine outside an all-night noodle shop on the national highway. And he was always afraid his mother or sister would find his secret cache when they cleaned up his room. But here in this innocent-looking bookstore just a ten-minute walk from his apartment were magazines which featured everything from prepubescent girls to garter-belted bondage queens. At first he went a little wild buying up the many porno magazines which were so readily available in Tokyo. He had to try at least one sample of every erotic variation offered, for his unrequited sexual longings were so strong that they spilled over into any area which was prohibited. The more prohibited it was, the more it excited him. Anything which was considered abnormal gave him a special thrill.

The closet of his apartment was filled with stacks of magazines which, just one year ago, he wouldn't have believed existed. There was only one type of magazine he hadn't yet been brave enough to purchase. Tonight he was strolling around as usual, pretending to be unable to find the book he was looking for, though really checking to see that there was no one here he knew. There were only three other customers — a salaryman browsing among the men's books, a woman near the news magazines, and a high-school boy engrossed in a comic book. It was late, near closing time. The proprietress was an old lady who sat behind the small wooden counter with a blanket over her knees listening to a tiny transistor radio playing postwar popular songs. She seemed to be nodding in time to an internal rhythm all of her own. On her lap drowsed a half-blind tabby cat. Fumio made his way slowly and surely to where the men's magazines were. As he glanced at the magazines displayed along the top shelf, his eye caught the Chinese characters for *Barazoku* (or 'Rose Tribe') on the spine of a digest-sized magazine tucked away to the far right. This was a well-known magazine for homosexuals which he hadn't dared to touch until now. His search for illicit thrills had not taken him that far yet. Naturally, he'd always been curious about gay men, for he couldn't understand what they could possibly see in one another. There used to be rumors back in high school that so-and-so was a homo, but Fumio hadn't believed any of them. It was just inconceivable to him that someone he knew would prefer boys to girls. It was a sign of unmanliness, a weakness, a failing.

Now he was beginning to wonder. Perhaps it was something which slept in all men, but was kept carefully out of sight, pushed out of the way. The feelings he'd experienced as he peeped at Tatsuya's body the other day could easily be considered homosexual in nature. He wondered if gay men were those who were so unsuccessful in their relations with women that they turned to other men as a substitute. Indeed, there was a part of him which —out of frustration or hopelessness — had toyed with the possibility of doing such a thing himself; even sex with another boy might satisfy his aching need. But it was only a joking sort of thought. He knew he wanted a girl more than anything in the world. Still, as he absent-mindedly regarded the difficult Chinese characters for 'rose' in *Barazoku*, he wondered if this magazine might help him answer some questions which had always bothered him. The salaryman nearby was flipping nervously through a girlie magazine. Fumio picked up a similar magazine and did the same, secretly eying the two copies of *Barazoku*. At this moment they seemed so out of reach. He noticed two other magazines next to them named *Adonis* and *Samson* which also sounded suspiciously homosexual.

He wished there was some way, short of picking them up and flipping through them, that he could verify their contents. Just then the proprietress announced in a quavery voice that the store would close shortly. The other customers quickly made their purchases and left. When Fumio saw that he was alone — he'd purposely lingered — he quickly picked up a copy of *Barazoku*, along with a comic book, and took it to the counter. He prayed he didn't look as guilty as he felt. But the old lady said nothing, merely totaling up the price. He wondered if it was possible that she didn't even know what *Barazoku* was.

She slipped his purchases into a bag, and with trembling fingers he scooped his change up from the counter, dumped it into his pocket and stepped out into the night feeling like a criminal. He'd never felt such excitement before — not even when he'd bought his first SM magazine, or the *lolicon* photobook. A homosexual magazine was the most forbidden of them all. He felt like an explorer stepping into a sinful world which he'd hitherto been too scared to even think about. He didn't allow himself the luxury of looking through *Barazoku* until he'd closed his curtains and locked the door. The cover was fairly innocuous, a tasteful drawing of a young man in profile. The back cover, empty except for a small arabesque design, gave no hint of the contents within. He opened the magazine. At the very front were several pages of photographs of a young man in his early twenties. The first picture showed him wearing swim trunks such as those which boys in high school wore. The trunks had been wetted — as if he'd just stepped out of the water — so that the outline of his genitals underneath could clearly be discerned. The following photos showed him progressively in various stages of undress and finally, completely nude. In the nude photos his genitals had been blacked out with what looked like magic marker. Yet this censoring had been done in a teasing manner which gave the viewer the barest glimpses of certain parts. Pubic hair, however, seemed to be acceptable to a degree.

The last photo showed the boy wearing black mesh briefs, and to Fumio's delight, everything could clearly be seen beneath them. Apparently, this did not violate the strict censorship laws. As long as genitals weren't brazenly exposed, a little leeway seemed to be permitted. Fumio thought the boy very handsome. He especially liked a photo which showed him wearing a baseball cap and white cotton briefs. The expression on his face reminded Fumio of a certain *sempai* in his soccer club back in high school. After lingering on this photo for a while, he turned the page. Another series of photos began, this one showing two men — a middle-aged one who never showed his face directly to the camera, and a young man of about twenty who was the passive partner in their sex games. They were posed in a variety of sexual positions which, to Fumio's eyes, suggested nothing so much as a parody of the normal male-female roles. Somehow, this thought reassured him.

He went on to examine the rest of the magazine. There were various letters of a confessional type, usually detailing first-time homosexual experiences, as well as articles dealing with gay lifestyles in other countries. In addition, there were comic strips, short stories, and a serialized novel, all dealing with gay themes. A large part of the magazine was devoted to a section in the middle called 'Rose Communications'. This was apparently a listing of men who wanted to meet other men. It was divided into geographic sections — from Hokkaido and Tohoku, all the way down to Okinawa. The entries — about 300 in all — were numbered, each containing a short description of the applicant, with his height, weight, and age. The men usually specified whether they wanted to meet a 'younger brother' or an 'older brother'. Some indicated that they didn't want any bald men or girlish men (called 'sisters'.)

Fumio read one of the entries at random, trying to picture the man who'd written it: 'No. 47, Funabashi City. Mr. Lonely 171-57-28. I am a 28-year-old civil servant, though people say I look young for my age. I enjoy sports and driving. I'm seeking an older brother who will be kind to me. I desire a serious relationship, beginning with friendship. Nearby prefecture preferred. No sisters, please. Send photo and telephone number. I will reply!' If a reader wanted to respond, all he had to do was send a letter along with a self-addressed, stamped envelope in care of the magazine indicating by number the entry he was interested in. The staff of the magazine forwarded it on to the address which they kept on file for two months. In this way, each party's privacy was protected. A standard application form was enclosed within the magazine for sending in entries. On the application form was printed the gentle advice: 'Please reply to every letter you receive. Do not use insulting language; remember the feelings of the other person. We do not look at the contents of letters; your secrecy is guaranteed. Pseudonyms are okay, but please tell your real height, weight, and age. No letters from readers under 18. No advertisements, no soliciting.'

There were entries for men who sought international pen pals or friends. These were followed by entries for people interested in marriage. The applicants were either gay men who wanted a woman (lesbian or otherwise) who would understand their needs, or women (lesbian or otherwise) who didn't mind marriage with a gay man. Both the men and women were no doubt being pressured by their families to marry, but didn't want to give up their sexual lifestyles. At the very end of 'Rose Communications' was a section for lesbian entries, women wanting to meet other women, but these were few in number. (Lesbians were apparently known as 'lilies' as opposed to the 'rose' people.) The last third of the magazine was given over to advertisements for bars, massage parlors, video shops, escort services, bath houses, and hotels, all gay in orientation. They were mostly in Tokyo (the 2-chome section of Shinjuku seemed to be a gay mecca) but there were ads from all over Japan, even such outlying places as Sendai, Kanazawa, and Okayama. Fumio checked to see if his home prefecture of Nagano had any gay bars. There were a couple in Matsumoto, the largest city.

He was surprised at the extent of this secret network. Apparently there were many more gays in Japan than he'd guessed. He'd always thought homosexuality was a rare aberration. Turning back to the photo spread at the very front, he was again struck by how handsome the boy was. Certainly he was attractive enough that, if he wanted to, he could get almost any girl he desired. Fumio wondered whether this boy was really homosexual, or had merely posed for the money. As he gazed in envy at the well-developed shoulders, the muscular back and upper arms, he wondered how it felt to be photographed in the nude. On television he'd seen an interview with a woman who'd posed for a men's magazine, and she'd confessed to getting an exhibitionistic delight out of displaying her body. It had probably been the same for this boy. Certainly, Fumio felt a reciprocal delight in being able to examine an attractive male body at his leisure, without the fear of being thought strange. It seemed perfectly natural, after all, to admire another boy's physical beauty, especially if he looked so much better than oneself. He couldn't deny that he was stirred in an almost sensual way by these photographs. But he felt that, rather than being excited by the boy's body, most of his excitement was generated by the idea that he was doing something forbidden. That idea alone had led him to buy many fetish magazines which hadn't really interested him directly.

Fumio looked at the photos in which the boy's genitals had been inked out. It seemed a little silly to censor what he could see anytime he wanted to, at a public bath, in the changing room at the school gym, or even in a mirror. In art books such as the one he'd seen in high school, one could look at classical Western paintings which showed a man's naked body in all its natural beauty. Surely there was nothing wrong in a man wanting to look at another man, or in secretly admiring him. He thought of Tatsuya standing before the mirror, gazing at himself with the critical detachment of someone who was so sure of his own looks that any found flaw could only be an added adornment to an otherwise perfect beauty.

Suddenly Fumio found himself wondering, with a hollowed-out feeling in his chest, if that stolen glimpse of his neighbor would dwell in his memory for the rest of his life, an ageless mental snapshot. He reached for the pack of Mild Sevens at his feet, tapped out a cigarette and put it between his lips. His fingers, he noted with a mild surprise, were trembling slightly. He shut the magazine and reached for the hundred-yen lighter on the bottom shelf of the bookcase. The tatami felt a little damp beneath him. It would be another muggy night.

4

A WHOLE new world gradually opened up before Fumio's wondering eyes. Until now he was like most people, for whom the gay world was only a myth half believed in or dismissed as a joke. However, as he was learning, it appeared to be a distinct, albeit invisible, society superimposed upon the everyday one, only perceivable to those in the know. Fumio's fascination with it was compounded of fear and awe. He felt a little like one of the 'secret Christians' in Japanese history who, because their beliefs were prohibited by the government, were brutally punished whenever they were discovered. Though he himself was not a member of the rose tribe, he thought he could understand what it must feel like to live each moment with the fear of discovery. He himself, in a vicarious way, caught a little of the sense of danger involved. He knew he could never divulge this new interest to his friends, and that was the way he wanted it. It was a secret he wanted to keep all to himself, a personal corner of his life into which no one was allowed to trespass.

The gay magazine was like a guidebook or map detailing a fascinating new country with its own set of customs, culture, even its own language. And yet this tribe of people lived in the heart of everyday Japan. Fumio wished he could explore their country more fully, infiltrate it as a spy and discover its secrets. He thought of himself as an anthropologist studying the habits of a curious culture, similar to his own but different enough to warrant his scientific interest. The *Barazoku* he'd bought had been thoroughly investigated, its contents perused and studied. Only the advertisements in the back remained, signposts pointing to further unexplored territory. Prominent among them was one for a gay movie theater. There were apparently several theaters in Japan which specialized in gay porno films: one each in Tokyo, Yokohama, Osaka, Hiroshima, Kokura, and Fukuoka. The one in Tokyo was located near Ueno station and was called, innocuously enough, World Masterpiece Theater. It was open week-nights until nearly twelve and all night on Saturdays. Curiously, it was one of the few gay entertainment facilities which was located completely away from the main gay center in Shinjuku 2-chome. That fact was important; Fumio was considering the theater as a possible site for an initial investigation. He was curious, first of all, just to see if it actually existed — that there was indeed a place where one could watch movies featuring gay men. He didn't have to actually enter it. According to the tiny map accompanying the ad, the theater was about five minutes' walk from Ueno station. This was apparently an area known for its many porno theaters. Should anyone he knew happen to see him walking in the area, he could always claim he was bound for one of the others.

He got up and took out a can of beer from his refrigerator and drank it down very quickly. It made him feel light-headed and expansive. By the time he was on his second can of beer he felt he was ready to head out. He hoped he didn't look as scared as he felt, for his heart was hammering as he stepped into the Tokyo-bound train. It was about eight-thirty and most commuters were heading back home to the suburbs in the opposite direction, so the car was almost empty. Though he tried to master his fear, a part of him still believed he might become frightened at the last moment and back out of this adventure.

It took about thirty minutes to get to Ueno, located almost opposite Shinjuku on the Yamanote loop line. This area of Tokyo was the edge of the 'shita-machi', the so-called old downtown which still clung very much to the old traditions. Ueno Park, the zoo, and the National Museum were located here, but with its many small machine shops and food markets, Ueno had a slightly sleazy atmosphere. One always felt that it had seen better days. It was also the terminal station for the Tohoku bullet train, the arrival point in Tokyo of people from the most provincial part of Japan, the northeast. Hence it drew shady characters waiting to take advantage of these naive, innocent new arrivals in the big city. Pickpockets and con artists abounded, as did yakuza pimps on the lookout for fresh young girls from the countryside.

At this time of evening the streets were fairly empty. There were relatively few people about, and all of them seemed busy going about their business. Here and there homeless people were seeking shelter for the night in the underpasses. Trying not to think lest he lose his courage, Fumio headed toward the main street. He was encouraged by the fact that most of the people walking around seemed well intoxicated. No one would pay the slightest attention to what he was doing — no one had the faintest idea that his destination was a gay porno theater. But what perhaps gave him the most courage was the fact that he was just an anonymous face in the crowd, one noted and then forgotten. It was a reassuring thought, and one which perhaps gave many people the courage to do things they might otherwise have been afraid to. That was one of the wonderful things about Tokyo. He'd never been in this part of town before but he easily got his bearings with the aid of the tiny map he'd clipped out of the ad. There were several porno theaters facing the main street but World Masterpiece Theater was apparently located in a narrow alley leading to Shinobazu Pond, about five minutes' walk from the station.

Fumio approached the alley and matter-of-factly turned into it as if he intended to go to Shinobazu Pond. At the far end, against the darkness beyond, he spotted the neon-lit marquee of the theater building. As he drew near it, he saw that the first floor housed the Ueno Star Theater, whose gaudy posters made it apparent that it featured hetero porno films. A stairway on the left-hand side of the front entrance led upstairs to two other theaters — according to a sign there, Japanese Film Classics and World Masterpiece Theater. The conservatively-named Japanese Film Classics apparently also masked a pornographic venue, though heterosexual in content.

Intending to walk straight on to the pond, Fumio found himself slowing his steps. Because there was no one else about, his confidence suddenly surged. He began wondering what a gay porno movie would be like. The idea of viewing a sex scene between two men seemed so novel that it might prove to be a refreshing change from his usual nightly fare of adult videos. And he'd come this far after all. Surely there was no law that said a straight man couldn't watch a gay movie for educational purposes. No doubt many other men had done the same thing. He looked around. There was no one in the alley to see him enter — and no one to care if he did. Without halting his stride, he turned his steps purposefully toward the left. Yet as he walked up the stairs he felt all the strength suddenly drain from his body. Halfway up, his steps became leaden and heavy and he had to force himself to move onward.

On the second floor he came to a corridor, in the middle of which was a circular counter. An old man about sixty years old was sitting behind it. To the left of the counter was a ticket-vending machine with buttons indicating choices for either World Masterpiece Theater or Japanese Film Classics. The latter was straight down the corridor and the former was down a narrow hallway to the left. Apparently the entrance had been purposely designed so that no one could tell from the outside which theater was one's destination. A customer coming up here could look as though he were headed for the hetero porno theater when in fact he was bound for the gay one... a convenient cover for anyone worried about being seen walking into a gay theater.

Fumio bought a student ticket for World Masterpiece Theater and handed it to the man. As he headed up the hallway to the theater he saw groups of young men in their twenties, mostly dressed in suits, standing around. At first he thought the seats inside were filled up and they were waiting for the next showing. A few of them were talking in low voices, but for the most part it was strangely silent. He opened a door and saw that it was a side entrance near the screen. He quickly shut it and continued up the hallway. At the end of it was a waiting room of some kind, a little dark, and this, too, seemed to be filled with young men. The rear corridor was likewise crowded. Fumio opened a back door and entered the theater proper. It was a smallish theater with perhaps about seventy seats. The whole rear area was filled with men standing around, leaning against the walls. Here and there at several places were niches formed by pillars jutting out from the wall, and these seemed to be popular.

To his surprise most of the seats were empty. Everyone seemed to prefer the rear seats and these were mostly filled, but those in the forward rows were virtually untaken. The few customers sitting there seemed to be asleep. Fumio tried to go forward but found his way blocked by a man's leg. As he bumped against it and pushed, it was withdrawn. He went forward and took an end seat about five rows from the front. His knees were shaking and his face felt hot. The theater seemed to him much too brightly lit up inside. He feared that someone he knew would see him here — though of course his logic told him that anyone he knew would be just as scared to be seen by him. Still, he couldn't suppress an uneasy feeling as he peered around in the dark trying to see the other customers.

He felt like a spy. Knowing that these men sitting all around him were homosexuals — real homosexuals — he felt all the excitement of an explorer coming upon a tribe of people he's read about in travel books but has never seen with his own eyes. He was unable to concentrate on the movie for a long time. He found his attention drawn more to the audience than to what was onscreen. In fact, no one seemed particularly interested in the movie itself. There was muffled conversation, yawning, smoking. (This was the only theater Fumio had been to in which smoking was allowed.) Fumio could see some of the men glancing furtively around. There was a tension in the air, a feeling of expectation which he could somehow catch just by being there. But it was a strangely stimulating atmosphere; he'd never been in a place where the feeling of anticipation was so palpable.

He was aware all the time of secret shiftings and creakings throughout the theater. These seemingly innocent noises spoke of a gnawing sense of longing, yearning. All during the movie there was constant moving around. Someone would sit down in a seat a few rows forward of him, watch the movie for about ten minutes, then get up and go. Another would stand along the side wall and watch the movie from there for a few minutes, then suddenly walk back to the rear of the theater. Presently a man sitting a couple of rows forward got up and headed toward a side exit. A moment later, another man from the other side of the theater also got up and went out the exit near him. It was almost as if their movements had been timed to coincide. Soon, another man who was sitting in one of the front rows abruptly got up and began walking slowly toward the rear of the theater. He stopped at a spot about two meters away from Fumio and leaned back against the wall.

Fumio was too scared to look at him. Out of the corner of his eye he could tell that the other was occasionally casting glances his way, so he turned his head just enough to see what sort of man he was. It was hard to tell without looking directly at him but he appeared to be an ordinary salaryman on his way home from work. He wore a normal business suit and was perhaps in his early thirties. Fumio felt he was being observed closely by the man yet he didn't have the nerve to verify it. The man even scraped his shoes loudly against the floor as if trying to get Fumio to look his way, but Fumio kept his eyes steadfastly on the screen. After a moment the man faded away toward the rear of the theater. With the blood throbbing in his ears and a hot flush on his face, Fumio tried to watch the movie. It was, in fact, something of a disappointment, cheaply made and badly photographed. The flimsy, almost non-existent storyline was pitiful, and Fumio could barely keep his attention on it. He'd expected homosexual porno to be more erotic, but compared to some of the adult videos he'd seen recently, this was tame stuff. The sex scenes were so obviously faked and very little nudity was shown. Even the mildest of hetero videos these days showed more of a man's body.

When it finally ended there was a brief break during which the lights remained dim. The second movie started right away and it was as dreary as the first. Obviously most of the audience hadn't come here to watch it anyway. Fumio doggedly attempted to watch it, aware all the time of little noises all around him, whispers, the doors constantly opening and closing. The minty smell of gum being chewed, and other mildly aromatic odors, added a sense of foreboding to his diligent effort. He badly felt the need for a cigarette yet didn't dare light one up. The second movie finally ended. Glancing at his watch he saw that it was a little past eleven o'clock. The curtains on either side of the screen closed and the lights came on. For the past ten minutes or so, the old man who had been at the counter in front had been banging doors and sweeping the corridors clean, and now he pushed open all the side doors and began cleaning the inside of the theater. Fumio got up to leave and saw to his surprise that only about eight people remained. When he'd arrived there'd probably been about fifty. Apparently they'd slipped quietly away all through the second movie, trickling out little by little.

He lingered until he was the last to leave. Outside, he saw that the Ueno Star Theater building had closed for the night. With its neon lights darkened there was a deserted atmosphere to the whole area. Fumio needed a cigarette badly. To his left the darkness of Shinobazu Pond was inviting. He began walking that way rather than toward the bustling main street with its bright, colorful lights. The darkness was soothing. He felt much more at his ease out here. Far across the pond the lit-up city seemed like a toy-scale model of the metropolis, the sounds coming from it faint and unreal. A hush prevailed all around Shinobazu Pond. Fumio gazed at the bizarre sight of the grotesquely huge water lilies covering the dark surface of its water. His nerves were still a little wrought up; he took out his pack of Mild Sevens and tapped out a cigarette with shaking fingers.

Sitting here and there on benches beneath the willow trees were boy-girl couples kissing. He chose a quiet spot and lit up the cigarette, took a deep puff and felt a soothing calm gradually envelop his body. Just then a man came up beside him, leaned against the railing and turned toward him with a surprised, questioning look. For a moment Fumio thought it was someone he knew but he couldn't place the face. As he was trying to recall the name to go with the face the other man walked away a little distance. Fumio gazed after him, still searching his mind for the missing name. Perhaps it was an absolute stranger after all, who had mistaken him for someone else. And then he saw the other stop again and peer straight back at him. Again Fumio had a twinge of doubt. Could it be someone he knew, who had seen him coming out of World Masterpiece Theater? He felt a chill of terror.

However, before he could do anything else, the man began walking off in the direction of the park. As Fumio watched, he stopped at a vending machine and pretended to be pondering what to buy, then glanced back. He walked on. Fumio felt as if he were being silently invited. It was like some sort of detective drama on television. Intrigued, he decided to follow.

The man had stopped at another vending machine further on and was looking back. When he saw that Fumio was following, he continued on. The secret, ritualistic nature of this silent pantomime gave it a dreamlike unreality. It was as if all of Fumio's volition had been suspended, and he was helplessly fulfilling a pre-ordained role in his destiny. They were going toward the park. Officially Ueno Park was closed after sundown but there was no way of enforcing this rule. As soon as it got dark, young couples made their way into the freedom of its shadows. Fumio knew that voyeurs also made a habit of prowling the dark to spy on the lovers, some of them carrying cameras with infra-red lenses. These were the so-called photo snipers who sold their pictures to sleazy magazines which specialized in stolen glimpses of intimacy.

The man he was following went straight up a narrow bicycle path. It was quite dark within the park. Fumio could pick out couples hidden in the shadows, the girls pressing against their boys. Some of them were kissing quite passionately, as lovers did in American movies. They didn't seem to care if anyone saw them or not. Fumio envied them; it was what he wished he was doing, instead of indulging in this bizarre chase.

Ahead of him the man continued on in a businesslike manner, occasionally glancing sideways, perhaps ensuring out of the corner of his eye that Fumio was still following. Strangely, Fumio felt no fear. They were taking paths which led into ever darker areas where few lights broke the all-pervading gloom. Here, the trees grew more thickly and in their heavy shadows the sounds of the outside world were strangely muted. In a little while Fumio spotted a public restroom among the trees. Either its lights were out or someone had broken them, for all was dark within it. The man hesitated outside this restroom and, peering back once more at Fumio, entered.

Fumio wondered whether he should follow. He knew it could be dangerous, and yet this bizarre pantomime had left his insides churning with excitement. He had never before experienced such a mixture of fear and anticipation. There could be no doubt now what the conclusion of this charade was intended to be. Yet he wanted to verify it. Peering around and seeing that no one was about, he stepped into the restroom. Inside, there was a strong smell of urine and damp cigarette butts. And to his surprise, there were about five men already inside. His first thought was that they were lined up to use the urinals. But that was ridiculous at this time of night. Upon closer inspection, they all appeared to be just standing around smoking cigarettes. No one said a word. It was all very strange. Perhaps from the excitement, he felt a strong need to urinate but he didn't dare use a urinal in front of all these men. He headed toward the toilet stalls where there would be more privacy. One of the toilet doors had been half torn off its hinges and hung a little crazily in the doorway. He headed toward the other one. When he pushed the door open, two men inside turned their faces toward him in surprise. One was standing and the other was down on his knees. Fumio muttered an apology and quickly left. As he rushed out into the darkness, away from the silent, smelly restroom, he felt as if he were escaping a sickeningly sordid world. It seemed to take him forever to get to the station.

5

WITH THE coming of autumn, cooler weather had returned. In his room, Fumio lay on his back, idly smoking a cigarette. The veranda window was open, and the temperature just right. If he leaned his head back far enough, he could just make out the clear turquoise sky high above, etched with rows of herringbone clouds tinged a flaming orange by the setting sun. The radio was tuned to the Far East Network, the US military radio station. Fumio couldn't understand a word the disc jockey was saying, but the sound of the American voice gave him a feeling of being in a far, foreign country.

He hadn't gone to school again today, having slept in late and idled away the whole day. For some reason, ever since coming back from his hometown visit to Nagano, he lacked the will power to do anything. Nothing seemed to interest him anymore. He'd thought that going home for the O-Bon festival would have cheered him up. But from his first day at home he'd yearned to be back in Tokyo with all its freedoms. In the stifling atmosphere of his home town the future had loomed as a dark wall before him, a gradually encaging prison. There was nothing to look forward to. He'd met his high-school classmates, many of whom already worked in the local economy. One boy had gone to work for his father's noodle shop, another worked in the town office as an employee of the waterworks department, still another was in training as a barber. They seemed happy enough with what they were doing, making money to buy the things they wanted — cars, audio equipment, cameras. But to Fumio their lives seemed so dreary — so much like a preview of his own that he'd become depressed.

Though he was only a second son and, unlike his older brother, wasn't expected to carry on the family business, he knew his mother expected him to return to Nagano after college and establish himself in his hometown, either as a public official at the town office or as a teacher. Secretly, Fumio had little inclination for either of these jobs but he really had no say in these matters. It was his duty to help his brother look after their mother in her old age. He would probably choose a wife (or have one chosen for him) through an arranged meeting, and settle down somewhere near his parental home. That thought also depressed him. He'd discovered that the girls in Nagano weren't as pretty as his memory had pictured them; they seemed so dowdy when compared to the sophisticated Tokyo girls. In his heart he was really most attracted to those girls who were obviously born and bred in Tokyo, who somehow managed to seem mysteriously sexier than their provincial sisters, more experienced and promiscuous. And the fact that they were so out of reach only added to their desirability. He knew some people might not understand that at all.

What it all came down to was that he could no longer feel as if he were a part of Nagano. His friends even kidded him about being such a Tokyoite, pretending to envy (but secretly disdaining) his newly-acquired sophistication. Fumio hadn't wanted to be one of those who put on airs about their Tokyo experience but it must have come out unconsciously. His brief stay here had changed him in many small ways which were difficult to enumerate clearly. So he'd come back to Tokyo as early as was decently possible. Sitting on the train approaching the capital, station by station he'd felt as if he were climbing higher and higher into a rarified atmosphere — the atmosphere of pure freedom. It was a freedom foreign to his hometown, and only to be enjoyed by the citizens of this metropolis.

Even lying here doing nothing in his tiny six-mat apartment, he felt as if anything were possible. But ever since his return he'd felt as if he were living on borrowed time. The knowledge that his freedom wouldn't last forever imparted a sense of urgency to his daily existence. It seemed such a waste of time to spend it studying hard at the university; he wanted to get the most out of his four-year stay in Tokyo before having to return home. Most of his college friends planned to find jobs in the capital after graduation so they couldn't possibly understand his anxiety. They were satisfied with going out drinking, trying to pick up girls, and visiting fashion healths when that failed. Fumio wanted more out of Tokyo than that. He didn't know what; he just knew he was restless and unsatisfied.

The image of Tokyo he'd created in his own mind — a fantasy fed by comic books and television, a city where exciting things went on all the time — actually existed out there, but he hadn't yet been able to find it. His lack of money was what restricted him. What he made from tutoring barely paid for his necessities, with a little left over for entertainment. He was provided only with teasing glimpses of all the treasures available... to others. Some of his fellow students at school had their own cars — foreign cars, even: BMWs, Porsches, Benzes. They hardly ever came to class, and spent their evenings at some fashionable disco in Roppongi or Shibuya. On weekends they enjoyed a leisurely stay at a ski resort or hot spring with their girlfriend of the moment. They were living the kind of life Fumio had always dreamed of. In contrast, he thought of his own life: the spoiled rich children he tutored in the evenings, the respectful way he had to enter their homes — and smile even when they said the most hurtful things. There were some children whom he felt he was only babysitting. He really worked too hard for too little, barely making enough money to scrape by from month to month. He wondered if he should find another job which paid more. But the only escape from tutoring was to become a day laborer, and though it paid well, it was hard, physical work. He seemed to be stuck with his present job.

The sun had set and the clouds had turned gray, then black, fading into the darkness of the sky as if they'd been consumed by a brief, fierce conflagration. Fumio got up, slid shut the veranda window and whisked the curtains closed. Feeling for the dangling string, he clicked the room light on. He lay on his side and shut his eyes for a moment.

The room began to reverberate to the low thunder of steps pounding up the stairs outside. He opened his eyes and immediately realized he had been asleep for quite some time. He glanced at his watch and noted it was past ten, about the time Tatsuya usually came home. Fumio listened for the footsteps to make their way to the room next door. Instead, they suddenly halted just outside his own door. There was a knock. "Yes." He got up and opened the door, wondering if it was Mori or some other friend come by on an unannounced visit.

"Good evening." It was Tatsuya after all, dressed up in an expensive-looking gray suit and looking quite attractive. He had a slightly embarrassed look on his face.

"Good evening." Fumio didn't know what to make of this visit, the first his neighbor had ever made except for the single time he'd come over to borrow a little soy sauce.

"I just dropped by to let you know that I'll be moving out at the end of this week."

"Oh." For some reason, Fumio felt a sharp disappointment. "Why are you moving?" A tiny spark of guilt played at the back of his mind: perhaps his peeping had been detected.

"This place is just too cramped, and too old."

"That's true." He found himself looking at Tatsuya's suit, so out of place in the surroundings. The other boy noticed it.

"I've come into a bit of money, so I guess I can afford it now."

"That's great. I envy you."

"Yes. Well... In a way it's too bad we never got to know each other. There was never really any time."

"That's true." Fumio thought of all the girls Tatsuya had brought to the room next-door, and of all the times he himself had eavesdropped on what happened there. He fought against the blush which threatened to expose his guilty recollections.

"I suppose I've been a trouble to you." Fumio started. Tatsuya's conventional phrase had seemed an ironic apology for those very moments.

"Oh no. Not at all." At a loss for words, he muttered, "Please come in."

"I don't want to impose."

"It's no bother. I was just lying around listening to the radio."

"In that case..."

Fumio brought out a can of beer and two glasses. "Please sit down." He couldn't shake the eerie feeling that Tatsuya was somehow out of place in this room — on the wrong side of the wall. It felt oddly as if an actor on stage had stepped right down into the audience to join one of the spectators. Fumio was keenly aware of the secret peephole hidden behind the picture on the wall at Tatsuya's back. As he poured the beer into the glasses, he noted Tatsuya's instinctive little bow of thanks. Indeed, there was an air of old-fashioned formality to all of Tatsuya's actions tonight which contrasted strikingly with what Fumio knew about his private life. The very fact that he'd come here to announce his departure showed that he observed all the proper ceremonies, if only out of a sense of obligation. This evidence of Tatsuya's provincial upbringing reassured Fumio, and allowed him to relax.

"Well, good luck, wherever you're going."

"Thanks."

They took a long drink at their beers. Tatsuya set his glass down. "Actually, I'm not moving too far away — only as far as Nakano — so we might still run into each other."

"I see." Fumio had almost said, "That's good." Though he felt much closer to Tatsuya than the other boy realized, he didn't want to give himself away. "I wish I could move out of here, too. But I'm from a poor family and can't afford it."

"I'm from a poor family myself. Why do you think I had to live in this cheap apartment for so long? My family runs a small farm in Ibaraki."

"Really? My family owns a small bicycle shop in Nagano." Feeling expansive, Fumio brought out another can from the refrigerator and began pouring out more beer for them both, but Tatsuya interrupted him to return the favor.

"Allow me."

"Thanks. You know, isn't it amazing that we're finally getting to know one another only on this final day?"

"True."

"We only saw each occasionally. Like that night you roared by in that sports car with that woman."

Tatsuya laughed. "I've always loved fancy sports cars. As a boy I collected car magazines, built plastic models of Ferraris and Porsches, took pictures of them on the national highway. So I can never resist an offer of a ride in one. In high school I had a friend who owned a secondhand Fairlady Z, and we would blast around all night on the empty roads among the silent rice paddies and the blinking traffic lights. The next day I would sleep through my classes. I'm still amazed at how I managed to graduate from high school."

Fumio laughed as Tatsuya continued in a more meditative mood. "I can't wait till I can afford my own car so I don't have to hitch a ride with someone else."

"Apparently you're on your way. Your prospects look good, I take it."

"I'm not making that much money. Yet. But I have hopes."

"Oh?"

Tatsuya looked uneasy. "I suppose I should tell you how I make my living now."

"Not if it's something you don't want to talk about."

Tatsuya laughed. "It's not that bad. I'm not doing anything criminal or illegal, don't worry."

"What do you do?"

"I work in a host club."

"A host club?"

"It's a club catering to women customers. I'm like a male version of a hostess. All our customers are women, and I serve them drinks, laugh at their jokes, flatter them. Take them out to dinner. That woman you saw me with the other night; she was a customer."

"What an enviable job." Only a boy with Tatsuya's looks had the option of getting paid for what most boys could only dream about.

"It's not as rosy as it sounds. Remember, we aren't allowed to choose our customers. Most of them are women who can afford the high prices. In other words, older, and not very attractive, either in looks or personality. If they were, they wouldn't have to come to a host club to seek male companionship."

"I see."

"Being a host isn't the fantasy many boys assume it is. We have to keep well-dressed at all times — which means our wardrobe costs are astronomical."

"Don't you get reimbursed somehow for it?"

"We receive little gifts, but we are expected to return those favors, too."

"And do you ever get to — "

"I know what you're thinking. But that, too, is a task. Just between you and me, sometimes I feel like a gigolo. It gets to be a grind, just like any job. When I first started, I had different expectations. Now I wish I could quit. I would if anything better came along."

"Then why do you do it?"

"Money."

"Wow. That's a pretty blunt answer."

"Isn't it? But it's true. I wouldn't even *touch* some of these women if they didn't pay me well for it. If you knew how much it's possible to make at this job, you'd be amazed. That's why I can't quit it." Seeing Fumio's reaction, he turned a little defiant. "Well that's what everything comes down to in the end, isn't it? Everything revolves around money — giving it, taking it, losing it, accumulating it, the feel of it between your fingers. That's what makes all the difference in how you can act: independent and arrogant, or cringing and subservient. Someday I'm going to have everything I want, without the need to worry about how much it costs. The whole point to living is to make enough money to have a good life. Don't you agree?"

Fumio nodded, but secretly he was a little dismayed by Tatsuya's blunt materialism. What scared him more was that he himself might harbor such longings in his own heart. Perhaps this concern revealed itself in his face, for Tatsuya's expression softened.

"But enough of this heavy talk. Come on," he suddenly announced. "Let's go out and have a good time. Pick up some girls."

"Where?"

"Roppongi, of course. Where else can you have fun at this time of night?"

Fumio knew that the all-night discos of Roppongi, the most fashionable after-hours place in Tokyo, were the best places to meet willing girls, but he'd never yet had the chance to go. "But I have nothing to wear."

"I'll lend you one of my suits. I have enough, believe me. Come on." He led Fumio to his own apartment next door. Entering it for the first time, Fumio couldn't help feeling a twinge of guilt. In a sense, he had already been an intruder here, so it didn't feel like the first time. Yet, from the inside, it looked somehow different from the view he had of it through the peephole. He noted the location of the mirror atop the dresser, and the bed against the wall. It was a large bed which took up almost half of the room's floor space, and was obviously the most important piece of furniture in here, a blatant symbol of where Tatsuya's priorities lay. Fumio tried not to seek the spot on the wall where the peephole would be, suppressing his itch to see just how visible it was. Tatsuya went to a vinyl-walled clothes rack and unzipped its flap. Suits were lined up neatly on hangers inside, but the space within was unable to contain all the suits which had spilled out and spread all across the room. Every available space on the walls was taken up by suits on hangers. In fact, the whole tiny room was like a closet space for these suits of all colors — gray, brown, blue, white, black, pale apricot, egg-shell.

As Tatsuya explained, picking through them, many were gifts

from women whose tastes he hated. "But I have to wear them to the club to please the customers who bought them for me." He picked one out at random and held it against Fumio. "You're about my size so there should be no problem. I'll give you this one."

"I couldn't accept."

"Don't worry. You can see I have enough to throw away. How about this other one, then?" Finally they settled on a light brown one which delighted Fumio. It had a rather loose fit, but that was the present fashion. As he looked at himself in the mirror, he felt a secret shiver go through him. The idea of wearing something which Tatsuya had once worn gave him an indescribable thrill.

"It looks better on you than it does on me," said Tatsuya. "Come on."

All the trains and subways had stopped running by now so they had to take a taxi. It was past the big night-time exodus of taxis from the pleasure spots of Tokyo so they managed to snare one in front of the station without much trouble. When they got to Roppongi, Fumio saw that it was still very much alive. Most of the people he saw on the streets would probably party all night and catch the first train home in the morning. He gazed with wide-open eyes at the crowds of young people, most of them girls walking about in groups of two, three, and four. Many foreigners were here, also, and he knew that quite a few of the girls were looking for dates with them. The sight of a Japanese girl walking arm-in-arm with an American or European man was not unusual here, though it might have raised a few eyebrows elsewhere. Expensive imported cars cruised by, more than he could count: Mercedes-Benzes, Ferraris, even a white Rolls-Royce. Tatsuya pointed out, quite casually, a famous comedian Fumio had often seen on TV.

They entered a disco called Dream. The doorman seemed to recognize Tatsuya and waved them in, past the lines of waiting people. As soon as they stepped inside, Fumio felt as if he'd entered another world. The decor of this most fashionable of nightspots resembled nothing so much as the inside of a warehouse, but that was apparently the intention. Loud, pulsating music seemed to come at him from all corners of the building, an almost visceral assault on his senses. Flashing lights made his head spin, and he all but stumbled after Tatsuya who was eagerly scanning the tables for a place to sit. All of them seemed to be taken, but Tatsuya didn't seemed perturbed. He told Fumio to wait, and walked over to a corner where two girls were sitting at a tiny round table. After chatting with them for a few minutes, the girls in one motion glanced over to where

Fumio was standing, and Tatsuya gave a little wave signalling for Fumio to join them.

At first Fumio felt out of place. Both of the girls were dressed in the latest fashions, as was everyone else in the place, and looked so sexy in their clinging body-conscious dresses which showed off every curve of their bodies. Apparently they were quite aware of the effect this had on the young men, but Tatsuya seemed completely at ease with them, joking and chatting with a fluency which showed he had quite a bit of experience with the disco scene. Fumio could easily see how women would pay to be entertained by such an attractive young man. It would be hard to resist his charms. He himself could only envy such a natural manner which casually betrayed considerable experience with all sorts of women. The conventional word 'handsome' was not quite the right word to describe Tatsuya's looks. There could be no doubt that he was handsome — extremely so. But in addition, there was a certain vulnerable, androgynous beauty to his face which made him a little too pretty for a male. It was a look which had always held a special attraction for young girls who worshipped those faces found in teen idol magazines: a cold, chiselled perfection that glittered like a carved diamond.

It was quite obvious that both girls were now completely under Tatsuya's spell, and Fumio could easily understand why. If he were a girl, he might find himself falling in love with this confident youth. Even in his boy's eyes, the other was attractive. He liked the slightly effete elegance with which Tatsuya held his cigarette as he talked. Far from putting him off, he found it charming and novel. After a few drinks, Fumio was able to join in on the conversation, but couldn't keep up with the witty phrases and repartee which seemed to float effortlessly to the lips of the other three. He noticed a pattern to these jokes after a while, and suspected Tatsuya might be spinning them out of a set repertory. Still, it was fun to listen to him just for the music of his voice, and the dazzling whiteness of his teeth when he smiled.

It was becoming clear that Tatsuya was more attracted to the girl named Naoko and was concentrating his talk upon her, while Fumio and her girlfriend Izumi mainly listened. Finally Naoko said, "Let's dance. I'm beginning to feel a little woozy."

"All right." By silent consent they paired off, Tatsuya with Naoko, and Fumio with Izumi. They danced until they were all exhausted, then left to go to an all-night pub nearby. The sky was getting pale and the sleepless revellers on the streets looked haggard and washed-out. Here and there, Fumio spotted girls kneeling ungracefully on the sidewalks, retching, then being helped to their feet by worried girlfriends. He wondered how this unexpectedly magical night would end for him. As he gazed at Naoko and Izumi, a pair of girls who were the very picture of Tokyo sophistication, he found it hard to believe that just a few hours ago, he'd been sitting all alone in his room hopelessly longing for just such an adventure. It was almost as if Tatsuya had come in answer to his prayers, to fulfill his stifled yearnings.

After a single drink each at the pub, Tatsuya looked at his watch and announced, "Well, what shall we do? It's getting late. Why don't we call it a night?" Everyone agreed. "Then," he continued, "how about if we split up and go our separate ways?" He looked at Naoko.

"Sure," she said, and got up to leave with him. They waved goodbye to Fumio and Izumi as they went out the door. Fumio was amazed at how quickly it had happened. Left behind at the table, he and Izumi looked at each other. "Shall we go?" he asked, not quite knowing what to do.

To his delight she nodded. "Why not?"

It struck him faintly that this was the first time he'd successfully propositioned a girl even though he had more or less taken Tatsuya's leavings. He knew that both girls had been out looking for adventure tonight, and that Naoko had been the luckier one—she'd gotten Tatsuya. Izumi had no doubt decided to settle for Fumio as a sort of consolation prize, if only to avoid the loss of face she'd have by going home alone.

The sun was beginning to brighten up the sky in the east and early commuters could already be seen here and there. Fumio wondered what to do next, but to his relief, Izumi took the initiative.

"I'm tired. Let's take a rest somewhere."

"Sure. Do you know a good place?"

"Follow me." She began leading the way, with Fumio following beside her. They turned up a side street which was much less crowded than the main strip. Fumio noticed that most of the people here seemed to be couples. Gaudy, neon-lit signs with names like Venus, Silver Dream, or Starlight hung perpendicularly over the entrances of narrow alleyways between buildings. Occasionally a couple would duck into one of these alleys, suddenly swallowed up by the night. Finally Izumi stopped. "How about here?"

Fumio peered down the alley and saw the concealed entrances of about three love hotels. Their signs hung like ghostly auras in the shadows. "Sure." He led the way inside and stopped before the entrance of the one called Toi et Moi. A check-in booth was just inside the door. Beside it was a lighted panel with photographs of the various rooms available. Apparently the lit photos indicated those which were vacant, the darkened photos the occupied rooms. Fumio selected one at random, clicking off the switch beside the photo. The check-in window had a blind which came down so that guests' faces couldn't be seen. He paid the money, and the hands — all he could see of the clerk were these hands, apparently those of a middle-aged lady — slid out the key to the room he'd chosen.

They took the elevator up to their room on the third floor, meeting no one on the way. Fumio later discovered in the room that a warning light just beside the door flashed if anyone was out in the hallways; this was to ensure that guests who were leaving wouldn't run into any arriving guests. Everything about the hotel was designed to save guests from any feeling of embarrassment. Fumio and Izumi had managed to pass from the street to their room without anyone seeing them. Inside the room Fumio looked around. He had never seen such a fabulous place. The most impressive thing in the room was its bed, a round, king-sized one. There were controls on the bedside console which — as he discovered — revolved the bed as well as operating the television, the radio, and various lights along the ceiling. In the center of the ceiling was a huge mirror. A pair of bathrobes with the hotel's name on them lay on the bed, a larger blue one and a more petite pink one. Inside a small refrigerator beside the bed were beer, soft drinks, and chilled wine. A make-up table with a hair dryer attached by its cord to the wall, a plastic brush and comb set, and even a complimentary bottle of perfume were obviously placed there for a girl to make herself presentable after a stay here.

The bathroom with its sunken tub was huge. No home in Tokyo could possibly boast such luxury of space. A ledge on the tile wall displayed complimentary bars of soap, toothpaste, toothbrushes, and shaving gear. The general decor of the place brought to mind the inside of a fairytale castle, all pink and soft. Fumio knew from watching TV that other love hotels were designed around various themes just as exotic — an Arabian seraglio, a tropical island paradise, a Swiss chalet. Amid the cramped, overcrowded apartments, office buildings, and shops of Tokyo, these gaudy love hotels were like islands of pure luxury where a pair of lovers could escape for two hours or overnight into a brief world which indulged their craving for voluptuous fantasy to the fullest.

Indeed, this room was a whole world removed from his tiny cramped apartment. It was like something out of a movie. "Quite a fancy place," he said. He knew that almost all girls, and many boys, had their first sexual experience in a love hotel, and that the designers of these rooms had taken that into account. The romantic motifs supposedly helped soften the fears of inexperienced girls. However, it was clear that Izumi was far from innocent. She didn't seem shy at all about being here, merely asking Fumio whether it was all right if she took a shower first. He nodded.

When the sound of the shower came on, Fumio, as calmly as he could, undressed and got under the sheets to wait for her. She returned after about ten minutes, a towel wrapped around her middle, drying her hair with another towel. Without a word she slipped under the sheets beside him. Her body was still warm and slightly damp from the shower, her skin a little sticky. She lay back with her eyes closed, her hair fanned out over the pillow. Fumio searched her face eagerly for any signs of resistance, but all he could sense was a silent, submissive waiting, a complete surrender to his will. This was — at last! — the thing he'd been waiting so long for. He felt as if he'd finally gotten permission to indulge his desires to the full. Yet his joy was tempered by a small cloud of doubt. He wondered if he really deserved this treat. On his own, he would never have been able to succeed like this. The young girl's body he was clasping was the equivalent of a parting gift from Tatsuya. It was only thanks to Tatsuya's clothes and Tatsuya's skillful patter that Fumio had been able to 'seduce' the girl. By some sympathetic magic, Fumio had 'become' Tatsuya for the evening. Like those shamans into whose bodies a departed soul will suddenly, almost violently, enter with a jerk, Fumio felt as if Tatsuya's soul had taken possession of his own body. Indeed, for Izumi, there seemed to be no question about it. Gazing down into her unfocussed eyes as he began making love with her, he could almost see, reflected in the frantic gleams of her pupils, the face of Tatsuya looking back at him.

6

TATSUYA WAS gone. The new neighbor who had already moved into the vacated apartment next door was a dowdy, bespectacled girl student at a nearby junior college who didn't interest Fumio in the least. Not once had he felt tempted to use the peephole. It would have been almost a profanation of Tatsuya's memory. With his departure Tatsuya seemed to have taken some vital substance out of Fumio's life — the possibility of adventure. For there could no longer be any doubt now: Tatsuya was one of those people to whom the things one read about in books and saw on TV actually happened.

Fumio had helped him pack on the morning after their memorable night in Roppongi. There'd been no mention of what had happened with their respective partners, but Fumio had felt as if, along with the suit, the night spent with Izumi had been a sort of parting gift. It was a night not soon to be forgotten. Fumio had made love with Izumi six times before falling asleep from exhaustion. The whole time it was happening, he couldn't get over the fact that she was letting him do it for free, that she actually wanted to do it. After their short sleep, they'd awakened about noon and quickly gotten dressed in time to leave before being charged for overtime. And though they'd exchanged telephone numbers when they parted at the subway station, Fumio knew he would probably never see her again. Without Tatsuya as a companion, such a night was not likely to be repeated.

But his influence seemed to have mysteriously rubbed off on Fumio somehow, for tonight something had happened which had never occurred before. He'd been tutoring a sixth-grade girl in the western suburbs of Tokyo when, after the lesson, her mother had asked him to stay for dinner. Happy to get a home-cooked meal for a change, he'd gladly accepted. But he'd had far too much beer to go with it; the mother had kept pushing it onto him and he could hardly refuse. By 10:30 her husband still hadn't returned from the office, and the child was asleep in bed. All alone in the kitchen with the mother, Fumio had begun to wonder if perhaps she were trying to seduce him. He'd heard it happened to tutors sometimes. She was about thirty-five years old and not unattractive if one went for older women. If only he'd been a little bolder, he might have responded to her offer... or at least tried to verify if one had been made. But then he quickly dismissed the thought from his mind: things like that only happened to people like Tatsuya, not Fumio.

He was just passing by a tiny park and, perhaps from all the beers he'd drunk, felt the need to use the restroom. After finishing up and rinsing his hands, he was about to continue on his way when, on a whim, he decided to check inside the toilet stalls. It was almost a habit by now. Ever since stumbling across that sordid scene in Ueno Park, he'd wondered if the same sort of thing went on in other parks. Whenever he spotted a public toilet, he would step in to check the toilet stalls for any secret evidence of homosexual activity. Every now and then, amid numerous heterosexual graffiti, he would spot a tiny, single word: 'Homo'. Occasionally there were more graphic signs of homosexual lust — lovingly detailed drawings of penises in full arousal, or hurriedly scrawled messages such as 'I want to meet a high school boy!' He was beginning to understand that secret gays were much more numerous than he'd ever imagined, though they were still very much hidden from the eyes of most people.

He stepped into the first stall and saw nothing. He stepped out again and entered the second stall. On the wall, at about eye level for anyone sitting at the Japanese-style toilet, someone had drawn an explicit picture of a muscular male torso, its loving attention to detail proclaiming its artist's inclinations even without the stark evidence of a fully aroused member. Fumio felt a shiver go through him. He'd always passed by this park after the lesson, but until tonight had never had the occasion to enter it. Located in the middle of a residential area, quite near a junior high school, it was one of those parks little visited even during the day, the type where one saw young children playing under the watchful eyes of their mothers. Nobody looking at it would have given it a second thought, much less conceive of anything illicit going on here at night. And yet this drawing surely indicated otherwise.

He stepped outside again. At this time of night the park was empty. Or so he thought. To his surprise he saw a young man sitting idly on a swing barely moving. Fumio hadn't noticed him when he came. Hurriedly, Fumio left the park and walked purposefully in the direction of the station. He barely noticed where he was going. His thoughts were on that scene he'd accidentally witnessed in the public restroom in Ueno Park a few weeks back. Even now, it disgusted him to imagine what the two men had been up to. For a long time, he'd been unable to understand the loathing with which gays were regarded by society. His image of homosexuals had been somewhat romantic: two attractive young boys secretly in love with each other, unable to openly express their love. The letters in *Barazoku* expressing a yearning for a friend or lover had a certain pathos to them, and Fumio had even sympathized somewhat with the loneliness the writers felt. Yet such romantic angst had nothing to do with the scene in the Ueno Park restroom. That sort of promiscuity was a little unsettling. After witnessing it, he could well understand society's disapproval of gay behavior. It was perfectly warranted.

The perimeter of the station plaza was lined with restaurants and stores busy now with late returning salarymen. Though he wasn't hungry, Fumio stepped into a Chinese restaurant and ordered a bowl of noodles. He hoped it would calm him down somewhat, for his heart was still pounding hard from the thought that the boy back at the park had been waiting there on purpose, hoping for a sexual encounter. Yet another part of him rejected that supposition: surely he was imagining it — such things just didn't happen in the quiet suburbs of Tokyo. That boy in the park had merely been resting on the swing. There was nothing suspicious in that.

The noodles came and he ate them, watching the sports news on the TV. The Giants weren't in the Central League playoffs this year so there wasn't much excitement in the reporting. Most of the other customers in the restaurant were reading newspapers. He finished the noodles and paid for them. But as soon as he stepped outside and turned toward the station again, his thoughts returned to the boy sitting on the swing. He wondered how long the boy would be sitting there.

At the ticket vending machine he bought a ticket for Koenji and headed toward the ticket gate. But just before he reached the station employee sitting there, he thrust the ticket into his jeans pocket, abruptly turned around and began walking back in the direction of the park. Perhaps the boy had already left, and he would be able to laugh about his foolish imaginings. He quickened his steps. As he neared the park he began to feel misgivings. If the boy were still there, he might misunderstand Fumio's motive in returning to the park. To his relief the boy was gone. A shadow behind the jungle gym moved. No, the boy was still here, but had moved over to the sandbox.

Not knowing what else to do, Fumio walked into the restroom. As he stepped up to a urinal, he glanced around to the entrance. The boy was standing there, a black shadow against the darkness behind. At Fumio's look, he stepped into a toilet stall, closing the door softly behind him. Fumio didn't hear the sound of the lock clicking. His heart began to pound. Things were moving much too fast. He stopped his charade of urinating and headed toward the entrance, determined to leave as quickly as possible. This was not what he'd planned on. But just as he was passing the stalls the toilet door creaked open. Startled, he halted, thinking the boy would step out. Instead, when he looked in, the boy was just standing there holding the door open, gazing at him with an expressionless look.

Fumio didn't know what to do. As he hesitated, the boy opened the door a shade wider. Feeling sucked in by forces beyond his control, Fumio stepped inside.

The door shut behind him and this time the lock clicked into place. The stall was a little cramped, and smelly. There was barely enough room for them both. Fumio couldn't believe he'd actually done it. Here he was, in a toilet stall with a total stranger, someone he'd never before seen in his life... someone who was (there could no longer be any doubt now) homosexual. Without any preliminaries, the boy reached down and brazenly rubbed the front of Fumio's jeans. Fumio felt as if he were in a dream. Everything was so direct; the main point was reached without the need for a gradual warming as there had been with Izumi. Did homosexuals always act as if they had so little time, rushing to do everything at a breakneck pace before it all dissolved away, before the fantasy faded... before the police came bursting in and hauled them away to jail?

Fumio tried to make his mind go blank. He could feel the boy begin to touch him intimately but it all seemed so distant that it had nothing to do with him. He could hear the faint noises of traffic on the thoroughfare a block away, the honking of car horns. He could even hear the conversation of passersby in a little lane about twenty meters distant. From a television set someplace could be heard a quiz program that he regularly watched. This was not erotic at all. He wished he had time to catch his breath, to mentally sit back and accept the fact of what was happening. Such a momentous event in his life needed perspective. It was hard to believe that it could happen at all, even to two anonymous boys in the middle of a city of eleven million people, in an out-of-the-way public park in a nameless neighborhood, in a dark toilet stall behind a locked door.

He closed his eyes and drew in his breath, but was startled into alertness when he felt the other boy begin undoing his jeans. He felt the sudden cool air against his skin as his pants and briefs were slid down his thighs. He was thinking: *If only we weren't here in this cramped, smelly toilet stall... If only I could relax.* All he could feel was an urgency, a nervousness. Just then the other boy dropped to his knees. An involuntary cry escaped Fumio: "No!"

The other boy drew back, startled, and looked up. It was the first word either of them had uttered. Now Fumio looked down at the boy's face and saw him for the first time: a boy of about high school age, the same age as some of the students he tutored. For some reason, Fumio couldn't help thinking of the boy's mother, and what she would think of her son like this, in a public toilet with a total stranger. He knew he could never go through with it. Quickly, he pulled his pants back on and zipped up. Without even looking at the boy, he unlocked the door, stepped out. Luckily, his cry hadn't been noticed by anyone — the park was still empty. Feeling as if the whole world's eyes were upon him he stepped out of the restroom and crossed the tiny park toward the station. But just as he passed the swings, he was startled to see the dark shadow of a man sitting there.

The orange glow of a cigarette got brighter, then faded. Fumio hurried past him toward the street. But even as he walked away he could feel the other's invisible gaze at his back, following him, following him, all the way home.

7

EVEN IN the short time he'd been collecting *Barazoku*, Fumio had noticed some changes in the magazine. More and more of the advertisements in back were being devoted to the new telephone services: sex tapes, message banks, dial Q2's, and telephone clubs. And though they were quite costly, he found he couldn't resist dialling in occasionally. Ever since the interrupted encounter with the boy in the toilet stall he'd felt a gnawing, unsatisfied yearning in his guts. The thought of what he'd almost done preyed on him. There was a small part of him which almost wished he'd gone through with it, though in fact, he knew he would never be able to seek his thrills in such a manner.

For one thing, the hurried, sneaking aspect of it put him off. Furtive encounters in places like that were just too sordid for his taste. And his innate sense of cleanliness wouldn't permit him to overcome his inhibitions; he feared catching some disease from a stranger. Yet, despite his feelings of repugnance, he often found himself reliving the encounter and wondering what would have happened if he'd been brave enough to go through with it. Because he didn't dare attempt it again, he found the telephone services a clean, safe way of indulging his fantasies. Though he sometimes felt ashamed at having to satisfy his desires in such a manner, he'd found the telephone services so fascinating that he was in danger of becoming an addict. The advertisement for a sex tape service had initially intrigued him: 'Don't dial in unless you have a box of tissues handy!'

When he dialled the number, a woman's voice on a computer had informed him of the charges: ten yen per twelve seconds. Then, after three rings, the line had been connected. Over the sounds of an indoor pool — splashing and echoey shouts — a young boy's voice had begun narrating: "My name is Seiji and I'm a second-year university student. I'm in the swimming club. Every day after school, I come to the school's pool to practice...." The scenario had continued: after practice one day, while Seiji is in the showers, the *sempai* whom he's had a crush on for a year comes in and begins showering. Seiji finds himself becoming aroused, so he turns to the wall to hide it. His *sempai*, wondering at the younger boy's sudden shyness, gruffly lectures him to get over any feelings of modesty. When Seiji reluctantly turns to face him, his *sempai*, far from showing any disgust, comes over to him. Amid the steam rising around them, they begin touching one another. "As my excitement became ever more intense, I found myself slipping down to my knees..." The tapes were apparently designed to climax with explicit sexual descriptions only after about two and a half minutes had elapsed.

Another telephone service was called Fruit Parlor, a so-called message bank, where one could have a message recorded and replayed continuously throughout the day on an endless tape. Again, after a woman's computer voice came on informing him of the charges, it had continued in a machine-like monotone: "For Banana dial, or boy-to-girl messages, press 2 on your push-button telephone. For Peach dial, or girl-to-boy messages, press 3 on your push-button telephone. For Strawberry dial, or girl-to-girl messages, press 4 on your push-button telephone. For Cherry dial, or boy-to-boy messages, press 5 on your push-button telephone. To fast-forward to the next message, press the asterisk dial. To access a message box, press — "

Fumio had pressed 5 and waited for the connection. After a brief pause, the tape came on, with the very human voices of the boys who'd left their messages: "Hello. My name is Toru and I'm a college student. I'm 20 years old, 175 centimeters in height and 65 kilos in weight. People tell me I'm above average in looks. I'm looking for a friend who will share my interests in music and travel. I don't want someone who just wants to play. If you are sincere and are seeking a long-term relationship, call my message box. That's Box number 45. I'll be waiting for you."

The next message came on immediately after. "Hi. I'm a 28-year-old salaryman who's looking for a good time. I take good care of my body and am used to getting compliments on it. My penis is 19 centimeters long, and it's hard right now. If you want to do something about it, let's get together tonight. I'm looking for some fun, with no strings attached. So, if you are young — about 18 to 22 —and want to meet someone who knows how to give pleasure, call my box. That's Box number 19. I can guarantee you a good time. You won't be disappointed. Don't forget: Box 19."

The next message had music in the background: "Hello again. I'm Tsutomu, from Box 82. Will Satoshi, who called my message box yesterday, please return the call? The last part of your message was not clear and I couldn't catch your telephone number. I'm interested in what you have to say. And incidentally, to all you crank callers out there, don't leave your messages in my box. Why don't you find another way to get your kicks? Again, Satoshi, I'll be waiting for your call. I'm in this afternoon until five o'clock. Thank you."

Fumio had enjoyed listening in on these messages (sometimes even on the other dials, for heteros and lesbians.) He was amazed at the number of boys who left messages, for he'd never been able to listen to the end of a tape. (The messages were apparently kept on file for about three days, then taped over.) He knew these services were paid for at some cost — usually calculated by the ten-second increment. A similar service was the dial Q2 system. Here, the caller was connected to a place where a number of young men were on call. Some of the ads had capsule descriptions of the boys, others even had photos. The ads usually said 'telephone sex OK', so Fumio had called in one night out of curiosity. He'd been connected randomly with a young man who introduced himself and began asking Fumio all sorts of questions (though not his name): his age, his occupation, his interests. Finally he'd asked if Fumio were gay. Fumio had demurred, hoping the other would talk more about himself. The other boy admitted that he was gay, and began talking about his homosexuality, though never in an erotic manner. Instead, he seemed intent on meeting Fumio. There was something a bit too professional about his manner, and Fumio suspected he was a prostitute. He'd rung off saying he wasn't sure about a meeting.

The only service he hadn't tried yet was the telephone club. He knew a little about how they worked from watching TV. Apparently a person could go to the telephone club and pay a certain fee to be able to sit for an hour in a partitioned cubicle and wait for calls to come in. Each tiny cubicle had its own telephone on a party line, and the first to pick it up on the ring got a chance to talk with the caller. How well one could interest the caller into meeting him depended on his verbal skills, for the idea was basically that the telephone club gave consenting adults a chance to meet each other. What happened after two people met was up to both parties, though most people assumed that such encounters led to sex. It was claimed that a certain number of professionals and semi-professionals used the service to find clients, but apparently the majority were just normal people looking for excitement.

From the ads in *Barazoku*, it seemed there were a couple of homosexual telephone clubs in Shinjuku. Maps were provided for each, and the accompanying diagrams even indicated the number of cubicles available. One evening, out of curiosity, Fumio picked up his telephone and called one of them. Someone answered on the first ring. "Hello?" The voice sounded young, and a little breathless, as if its owner had been waiting eagerly at the other end of the line.

"Hello?"

"How do you do. What's your name?"

Fumio gave the false name he'd had ready, and asked for the other's, knowing the other would probably do the same.

"How old are you?"

"Nineteen," replied Fumio.

"Are you a student, by any chance?"

"Yes."

"I thought you sounded like one. I'm a student, too."

"I'm glad to hear that," said Fumio, relieved.

"Is this the first time you called a telephone club?"

"Yes. And I'm a little nervous."

"Don't worry. Everyone is, at first."

It was all so polite. The other boy sounded sincere and natural, and his questions weren't at all in the professional manner of the Q2 boy. Still, Fumio was on his guard when the inevitable subject was broached.

"So... are you... gay?"

"Are you?" Fumio countered.

"Yes. I am. There: I confessed, now it's your turn."

"I'm... not sure," he equivocated, feeling for a credible storyline. He still felt a little like an imposter calling in when he wasn't the least interested in an actual encounter. "I'm very curious about the gay world," he confessed finally, feeling protected by the anonymity the telephone provided.

"Many people are. So that means you've never had an experience?"

"Never."

"Are you interested in having one?"

"I don't know." He felt his face flush, surprised by his own answer.

"Do you like girls?"

"Yes." He was about to add "of course," as if in reply to an obvious question.

"But you're also interested in boys."

"In a manner of speaking. And you?" He wanted to hear the other talk. "Which are you interested in?"

"For me there's no question. I don't think I've ever liked girls.

From the time I became sexually aware, there was never any doubt in my mind about my orientation. It was boys from the start, beginning with my junior high school classmates, then my physical education teacher, my high school friends, my college friends."

There was a freshness about the way they were talking which thrilled Fumio. He'd never thought he'd be able to speak so freely with another boy about such things. He'd assumed the conversations would be more sexual in nature, but this was turning out to be a sort of confessional. And it was not unpleasant. He wanted to find out more. Feeling his throat go dry, he asked: "Have you had any experiences? I mean, with other boys?"

"Just once."

"When?"

"Back in high school. I was spending the night over at a friend's house. Late at night, after his parents and sister had gone to sleep, we were up in his room watching adult videos. Well, one thing led to another, and soon we were masturbating together. That sort of thing happens a lot, I hear, even among boys who aren't gay. But you can imagine how I felt. Seeing my friend like that, I couldn't refrain from carrying it further. I knew I might never have another chance. So, making a joke out of the whole thing, I managed to convince him to let me..."

"What?"

"You know... with my mouth."

Fumio felt his eyes go hot. "You actually did that?"

"Yes. It was like a dream come true."

"And what was his reaction?"

"He seemed a little embarrassed about it afterwards, but apparently took it all in his stride as part of the usual boys' play. It was never again mentioned afterwards between us, though."

"And after that? Were there any other experiences?"

"No. I guess I'm still very much afraid of being known as a homosexual. That's why I came here to the tele-club. I thought I might be able to meet someone I could talk to about myself."

"I see."

"How about you? You must have some interest in homosexuality or you wouldn't have called this number."

Fumio hesitated. As the other boy realized there was no answer forthcoming, he continued his questioning: "You said you've had no experiences with boys. How about girls? Have you ever slept with a girl?"

"Yes."

"And did you enjoy it?"

"I suppose so."

"You don't sound so thrilled about it."

"Well, it wasn't quite what I'd expected. I mean, I thought there would be more to it. There seemed to be something lacking. I don't know if I can explain it so well."

"Try."

"Well, actually... You see, in a way, it all seemed so mechanical. As if I was only going through the motions. I found myself wanting more."

"What more could you want?"

"I don't know. I wonder if there's something wrong with me. I find myself doing things."

"What sorts of things?"

"One time I went to a gay movie theater."

"There's nothing wrong with that."

"Afterwards, in the park, I saw something. In the restroom. How can people do such things?"

"Were you disgusted?"

"Yes."

"Have you ever thought of doing such things?"

"Not in a park toilet."

"Then someplace else?"

Fumio considered. "If I liked the other person... maybe. That is, it's not completely out of the question."

There was a pause, during which Fumio became aware of what he had just confessed to. His hand holding the receiver felt cramped; he realized he was clutching it too tightly. He transferred it to his other hand just as the other spoke: "Would you like to meet?"

"Meet?" Fumio tried to picture how the other boy looked. "No, I'm not ready for that yet. As I said, I'm only curious about these things."

"I'm not going to seduce you. All I want is to talk with you. Besides, it'll cost so much less than what we're paying now."

"That's true."

"This evening, if you're free."

Fumio hesitated.

"How about nine o'clock this evening?" The other boy had tried hard to keep the eagerness from showing in his voice.

"Where?"

"Does Shinjuku station sound all right?"

"How will I know you?"

"I'll be carrying a rolled-up magazine, maybe *Focus* or *Friday.* Why don't you carry one, too, so I'll recognize you? Let's meet on the Chuo Line platform, the Tokyo-bound side, where the first car stops. How's that?"

"I don't know..."

"I'll be there tonight anyway. I'll be waiting there."

"..."

"Goodbye."

"Goodbye." As Fumio hung up, he glanced at his watch. It was only seven-thirty.

8

SHINJUKU STATION was crowded, as it usually was at this time, with commuters heading home and pleasure seekers arriving for the night. Jostling his way through the throng, Fumio slowly made his way toward the rendezvous point specified by his partner on the telephone. He had decided, after some self-debate, that he wanted to see how the other boy looked: to match a face to the voice which had delivered such a personal confession. His own identity need not be revealed; he planned to continue walking straight on after confirming who his partner was, a passing stranger in the faceless crowd. A little nervous despite his efforts at self-control, he headed toward the front end of the platform. He'd purposely taken a car near the middle of the train so he wouldn't be suspected.

The crowd on the platform gradually began to disperse as people flowed toward the various exits. Fumio glanced at the benches in what he hoped was an offhand manner giving no indication of the anxiety he felt. There was a young man sitting at the far end of the last one, lightly riffling through a *Focus* magazine. He had to be the one. Despite his desire to see the face, Fumio was so nervous that he couldn't bring himself to look up. Strangely enough, however, it seemed that the other was peering intently at him, even though he wasn't carrying the requested magazine. As impossible as it seemed, Fumio wondered if he'd been recognized as the voice on the telephone. Steeling himself, he glanced up at the boy, not registering the face for an instant, so nervous was he about his deception.

"Is it you, Fumio?"

The other had spoken to him first. Sitting on the bench, rolling the magazine nervously in his hands, was Mori, his college friend from Nagano. Fumio hoped the shock didn't show on his face. For a moment he had an irrational impulse to flee, before he realized his own secret was still intact. Mori could have no idea that it had been Fumio who had called the telephone club. The two friends continued to look at one another in speechless surprise. For a moment Fumio wondered why he hadn't recognized his friend's voice on the telephone, then realized that because they'd both been speaking Tokyo dialect, they'd inadvertently disguised their identities. Still, even with the evidence before his eyes, he couldn't believe Mori was gay. His image of homosexuals had been formed by the attractive boy models in *Barazoku*, and he couldn't reconcile it with his plain-looking, normal-acting college friend. Gay men were supposed to look and act the part — flamboyant, effeminate, and attractive. Because this image was so strong, he couldn't help wondering if Mori had been here with a *Focus* magazine purely by coincidence, and had actually been waiting for someone else. That seemed the more likely explanation. However, if it were true that Mori had indeed been the one who'd made those confessions, it would be a great relief somehow to learn for sure that one of the people he'd known personally was secretly homosexual. With the dawning of this possibility, Mori suddenly assumed a completely different personality.

Finally Fumio found suitable words for the situation. "I thought I recognized you." Mori, too, no doubt realizing now that Fumio had no idea of his intended tryst, made his expression more natural. Still, he couldn't hide a certain furtive look in his eyes, as if he'd been caught at something illicit. Apparently he was nervous at the thought of his 'real' partner on the telephone showing up now. And he didn't want to be caught in such an awkward situation.

"What are you doing here at this time of night, Fumio?"

"Looking for books at Kinokuniya bookstore. I couldn't find the one I wanted, so I was heading down to Kanda Jimbocho when I saw you on the platform." He found the lies coming effortlessly to his lips. "Boy, was I surprised to see you. It's been so long. How long has it been?"

"I can't remember..."

Fumio felt a strange sense of displacement come over him. It was almost as if he were standing outside the scene, watching it all with the detached attitude of a spectator enjoying a movie, knowing something the protagonists don't. As he realized that he was completely safe, a subtle streak of cruelty awoke in him.

"What are you doing here, Mori? Waiting for someone?"

"Yes." Mori glanced at his watch in an irritated manner. "But I don't think they'll show. I've been waiting over an hour now. Would you like to go someplace?" It was obvious he wanted to get away from there as quickly as possible.

Something in Fumio was delighted at the agitation he was causing in his friend. "No. Let's stick around a bit longer. Sometimes people get delayed for the most trivial reasons. Who are you waiting for?"

"It's no one important. It can wait till another day."

"Is it a girl, by any chance?"

"Listen," Mori said, looking at his watch again, "why don't we go someplace and have a drink? I can really use one."

Fumio decided he'd teased his friend enough. "All right." They went down the steps nearby and turned left at the bottom. Mori led the way toward the west exit of the station. The pub they found was innocuous, filled with businessmen and office ladies laughing and joking away the stresses of the working day. As soon as they finished their beers, they switched to their usual high sours. Perhaps out of relief, Mori was drinking them at a much faster rate than was usual for him. Fumio, looking at his friend with new eyes, found himself wondering what other secrets lay hidden behind the bland, innocent exterior of his face. The confessions on the phone had certainly revealed a much more passionate secret life than anyone would have guessed from looking at him. Fumio thought of the night they'd all gone to Petit Doll, largely at Mori's instigation. Had he been trying to 'cure' himself with a visit to a fashion health parlor?

"So, what have you been up to, Mori?"

"Nothing much. Just the usual. And you? Are you still tutoring?"

"Yes. Isn't it pitiful?" They'd both reverted to Nagano dialect, and the change made Fumio feel more relaxed. It now seemed so strange to imagine the confessions they'd both made over the telephone when they'd been anonymous voices. He wondered if it would be possible to speak of such things in the open, now that they were actually face to face, though only he himself was aware of the real situation. For a moment he toyed with the thought of confessing that he'd been the caller on the phone. It would be interesting to see what Mori's reaction would be. After all, he had much more to lose by it.

"You're not talking too much tonight, Fumio. Do you have any problems you're worried about?"

"Me? No. I was just wondering what all the others are doing. I haven't seen much of the old gang lately. Can you bring me up to date on them?"

"There's not much to relate. Harada found a girlfriend and is living with her now."

"Oh? I'm surprised. Where is she from? Is she a Tokyo girl?"

"No, she's from Akita."

"Even more of a country hick than us."

"That's true. She's a nice girl, actually. I met her once."

"How about Kurita? I thought he would be the first. He has the best looks of all of us."

"Kurita is still unattached. But I think he has a girlfriend back in Nagano he hasn't told us about. It's my guess that he's serious about her."

"Hm. Everyone seems to have secrets these days. How about you, Mori? Do you have a girlfriend?"

"Me? No." He took a nervous sip from his high sour. The lenses of his glasses flashed back the reflection of the lights over the bar counter behind Fumio. Buoyed by a spreading intoxication, Fumio decided to probe gingerly into more personal aspects of his friend's life.

"Have you ever been back to that fashion health we visited that time... what was its name?"

"Petit Doll? No. Of course not. I can't afford those kinds of prices."

"But you're a doctor's son. You're supposed to be living it up while in Tokyo."

"I wish I could."

"If I had your kind of money, there'd be no stopping me. I'd be the emperor of the night," he joked, laughing. "I would get to know my way around Shinjuku, at least."

Mori laughed feebly, and Fumio picked up a piece of dried squid and brought it to his mouth. For a while they said nothing more. Mori had turned thoughtful. He was twirling his glass around, making the ice in it tinkle, occasionally bringing it up to his mouth to take a drink. When he'd finished off his cocktail he signalled to the waiter for another. Fumio noticed that the waiter was quite attractive, and wondered if Mori felt any interest in him. It was a thought which gave him a strange, muted sort of satisfaction; it made him feel worldly to be so open-minded about such a possibility.

"Fumio?"

"Hm?"

"About that time we all went to Petit Doll..."

"What about it?"

"Do you remember what happened that night?"

"Of course. We envied you because you took so long. You really got your money's worth, didn't you?"

Mori gave a brief laugh, then fell silent. "Listen. Do you promise not to tell the others?" He spoke in a low voice, looking around to ensure he wasn't overheard, a superfluous precaution in this noisy pub.

"What?"

"The reason I took so long is quite different."

"Different?" A premonitory chill crept up Fumio's neck.

"I couldn't get an erection. That's the real reason I took so long. Finally we just gave up. I made the girl promise not to tell anyone."

Fumio felt unable to say anything.

"I guess I was nervous," continued Mori, speaking more rapidly now. "That's what the girl told me. It happens to a lot of guys, she said, a lot more than you might think. She says almost all the guys that go there are very drunk, and alcohol causes temporary impotence."

"We *were* drinking quite a lot that night."

"Yeah." Mori fell silent again, seeming to ponder on what he was about to say before continuing. "And another thing. I think I watch too many porno videos. I'm afraid I'm coming to rely on them too much for stimulation. I'll probably never be any good with women when it comes down to the real thing. What'll I do?"

"Don't worry," Fumio reassured him, not knowing what else to say. "I'm sure there's no problem with you physically. You just have to relax, that's all."

"Do you think it could be something else?"

"What do you mean?"

"I mean my problem might be deeper than that."

"I don't understand."

Mori lowered his voice even more, speaking so softly that Fumio had to lean in closer to hear what he was saying. "I have this fear.... What if I'm homosexual?" Fumio felt his blood freeze. "What are you talking about?" He wondered now if his voice over the telephone had been recognized, and that Mori had been playing with him all along, or was gradually working toward an atmosphere in which he could finally make his confession.

"It's possible I couldn't get excited by the girl in Petit Doll because I'm unable to."

Fumio forced a laugh. "Don't worry, Mori. I'm sure it has nothing to do with it. You're the most normal person I know."

"That doesn't mean I might not have abnormal urges occasionally."

"Abnormal..." Fumio felt the resonance of the word linger in his mind like a solid temple bell just rung. His ears felt hot and his mouth was dry. "A lot of boys probably have the same fear. It's nothing to get worried about."

"Do you?"

"Do I what?"

"Worry that you might be homo?"

"Of course not," he fired back, then, seeing the disappointed expression on his friend's face, softened the denial. "Uh... well, maybe I do, sometimes. But it's all a lot of pointless anxiety. You should just forget about it."

"Did you ever wonder if anyone we know might be 'like that?'"

"You mean homosexual?"

Mori nodded slowly. "I mean, think of it. What if one of your friends was homosexual and you didn't know it? It's possible, isn't it?"

"Anything's possible."

"What if you were one?"

"What?" A bright light seemed to flash before Fumio's eyes. "Don't joke about things like that."

"Sexual feelings are so tangled up sometimes, so mysterious and hard to explain, even to yourself, that anything is possible. In this world, anything is possible."

Firmly, decisively, Fumio stated: "I like girls. Period. There's nothing wrong with me."

"I'm not saying there's anything wrong with you. When you come down to it, there's probably nothing wrong with any of those tastes we call abnormal. As for me, well, I like girls, too, but — " Suddenly he seemed to lose confidence in what he was about to say but he pressed on. "Sometimes I feel so — "

"Yes?"

"I wish I had the courage."

"The courage?"

"To do things."

"What things?"

Mori looked down at the table and began carefully picking apart the piece of dried squid on the plate before him. There was a long silence. The song being played was a suggestive hit single by one of the many girl groups which were so popular now. Fumio wondered if this were his moment to admit that it was he who'd phoned the tele-club. He felt almost breathless. He knew somehow that a secret message had been conveyed, that Mori had just revealed a glimpse of his soul. Everything from here on in could only lead to a mutual confession, or complete denial. Now that he thought of it, Mori's mannered, oblique way of getting to the point had slowly proceeded according to some ritual design, and could have happened in no other way.

Fumio felt himself begin to shiver, and Mori noticed it, for he said, "Are you cold? Maybe the air conditioner is on too high?"

"No... no."

"What is it?"

"I think it's about time I got home. I have to study for a test tomorrow."

Mori looked at his watch. "I didn't realize it was this late. And here I've been, keeping you here with my trivial talk."

"No. I enjoyed it. Really."

"It was good to see you after so long. Don't keep yourself hidden away so much anymore."

"All right."

Mori reached into his back pocket for his wallet. "And it's my treat."

"No, it's okay. I just got paid yesterday."

"I'm the doctor's son, remember? I can afford this much, don't worry."

"Well, all right. If you insist. But remember: the next one's on me. All right?"

"Sure."

As Fumio got up to pull on his windbreaker, the waiter called out in a loud, ringing voice: "Thank you very much for coming!" But Mori had made no move to get up. He remained seated, the plate of dried squid before him, his hands cupped protectively around his drinking glass.

"I'll see you, then," said Fumio, moving toward the pub's entrance.

"Fumio?"

"Yes?" He turned around. Mori was looking up at him from under a lowered brow.

"You won't... tell the others... about my fears?"

"Of course not." Fumio felt a rawness in his throat. "I'm your friend, aren't I?" He was afraid to say any more.

9

FUMIO HAD wanted to visit a gay bar for some time now, and his accidental discovery about Mori somehow lent impetus to this longing. The knowledge that someone he knew was actually homosexual gave a certain legitimacy to his ongoing curiosity about the rose tribe. Actually, going to gay bars was not such an unusual thing for many young people. In fact it was quite fashionable now to know at least one to which you could take your friends. The proprietors of gay bars were known to be talkative, interesting and funny; at least a customer was never bored there. Transvestite bars were especially popular since the so-called 'new-halfs' kept their customers laughing by acting outrageously, joking, gossiping, and performing unmentionable party tricks. They were true entertainers in every sense. The theory was that they had to work twice as hard as real women to keep a man interested — whereas a true woman only had to sit there, pour drinks, and laugh at a man's jokes to keep him satisfied.

But Fumio didn't want to go to a gay bar with a group of friends just to get drunk and have a good time. He wanted, if possible, to be able to speak with a gay man frankly and openly. And he wanted to do it in such a way that his friends would never find out about it; they were sure to misunderstand his motives. He had to go alone. The problem was finding a good bar. He didn't want to go to one in Shinjuku where he was likely to run across someone he knew. He needed one which was out of the way, and which very few people would frequent. The back pages of *Barazoku* listed the bars geographically, and he scanned the areas a little bit away from the heart of the city. The western suburbs of Tokyo seemed the most likely place to look. An advertisement for a bar called Aladdin intrigued him: 'small, comfortable, and friendly atmosphere'. An accompanying map indicated it was located all the way out in Tachikawa, a part of Tokyo where Fumio's friends probably never went. It was a residential suburb, and Aladdin was probably the only gay bar in that part of town.

Fumio decided to chance it. Carefully, he tore the advertisement out of the magazine and slipped it into his wallet. The south side of Tachikawa station was apparently less developed than the north. There were no large department stores or fashionable boutiques, only the familiar shopping arcades which one saw in all medium-sized cities. For Fumio, this felt very much like being back in

Nagano.

It was a cold night with a chilly wind blowing from the north. He could see his exhaled breath like a comic-book speech balloon, and it reminded him of how, as a boy, he used to play at being Godzilla on cold winter mornings in the school playground. He'd never been to this part of Tokyo before, so he first scouted out the area, walking to his destination and passing the alley where Aladdin was located several times as he familiarized himself with the streets. Aladdin had its lighted sign out in the street like any number of bars along here, and nothing distinguished it from the rest. Still, Fumio didn't have the nerve to enter right away. He stepped into a nearby Beef Bowl and had a light dinner along with a beer. He quickly finished off the beer and ordered another one.

By the time he left he was feeling a little more relaxed. Still, the idea of stepping through Aladdin's door made his knees feel weak and he had to pass it a couple of times before he could buck up his courage and force himself to enter just as he was going past it for the third time. His heart was literally pounding as he pushed open the door. The moment he stepped in, everyone in the bar turned to look at him. He had a feeling he'd interrupted an ongoing conversation.

"Welcome," said the boy behind the bar. "Please have a seat." Fumio sat down on the nearest stool and said hello. The boy handed him a warmed-up hand towel and Fumio heard the men behind him resume their conversations. "What would you like to drink?" The young bartender was quite attractive, and not at all gay-looking. He seemed ordinary enough — probably a college student like himself, working part-time.

"A beer, please." He wiped his hands on the towel. The boy set the beer before him and went back to his interrupted talk with a quiet-looking man at the other end of the counter. As Fumio drank his beer he listened in on the talk around him. It seemed to be quite normal, what one might hear in any bar. Nothing would lead him to suspect that this was anything other than a neighborhood bar. He got the impression that most of the customers were regulars who came almost every day after work. There was a poster of James Dean behind the counter and another of a handsome man he didn't recognize. But did that make this a gay bar? Fumio began to wonder if he'd made some sort of mistake.

Then a man a few stools down talked in a somewhat louder voice; Fumio caught the word 'homo'. He didn't bat an eye. He felt as if he were being tested, or warned that he was in a gay bar; perhaps the patrons thought he might have come here by accident? A few minutes later he again heard someone talk about 'gays'. The man who said it then glanced at Fumio to check his reaction, but Fumio merely smiled and went on drinking. This seemed to do the trick. It was as if he'd passed the test, and the ice was immediately broken. The talk all around him resumed in a much more natural manner, and the men seemed to pick up their conversations from where they'd left off when Fumio had stepped in.

The bartender came over to him. "My name's Yuji," he said. "What's yours?"

Fumio hesitated, then decided he had nothing to lose by telling his real name. "Fumio."

"Oh, we had another Fumi-chan who used to come here before, but he stopped coming two or three years ago. He was transferred to a branch office in Osaka. Where are you from?"

"Nagano."

"Shima-chan over there is from Nagano." The man pointed out by Yuji heard his own name, looked over and smiled. Yuji said to him, "This is Fumi-chan from Nagano."

"What part of Nagano?"

Fumio told him.

"I know it well. I was born just a few kilometers from there."

A drunken-looking man sitting nearby said, not unkindly, "Well, well, this is practically a family reunion."

Fumio laughed. The tension he'd felt ever since coming inside immediately vanished. There was such a relaxed atmosphere in here that he couldn't help feeling relieved. And, though this was his first visit here, everyone seemed genuinely kind. He felt he was among friends who were eager to include him in their ranks. One strange custom he noticed (which probably helped give it a relaxed atmosphere) was that everyone used nicknames when addressing one another. The diminutive suffix 'chan' was preferred, as if everyone were a longtime friend. (Normally it was only used for small children or very close acquaintances, never for grown men.) This was unusual in Japan where the suffix 'san' was almost always used out of respect.

To Fumio's surprise, even older men were called "Yama-chan" or "Hara-chan" by younger ones. He'd never before been in this kind of atmosphere, a democratic limbo found nowhere else in Japan. It was like being in another country. Normally, one was always aware whether one was addressing a superior, an equal, or a subordinate. Here, all those rules were suspended. He could talk to anyone like a friend or age-mate; identity was fluid. There were no last names.

Rank, status, even gender meant nothing. (Some of the men seemed more comfortable with feminine forms of speech.) This was rebellion against everything outside Aladdin's doors, against all of society.

"Mind if I sit next to you?" said Shima-chan.

"Not at all."

The man appeared to be in his mid-thirties and looked like an ordinary salaryman. As he sat down next to Fumio, he began asking him about his school, his major, his part-time job. It was light, friendly conversation which might be overheard at any normal drinking place. Fumio found himself warming up to this fellow native of Nagano. Shima-chan hadn't visited his hometown in three years and Fumio brought him up to date on many local happenings. They mentioned all the places they knew in common. Then they came around to the subject to which fellow provincials always seemed to gravitate.

"What do you think about living in Tokyo, Fumi-chan?"

"To tell you the truth, I like it. When I went back home last summer, everything seemed... well, after being here, it all seemed so drab, so limited. I actually felt out of place there and couldn't wait to get back here."

Shima-chan laughed. "I was the same the first time I went home. Many of my friends seemed to resent the fact that I was able to live and work in Tokyo. They didn't come right out and say it, of course, only hinted around, you know, like they do."

"Yes. But many of my high school friends said they envied me. When I told them about life here, I must have left out the loneliness and homesickness, and the tiny cramped apartment I have to live in. They pictured my life here as it is in those trendy TV dramas."

"As if everybody here lives like that, eh?"

"Mm. My relatives told me my speech had become Tokyo-like. They thought I was putting on airs, and I resented that. I'm still very proud of my roots but people back home don't realize that here you have to speak like everyone else, otherwise you stand out."

"I know, I know," laughed Shima-chan. "I still have the same problem. But living in Tokyo hasn't taken the country out of me. Whenever I get a phone call from home I revert to Nagano dialect. And as soon as I hang up I'm speaking standard speech. It becomes second nature."

"But it's not easy. When I first came here, I made an effort to sound Tokyo. In my mind I thought I was pulling it off. But people would laugh and tell me they could guess my roots. So I did an about-face and started speaking with a thick Nagano accent — one that I would never have used at home."

"Exactly. And the thing is, the people who most pointedly note your rural origin are those who've just come up from the country themselves, the ones who've managed to blend in. They delight in seeing the distance they've come, the contrast they provide with someone just arriving. Most real Tokyoites could care less that you're provincial. We country people have a complex, I guess. But we shouldn't. We probably outnumber the real Tokyoites. Just about everyone in Tokyo is from someplace else, and I don't see why we should try to hide it."

"I agree." Fumio felt a genuine liking for Shima-chan who, unlike many of the older men he knew, was worldly and experienced without being condescending. As if guessing his thoughts, Shima-chan suddenly asked him: "How old would you say I am?"

Fumio looked at him. Older people always asked him this question, and he always tried to answer about two or three years younger than what he really thought. He knew this pleased them. "Oh, about 30, 31?"

"I'm 38," said Shima-chan, pleased.

Fumio was surprised. "You look so much younger," he said truthfully.

"Living in the city keeps you looking young. Whenever I go to a high school reunion back home, my schoolmates who've stayed in Nagano always look so much older."

"Do you think you'll ever go back for good?"

"I don't know." He lapsed into thought for a while and seemed about to admit something, but then thought better of it. Perhaps it would have been a personal confession. "How about you?"

"I have to return after I graduate." The thought suddenly depressed him.

"Oh, that's too bad."

"Yeah." A couple of customers at the other end of the bar got up to leave, and Fumio looked at his watch. The time had flown and it was almost time for the last train.

"Are you leaving?" asked Shima-chan. There was a hint of disappointment in his voice and Fumio wondered if he'd be propositioned. He half-hoped he would be.

"I'm afraid I have to. I have an early class tomorrow." No one else in the bar seemed worried about missing the last train; they probably lived nearby or could afford to take taxis home.

"Will you be back again?"

Fumio thought. "I guess I could come back next week."

"Good. I'll be looking forward to seeing you."

"I enjoyed meeting you, Shima-chan."

"Me, too. Good night."

"Good night." He paid for his beer and found to his delight that it cost much less than what most drinking places charged. Outside, the night had turned much colder. He buttoned his coat and turned up the collar. All in all he felt satisfied with his first visit to a gay bar. Aladdin had been much less wicked than he'd expected. With Shima-chan there'd been no talk at all of sex though Fumio had overheard some of the other patrons discuss it openly. He was glad Shima-chan had refrained, though. It would have put a burden on their talk.

10

WHEN HE returned to Aladdin the following Tuesday, Fumio experienced much less uneasiness about going. He walked straight there from the station, knowing full well what to expect when he stepped in the door. Until the night before, though, he hadn't been sure if he'd make another visit. After all, one visit had been enough to satisfy his curiosity about gay bars. Unlike his previous image of them, the men in them hadn't seemed like perverts at all. His fear that they would try to seduce him had been completely unfounded. A part of him had even been a little disappointed that his venture into sin had proved so mundane — an evening of good conversation with an intelligent older man. There had been nothing overtly gay about Aladdin at all except for the special atmosphere of the place. He realized that he hadn't even thought to ask Shima-chan if he were homosexual. In fact, there was no guarantee that all the men in Aladdin had been gay. Shima-chan might well have been a normal man who merely enjoyed the unusual ambience of the place. After all, Fumio himself was not gay, yet had had a good enough time there.

As he stepped inside, Yuji greeted him cheerfully by name from behind the counter and Fumio returned the courtesy. He noticed Shima-chan right away. To his surprise, the older man was dressed up in a nice suit and tie. Fumio felt flattered at the trouble he'd taken, but a little awkward. He wondered if this was how a girl felt when a man dressed up to please her. And in a curious way, he was relieved to discover that the older man had been attracted to him after all. He sat down on the stool next to Shima-chan and they began speaking as if they'd known each other much longer than one week.

Most of the men who were here tonight were the same ones that had been here last week, and as the evening wore on, they had no compunctions about joining in on the conversation between Fumio and Shima-chan. Soon the talk was general. Aladdin was cozy enough that anyone in the place, no matter where he was sitting, could easily speak with any other person there. This time some of the men cautiously told Fumio about their homosexual experiences. One man had been in a hetero porno theater where he was approached by another man. They'd gone off to a hotel. Later, as he was dressing, he discovered that his wallet was missing. The next day he got a phone call at the office. It was from the man of the night before: he'd gotten the telephone number from a business card in the wallet. He threatened to blackmail if he didn't pay up.

"And did you pay him?" asked Fumio.

"I had no choice. I paid the money and never heard from him again."

"Wow."

"You have to be careful," he said.

"I will," said Fumio, thinking about the man he'd followed outside World Masterpiece Theater. He felt so worldly and sophisticated to be the recipient of these confidences after only his second visit. It indicated that he was trusted by everyone here. This was exactly what he'd been looking for when he'd scanned the advertisements for gay bars in the back pages of *Barazoku.* He wished he'd come here much sooner.

A fey-looking man sitting several seats down interrupted his ongoing conversation with another customer to ask Fumio: "And how about you, Fumi-chan? Are you a cherry-boy?" They all laughed good-naturedly as Fumio scratched his head in embarrassment.

"Don't tease him," said another, and the matter wasn't pursued. When the laughter had died down, Shima-chan turned to Fumio. "You're not a regular at this bar. What made you decide to drop in?"

"I don't know. Mostly curiosity. I found the advertisement for it in the back pages of *Barazoku.*"

"I see."

Fumio felt his face get hot. "I guess it was a dare I took with myself."

"So you're new to this world."

"Very new."

"Don't be put off by the bizarre characters you see here."

"I don't find the people here bizarre in the least. They're quite gentlemen."

"Hear! Hear!" sang out the fey-looking man, amid much laughter. Shima-chan went on: "The first time I entered this world, I was scared, too."

"When was that?"

"I was about your age, I think. In college. All through junior high school and high school I had strong feelings about some of my classmates — male classmates. And I thought I was the only one in the world to feel them. Did you ever have that feeling?"

"I'm not so sure... " Fumio recalled that he'd always been a little attracted to certain *sempai*, especially in the soccer club. But it was quite common in high school for younger boys to look up to, even idolize, attractive older schoolmates. Fumio had secretly nursed vague yearnings for the ace striker on the soccer team, but they had never turned sexual in nature. As far as he knew, all his sexual desires had been focussed on girls, as they still were. It was just that girls were so out of reach.

He turned to Shima-chan. "Don't you find women attractive?"

"Attractive? Yes. But I feel nothing sexual for them."

"I see." Fumio felt a shiver go through him. At the same time he was relieved, for he himself did feel sexual desire for them. He was obviously not a candidate for fulltime membership in the rose tribe. Yet Shima-chan's open confession thrilled him. He had been toying with the thought of extending his explorations even further, and had half decided that if he were ever going to have sex with a man, it would be with someone like Shima-chan. The idea, at least, didn't disgust him. But so far Shima-chan had made no move toward a proposition, and a part of Fumio felt let down. From the way they had gotten along, he was almost sure Shima-chan was attracted to him. But perhaps he was merely being kind-hearted, doing his best to make the newest member of the group feel welcome here.

However, as the time approached for Fumio to leave tonight, Shima-chan casually offered to give him a ride home. Feeling almost relieved, Fumio accepted without hesitation. They went outside together and lined up for a taxi in front of the station, for all the world like two fellow office workers going home after a couple of drinks. Once they were inside the taxi, Shima-chan asked him, "Do you have to go straight home?"

"Not really." Fumio felt his heart begin to race.

"All right. There's another place I'd like to take you."

"Sure." It turned out to be a pub, not a gay one, where many young people gathered. They had a few more drinks here and continued talking about innocuous subjects: baseball, popular music, scandals in the entertainment world. Perhaps because this was the first time they were away from Aladdin, there was a refreshing naturalness to their conversation which had been lacking back in the gay bar. However, Fumio found himself thinking so much about what might happen later tonight that he was barely paying attention to what the other man was saying. He cast a furtive glance down at his watch, but Shima-chan apparently noticed it.

"Shall we go?" he asked, looking at his own watch. "I didn't realize the time."

"All right."

"But I'd like to take a little walk to clear my head. I'm afraid I drank a little too much tonight."

"Me, too."

They stepped outside and began to walk. Fumio noted for the first time the presence of many business hotels in the area. However, from the looks of the young couples walking along nestled closely together, it was obvious what kind of hotels they really were. Shima-chan noticed the direction of Fumio's gaze and confirmed his guess. "Yes, this is where they all come," he said. "Looks like they're out in full force tonight."

Fumio didn't have the strength to say anything.

"Have you ever been in a love hotel?" asked Shima-chan.

"Just once," said Fumio truthfully.

"Only once? A healthy young boy like you?"

"I'm not exactly the most popular boy on campus," laughed Fumio. "So it's not as if I have that many opportunities to go. That one time was a fluke, really, and came about quite by chance."

Ahead of them, a young couple, looking furtive, slipped into one of the recessed entryways. Shima-chan nodded in their direction. "You can tell at a glance that this is their first visit together. A couple which has had many trysts don't have that guilty look about them."

Fumio laughed uncertainly. "That's how I must have looked when I went in." Glancing up at the facade of the building they were passing, he mused aloud, "I wonder if these hotels are as fancy as the one I stayed in."

"That depends on what you mean by 'fancy'," said Shima-chan with a slight laugh. "Would you like to step inside one and see?"

"Sure."

It was all so casual, so smooth that Fumio felt no resistance. But as he thought of the enormity of what he'd just done, a queasy feeling grew in his stomach. He stayed a little ways in the shadows as Shima-chan paid for the key at the check-in booth. As with the first hotel, a blind hid the clerk so that only her hands were visible. Together they walked up a flight of stairs in a stairwell which had been purposely darkened. Fumio kept his face averted just in case they should encounter another couple descending, but they met no one. It wasn't until they'd entered the room and locked the door behind them that Fumio realized how skillfully Shima-chan had wafted him into this hotel room.

Looking around, he saw at a glance that it was a lot less luxurious than the one he'd been in with Izumi. The air felt slightly stuffy.

"Well, shall we watch some TV?" said Shima-chan, as if that had been their sole purpose in coming here.

"All right."

"Make yourself at home. I'm sure they have some drinks here."

"Nothing alcoholic for me, thanks. I've had quite enough to drink already."

The older man opened the refrigerator and peered inside at the contents. "How about a can of oolong tea, then?"

"That sounds good."

He dug out a can and handed it to Fumio. "Here you are."

As Fumio reached for it, he noted with some shame that his own hand was shaking slightly. Shima-chan paused, a concerned look on his face. "You're not scared, are you?"

"This is my first time with a man," Fumio blurted out.

Shima-chan smiled. "I guessed that already. Don't worry. We don't have to do anything tonight if you don't want to. I don't want you to think — "

"It's all right. It's just that I may be a little nervous, so please understand."

"I understand. I'm very nervous, too. You see, I didn't know if you were interested in anything more than friendship. I half thought you would bolt and run away when I mentioned 'love hotel'."

"Well, I'm here now. And I'm completely in your hands." He all but bowed as a freshman employee might bow to a section chief.

Shima-chan smiled. "Why don't you take a shower? It'll probably help you relax."

"That sounds good."

Fumio went to the little nook in front of the shower room and began undressing, hanging up his clothes on the hanger provided. When he glanced back to the bedroom he saw Shima-chan apparently absorbed in watching the TV. He stepped into the shower room and turned on the water, adjusting the spray until it was a gentle, warm rain. It was indeed refreshing. He felt his stiff muscles soften under the water's light massage.

Shima-chan stuck his head in at the door. "How's the water? I hope you don't have it too hot."

He stepped in and Fumio saw he was nude. The older man came to join him under the spray and strangely enough, Fumio felt no qualms about it. As they took a shower together shifting about under the jetting water, Shima-chan's hand seemed to slip accidentally onto Fumio's body. Fumio said nothing, and the hand remained there. Heart pounding, Fumio closed his eyes. They got out and dried off. As they sat down on the bed Shima-chan gently pushed Fumio onto his back. Fumio thought about his encounter with the boy in the toilet stall, and oddly this seemed merely a continuation of that, as if no time had elapsed since then. He felt very nervous and just lay there stiffly. A curious sense of dislocation seemed to come over him. He realized he knew almost nothing about Shima-chan — where he lived, what he did for a living, or even if 'Shima' was the prefix of his real name. A week ago they'd been absolute strangers, completely unaware of each other's faces. Until a little while ago they'd been drinking together like fellow office workers. And now here they were, both lying nude atop this bed, engaged in the most intimate contact possible between two people. In the midst of these strangely dispassionate thoughts he felt an odd voluptuousness come over him. He looked at Shima-chan. Though he wasn't a bad-looking man, Fumio would have preferred a girl. But no girl would do this for him.

Shima-chan stopped what he was doing and gazed up at him. "I want you to fuck me," he said in a soft voice.

"I don't know if I can."

"You can, don't worry." Fumio watched expressionlessly as Shima-chan reached into the drawer of the night table and pulled out a small bottle containing an amber-colored jelly.

"Do you know what this is?" he asked Fumio.

"No."

"It's a lubricant. To make it easier."

Fumio swallowed. Shima-chan lay down beside him on the bed. Fumio had never known that a man could look like this, so passively expectant. The soft look in his eyes, the gentleness of his movements and gestures seemed to endow him with a magical femininity which permeated his torso and limbs. Outside this room Shima-chan had been a respectable-looking man in his thirties dressed in a business suit. And now he'd been transformed into a nebulous, desirous creature whose skin seemed so much softer.

Fumio felt a dreamlike unreality as he began going through the motions. He commanded much more self-possession that he would have expected. Yet at the core of his being was a tight ball of nervousness which seemed to grow heavier and heavier. He felt a little too detached from it all. A voice in his mind said, this is not real sex. Real sex is with a girl. This is play sex. Shima-chan lay passive and silent beneath him, a drawn look on his face.

Afterwards, as he lit up a cigarette, Fumio felt a sense of letdown. He asked himself if the experience had been pleasurable. As before, after his experience with Mariko in Petit Doll, and later with Izumi, he wondered: is this all there is?

Seeing Fumio's pensive mood, Shima-chan said, "I remember my first time. I, too, felt ashamed. But after several more times, you lose the shame. Don't worry."

Fumio said nothing. The older man reached down for his own pack of cigarettes. "You were so much better than I was my first time — so assured of yourself, so good."

"Thanks."

"Do you ever dream about taking it up the butt, Fumio?"

"No," said Fumio, a little startled by the bluntness of the question.

"There will come a time when you might wonder what it's like, or even want it. Take my advice: don't. Don't ever do it. Stay as you are. Because once you do it, you're changed forever. You can't go back to what you were: you'll become just another homo like me. Do me a favor — stay a man."

Fumio nodded, surprised at the self-loathing revealed in Shima-chan's warning. But he wasn't worried about himself in the least. He knew he was all right. He had no desire to become a homosexual.

11

SITTING AT the counter in Aladdin, Fumio was nursing a beer as he idly flipped through an American gay magazine. It was still quite early — just after opening time — and he was the only customer here. In the corner, a kerosene room heater was keeping the place warm, the tea kettle atop it whistling softly. Yuji was behind the counter, wiping glasses and arranging them in neat rows on the shelf below. He paused for a moment and folded up the piece of cloth he was using, placed it on the counter-top.

"Fumi-chan, I hear you went to a love hotel with Shima-chan

the other night."

Fumio looked up. "Who told you that?"

"Oh, word gets around. You know homos — they just can't keep a secret. They're the worst blabbermouths in the world. Especially the ones in here."

A little incensed that Shima-chan had made public their secret tryst, he muttered, "It's not true. We had a few drinks together and he took me home by taxi."

Yuji smiled knowingly and went back to wiping the glasses.

"Shima-chan was very nice to me," continued Fumio, "so I agreed to go out with him that night. But nothing happened. It's not like you think." Though he knew there was no point in denying it, he went through the motions anyway. He even experienced a certain satisfaction from his coy denial. Ever since his second visit, he'd been the recipient of numerous friendly propositions which he'd laughingly parried. This sudden popularity was flattering, as he'd never considered himself sexually desirable, and he was quite pleased at being so sought after here, unlike the outer world where his presence went largely unnoticed by everyone. But he knew his desirability probably had a lot to do with the fact that he was the youngest customer here; most of the others were in their thirties and forties. (Yuji, as a bartender, seemed to be off-limits by some tacit acknowledgement. Otherwise, with his handsome looks — he was the spitting image of a famous baseball player on the Seibu Lions team — he was sure to be pestered endlessly by the regulars.)

"There are no secrets in Aladdin," said Yuji, a little apologetically.

"Apparently not." From the conversations Fumio had heard, everyone seemed to know about everyone else's sexual idiosyncracies. Many of the regulars had apparently slept with one another at some time in the past, and now they occasionally joked about it in an almost nostalgic manner. Fumio found this promiscuity rather liberating. Not all the men, though, were quite as free with their affections. A couple of them were steady lovers who'd been true to each other for the past eight years.

The door opened and both boys turned to see who it was. For a moment, Fumio only saw the light gray suit against the darkness beyond the doorway. A cold wind blew into the bar.

"Welcome," said Yuji. "Please have a seat."

The other stepped in and Fumio took a moment to recognize Tatsuya, his former neighbor, as handsome as ever. His first impulse was to hide his face from an instinctive sense of shame. But the next moment he felt a wild joy at the thought that there was no need to do such a thing. Tatsuya, too, recognized Fumio right away, but it was impossible to read his thoughts. He didn't seem embarrassed, though, or upset in the least. He merely nodded to Fumio and sat down next to him. "It's been a long time," he said.

"You know each other?" exclaimed Yuji.

"We used to be neighbors," said Fumio.

"It is a small world. What would you like to drink?"

"A high sour." Yuji mixed up the cocktail in silence and placed it on a coaster before Tatsuya.

"I'll let you two get re-acquainted," he said, tactfully moving off to the far end of the bar, where he began busying himself wiping glasses. Fumio could barely restrain his joy at being with Tatsuya again, after having relegated him to the realm of memories. It felt as if he'd suddenly stepped into a garden in full bloom. His joy was given keener poignancy somehow by the possibility that Tatsuya had secretly been gay all along... despite the evidence of all the girls he'd bedded. It hardly seemed likely, but Fumio was beginning to believe that anything was possible in this world. After all, out of the hundreds of gay bars in Tokyo, Tatsuya had stepped into this one, on this night. Fumio had been warned that the gay world was a small, limited one, whose secret boundaries imposed a claustrophobic — indeed, incestuous — closeness upon its denizens. Yet he wanted to believe that some kind fate had brought them back together in answer to his unstated wish.

The question he was dying to ask would have to wait until a decent interval had passed: had Tatsuya come here merely out of curiosity? Or to meet friends? Or was he seeking adventure? For Fumio, the expectation of the answer was in itself a source of pure joy.

"The last I heard, you were working as a host," he said to Tatsuya. "Are you still working there?"

"No. I quit about two months ago."

"Why? You seemed to be enjoying it."

"It was all right at first. But things changed."

"How so?"

"In the beginning — this was when I first came to Tokyo — I only worked there a couple of nights a week. The clientele back then was mostly older women who fawned over me, bought me expensive presents, and were quite blunt about their sexual needs."

"That doesn't sound so bad."

"It wasn't. I didn't mind that part, though basically it was just work. And flattering them, play-acting romance... that all came with the territory. I was certainly paid well enough for it."

"How has that changed?"

"Recently, there are fewer older women coming. Most of the customers now are younger women, usually hostesses themselves, who make a lot of money and want to spend it lavishly. I guess they're driving out the older women."

"I would think hostesses wouldn't have any trouble finding boyfriends. Why should they have to go to a host club?"

"Well, they work most of the night and sleep most of the day, so they usually don't have much opportunity to meet men outside of work. And the customers in their clubs are, for the most part, middle-aged lechers who have only one thing on their minds. So, to meet young men their own age, they end up going to host clubs."

"Surely you didn't mind that."

"Actually, younger women are a lot more trouble. Whereas older women are happy to have a young man to dote upon, young girls expect to be petted themselves. They're used to being fussed over, and for all the money they spend on the hosts, expect to be compensated in return with gifts, outside dates, and romance."

"You mean they actually expect to buy love?"

"The romance is feigned and play-acted, and both parties know it. But from the girls' point of view, this sort of relationship even has its advantages. It's cut and dried, there's nothing messy or binding in it, and they have their fun. When they get tired of it, they move on. But all the emotional baby-sitting is hard on the hosts. It wore me out. I got so tired of it that I opted out for a much easier job. Remember I said I was only doing it until something better came along?"

"That's true. And so you have a better job now?"

"Yes."

"What do you do?"

"I'm still a host, only now I work in a gay club."

"I see." Fumio hoped his face had remained as calm as his voice. It seemed incredible to him that Tatsuya could speak so calmly about switching from women to men. But it only added to the aura of mystery surrounding him. No doubt part of the fascination Fumio felt for Tatsuya lay in the fact that he couldn't hope to understand him — perhaps ever. "Is it much easier being a host for men than women?"

"They pay so much more, and don't require as much extra effort outside the job. Tonight is a rare exception. I was told to meet a client here."

"So that's what you're doing here."

"Right." Tatsuya took a drink from his glass. "I must admit I was a bit surprised to see you here, though." There was nothing accusing in the look Tatsuya gave him, merely curiosity. But Fumio felt himself blush.

"It's not what you think. I'm not — "

"Oh?" Tatsuya laughed. "Don't worry, it doesn't mean a thing to me whether you are or not. It's just that you looked so guilty at being caught here. Besides, just because you're here doesn't mean a thing. Look at me. I'm as *nonke* as they come."

"What's *nonke*?"

"A straight. A non-homosexual. A heterosexual."

"But your work — "

"Just because I work in a gay club doesn't make me gay. A lot of the other hosts there are *nonke*. They have girlfriends and everything, and only work in the club for the money. One or two of them are even married, though their wives don't know the details of how they make their living."

"That's amazing. Do the customers know that their hosts are actually heterosexual?"

"When we're with customers, we're expected to act completely *nonke*. In fact, that's what the customers want. Their fantasies are for straight boys. Even the hosts who are out-and-out homosexuals have to play at being *nonke*."

"How about if — "

"Yes?"

"You spoke earlier about the women being blunt about their physical needs... "

Tatsuya laughed again. "In a gay host club, there's not much romance involved. Everything is straightforward and to the point. No roundabout routes to arrive at where *they're* going."

"I see." Fumio couldn't trust himself to meet Tatsuya's look.

"Are you shocked? You shouldn't be. Remember I told you I'd do anything if the money was good enough? Well, I'm doing it. Actually, it's not as bad as you might think it is. You get used to it after a while."

"Won't it change you, though? What if you can't go back?"

"I'm not worried. I know where my priorities lie. In my mind I can separate it, the work from the play."

"So the money must be very good, then."

"It is. In fact, you'd be surprised at just how much money can be made at this. The men who come to host clubs are usually successful men in their fields — mostly in their forties and fifties — who have no trouble paying for their pleasures: doctors, high-ranking businessmen with major corporations, entertainers, you name it."

"Entertainers?"

"Sure. There's plenty of them. I've been with a few I recognize from television, actors of my mother's era who are no longer very much in demand. I wonder what the old lady would say if she knew I was sleeping with some of the idols of her youth."

He gave a melodious laugh which sounded so boyishly innocent that Fumio could hardly believe it had come just after such a shocking confession. What had surprised him most was the light manner in which Tatsuya spoke of sleeping with men. Yet somehow, it only made him that much more seductive. Tatsuya was looking straight at him. "You could be making a lot of money as a host if you wanted to."

"Me? You're joking. Maybe if I was as handsome as you."

"What are you talking about? Anyone can be a host. They're always looking for new faces."

From reading the advertisements in *Barazoku,* Fumio knew that what Tatsuya said was true. There were many kinds of places which catered to gay men's needs — host clubs, gay bars, massage parlors — and almost all of them were constantly seeking new workers; every ad was accompanied by 'Hosts wanted' or 'Part-timers needed, urgent' or 'No experience necessary' or 'You can work out of your own home'. (This last was from one of the so-called 'boy delivery' services.) And from looking at the prices they charged customers, it was obvious that these places paid quite well.

Fumio shook his head. "I'm such a potato boy that they'd laugh me right out of the club." His complex about his roots had returned after seeing Tatsuya again, and the derogatory term for a young man from the provinces — potato boy — had slipped out unconsciously.

"But don't you see? That's an advantage. The other boys have been around so long that they're jaded. They've lost that magic charm a newcomer has. There are plenty of men who are interested in just what you are. You remind them of their youth in the country. Their greatest desires are for normal-looking boys like you. They aren't the least bit interested in those flamboyantly good-looking youths. The less homosexual you look, the better. What they really want is a *nonke.* To look at you, you're someone who doesn't have the slightest tinge of homosexuality in his character."

"I never thought it would be an advantage to be a potato boy."

"In this world it is. That plus your youth will take you a long way."

Fumio thought of the night he'd spent with Shima-chan, and knew that what Tatsuya was saying was probably true. If so, he was foolish to give away for free something for which he could be making a lot of money. Still, he'd never thought of himself as the type to work in the 'water trade'.

"I don't think I'm the type to be a host."

"If you don't like drinking and partying, there are always other ways. The best thing is to hook up with a rich 'papa' who'll look after you."

"A 'papa'?"

"A patron — an older man who takes care of all your financial needs. He'll set you up in a place to stay, give you enough money for daily needs, plus have some left over for play. I know boys who were made for life just from meeting a good older man. Cars, condos, overseas travel. It can be a very good life. And there's plenty of older men out there looking for a young companion. You'd be surprised." Tatsuya lowered his voice. "But if you stick around here you'll never meet anyone like that. There's no one here who's in that class. This is too country. You have to go downtown to Shinjuku or Roppongi. If you like, I can introduce you to people who can help you. But don't tell anyone here I told you about it. They would hate me for it."

Fumio was about to ask some more questions when the door opened. From the other end of the counter, Yuji called out cheerfully to the new arrival, "Welcome!" Fumio looked at the man who had just entered, a short, fat man wearing glasses, with balding hair. He looked like the prosperous president of a medium-sized company making machine parts. From the opened door behind him came a blast of cold air.

"Kin-chan!" said Tatsuya in a false-sounding voice, "I thought you'd never come."

The glasses of the older man fogged over from their sudden contact with the warm air in the cozy bar.

12

PERHAPS BECAUSE it was still too early in the day, there was nothing to indicate that Shinjuku's 2-chome was the wicked hub of Japanese gay life. But Fumio felt a real excitement about setting foot for the first time into this sexual *dejima.* From hearsay, he knew that this whole area was peppered with bars, bookstores, and adult toy stores catering to a mainly gay clientele. There were bars for young men, bars for older men, and bars where they could meet each other; bars where overweight men convened — and bars for attractive young boys who were interested in overweight men. There were SM places with leather, chains and whips for decor. There were bars where foreigners met, and where they could meet Japanese boys who went for foreigners. There were transvestite bars where men chatted with and fondled new-halfs. There were transsexual bars where straight men got the thrill of their lives by picking up a hybrid beauty. There were salons where salarymen, doctors, and lawyers came after work to change into women's clothes (with the aid of stylists and make-up artists) to meet and chat with others of the same persuasion. Perhaps ninety percent of all the gay bars in Japan were located here. Fumio had seen underground maps which identified all the different bars and the types of bars to be found in 2-chome but he was told that they were constantly in need of updating, for the names and ownership changed so often.

Tatsuya was taking him to Genji, the host club where he worked. Fumio had often seen its advertisement in *Barazoku*; apparently it had been in operation for over twenty years now. The last line in the ad read: 'Visitors from the provinces welcome'. Fumio was surprised at the numbers of ordinary-looking men he saw walking about. He knew many straight people liked to come here to relax after work, but if he'd been alone, he would have felt some anxiety about being seen in the gay Mecca of Japan.

"Here we are," said Tatsuya.

Fumio looked at the building they were standing before. It looked innocuous enough. Like any number of other emporiums around it, it was a six-story entertainment center honeycombed with restaurants, night clubs, and drinking establishments. A lighted neon sign in the vestibule identified all the different stores and shops located within, most of them bars and pubs from the sounds of them. Genji was the only business on the second floor and its name alone gave no indication of its specialty. It was only one establishment in the vast water trade of this thriving entertainment district.

Tatsuya led him up the stairs to the second floor where they came to a short hallway with a door at the end of it. The name 'Genji' was written upon it in English, and beneath it in Japanese: 'Members' club'. They pushed their way in. At first glance, it looked like an ordinary gay bar, in a cramped space with a counter on the right as he entered, and another doorway at the far end. There were no customers this early in the evening, but an attractive young man dressed in an expensive-looking Italian suit was behind the counter wiping glasses. He looked up at their entry.

"Hello, Tat-chan. What brings you here so early?"

"I have a friend who wants to work here."

"Oh?" He looked at Fumio in a friendly manner. "I'll go get 'master'." He came out from behind the counter and disappeared into the curtained doorway.

Fumio picked up what looked like a photo album on the bar counter. Opening it, he saw that it was filled with pictures of young men. Beneath each photo was the boy's 'Genji name'. Apparently a customer could choose his companion for the evening from among them. Fumio looked around him. His image of the place (from the prices it charged) had been of an elegant supper club. Instead, it appeared to be rather seedy, though with feeble attempts to give it a classy image. The carpet was worn in spots and the decor wasn't of the finest quality. Presently the boy returned to his place behind the counter, and in the doorway appeared a man who seemed to be the manager of the club, a normal-looking man in his middle forties who, Fumio guessed, wasn't homosexual.

"Hello, Tat-chan. And this is your friend?"

"Yes. This is Fumio." Fumio bowed his greetings.

"Right this way, please."

Fumio followed him in. Beyond the doorway was a narrow aisle, lined on either side by partitioned cubicles with accordion curtains in their doorways. Apparently, these were those 'private rooms' mentioned in the advertisement; once the customer chose his boy, he was shown to one of these rooms where he had all the privacy he needed. As Fumio passed by an open one, he glanced inside. It was a tiny space just large enough to hold a couch with a side table next to it, a video player, and a large TV monitor. Atop the side table was another photo album like the one he'd seen on the counter, and beside it, a box of tissues.

In the office at the end of the corridor — a cramped room with a desk, a telephone, and a small safe — the manager waved Fumio to a seat.

"I assume this is your first stint as a host?"

"Yes."

"I see. Do you have many other suits?" he asked, eying the one Fumio had on.

"Just this one." It was the one Tatsuya had given him.

"Well, you'll have to buy yourself a few more. And you'll need a good haircut, too. If you can't afford it, we will take care of initial expenses — which will come out of your wages, of course. The customer likes to have well-dressed, clean-looking boys to look at."

"I see."

"A lot of host clubs these days like their boys dressed casually, in jeans, t-shirts, and sneakers, but most of our clients are older and well established. They might like to take you out on a dinner date at a nice restaurant, so you have to look presentable at all times. Also, you'll be expected to take turns working behind the counter helping O-Tama. That'll give our regular customers a chance to learn your face. Eventually, you might become well enough known to be asked for by name." O-Tama, as Fumio later learned, was a middle-aged swishy queen, whose main job was to keep conversation going, and to set up meetings between clients and hosts.

"What do I do behind the counter?" asked Fumio.

"O-Tama will make the drinks and snacks, so all you have to do is light the customer's cigarettes for him, pour his drinks, make small talk. Laugh at his jokes. O-Tama will be sure to pick things up when conversation lags. He's good at that. Just act naturally, and everything will work out fine."

"I see."

"Most of the time though, you'll be up in the waiting room with the other boys until you're requested by a customer. We'll take your photo tonight and have it in the menu book by tomorrow."

"What happens when someone chooses me from the menu book?"

The manager looked at him. "Most of our customers want to use one of our private rooms. You'll accompany him there. Once you're inside, just do what the customer wants you to. Don't worry about any strange characters; we have a respectable clientele here. Anyway, the customer has to negotiate with O-Tama before you're called for. When your picture goes into the menu book, let O-Tama know exactly what you're willing to do, and he'll pass it on to the customer. You'll never have to do anything you don't want to."

"I see."

"For a private room date, you'll get fifty per cent of what the customer pays, we get the rest. On an outside date you get to keep sixty."

"What's an outside date?"

"If it's agreeable to both you and your customer, you can leave the club to go out for dinner, for a drive, to a hotel, whatever. The customer pays a little extra for this, of course. Also, we sometimes get outside calls for a 'boy delivery'. You go out to meet him whever he likes, usually a nearby hotel, but sometimes out in the suburbs. He'll pay all the travel expenses, plus the upfront fee. You keep all the travel expenses, and we take thirty-three per cent of the delivery fee. If he wants to tip you for any extra personal services, that's his business."

"I see." Fumio felt a shiver go through him at the matter-of-fact way he said this.

"What you do with the customer once you leave the club is your business," said the manager. "But please remember that the reputation of the club is important, so if you do anything bad, it might come back to you. You'll find it hard to find a job anywhere else."

"I quite understand. Please don't worry about me on that score."

Fumio had heard that the *yakuza* were often involved in the management of these places, and he didn't dream of crossing them. The *yakuza* got their revenge in most drastic ways.

"When can you begin working?"

"Tonight."

"Good." He called out to the other room. "Tatsuya, why don't you show Fumio to the waiting lounge."

"Sure." Tatsuya's answer came from the bar where he was chatting with the boy on duty.

The manager turned to Fumio. "Tonight just take it easy and learn your way around. From tomorrow, you'll begin working the counter, all right?"

"Thank you very much."

Outside at the counter, Fumio posed as the boy on duty snapped a photo of him with a cheap camera, then he and Tatsuya went out the front door and took an elevator up two floors. They came to an unmarked door, where Tatsuya pushed the buzzer and entered. As Fumio followed him in, he saw that it was an ordinary one-room apartment, unadorned except for sofas, a coffee table piled high with comic books, and a television set. Six young men greeted them in cheerful voices. Cigarette smoke hung in the air and snack foods were scattered on the table. Apparently this was the waiting room where unengaged hosts stayed until called for. A telephone sat on the floor under the coffee table.

Tatsuya introduced Fumio to the group. It was a little like being introduced to the members of an extra-curricular sports club. The boys were all cheerful, and at their ease. Tatsuya was apparently the Number One host here.

Upon being presented, Fumio made a polite bow and introduced himself as he would have done to anyone. He tried to make his demeanor polite and unassuming, and was relieved when the boys welcomed him warmly.

As they introduced themselves, Fumio noticed that each boy used his 'Genji name', the personal pseudonym adopted by most people who worked in the water trade. Though they were all friendly to him, Fumio wondered if there was any rivalry among them, and whether they saw him as another competitor for customers. They were all so good-looking that he was sure he would be the least of their worries.

He noticed that they fell into two basic types: the sportsman type and the Johnny type. The Johnnys were slender and boyish like the breed of singers idolized by junior high school girls. Some of them looked no more than fifteen or sixteen, but since there was a minimum age limit for working here, they had to be at least eighteen in fact. Fumio, with a body built up from three years on his high school soccer team, felt he would belong to the sportsman group.

"What name would you like to use?" asked Tatsuya. "As you probably noticed, everyone uses a false name here."

Fumio thought for a moment, then said, "Why not use my real name — Fumio."

"Sure. I do the same thing myself." Tatsuya sat down and lit a cigarette as the others went back to what they'd been doing, watching television, reading comic books, or chatting idly.

Apparently business was a little slow tonight. There were only a handful of regulars who'd asked for their usual hosts. Quite some time had passed, and Fumio was beginning to think that boredom would probably be the biggest challenge in his new job when the telephone under the coffee table rang.

The boy who answered it spoke for a few moments, then announced to the room at large: "Looks like Fumio already has his first job. An outside call just came in for a 'delivery service'. A customer in a nearby love hotel wants to order up a boy, sight unseen. His only stipulation is that the boy look *nonke*, and be fresh blood."

"That sounds like you," said Tatsuya to Fumio.

"Do you know who it is?" asked someone.

"The Professor."

Tatsuya turned to Fumio. "This is a regular, a professor who teaches at R University. He always asks for university students, from his own university if possible." R University was quite close to Fumio's college; the two schools were traditional rivals. "You fit the bill perfectly. Are you ready to make your debut?"

"Will I be all right, do you think?" Fumio felt uneasy at the prospect.

"Oh, don't worry. He's a very nice man. And tips well, too. Come on, I'll take you to his room."

The boy who'd taken the call had written down the hotel's name and room number. Apparently there was a love hotel nearby which was used exclusively by the gay patrons of the clubs all around. Genji had an arrangement with it, and most of the boys felt safe there. If there was any trouble with a customer, the bouncers at the front desk wouldn't hesitate to come and help them.

They went straight there from the waiting room, taking the elevator down four floors to the street level. Outside, there was quite a crowd of men walking about, and Fumio had the strange illusion that all their eyes were trained upon him — as if they knew just by looking at him what he was doing.

The hotel was nearby, about a two-minute walk, and didn't look like a love hotel. There was a respectable appearance about it, and Fumio would never have guessed that it was used for gay trysts.

"How much do these men pay?" he asked.

"For an outside date, 15,000 yen for a short time, that's two hours, or 20,000 for an all-night. If he wants to save money, he can use one of the private rooms in the club — that's only 10,000 yen. For a boy delivery, you're sure to receive a tip. That's one of the advantages of working at a well-established place like Genji: the clientele aren't stingy with their money."

"How much should I expect to be tipped?"

"Tipping ranges anywhere from 10,000 to 100,000, depending on who it is and what you do. None of our customers are into the hard stuff or the wierd stuff, so don't worry. Basically, the nicer you treat them, the better your tip will be."

Fumio tried not to let his amazement show, but he was exhilarated by the amounts mentioned. It was certainly a different world from that of a lowly-paid tutor.

"A word to the wise about tips, Fumio. When you tell O-Tama what you will and won't do, leave one service that you'll do for tips only. You'll pick up more money that way; we all do it. Most of the other boys have set rates for it, but I've learned that when the customer asks you 'how much?' and you tell him, 'I'll leave that up to you,' you'll get paid far more than if you come right out with a set price."

"I see."

They had no trouble being passed up to the professor's room. As Tatsuya raised his hand to knock on the door, Fumio blurted out: "I'm scared. My heart is thumping away in my chest like crazy."

"Don't worry. Take a deep breath. It's nothing. Just an old man. If you don't feel like going through with it, just tell me. I'll make up a reasonable excuse."

"All right. Thanks."

"Are you sure you're all right?"

Fumio nodded, swallowing. Patting Fumio on the shoulder to encourage him, Tatsuya knocked on the door and they entered.

13

A DISTINGUISHED-LOOKING man in his fifties was sitting on the bed. Tatsuya introduced Fumio while the professor looked him over critically. Seeming satisfied with what he saw, the older man briskly reached into his suit pocket and handed Tatsuya the money for a short time, and Tatsuya left.

After he'd gone, the professor seemed to relax. "Why don't you sit down, Fumio? Would you like something to drink?"

"Yes, please."

"A whiskey and water?" He got up to fix the drinks.

"Allow me, sir." Fumio went over to the side table where a bottle and a couple of glasses had already been set out.

"The water's in the decanter over there."

Fumio felt himself begin to shiver slightly; he wished Tatsuya had stuck around a little longer to break him into this work. He felt completely lost without any support or advice.

"I understand you're new to Genji, Fumio."

"Yes. In fact, I'm not even registered yet; I just started tonight."

"This very night?"

"Yes."

"That is a pleasant surprise. Some of the boys there have been working so long they should be receiving retirement pay. What made you want to be a host?"

"The money. I thought it would be a good way to make a lot in a short time."

The professor chuckled at this straightforward answer, peering more closely at Fumio. "You're a university student?"

"Yes."

"Well, I teach political science at R University. Where do you go to school?"

Fumio told him.

"Ah. Quite a few professors in your school are gay. If you like, I can introduce you to some of them. It'll help you get through college. As long as you know the right people you can easily make it to graduation with almost no studying. That gives you that much more time to play around, which is really more important for you than study, at your age."

Fumio handed him the drink and waited for the older man to take a sip before drinking his own.

"Now if you were one of my students, you'd be guaranteed to pass the course, and with good marks, too. Have you ever worked at other host clubs? I don't recognize you."

"No. This is my first experience at this kind of job."

"I see. You have a very nice build. Do you play sports at school?"

"No," Fumio stammered. "I was on my high school soccer team, though." He was too ashamed to tell him that because of his work as a tutor, he had no time for extra-curricular activities in college.

"Oh, good. Tell me about your experiences."

Fumio told him, hesitantly at first, but more and more animatedly as he realized the older man was fascinated by the normal things that went on in a soccer club. The professor wanted to know all the details — how the locker room smelled, how dirty the boys' uniforms got, how rough the games were.

"Was there any bullying or punishment within the soccer club? I'm sure there was."

"Oh yes. Whenever junior players made mistakes on the field, they were punished later in the clubroom by the *sempai.*"

"How?"

"By being whacked on the bare back with a belt. Not only were we not allowed to cry out, we actually had to yell 'Thank you!' at each stroke."

"I see." There was a glow in the professor's eyes that spoke of sexual warmth. Fumio sensed that the older man had never gone out for sports of any kind as a youth and had a special kind of longing for the gruelling regimen undergone by sportsmen.

"Do you have a girlfriend, Fumio?"

Fumio blushed. "No. I don't have the looks girls go for."

"Nonsense. You're quite handsome. And have a nice build, too. Will you take off your shirt so I can have a good look at you, please?"

"Of course."

Wordlessly Fumio began unbuttoning his suit jacket.

"Slowly, Fumio, more slowly. I want to enjoy it." The professor, turning a knob on the console by his bed, adjusted the lights so that the room was bathed in a mysterious twilit atmosphere, and watched intently with his slightly hooded eyes as Fumio undressed. Staring at the amber shadow cast on the wall by his glass of whiskey, Fumio slipped off his jacket, undid his tie, and unbuttoned his shirt. When his upper torso was completely bare, he stood at attention like a soldier.

"Now turn around."

Fumio felt as if he were a model for an artist or a photographer — the professor's eyes seemed to be drinking in every bit of his bare flesh. The feeling was far from unpleasant — quite flattering, in fact. He began to understand now what Tatsuya had meant when he'd said that many men longed for the normal-looking classmates and friends they'd known as youths.

"Now your pants, Fumio."

If there were many more men like the professor, Fumio had no doubt that he could compete in this business with those more conventionally attractive boys. He wondered how much money he could make in a month at Genji. In a year.

"Now come over here, Fumio. That's right."

The professor remained seated on the bed as Fumio stepped hesitantly up to him.

"Don't be shy... "

Fumio felt the older man's hands come to rest on his hips and tried not to wince. But he had to close his eyes when he saw the other's thin, sensitive lips part in a lewd pucker. He told himself that this was, after all, no different from what he'd experienced in the love hotel with Shima-chan. But he felt unclean, nevertheless.

Afterwards the professor gave him a 50,000-yen tip and asked to see him again sometime. The whole thing — from the moment Fumio was introduced to the man, to the time he returned to the waiting lounge — had taken little more than an hour.

Fumio remained in the lounge until two o'clock but had no other work. Many of the boys had already left at about twelve in order to catch the last train home. Others could afford to take taxis. Because Fumio was the junior man there, it was his duty to clean up the lounge after everyone left. Tatsuya, however, stayed after to help him with the work. When they were done, he said, "Are you doing anything tonight?"

"Not really." Fumio had already decided to wait for the first train in the morning.

"Why don't you come along with me?"

"Where are you going?"

"On a drive. It'll help you get rid of the bad after-taste from that old geezer."

Tatsuya had recently bought a Ferrari, and had it parked in an underground garage nearby. He told Fumio how he liked to take it out onto the expressways in the early morning hours after work.

"Whenever other guys see me in this thing, they can't resist challenging me to a race. I always accept because I know I have the faster car." It obviously afforded him a sweet gratification to humiliate anyone brash enough to challenge his supremacy. Apparently, he never had any trouble finding a competitor, though. The Chuo Expressway in the early morning hours just before dawn, when there was virtually no other traffic, became a sort of race strip where young men pitted their cars against any and all challengers. Fumio got in and sat in the passenger seat, feeling a sense of anticipation. Even before they'd reached the on-ramp of the expressway, a sporty car pulled up next to them at the traffic light and revved its engine in challenge. Tatsuya signalled for the other car to follow, then slowly pulled up the ramp to the toll-gate window. The Chuo Expressway seemed almost deserted at this hour. Fumio gazed blankly at the endless rows of yellow-orange lights suspended over the roadway before him as far as he could see. The sky in the east was already getting light.

Tatsuya allowed the other car to catch up and even pull ahead a little before stamping his foot down hard on the accelerator. Fumio felt himself being yanked back into his seat as the highway lights above became a blur. His heart hammered madly and he didn't dare look at his friend. He was amazed at the confident way Tatsuya drove — as if fearless of death, or even inviting it. This expressway was notorious for the way its sinuous curves wound over the mountains west of Tokyo. Many young men had killed themselves there. Flowers sometimes decorated the places where they'd met their end. A keen thrill shot through Fumio like a drug, giving him a light-headed, drunken clarity of vision. The world outside looked like a 3D picture postcard. At this moment he felt that a sudden death on the highway with Tatsuya at his side would be the most beautiful and romantic way to end his life.

There was a lot of unexploded power in Tatsuya. He was one of those young men who seemed to live in a constant blaze of glory, always existing in the exact center of each moment, a natural hero. Because Fumio felt that Tatsuya had the looks and confidence to do whatever he liked, he was puzzled why he seemed satisfied to remain a mere host.

The other car slipped further and further behind them as if being sucked back by their draft, and apparently got off the expressway at the Hachioji interchange. Tatsuya grinned at Fumio, a look of triumph in his eyes. "I live for these moments," he said. "Nothing feels better than winning against an opponent." He looked like a young man in a primitive tribe who has just killed the biggest game, or has just beaten out his rival in a brutal contest of arms, winning the hand of the chief's daughter. Fumio eagerly partook of his friend's happiness. But the magic in the moment was fleeting, for he had a sudden presentiment that Tatsuya would die young. Fumio couldn't picture him as a middle-aged man no matter how much he tried. Tatsuya was the very embodiment of youth and would always stay as young as he was at this moment.

They pulled into a rest stop where a couple of trucks were parked, and entered the all-night eatery. It turned out to be a vending machine restaurant, empty but for a couple of truck drivers lingering over their styrofoam bowls of noodles, reading their sports newspapers. Still feeling a little shaky after the race, Fumio lit a cigarette and felt calmer as he smoked it. He tried not to think how fast they'd been going. Tatsuya bought a bowl of hot noodles and began slurping it up noisily. Watching him, Fumio felt he looked curiously boyish — it was easy to picture him as a young lad in elementary school. Again, he thought of how alive his friend was, investing every action — even eating noodles — with a unique grace. Tatsuya was so vibrant that each moment of his being seemed precious and meaningful. Fumio himself was very rarely vouchsafed these moments when he fleetingly glimpsed something beyond his everyday world, a glowing vision of heroic destiny, romantic glory. He felt he was never really living up to his full potential, that there was always a thin, transparent barrier between himself and what was called Life. Only boys like Tatsuya were really alive.

Tatsuya finished his noodles, drank some of the soup and broke the disposable wooden chopsticks in two. "There, that takes care of that." He pulled out a pack of cigarettes and tapped one out, gazing abstractedly at Fumio. "Well, what do you think about your new job?"

"The money is good. Very good. Because of it, I guess I can put up with a lot of things."

"You'd be surprised at the things you will do for money. I know I surprised myself. But it feels good to know you can buy things. Anytime."

"Yeah." Fumio, without touching his wallet, could feel the weight of the bills he'd put in it tonight, and their presence seemed to give him a satisfying glow inside.

"Just don't let your mother know how you make your extra pocket money."

"Right."

Gazing at Tatsuya's profile, Fumio realized how little he actually knew about his friend. He really knew next to nothing about Tatsuya's private life, and nothing at all about his real nature. But that mystery only added more depths to his allure.

"Tatsuya, what do you plan to do after all this? I mean, you can't expect to work as a host forever, you know."

"Don't remind me of that." He sucked abstractedly on his cigarette and blew the smoke out of the corner of his mouth. "My dream is to become a big star someday, in the entertainment business. But I don't know. I just take life as it comes, day by day. I know something will come up. It always does." His slightly crooked smile was a half-hearted plea for understanding.

Strangely enough, Fumio felt that something probably would come up eventually. It had to. And Tatsuya's only duty until then was to wait for that moment to come, fulfilling all the expectations of a life destined to rendezvous with glory. Fumio had sensed something special about Tatsuya ever since meeting him, ever since that night they'd gone out together and picked up those girls without any effort.

"Do you still go out to Roppongi a lot, Tatsuya?"

"Yeah. Every now and then. It's another way to relieve the stress of working at Genji."

"Do you have much time for girls?"

"Sure. But I'm getting a little tired of that scene, actually."

"Getting ready to settle down?"

"No way. I tried that and it didn't work."

"Oh? You had a steady girlfriend before?"

"Yeah. My only one, believe it or not. But we broke up long ago."

"When was that?"

"I can't remember. Oh yes, I do. It was just before I moved into the apartment where I met you. That was the reason I moved, in fact."

"Why did you break up?"

"I really don't want to go into that right now. It's a long story, believe me. Let's just say she hurt me in a way I could never forgive... as a result of which I found myself beginning to hate women. At least, I wanted nothing more to do with them for the rest of my life. Maybe that's why I'm the way I am now." He lapsed into silence.

"Have you tried meeting someone new?"

"Sure. But each new girl I met only confirmed the deadness of my feelings. It was all over. They were just turning into playthings, a way of relieving my stress. In my heart I despised them all."

Fumio felt a vast emptiness hollow out his chest. He could sense the deep loneliness in his friend, an almost bottomless despair. And he was afraid to look inside his own heart for fear of finding the same meaninglessness there.

"Then is there anything you care for, Tatsuya? I mean, besides cars."

Tatsuya reached into his jeans pocket and pulled out the car key. The keyholder was shaped in the likeness of an ancient Egyptian hunting hound. "Let's change the subject, all right?"

"Sure."

The two truckers got up and left, and the boys now had the place to themselves. But Tatsuya seemed restless.

"How about if we step outside for some air?"

"Sure."

From the parking area they could see the lights of the city stretching out before them like a dazzling crystal carpet. Cars blurred by them on the expressway, causing the ground beneath to quake as if buffeted by phantom winds. There was a distinct chill in the air. Despite the cold, Tatsuya was wearing only a t-shirt and jeans. He looked so sexy in them that Fumio felt a shiver go up his spine. In the early morning light the mountains in the west appeared to be emerging from a gauzy curtain of pale smoke.

14

FUMIO ALWAYS felt unclean after coming off an evening of work at Genji. Sometimes it was so bad that he dropped in at a sauna before going home, as if the cleansing steam had the power to erase the foul memory of being caressed by middle-aged men. He wondered whether he should go tonight. It was 1:30 in the morning and he was standing on the sidewalk of one Shinjuku's main streets. It was the season for year-end parties, and the usually festive atmosphere of the nightless town was made even more so by the crowds of revelers. Tonight had been a busy night at the host club and Fumio felt he could use a sauna to help him wind down. But, standing here in the wind like this, the cold air chilling him to the bone, he suddenly decided to go straight home.

It would be difficult to get a taxi to stop for him at this time of night, though. The river of them flowing by on the street all seemed to have their fare meters engaged. Finally he spotted one with its flag up and gestured wildly for it to stop. To his relief, it began slowing down; he stepped out into the street. Just as he did so, however, a young woman hurriedly brushed past him. Apparently she'd been waiting for a taxi, too, and had assumed it had slowed down for her. The taxi driver was looking at neither of them, so it was difficult to say.

Fumio and the girl looked at each other. She spoke first. "Excuse me, I think that was my taxi."

"I think he was stopping for me, actually," argued Fumio, even though he didn't really care one way or the other. She was in her early twenties, and quite attractive, though she'd obviously had a little too much to drink tonight: her speech was somewhat slurred, and she was a bit unsteady on her feet. Just as they were confronting each other, a third person, an older man, slipped into the taxi, and the driver, apparently not caring who his fare was, drove away.

Fumio and the girl looked at each other in surprise and burst into laughter. "Well, now neither of us has a taxi," she said.

"And I was going to offer to share a ride with you, too."

"I would have accepted."

"So, what do we do now? Wait for another taxi to come along?"

"I'm tired. I don't care where I go. I just want a little rest."

"Come on, then. I know a good place," said Fumio. They began walking toward the Kabuki-cho area. "What are you doing all alone out here, anyway?"

"I just had a fight with my boyfriend. After he left, I had nothing better to do than get drunk. I don't care anymore."

"You should be more careful. There are a lot of bad characters around here."

She looked sideways at him as they walked along. "Are you one of those 'bad characters'?"

"Me? Oh no. You can see by my face that I'm honest."

She looked at his expensive suit. "Do you work here?"

"Part-time — as a waiter in a club. I'm a student, actually."

"I didn't think you looked the water trade type... "

"I'm not."

Since he'd started working at Genji, Fumio was living a double life. During the day he was a college student — a sleepy one who nodded over his notebooks, but who made sure to show up for the minimum number of required lectures. But at night, after a short nap after school, he was dressed up in suits of the latest fashion, catering to the whims of rich, middle-aged gay men. No one would have guessed that the plain-looking boy on campus in his jeans and windbreaker was transformed at night into an elegant butterfly flitting from customer to customer. For Fumio was becoming much sought after as a host. From his time behind the counter, he quickly learned how to be a good companion for the men. The important thing was to look cheerful, and to greet the regulars by their names. But there were other tricks of the trade he picked up by watching O-Tama, the middle-aged queen, at work: how to flatter the older men by laughing at their jokes, listening to their gripes about work, soothing their hurts — in short, glorifying their egos. Also, since most of these men were quite successful and intelligent, Fumio made it a point to read the newspaper every day from front to back so that he would be up on any topic which might come up. And in listening to their comments on financial and political affairs, he found he was getting a better education than any he might receive in college. For their part, the men liked a young boy who could keep up with them, and they rewarded him with innumerable presents: Rolex watches, gold necklaces and bracelets.

Though many men enjoyed chatting with the hosts at the counter, by far, most of the customers only came for sex. Tatsuya was still Number One host in Genji, of course, but Fumio was getting his share of short-times, all-nights, and outside dates. He usually had one, sometimes two customers a night. As much as he disliked having to perform sexually with middle-aged men, he learned to make it seem as if he enjoyed it. The tips he received were well worth the effort.

There were some men who were so shy that they went straight to one of the cubicles in back, from where they made their choice of a boy by consulting the menu book. Some were so nervous they couldn't say a word when Fumio went to them, so he had to do all the talking, even instigate the action. But by far, most men, when alone with a host, couldn't stop talking. Since the sex was usually over very quickly, the rest of the hour was spent in talk. Some wanted to hear all about Fumio's sex life, others just wanted to learn why a boy like him was working as a host. Most of them, however, wanted to talk about themselves, to open up about their deepest secrets. It was as if the act of sex had been the key to unlocking their reticence.

Fumio guessed that many gay men were lonely and had no one with whom they could truly open up. He felt as if he were being paid to listen to their troubles... as if the sex had only been an excuse or pretext for meeting him in private, the ice-breaker of the conversation. (Indeed, in some cases, the men didn't even require, or want, sex. All they wanted was a private companion with whom they could openly discuss their homosexuality.) Fumio couldn't understand it. But he didn't care as long as they paid well. And the better a listener he was, the more they paid.

The money was coming in. Shortly after starting work at Genji, Fumio had opened up a bank account and now he delightedly watched his savings grow. Finally he was able to buy all the nice things he'd always wanted — clothes, neckties, accessories. Part of this wardrobe was necessary for professional reasons; hosts were required to look as nice as possible in the club... meaning as expensive as possible. His dream was to save up enough money to buy a car and move to a nicer apartment, perhaps even a condominium. He was having a hard time now finding enough space to store all his new suits in his cramped closet.

His improved wardrobe helped him a lot with girls, as did the greater conversational ease and confidence he'd gained as a host. He was amazed that these mere external changes in him could have such a drastic effect on his life. Inside he knew he was basically the same potato boy who'd just come up from Nagano. All he'd done was put on designer suits, go to a men's aesthetic salon, and begin frequenting an expensive hair-stylist. But as far as the world was concerned, he'd become a completely different person. In Tokyo everything was illusion. Even his background could be changed. Taking his cue from Tatsuya he found he could easily create his own scenario about his past or his present, making it much more glamorous than it was. The two boys let on that they were students at Keio University, a very prestigious school in southern Tokyo, and that their families lived in Dennen-Chofu. These names alone were like magic talismans guaranteed to soften up girls for the final conquest. Actually it was quite simple for the boys to impress girls with their expensive clothes alone, and the ease with which they spent money. But deep down, Fumio knew it was Tatsuya's presence which assured his own success with girls. It was Tatsuya's extraordinarily good looks which were the most irresistible bait for them. Still — and this was what

Fumio found most fascinating about him — despite his seemingly effortless success with girls, Tatsuya continued to despise them. In fact, he seemed to look down on them precisely because they gave in so easily to his demands. Fumio found him quite mercenary, even ruthless in his treatment of them sometimes.

Tatsuya had once shown him his notebook in which he kept detailed records of the women he'd slept with. In it he graded them on a scale of one to ten, first on their physical attributes, then on their sexual performances. Special emphasis was paid to anything which might add spice to the conquest, rating a single or double star by the entry: pairs of sisters he'd bedded, mother-daughter conquests, three-ways, etc.

Fumio, too, became caught up in this sport-like game. He never went with the same girl twice, and luckily, most of the girls themselves never expected anything other than a pleasant one-night stand — they, too, slept with boys as if it were some sort of sport. Sometimes the boys traded girls in the middle of the night, Tatsuya sending his girl over to Fumio's room with the message that they were to swap partners. One of the things Fumio liked to do when he and Tatsuya had these 'swaps' was to question the girl about Tatsuya. Far from objecting, she was usually eager to provide him with the most intimate information. Fumio felt no jealousy even when it was obvious that the girl had preferred Tatsuya to him. In fact, he got a perverse joy out of the knowledge.

Apparently, Tatsuya's sexual technique was quite good, honed by his experiences with women of all ages. The girls said that most of the boys who went to bed with them were relatively inexperienced, a little too eager and quick. Tatsuya, on the other hand, was what was known in present parlance as a 'technician', experimenting with positions, tempos, seeking out the particular thing which most excited the girl he was with, and coolly toying with her.

These intimate revelations about Tatsuya gave Fumio a strange satisfaction. And to be holding the girl who had just left his friend — whose skin was still warm from contact with him — made it that much more exciting. It was all like a mad, adolescent daydream, the kind Fumio had often spun out in fantasy. And at first it was paradise. But gradually, a change had started to come about. The endless numbers of girls all blended in Fumio's mind with one type, and the game was ceasing to have any excitement. It was all so easy.

It now seemed amazing to him that he'd ever been in awe of these girls in their skin-tight dresses, that he'd felt shy and out of place in their presence. As he got to know them better, he found that they were really not as self-assured as they appeared on the surface. Many of them had come up from the country themselves, or from the neighboring prefectures of Chiba and Saitama. For them, he was the glamorous city boy, the type they desired. Now that he knew them for what they were, the Roppongi girls actually began to bore him. In his eyes, they were so vapid, saying the same things in the same manner. He knew they'd picked up their studied sophistication from a limited number of fashion magazines, without which they would be lost. For the magazines told them everything: which brands of clothing were in, which places were fashionable, which phrases and topics were popular. The girls themselves seemed like nothing more than illustrations in a fashion manual, the only differences among them stemming from the particular magazine each had studied. Fumio and Tatsuya learned to distinguish them by the perfume they used: Chanel No. 5, Poison, or Nina Ricci. And between themselves, they eschewed the girls' given names, calling them instead by the brands of clothing they wore.

These girls spent money as if they were naturally entitled to it. Whether they were students or workers, most of them still lived at home with their parents, who paid for all their living expenses. All their allowance money or salaries went on clothes, restaurants, or travel. Many had been to Europe or America several times.

But this fast life was only temporary for most of them, and they knew it. Eventually, their playtime would end... they were living on borrowed time. All of them fully intended to marry by the age of 26 and had no illusions about what their lives would be like after that. Most would marry ordinary salarymen who could never afford to keep them in their present lifestyle. This was their last chance for fun — for sex without any responsibility. Sleeping with boys was a way of dramatizing that sense of adventure, the last fling before settling down to boring wedded bliss.

Most of the girls Fumio met in the discos had more than one boyfriend, each of them pigeon-holed according to his purpose. Boys like Tatsuya and himself were for meeting in discos, dancing with, and sleeping with. Other boyfriends were there to take them out to dinner, to drive them places, to go shopping with. And somewhere else there was a boy — perhaps ordinary-looking, dependable, dull — earmarked for marriage.

Fumio stared blankly up at the ceiling of the hotel room, watching with detachment the faint blue smoke from his cigarette curling, expanding, fading. It was seven o'clock in the morning and he had just made love again with the girl he'd picked up the night before. As he turned to gaze at her face, slack and a little bloated-looking, he thought to himself: why is it that all women's faces look alike at this moment? He could superimpose her face on the faces of all those forgotten others and not tell the difference.

She opened her eyes and seemed a little startled to meet his impassive gaze. "I'm going to take a shower," she said.

He nodded, watching her walk nude to the bathroom. He crushed out his cigarette and began pulling on his clothes. This was the glamorous city life he'd dreamed of in far-off Nagano. This was what it felt like to sleep with the richest, most elite girls of Tokyo. The sound of the shower came on and he hummed to himself as he knotted his tie.

When he finished dressing, he sat down on the bed again and gazed forlornly at the girl's clothes lying sloppily on the floor where she'd shucked them off last night. They looked like nothing so much as the discarded shell of an insect which is doomed to die in the space of one summer. He wondered idly if there would come a time when he was no longer sexually aroused by girls.

After the girl finished dressing they left the hotel, he to go to school, she to go home. They parted at Shinjuku Station. In the train for Yotsuya, Fumio took off his tie and undid the top button of his shirt. To look more like a student, he would put his expensive suit jacket into a coin locker at the station.

The train entered the tunnel just before Yotsuya, and as Fumio moved toward the door, he felt a tap on his shoulder. Turning around, he came face-to-face with Professor Akiyoshi, his first customer as a host. They now saw each other quite regularly at the club but this was the first time they'd run into each other during the day.

"Good morning, sir."

"Good morning."

They chatted as if they were just a student and his teacher who'd happened to take the same train this morning. At Yotsuya Fumio started to get off, but the professor held him back.

"Would you mind coming with me to my school?" he asked casually.

Fumio saw the secret entreaty in the older man's eyes and nodded.

It was the policy of Genji that customers could make outside dates with the boys — for a fee, of course. But normally, dates were arranged for early evening, just before the club opened. This early in the day, no one would know about their meeting and Fumio could pocket the full tip without having to give the club its cut.

They got off at the next station, Ochanomizu, which was within walking distance of the professor's school. At this time of the morning, there were very few students about. Fumio felt the air cool and crisp against his cheeks. They were walking through a small woods on the campus when a bird chirped somewhere above them, sounding an incongruously pastoral note among the bare-limbed trees. Fumio searched among the branches but couldn't find it.

As they approached the faculty building where Akiyoshi had his office, the older man whispered, "I saw you with that girl."

Fumio started, but said nothing.

"Did you spend the night with her?" the professor asked in a trembling voice.

Fumio saw he had nothing to gain by lying. "Yes."

The expression on the older man's face underwent a subtle change. There was a barely noticeable trace of something very much like eagerness.

"A very pretty girl. That tight dress she was wearing showed off every curve."

"You're not mad at me?" asked Fumio, amazed. The professor, far from sounding jealous, actually seemed excited.

"On the contrary. Like many dirty old men my age, I'm thrilled by the sight of a sexy young girl. But in my case, I'm thinking of the handsome young man who is sure to be her boyfriend. So my thrill is only vicarious." He sniffed the air around Fumio. "I can still smell her perfume."

He escorted Fumio to his private office and locked the door behind them. Swishing the curtains at the window shut, he dropped to his knees before the boy and pulled him close.

"Did you enjoy her last night?" the professor crooned.

"Yes."

"Was she very nice to you?"

"Yes."

Fumio heard a sniffing sound.

"Oh yes. She was. I can tell." He closed his eyes as if he were in ecstasy. "Ah. This is the smell of a *nonke*. No homo has this smell — the fragrance of young girl. I love the smell of her on a boy. It makes the perfect spice, the perfect seasoning."

Outside the window, faintly, could be heard the sounds of a group of girl students passing by.

Fumio stared down at the older man as if confronted by a particularly grotesque species of insect. The professor glanced up at him in a coquettish manner.

"Fumi-chan, that's what I love about you. You're so cold. So cruel. You despise an old homo like me, I know you do. How can I compare with a luscious young girl like that? A young girl who can give you what I can't... "

Fumio saw that Akiyoshi loved the masochistic scenario he was spinning out, in which sexual humiliation gave him the perfect setting for his exquisitely refined mode of pleasure. He needed young *nonke* college students like the ones he taught, who looked up to him, respected him, and — perhaps at the same time — despised him.

The professor began moving his face from side to side, burrowing his nose into the pit of the smell's source. Against his will, Fumio instinctively shoved the older man away. But, far from objecting, the professor welcomed it. The look on his face was very much like that on the young girl's face in the hotel earlier. For Fumio, there was really no difference. It was all part of the universal game whose rules were defined by the exigencies of supply and demand. He shut his eyes so his disgust wouldn't show, and wondered idly how much the tip would be this time.

15

WHEN THE door chimes sounded, Fumio went to the door and peeked out the spyhole. It was the professor standing outside with a raincoat folded over his arm.

Fumio opened the door and greeted him.

"Welcome home." Though the professor only came by once a week, he insisted on this phrase being used each time. It was a travesty of the proper wife's greeting,and no doubt he got a thrill out of hearing it from Fumio's lips.

Fumio took the professor's raincoat and hung it up.

"Would you like something to drink?"

The older man looked a little tired. "I think I'll take a shower first."

"All right. I'll get the bath towel and robe ready."

As soon as the professor went in to take his shower, Fumio poured some of the professor's favorite brandy into a glass, then poured some for himself and sat back in the armchair to wait.

He had been here for a month now and still couldn't get over the feeling of newness. Compared with his old apartment, this condominium was a dream residence.

After being installed here by the professor, he'd stocked it with the latest in video and audio equipment — all at the professor's expense. Sitting here in the evening listening to music, he could gaze out the window at the tall skyscrapers of western Shinjuku glowing magically in the dark sky. The professor had arranged with his bank to have the monthly rent automatically deducted from his account for the next two years. In addition, he gave Fumio a regular allowance of 400,000 yen to spend as he pleased.

Fumio had, after much persuasion, finally given in to the professor's pleading to quit work at Genji and become his kept boy. The older man had grown increasingly averse to the idea of having to share his favorite with anyone who had 10,000 yen. His desire for a long-term commitment with Fumio was also, he said, the culmination of a lengthy search; he'd always dreamed of being the steady patron of a promising young man.

Fumio was torn between his desire to enjoy the pampered life of a kept boy, and his personal disgust for Professor Akiyoshi. He'd consulted Tatsuya about it. He wouldn't dream of taking such a major step without asking his friend's advice. Indeed, he felt he was secretly seeking to do Tatsuya's bidding.

Tatsuya had seemed surprised at Fumio's hesitation. "What's the matter? Go for it. It's the best thing that could have happened to you. This is the break you've been waiting for."

"I know. But I feel a little uncertain about it."

"Why? He'll set you up in a place to live, give you a steady allowance. What are you worried about?"

"Well, I feel my freedom would be restricted. It won't be like it is now, when I can do whatever I like, anytime I like."

"Don't worry. Being a kept boy isn't as restrictive as you imagine. You'll still be free. He isn't going to be around you all the time — after all, he has his job and his family. And anyway you can always break out of the arrangement whenever you get bored with it. There are many ways."

"So you recommend I should say yes?"

"Of course."

The professor's terms had been quite generous. Fumio was able to dictate the arrangements to his own satisfaction. Together, the older and younger man had gone condo-hunting and found this one in Ogikubo. Fumio had been living here a month now. He discovered that he didn't feel cheapened by his new status; for him it was merely a practical arrangement by which he got what he wanted, and the professor got what he wanted — and both parties were satisfied. Other young men had looked to a patron for support and done quite well by it, getting excellent jobs with the best companies merely through their acquaintance with an older established gay man. Fumio felt he might have that sort of chance. And if it didn't work out, he could always return to Genji.

He rather liked being a kept boy, actually, though it did have its drawbacks, mainly boredom. Now that he didn't have to work for a living, he found time heavy on his hands in the evenings. The professor usually dropped by only about once a week for dinner, an evening of drinking and talk, and afterwards, sex. He never spent the entire night with Fumio, going home to his family around one or two o'clock.

Outside of these weekly meetings, Fumio was free to do as he liked. The professor allowed him (indeed, encouraged him) to date as many girls as he wished, provided it didn't disrupt his studies in school; the older man took a concerned interest in his young protégé's education.

During the day Fumio still attended classes at college though school didn't interest him in the least. He went to the minimum number of required classes and whenever he could skip out, did so, paying other students to sign the attendance sheet and take notes for him.

It was so easy to graduate from college once one entered that people who did study seriously were taken for grinds. Like most university students, he wanted to get as much fun out of his college years as possible, for these four years of relatively idle time were his last chance to really enjoy life. Given Japan's system of 'examination hell', this was probably inevitable. The best years of his life — that period of youth which would never return — had been spent with the smell of ink and textbook pages, and he regretted it. He'd slaved away at his studies all through junior and senior high school in order to get into a good university, and now that he'd done so, he intended to make the most of it. Once he graduated, he knew he would be grinding away as a petty official back in his hometown, and, being the junior member of the office, would have to bow and scrape before his superiors.

The thought of his future depressed him. It seemed foolish to plod away at his studies just so he could get a 180,000-yen a month job, when he could make four or five times that much now by working in a host club. (The monthly allowance Akiyoshi gave him was more than the salary of most employees who'd worked with a company for ten years.) The homosexual world, despite its unsavory aspects, had been good to him. Yet he wasn't bound to it; he knew he could step out of it anytime he met the right girl. He still planned to marry and have a family. It was, after all, what all men did. But it would be very difficult to give up his present life — the money was so good and so easy to make. He'd be foolish not to take advantage of this opportunity while he was still young. His future surely held nothing as exciting as what he was living through now.

The sound of the shower stopped, and a few moments later the professor came out wearing his bathrobe, rubbing his hair dry with a towel. Fumio handed him the brandy and took the towel from him.

"You've had a hard day," he said, another of those phrases the proper wife would use in the situation.

"Yes. Those television spots really pay well but they take a lot out of you."

The older man began talking about his day. Recently he was quite busy as a panelist on numerous television talk shows. In fact, he'd just come from a meeting this afternoon with some executives at Asahi Television. His area of expertise — US/Japan relations — was very much in demand at the present, and the invitations to speak on various news programs never seemed to let up.

"Did you see me last night on News Station?"

"Of course," said Fumio. In fact, though he'd had the television set on, the sound had been turned down so he could listen to a new Southern All Stars CD he'd just bought. "I liked the tie you had on. It made you look so much younger."

"Do you really think so? It was a present from my daughter."

"Are you sure it was your daughter and not some handsome young boy?"

The professor smiled, delighted at this show of jealousy. Fumio had become adept at flattering older men like this, with the sort of standard host patter which had become an almost ritual ceremony with his patron.

"You know I wouldn't cheat on you, Fumi-chan, after all the trouble I had getting you out of the club."

"Well," he said, pretending a pout, "she has good taste, anyway."

"And how was your day, Fumi-chan?"

"The usual."

"How are you doing with your schoolwork?"

"Fine." He knew he really should have been studying for the upcoming finals and writing his paper for his world history class, but he hadn't even started yet. He was thinking of paying someone to do it for him.

"You don't seem too interested in your studies. If you don't do it now, you might regret it someday."

"I thought you were the one who told me I shouldn't spend too much time studying."

"Well, to a certain extent. But you do have to think about life after college, you know."

"That's still a long way off."

"Much sooner than you think. What are you going to do after you graduate?"

"I'll probably go back home and become a teacher or official. That's where my studies are taking me. My mother wants me to come home."

"Is that what you want to do?" He looked hard at Fumio.

Out of respect for his mother, Fumio couldn't answer, and the older man understood. He sat back in his deep armchair and appeared to be contemplating something. Finally, he said, "You know, I run a small *juku*. Not under my own name, of course, but under my wife's."

"Oh?" This was the first time Fumio had heard of it. He knew that college professors made a lot of money through their teaching and writing, but hadn't suspected this business aspect of his patron's life. Now he understood where much of Akiyoshi's money came from. *Jukus* — or cram schools specializing in preparing students for entrance examinations to prestigious universities, high schools, even junior high schools — were big business in Japan where educational cachet meant so much to one's career and social status. They seemed to be springing up everywhere. In Tokyo, it was hard to find a child who didn't attend one.

"Where is the *juku* located?"

The professor told him, and Fumio recognized the name. He'd often seen advertisements for it in the papers. Far from being a small *juku*, it was one of the most well-known in western Tokyo. His patron was far richer than he'd suspected; and he couldn't wait to tell Tatsuya about it.

The professor seemed pleased at the impression he'd made on Fumio. "I've been successful enough with the first *juku* to open up another one in Mitaka. It looks like things will be quite busy there in the near future, and I could really use someone I trust to head it — a young person who is capable and ambitious. It'll be a well-paying job and allow one to make many important connections in the education field."

"What are you saying?"

"That you should study harder. And after you graduate, if you wish it, you'll have a job waiting for you. At first you'll start out as an instructor, of course, but with the understanding that you'd work your way up to the director's position. It's a nice living, let me assure you. But of course, having a job here in Tokyo might be going against your mother's wishes."

Fumio knew that the position would enable him to earn much more than he could ever hope to make back home, allowing him to send an allowance to his mother every month. The offer did sound tempting. The work would be challenging, well-paying, and above all, allow him to stay in Tokyo.

"It sounds very good but I'd have to consult my mother and brother."

"I understand. It's not an immediate thing, so give yourself plenty of time to think it over. You could even break into it gently during your student years, as a part-time instructor... to see how you like it, how you take to it. I realize you might prefer a government job with all its benefits and security. But if you decide to go with the *juku* you have my guarantee that I'll look after your welfare no matter what happens."

Fumio needed time to think. He hadn't expected things to move so fast. The professor saw his concern and tactfully changed the topic. "And how about your romantic life? Been seeing any girlies lately?"

Since quitting Genji, Fumio hadn't played around with girls very much. It had all become such a boring routine that he'd decided to take a break for a while. In fact he spent most of his days working out at a health club to which Akiyoshi had bought him membership. And whenever possible, he went out with Tatsuya. Though the professor hadn't expressly forbidden him a male friend, Fumio felt it would be impolitic to mention his friendship with Tatsuya. The older man might see it as a betrayal, no matter how platonic the relationship was.

Fumio shook his head.

"What? If you aren't spending your time studying, or going out with girls, what are you doing?"

To divert the professor's questions, Fumio said, "Chasing girls seemed too frivolous a way to spend my time."

"Nonsense. You're only young for a short while. Here you are in the prime of your life — and with the time and the money. You should be making the most of it."

It seemed to please Akiyoshi to think of his young protégé as a ladies' man. He was always begging to hear about Fumio's conquests, and Fumio was sometimes hard put to come up with new tales. Occasionally he borrowed some from Tatsuya, who had an endless store of them. Sometimes he suspected Akiyoshi knew he was making them up but kept silent about it, playing along with the game. He didn't feel like playing storyteller tonight, though. "The girls in my school like to play hard to get. And I'm coming to feel they aren't worth the trouble of going after."

"That's their loss," laughed the professor, then cleared his throat. "You should think about shifting your sights to the girl students in my school. They're a really promiscuous bunch." He enjoyed belittling his girl students before Fumio; for an academic man, he seemed to know an awful lot of gossip about them — the ones who'd had abortions, the ones who were sleeping with professors. "They don't know a thing about what they're supposed to be studying, but when it comes to bedroom lore, they're indefatigable in their quest for knowledge."

"College girls in general are so vapid. They're really the stupidest creatures you can imagine."

The professor chuckled indulgently. "But don't you see? That's just their charm. Frivolous, empty-headed and cute: the perfect female companion for a man. They can never understand the real things which bond men together, of course, but that doesn't mean you can't play around with them."

Fumio sipped his brandy in silence. All of a sudden the professor took off his glasses and rubbed tiredly at his eyes. He looked helpless and lost without his glasses. Setting them on the coffee table, he peered short-sightedly at Fumio. "You know something, Fumi-chan? The worst thing you can do in life is to waste your time. It flies by so fast. Before you know it, you're old and ugly. Unwanted."

"Don't say that, Sensei. It's not true."

"It is. Once you're an old man there's nothing to live for. Nothing."

Fumio spoke a little more sternly. "Sensei, pull yourself together." The older man's bathrobe had fallen open a little, partly exposing his scrawny chest. Fumio couldn't help but picture the saggy flesh beneath the robe, and the solitary strands of gray hair poking out from the nipples.

"Fumi-chan, I get so lonely sometimes... "

Fumio put his glass of brandy aside and glanced at the clock.

This was the part he liked least about being a kept boy.

16

THE DOOR chimes sounded and Fumio looked at the clock — it was four in the morning. The professor had already gone home and Fumio was drinking brandy and watching a videotape of an old Ishihara Yujiro movie. Wondering who it could be, he got up and went to the spy-hole. It was Tatsuya, his suit jacket off, his tie loose, drunk.

Tatsuya occasionally dropped by Fumio's apartment before or after work, and because he was putting in long hours recently, it wasn't unusual for him to come by just before sunrise. Knowing Professor Akiyoshi might be upset if he were to catch them together, they'd worked out an elaborate code on the telephone to communicate whether it was safe to visit. But for some reason Tatsuya hadn't employed it tonight. Fumio was a little angry as he opened the door to let him in. Tatsuya immediately apologized for the unannounced visit, explaining that he'd had to spend a lot of time with a boring customer, a high-ranking official in the Treasury Ministry, and had drunk far more than necessary.

Fumio brought him a glass of oolong tea to help him sober up a little, then refilled his own glass with brandy. Tatsuya sprawled out on the sofa, his hair falling into his eyes, his suit disheveled. When he spoke, his speech was a little slurred. "So how's your *pato-chan* been? Still treating you nice?"

"He left just an hour ago."

"Oh? Close call, wasn't it?"

"It's not funny, Tatsuya. If he ever caught you coming here, he might kick me out of here."

Tatsuya didn't answer, lighting up one of his favorite Egyptian cigarettes and puffing languidly on it. He let out a huge plume of smoke. "You know, it's silly meeting like this, as if we were a clandestine couple or something."

"Hm." They sat watching the movie for a while until Fumio remembered what Akiyoshi had told him earlier. "Say, I finally discovered how the professor can afford to keep me in luxury."

"How?"

"He runs a couple of *jukus* in the suburbs."

"Oh?" Tatsuya kept a straight face but Fumio could tell he was impressed.

"That's a good line of business to be in, these days," added

Fumio, disappointed by his friend's lack of response. "A lot of money in it."

Tatsuya's expression suddenly turned a little fierce. "Yeah, right. And what do they do once they make the money? Treat everyone else like filth, without thinking about their feelings."

Fumio was somewhat startled by this unexpected outburst. "What's wrong, Tatsuya?"

"I don't know. I think I'm getting tired of this life. Sometimes I just want to give it all up and leave, go someplace far away where I don't have to cater to a bunch of old homos pawing at me."

"I know what you mean. But we have it so good. It would really be hard to give all this up." He waved his hand around, taking in with a sweep the audio system, the television, videos, the imported furniture. Through a half-open closet door could be glimpsed a row of Italian and English suits hanging inside.

"I could give it up in a minute," said Tatsuya, "if I met the right person."

Fumio knew now that something had happened to his friend tonight, but he didn't press the matter. In silence, they watched the rest of the movie. When it ended, Fumio turned the video off with his remote control, and the monitor automatically switched to television. An early morning news program was on. Fumio refilled his own and Tatsuya's glasses and then stared blankly at the news about a small airplane disaster in the Philippines. All the passengers had been killed.

"If I'm to die, that's the way I'd want to go — quick and painless."

Fumio was shocked at this toneless statement by Tatsuya. He himself had just been thinking how wonderful life was. The deaths of all these strangers had incongruously infused him with the happiness of being alive. "What are you talking about?"

Tatsuya looked at him and Fumio saw only a deep sadness in his eyes. This time he couldn't keep silent about it. "Tatsuya, something's happened, right?"

"Yeah. She telephoned tonight. She wants to get back together again."

"Who does?"

"Do you remember that girl I mentioned to you once? The one I used to live with?"

Fumio did remember — and with the memory came an unexpected surge of jealousy. He wondered at his own response. Was it because the image he'd cherished of his hero had been shattered? The cruel and heartless Tatsuya who'd toyed with girls had been a sort of masculine ideal for him. Now that idol had been tarnished: Tatsuya had turned out to be human after all, capable of feeling deep emotions for a woman.

Fumio tried to guess what sort of woman could have captured his hero's heart in such a way. All the girls Tatsuya had chased till now had been anonymous faces and bodies; this one was the only one who had had any real existence. As Fumio tried to picture her in his mind, he realized that all he felt for her was a blind hatred. She was coming back to take Tatsuya away from him. Gazing at his friend's handsome profile, Fumio felt a twinge of anxiety about the nature of his own feelings. He knew Tatsuya despised those boys who became overly emotional about their friendship, who pledged eternal faithfulness to each other. It was just that sort of behavior which disgusted him about girls, and he would never tolerate it in a male friend. And yet Fumio felt that Tatsuya was drawn to him in much the same way as a boy was drawn to his girlfriend. They shared things together that they never shared with anyone else.

Fumio, for his part, had never felt for a girl what he felt for Tatsuya: the joy of just being with him, of spending meaningless but lovely moments together, of sharing experiences. He was happiest just walking beside Tatsuya, or watching a movie with him, eating at a restaurant, singing songs with him in a karaoke room. And yet this happiness was tinged with the inevitable disappointment he knew was in store, for it could not last forever — two boys just could not go on like this. They had to grow up someday and enter society, become responsible members of the community. And that eventuality imparted to the time he spent with Tatsuya the intangible sweetness of a forbidden fruit. Each moment was so precious and wonderful precisely because it had the insubstantiality of a dream. And though each such moment was bought by the betrayal of his patron, Fumio felt no guilt about it. He could only feel resentment toward Professor Akiyoshi... as if the older man were purposely, jealously, strangling his own freedom, his own precious moments of youth.

"I just don't know what to do," Tatsuya said.

"Do you mean you don't want to return to her?" Fumio hoped his voice hadn't sounded too eager.

"No, it's not that. It's just — hearing her voice after all these years — I couldn't believe how moved I was. As if my feelings hadn't changed at all... "

"Then why don't you go to her and find out? Test your feelings by confronting her. She might have changed. You never know."

"She's still in Osaka now. She's thinking of quitting her job."
"What does she do?"
"She's a hostess."
"I see."
"Can I sleep over tonight?" asked Tatsuya suddenly. "I don't feel like going back to my own place and sleeping alone."
Fumio didn't reply immediately. Tatsuya had never spent the night over before — they'd both been too worried about Akiyoshi. And though it was unlikely the professor would return tonight, it was still a great risk. However, Fumio felt that his friend was so upset that it would be unkind to refuse.
"Of course."
"Thanks. You're a real friend. I don't have anywhere else to go, you know. There's no one else who understands me like you do."
"Don't say that."
"No, it's true. I may be bubbling and vivacious on the outside — the Tat-chan all the people at Genji see. But they don't have the least idea what I'm like inside. You're the only one who does."
Tatsuya's sudden sensitivity unnerved Fumio a little; having never encountered it before tonight, he couldn't quite believe in its sincerity. He'd only known the cold, rather manipulative young man who slept with girls as if engaged in a savage sport. Still, he was strangely moved by his friend's outburst, and wanted to show that he was able to respond in a suitable manner.
He led Tatsuya to his bedroom closet to find an extra pair of pajamas, then watched silently as his friend began taking off his suit. Fumio had slept with older men for so long that he'd almost forgotten what a healthy young body looked like. He recalled the first time he'd seen Tatsuya nude through the peephole that summer afternoon, a vision so potent that it still thrilled him to picture it.
He sank down onto the bed, his knees trembling a little. Under his own bathrobe he was wearing only a pair of bikini briefs. He crossed his legs and re-arranged the folds of his bathrobe. Tatsuya stood before the full-length mirror on the closet door looking at himself. He was wearing a pair of black briefs which hugged his hips so tightly that nothing was left to the imagination. Fumio felt like the hero of a children's storybook who has just stumbled across stolen treasure. A haze seemed to come before his eyes as he heard himself say: "Your bottom looks better than most girls'." A little light-headed, he had the illusion that he was addressing the Tatsuya he'd spied through the peephole on that far-off day.
Tatsuya looked over his shoulder almost coquettishly. "Do you

think so?"

Fumio nodded. Tatsuya turned back to the mirror, and in it, the reflection of his face was gazing thoughtfully at Fumio. It was not unlike that uncomfortable feeling produced by barbershop mirrors, when the barber talking with the customer addresses his remarks to the mirror.

"Fumio, do you have a steady girlfriend?"

"No."

"Are you still playing around?"

"Not much, these days. I guess I'm getting a little tired of that sort of thing."

"I know how you feel. If you keep it up, you'll eventually end up despising women, like me. I wouldn't want that to happen to you — I'd feel responsible."

"I think I despise them already."

"What makes you say that?"

"I get no pleasure out of it anymore. In fact, I haven't slept with a girl in over a month."

"Then you must be quite lonely. Of course, you always have your 'papa' to keep you company." He laughed.

"Maybe that's why I look forward to seeing you so much."

"Watch it, Fumio. If you're not careful, you'll turn homo." Tatsuya smiled the professional smile of a host, then hooked his thumbs under the elastic of the briefs and pulled them down. Fumio looked away.

"Don't do that."

"Why not? Because your 'papa' will scold you?" Fumio felt his ears burning. Tatsuya's teasing had struck a little too close to home. And yet it made things easier, for now that the topic had been introduced as a joke, it could be continued in another vein. Something unnameable swept furiously through Fumio, making him sway giddily. He sought the first words which came to his mind, regardless of consequences, and even unsure of their very meaning.

"Tatsuya, let's make love."

He'd used the fashionable English phrase, perhaps to soften the directness of his request. And he hoped it had sounded light-hearted, almost a joke. But when he looked up to face Tatsuya, he felt something like an electric charge go through him. There'd never even been a hint before that their friendship might be tinged with eroticism.

Tatsuya didn't say a word. But he didn't leave, either. Fumio undid the loose belt of his robe with shaking fingers. He lay back on the bed. Tatsuya began walking over to him. Fumio closed his eyes. As he thought of the consequences of his blurted request, he recalled Shima-chan's warning the first time he'd made love with a man: "Fumi-chan, never, never let a man do it to you. If you do, you'll never go back." Fumio had always felt it was unnatural for a man to assume the passive role, and he despised those men who did. To him it was unthinkable — for it made a woman out of a man. His attitude had been that if he had to have sex with another man he would be the aggressor — that was safely heterosexual. After all, one didn't compromise one's masculinity just because one's partner wasn't a woman. In the past, the toughest samurai warriors had slept with their pages so that their pure masculinity wouldn't be sullied by the weakness of a woman's character. Fumio didn't believe that sort of thing, but he did feel that a man was still a man even though he slept with a boy, provided he assumed the man's role.

There was also the professional aspect. If word got around that he had become a 'sister', his status would diminish in the eyes of all the men who'd paid to have sex with him — who'd paid for a man. Yet all these considerations seemed to melt magically away when Tatsuya slipped onto the bed beside him. As he smelled the alcohol fumes coming from his friend's body, and looked at his firm muscular chest, arms, shoulders and thighs, he knew he would surrender. Tatsuya was his superior in every way — much more attractive, much more masculine. It was only natural that Fumio would become the girl for him.

As for Tatsuya, there was no question that only he could assume the masculine role. And he did. Fumio's initial reaction was: "So this is what it's like." After some moments of initial awkwardness, it gradually dawned upon him why they all liked it. What surprised him more than the physical pleasure was the purely mental gratification of assuming the passive role. There was a feeling of liberation in letting the other assume control. It made him feel vulnerable and submissive, as if he were serving a beloved master.

Sex with girls had never done this for him. He felt as if a hard outer husk were being stripped away to reveal the delicate tender white fruit within. He might have been the passive one all his life and not known it until now. That might be why he'd been so afraid of it before. He had been afraid he would like it. He gazed in quiet awe at Tatsuya's face, with its look of unfocussed concentration. The tiny gold chain he wore around his neck was bouncing up and down, thin and shiny against the healthy nut-brown color of his skin. And the smell of masculine sweat which seemed to perfume his body was a heady new brand — strong, virile, and young.

Tatsuya's lips curled back, baring his teeth. Abruptly, he stopped and appeared to be listening intently as the merest tremor passed through his body. Fumio felt that shiver as a secret message of love. Then Tatsuya dropped onto his stomach beside Fumio, breathing heavily. His broad muscled back glistened with sweat. As Fumio gazed at the sexy swells of flesh, a thought came to him, as if it had just emerged from behind a cloud. With a sense of wonder, he said to himself: "I'm a homo." With this simple, elegant statement, everything at once became clear. All the confusion in his soul became unravelled. He wondered why he hadn't thought of it before. It was so plain. The explanation for all his vague discontents had been so obvious and he'd blindly denied it. All his half-guessed conjectures, false leads, and hypotheses had been dead ends. The simplest explanation had been the correct one after all.

Strangely enough, this new knowledge didn't pain him at all. Instead, he felt a calm contentment as if he'd opened himself up to someone else for the first time. He'd finally confronted his own fear and discovered the truth about himself; his real fear had been of the confrontation itself, and once it had occurred, the initial anxiety dissolved away like mist. There was nothing to hide from now.

The two boys lay side by side, their breathing slowly coming back to normal. Fumio felt as if he'd given something up, not just his virginity but something infinitely more precious: his boyhood illusions. Nothing else mattered anymore after this. He only wanted to be held in Tatsuya's arms. His entire being was suffused with an aching tenderness which sought an outlet. But Tatsuya merely turned away from him and tried to sleep.

Gazing up at the ceiling, Fumio said, "I wish we could go someplace far, far away. Another country, perhaps."

Tatsuya stirred. "Or Hokkaido." Fumio knew that for Tatsuya, Japan's northernmost island was a sort of dream country. There, spaces were wide open. The roads stretched endlessly onward, past rolling fields, farms and ranches, under a clear blue sky which was vast and eternal. Tatsuya dreamed of taking his Ferrari there and opening it up to the full — to see exactly how fast he could go. If he went fast enough, he just might shatter the reality barrier and burst into a fabulous new world. "If only we had the money." Fumio was merely talking for the sheer pleasure of hearing his friend's voice.

Tatsuya turned onto his side to look at him. "We do."

"Where?"

"If you have the courage to reach for it."

They looked into each other's eyes and Fumio read a seriousness there he'd never seen before. He felt as if he were being challenged to test the strength of his friendship for Tatsuya. The answer was already given.

17

AS TATSUYA had instructed, Fumio called Professor Akiyoshi at the university and made a daytime date to meet at a Skylark restaurant near the school. The older man was agreeably surprised at this unxepected request; perhaps he flattered himself that the younger man couldn't wait until their next meeting. He quickly agreed to meet Fumio, though it meant having to cancel a professional lunch date. Sitting in the restaurant at the appointed time, Fumio imagined himself as an actor in a movie. He could actually see himself as others saw him — a well-dressed young man who looked completely at ease with what he was doing. For the first time he felt as if he were living life with the same intensity as Tatsuya.

Professor Akiyoshi, when he walked through the door, spotted Fumio immediately, and his joy at seeing him was unfeigned. He sat down in the seat opposite and picked up the plastic-coated menu before him.

"I'm not used to eating in family restaurants like this," he said.

Fumio made some suggestions on what to order and the older man went along with them. The lunch progressed pleasantly enough as the two chatted about familiar topics. In his cheerfulness the professor seemed so much younger and alive than he'd ever been before, and Fumio was amazed at the change in him. When the meal was over and the two were sitting over their coffees and cigarettes, Akiyoshi asked, "To what do I owe the pleasure of your company, Fumio? Not that there need to be a reason."

Fumio had almost decided not to go through with what he'd come to do. He'd told himself that if the professor said nothing, this would be just a lunch date. But now that the issue had been broached, he felt moved to action by powers beyond his volition. He reached into his inside jacket pocket and pulled out an envelope. Without a word he placed it on the tabletop and slid it over to the professor. It was a letter addressed to the professor's wife.

The older man blanched. Something in his expression indicated that this was something he'd feared all along... but also that living with this fear had probably given him a secret thrill, infinitely enriching his attachment to his young protégé. "Is this what I think it is, Fumio?"

The younger man stared down at the tabletop.

"This is blackmail, Fumio. I never would have expected such a thing from you. You seem so decent. Tell me it isn't true."

Fumio tried to make his expression and voice hard. "There's no such thing as decency in this world." He still couldn't face Professor Akiyoshi's pained expression, however. He tried to instill some courage in himself by thinking of Tatsuya waiting in his car nearby to help if anything went wrong. Tatsuya had easily discovered the professor's home address and telephone number by making a few calls to the *jukus* run by his wife. He seemed to know so much about such things.

The professor sighed audibly. "Well, then, obviously I have no choice. Meet me in my office this afternoon at five. I'll have the money ready for you." He got up and left, seemingly in complete control of the situation. As soon as he'd gone, Fumio felt his knees begin to shake. He really had nothing personal against Akiyoshi and wished things didn't have to turn out this way.

Outside, Tatsuya was waiting in his Ferrari, its engine idling, the car stereo playing a Southern All Stars tape. "How did it go?"

"All right. He said to meet him at his office at five." He slid into the passenger seat as Tatsuya put the car into gear. "I'm worried. Do you think he'll tell the police about it?"

"No way. He has a lot more to lose by that than us." The boys drove around the city for several hours to kill time. Fumio became more and more nervous as the moment for the meeting approached. He kept hoping, indeed half expected, the whole thing to turn into a joke. But at five o'clock they drove to the professor's school and parked in a side street near the campus. The school appeared deserted. Though Fumio had been here once before, Tatsuya had gone through the trouble of scouting out the territory and outlining the exact route he wanted Fumio to take to the professor's office.

Fumio felt as if he were sleepwalking. The school buildings had the appearance of stage sets, and the darkening clouds above were like paintings on a backdrop. When he knocked on the door of the professor's office and walked in, the older man was sitting alone at his desk with a resigned look on his face. They didn't make any conversation but got right down to business. Akiyoshi opened a drawer, pulled out a thick envelope and dropped it onto the desk. After peering around to make sure no one else was hiding in the office, Fumio picked up the envelope and glanced inside. It was stuffed with thick wads of ten-thousand yen bills.

"That's not blackmail money — it's your separation money," said Akiyoshi. "I suppose I should consider myself lucky to be rid of you. Don't ever bother me again. That amount should be sufficient for your needs."

"All right."

"It's not the money which hurts me so much as your betrayal. But it probably goes with the territory. Let's just say I'm a wiser man now."

Fumio remained standing there uncertain of what to say.

"Now get out of my life and stay out, or I'll notify the police next time."

"Sure." He started to leave but hesitated, vague words of apology beginning to form on his lips. Just as he was about to say something, he saw Akiyoshi's stern visage crumple and almost give way to tears. As Fumio had suspected, the older man had been putting up a brave front. A twinge of pity blossomed in his heart but he quickly suppressed it. He turned to go, but the professor called out after him. "Fumi-chan. I still love you. You know that, don't you?"

There were tears in his eyes but Fumio could only feel a disgust now at the grotesque spectacle the middle-aged man presented. "I'll miss you, Fumi-chan. I'll never forget you in spite of this. You don't know what you're doing. You're young and foolish — your ambition is making you blind." Then, contradicting his earlier words, he almost sobbed out: "You can always come back. You were the only one for me."

Though Fumio couldn't stand such melodramatic nonsense he was beginning to be moved in spite of himself. Before he could change his mind he quickly left. In the car, Tatsuya appeared more nervous and impatient than he'd let on before. But when Fumio waved the thick envelope at him he burst into a boyish grin and gave an OK sign with his thumb and forefinger. Fumio got in and they roared out of the side street, the Ferrari's tires squealing.

"Count the money, Fumio. How much is there?"

Fumio did so, with trembling fingers, and discovered that the professor had paid out five million yen. Tatsuya gave a shout of triumph. They drove onto the Shuto Expressway, joining the evening traffic jam on the elevated loopway. The excitement of planning, discussing, and preparing for the blackmail scheme had energized them for the past few days, and now, even after its execution, still burned inside them, perhaps more strongly than ever. All the tension which had keened through their nerves during the whole ordeal now seemed to radiate out of them, charging the air with electricity.

"How will we spend all this money?" It was more cash than Fumio had ever seen at one time in his life. He felt a giddy drunkenness at its heavy weight in his lap.

"Don't worry. Money always has a way of getting spent. I've learned that." They were heading for the junction connecting the Shuto with the Chuo Expressway. Instinctively, they wanted to get as far away from Tokyo as possible, as if putting some distance between themselves and their crime would help erase it. As traffic speed began picking up, Fumio slipped the envelope onto the back seat, leaned his seat back and gazed out at the cityscape. All of Tokyo seemed to be spreading outward, as far as he could see, the smaller structures like an ocean of flotsam and jetsam washing around the bases of the tall buildings. Beneath the dark purple sky the lights of the city were winking on here and there like fireflies. Ahead of them, to the west, the sun had just set, turning the mountains there into an intricate black cut-out silhouette of ranged peaks. Most prominent among them was Mount Fuji with its perfect cone shape, the quintessence of Japanese beauty, whose fresh outline never failed to move Fumio no matter how many times he saw it.

"Nice view, huh?" said Tatsuya, noticing Fumio's rapt study.

"Yeah. It is."

"But I soon get tired of views, myself." He had already returned his attention to the road. Fumio gazed in silence at his friend. He was still in an acute state of excitement from their successful blackmail, an excitement which had all the feverish intensity of sexual arousal. Indeed, what they'd done together today constituted, for him, a sexual act. It had been better than sex — better, indeed, than anything he'd ever done in his life. He was a criminal now, a co-conspirator with Tatsuya. He wondered if Tatsuya felt the same way. There was a sub-current of expectation surging through his own heart, and somehow he felt it was impossible for the other to remain unaffected by it.

Whistling a disjointed tune, Tatsuya reached into the glove compartment and pulled out a pair of sunglasses. When he put them on, he assumed a jaunty, cocky air, the attitude of a young man who has everything in the world going for him. This show of arrogant confidence charmed Fumio, made something melt inside him.

"You look so sexy in those sunglasses."

"Do I?" He looked at himself in the rear-view mirror.

"Yes."

Tatsuya pulled the Ferrari into the left lane, accelerated past the slower-moving cars in front of them before pulling into the fast lane again. Without a word, Fumio reached his hand over and let it rest on his friend's thigh.

"Don't, Fumio." Since the night they'd made love on Fumio's bed, there'd been no mention of what had happened. By mutual consent, it was a topic they avoided. For all practical purposes, it hadn't happened at all.

"Slow down, Tatsuya. Do you want to be stopped by the police, after what we just did?"

Tatsuya eased his foot off the accelerator; Fumio's touch had apparently unnerved him, too. But Fumio didn't move his hand from his friend's thigh. Tatsuya didn't say a word. With an impatient grunt he lifted his foot off the gas and the car decelerated abruptly. Fumio saw they were pulling into one of the small emergency highway ramps located at intervals along the Chuo. The green emergency telephone stood in the cluster of bushes lining the outer perimeter of the ramp. As they pulled to a stop right next to it, Fumio could still feel the cars and trucks roar by them on the expressway, shaking the parked Ferrari. They were about twenty meters from the main flow of traffic, isolated on their little island of quiet. Tatsuya said nothing, just sat in the driver's seat looking straight ahead.

With a surge of joy in his heart, Fumio realized what it implied. The sound of other vehicles passing by them on the expressway only heightened his awareness. He knew he was on the brink of a moment of truth. As in a dream, he watched his own hands at work laying bare the evidence that, despite his earlier protest, Tatsuya was far from unwilling. Perhaps for him, too, the crime they'd committed had been sexual. Fumio savored its ripe fragrance for a moment, then slowly bent down, out of sight of the drivers going by, and as the sounds from outside rapidly faded from his consciousness, all of reality became drained of its meaning.

Tatsuya accepted Fumio's slavish tribute with the assured mastery of a natural conqueror, the natural beloved. He was so cold and distant, but not — not! — out of reach. Fumio felt his friend's fingers rake distractedly through his hair, then clutch tightly at his scalp. Nothing could match the satisfaction of this moment: everything had just come together... his first lonely days in Tokyo, charged with illusions and hope... his tentative forays into the homosexual underworld... and his friendship now with the handsomest, most virile young man in all of Japan.

This, he thought, swallowing, was the taste of happiness.

18

THOUGH THE television set was on, Fumio could clearly hear the words through the closed door. Mayumi's voice had a shrill edge to it whenever she was angry, and now she was making no effort to keep it down. It seemed she was having one of her periodic spats with Tatsuya.

"What do you see in him?" Her voice had risen to a whine. Fumio had been lying on the sofa half-asleep in front of the television set when he'd been awakened by the commotion in the next room. Feeling ashamed of his own curiosity, he now edged a little closer to the wall, the better to hear the couple.

"Will you keep your voice down?" Tatsuya sounded uneasy. "He's sleeping." Their talk became subdued for a while, until Mayumi's voice gradually started getting more shrill again. Fumio knew she was purposely speaking loud enough for him to hear, despite Tatsuya's pleas.

"I don't care if he hears. And I'm tired of having to share rooms with him. Why can't we be on our own?"

"He's not bothering you, is he? And it's his condo, really."

"But you're paying half, aren't you? You're entitled to a say."

In reply, Tatsuya lowered his voice and Fumio couldn't hear what was said. But then Mayumi's response was clearly audible through the wall.

"Why are you always sticking up for him? Who's more important, me or him?"

"If you don't shut up, I'll knock your teeth in."

"Go ahead and try — if you dare."

"Bitch."

"You're a big man when it comes to speech, but when it comes to action, you're worse than a woman. I wonder about you sometimes."

Fumio lay there listening to all this, a bit fascinated, as if it didn't concern him in the least. The injustice of it didn't even enter his mind. He was only interested in Tatsuya's replies. He prayed that Tatsuya would throw her out, so the two of them could live together in peace again. Before Mayumi had moved in, things had been so much better. Shortly after getting the money from Professor Akiyoshi, they'd split the profits and gone their separate ways for a while. Because the professor had made no attempt to have Fumio evicted from the condominium, no doubt hoping he would return to him, Fumio had continued to live here. He'd grown accustomed to the place and thought of it as his own. Even when the rent was cut off, he had started up his own direct deposit account.

As expensive as it was to stay here, the separation money he'd collected from Akiyoshi was more than enough to keep him in good living for quite some time. Then, a couple of months ago, Tatsuya had approached him with the idea of moving in together. Fumio had immediately agreed. However, having Tatsuya with him under the same roof had been a species of torture. Fumio's initial feelings of hope and expectation had given way to despair once he realized that his friend had no intention of repeating what had happened in the car. There had been nothing more between them since that intoxicating celebration of their successful blackmail. The subject was never brought up, and Fumio didn't have the courage to mention it, much less try anything. He was afraid of driving Tatsuya away.

In his darker moods, Fumio wondered if his friend had seduced him from the start solely for the purpose of getting him interested in the blackmail plan. After all, Tatsuya had gotten half the earnings without doing anything other than suggest the plan. Strangely enough, however, that thought didn't bother Fumio — even if it should be true. In fact, there was a part of him which relished his new subservient role in relation to Tatsuya; he rather liked this feeling of serving as a disciple to a heartless and beloved master. It was as if he'd discovered a new, untried variation of romantic fulfillment: sacrificing his own pleasures for those of another. Fumio had given up his double bed to Tatsuya, taking the living-room sofa for himself. And it was Fumio who did the laundry, cleaned the house, went shopping for food, and cooked their meals. He didn't mind it at all. It seemed more natural this way, a balance demanded by nature. His only hope was that Tatsuya — as he saw how faithful Fumio was — would grow to appreciate the sacrifices.

Even when Tatsuya began bringing girls into the room, Fumio didn't complain; it only confirmed Tatsuya's virility and attractiveness. Tatsuya would inform Fumio that he was going to have company, and Fumio would uncomplainingly find something else to do for the evening. The thought of having to overhear his friend having sex with a girl pained him so much that he sometimes stayed in an all-night porno movie theater to pass the time till morning. (Never on these occasions was he tempted by the middle-aged men who fumbled at him as he was nodding off.)

Though this cruel master-slave relationship pained him sometimes, he felt it was better than nothing at all. His biggest fear was that his friend would disappear into the labyrinth of Tokyo never to be seen again. It could always happen — the city had swallowed up many others before. The tenuousness, the fear that was always there, made his situation so much more precious than the usual live-in partnership that he was almost satisfied with it. He secretly pretended they were living together out of love, and that he was the domestic partner in a marriage-like arrangement. He fantasized that Tatsuya was only trying to stoke his jealousy by having these affairs with women. After all, it had been Tatsuya's attractiveness to women that had captivated him in the first place. Tatsuya's blatant heterosexuality only made him that much more desirable; now Fumio could understand why Professor Akiyoshi had built such a cult around *nonke* boys. Somewhere in his heart, though, was the hope that Tatsuya would someday give in and change, let down his armor just enough to allow a glimpse of more tender feelings. Until then he would have to play the faithful wife who puts up with her husband's infidelities solely because she knows he will return to her in the end — if only for the reason that he has nowhere else to go.

However, even Fumio had his limits. There were times when he became so upset by Tatsuya's cavalier treatment that he would sulk for days, and refuse to do the housework. The air would become tense with unspoken resentments. But Tatsuya seemed to know exactly how far to push Fumio; all his experiences with various girl friends of differing temperaments had made him an expert in human manipulation. Whenever he sensed that Fumio was reaching the point of rebellion, he would casually walk naked from the shower room to his bed and call out: "Fumio, I wonder if you could give me a massage. My shoulder muscles are killing me." And Fumio, all his pique vanishing at this peace offering, would willingly kneel beside his prone friend and knead those magnificent shoulder muscles, pressing his thumbs down along the back muscles as directed.

There was always the hope that this service would modulate into something more intimate. But he never dared. Usually, after about an hour, Tatsuya would be dozing peacefully, and despite his aching need, Fumio would gently lay a towel or blanket over his sleeping friend's body and creep away. These massage sessions were so pleasing in themselves that he grew to treasure them, angling for them in his own devious way, pretending sulks he didn't actually feel, just so he could arrange for another one. It always worked; and from the next day, peace was restored, and life went on as before.

This punishing cycle took up a lot of his energy, but Fumio didn't mind — at least he was vouchsafed the pleasure of touching his friend's body. He had begun going to school regularly again, attending classes with a sense of purpose which would have gladdened Professor Akiyoshi. After school, he cooked dinner for the two of them, seeing Tatsuya off to work before settling down to study. Tatsuya still worked at Genji, and by the time he came home in the early morning hours, Fumio was usually fast sleep. When Fumio left for school in the morning, it was Tatsuya who was fast asleep. They were on different schedules, and didn't have much chance to see each other very often, but there was a sense of domesticity to Fumio's life which left him with a feeling of happiness.

A couple of weeks ago, however, he had come home from school to find luggage and boxes stacked up in the living room. Without a word to him, Tatsuya had invited Mayumi to stay with them. She'd been kicked out of her condominium in Azabu by her 'papa' when he'd discovered her relationship with Tatsuya. (Tatsuya had greatly increased the risk of this by recklessly making love with her in the very bed the older man had just vacated, as if daring the fates to punish him.)

Though nothing was ever said about it, Fumio gathered that this was the girl Tatsuya had been so infatuated with all this time, the one who had broken his heart. Fumio saw nothing extraordinary in her. He'd met numerous other girl friends of Tatsuya's, and many had been prettier, sexier, and far more fashionably dressed. It was a riddle to him how this girl, out of all the girls in Tokyo, could have been the one to snare his friend's deepest affections. Though rather coarse in manners and speech, she was a fashion model who was beginning to make something of a name for herself in a small way. She modelled under a different name, but Fumio had seen her photos in various magazines, usually in a swimsuit designed to show off her well-proportioned body. Like Tatsuya, she, too, was hoping someday to make a name for herself in the entertainment world — her 'papa' had been connected in a vague way to various talent agencies.

Fumio half suspected that Tatsuya's interest in her might be rooted in his hope that her success would propel his own. For Mayumi had a confidence in her future success which bordered on arrogance or mania. She preened herself before the mirror with a self-absorption into which she could become lost for hours. She was always flipping through magazines looking for herself in them. And whenever she had a bit part in a television drama — even as a passerby — she was careful to spot herself, pointing herself out with pride. One time she told Fumio that she was to appear on a news documentary as one of several girls being interviewed in Roppongi. When she discovered that the segment had been cut, she was in a dreadful pique.

She was indefatigable in seeking out anyone who might further her career. Her conversations consisted almost entirely of the singers, actors, or producers she'd met at this club or that disco. Most of her time at home was spent boning up on the entertainment news, learning the names of people who might be good connections someday. Chewing mint-flavored gum, her feet propped up on the coffee table, she watched TV with an absorption which was just short of pathological. She seemed hypnotized by the screen, and when Fumio spoke to her at such times, she sometimes couldn't even hear him.

She was biding her time, just waiting for her moment of fame to arrive, and until then, took it for granted that she would be waited on hand and foot by Fumio, whom she saw as someone with no future. She quite naturally assumed a star's prerogatives, even at this early stage of her career. Therefore, she made no attempt to make things easier in the house. She did very little cooking, and most of it was instant food. She was happy to leave all the housework to Fumio. And she had messy habits. Fumio had to pick up after her all the time. He was angered by the sight of her stockings hanging on the curtain rail to dry. One time he had opened the toilet lid to find that she hadn't even bothered to flush. He was amazed that any girl could be so slovenly and undisciplined in her habits. He knew she did it partly out of spite, for she made no secret of her irritation at his presence. And though it was he who kept the house running and paid the rent (despite her claim, Tatsuya was a little lax in keeping up his part of the bargain in this), Mayumi acted as if she were the one who had to make concessions to keep the peace.

Tatsuya had apparently never told her that Fumio was gay, but she seemed to instinctively sense a rival in Fumio. For her, the presence of a male friend was just as irritating as that of another girl. As it was a common practice for college boys to room together, she didn't find it odd that two boys were sharing, but she did feel puzzled that her lover should choose such a dull friend for a roommate. "He's an old friend from school," was all the explanation Tatsuya gave.

Things had become quiet in the next room, and Fumio was concerned that they might be making up their spat in the usual way — he loathed hearing Mayumi's cooing moans through the wall. But he knew Tatsuya had to go to work tonight at Genji. That was another unusual aspect of their precarious menage à trois: Mayumi seemed to have no idea what Tatsuya's job was. She apparently thought he was still a host in a club catering to women. Fumio suspected that her recent bad moods were brought on by sexual jealousy more than anything else. Because Mayumi and Tatsuya were having sex less and less often (and Fumio knew this because it was so difficult to keep it secret in their home), the frustrated girl apparently suspected her lover of playing around with other women. Having been a hostess once herself, she knew exactly what was involved in a host's job. It gave Fumio a measure of satisfaction to know that Mayumi's fears were so misplaced. He wondered what she would think of Tatsuya's real customers — many of them perhaps the very same actors, singers, and producers she saw at discos. At the same time, he marvelled that it was in his power to completely destroy the relationship between the boy he worshipped and this shallow, stupid girl. Apparently Tatsuya counted on Fumio's devotion to keep quiet about it... and that was enough for Fumio.

The bedroom door opened. Tatsuya was dressed up in a new pale gray Armani suit bought for him by an admirer. He nodded to Fumio. "I'm going to work."

"Don't forget to take your umbrella." The rainy season had set in, and Fumio always checked the weather report for the chances of rain overnight. Tonight there was a fine drizzle outside, likely — according to the forecast — to turn to heavier showers later on. "Take care of yourself."

"All right. See you tomorrow."

"Bye-bye." As he saw his friend off at the door, Fumio secretly thought of himself as the wife seeing her husband off.

Mayumi came out of the bedroom dressed in jeans and a loose t-shirt, smoking a cigarette — the Egyptian brand Tatsuya favored. She blew out smoke and picked up the remote control for the television, switching it to a variety show without even asking Fumio's permission. Feigning unconcern, he picked up a comic book and began flipping through it. "I thought you were going out tonight, Mayumi."

She didn't answer, her attention seemingly focussed on the television screen. Sitting down cross-legged on the floor, she leaned over to crush out her cigarette in the ashtray, and her t-shirt bagged open so far that Fumio could clearly see her pink-tipped breasts. Though he quickly looked away, she tugged at the neckband of her t-shirt in a way which made it obvious she knew he'd seen. Fumio knew she'd done it on purpose. It was in her nature to be flirtatious — at least whenever she thought she could get something out of it. But there were times when she seemed to use her sexuality as a weapon for the sheer pleasure of using it... as a test of her own power over others. No doubt it had been developed as part of her strategy for success, but sometimes it seemed her seductiveness had gotten to the point where she couldn't help it anymore — it had become second nature. She would wear the sexiest clothes when she came out to the living room to watch TV — an over-sized man's t-shirt with only panties on underneath, or a sheer negligée — and she made the most feeble attempts to cover herself. Or she would call out from the shower, "Fumio-kun, would you bring me my towel? I forgot to bring it in with me." And when he took it in, he could see, beyond the glass shower door fogged up from the steam, her flesh-colored form.

He always tried to keep the displeasure from showing on his face, but sometimes he couldn't hide it. She, for her part, seemed frustrated that nothing she did succeeded in capturing his interest. One time she'd even chided him openly about it. "What's the matter?" she'd taunted. "Don't you find me sexy enough for you?"

"I find you very sexy," Fumio had replied, without a smile.

"Then why don't you do something about it? Some of his other friends do, you know. I mean, at least try."

"I couldn't do that to Tatsuya."

She tisked her tongue. "You're so straight, you know that? Doesn't it make you sick to know how boring you are? What a dull life you must lead."

"I have all the fun I want, thank you."

She made a face. "Well, I wouldn't want to have your kind of fun."

Fumio thought he could guess what was behind her seductive games. She was getting back at Tatsuya for what she perceived as his lack of affection. Fumio was merely the tool to stimulate Tatsuya's jealousy.

Mayumi got up suddenly and went to the refrigerator, took out a can of beer, popped it open and began drinking straight from the can. Walking slowly back to the sofa, she sat down again and boldly crossed her legs, returning her attention to the television screen. Without comment, Fumio got up and went to the kitchen to make himself a cup of instant noodles. Pouring the hot water into the styrofoam cup and covering it up again, he carried it out to the living room. Then, sitting down in front of the television and completely ignoring her, he pulled off the top and began slurping them up. By the time he was finished, Mayumi had gotten bored with what was on television. She was now sitting on the floor, her knees drawn up, painting her toenails a ghastly purplish color. As loath as he was to do so, Fumio couldn't help but watch her at this operation — just as he knew she wished. She glanced up at him suddenly, catching him looking. He turned his face away.

"Don't you have anything better to do tonight, Fumio?"

"No."

"You must get bored coming straight home from school every day." She looked closely at him. "Don't you even have a girlfriend?"

"No."

"I suppose not. I can't imagine the girl who would see anything in you." Fumio didn't answer. "Still, it must be frustrating to be living together with Tatsuya and me. You know... doing the things you can't do..."

She had a faint smirk on her face but Fumio didn't want to give her the satisfaction of knowing he noticed it.

"There's more to life than that." He felt himself blushing even as he said it.

"Don't you stop to think you might be in the way sometimes? For instance, when we want our privacy?"

"You have enough privacy during the daytime. I'm outside all day."

"I get it!" she said, clapping her hands, "you get your kicks from listening in on us, is that it?" Fumio was pained by the crudity of the statement. It wasn't so much what she said, as the intent behind it. She was choosing her words carefully to find those which would hurt him most.

"I'm not a pervert."

"I didn't say you were. If you were, you would try to sneak a peek sometimes when I take a shower. You never do."

Fumio knew she often left the bathroom door slightly ajar, as if accidentally, and he'd taken care never to be near it whenever she was taking a bath.

"And besides," she went on, "Tatsuya would never let you stay alone with me like this if you were one." The faintly disgusted look on her face seemed to imply that she despised him for being so straight, for showing so little of the lust which most normal males would have shown. She fell to thinking at what she'd just said, as if struck by something. "You know, I've always wondered why he isn't more worried about you and me being alone like this. Usually he's so jealous when I'm with another boy. Does he have such a low estimate of your ability to seduce a girl?" She looked at him mockingly, then said, choking back a laugh: "Or are you impotent?"

Fumio felt a flash of rage. "I'm not impotent. And anyway,

what makes you think you're so irresistible and desirable? I find that a very arrogant assumption."

"Because I know what men are after. My whole life has taught me what they want, and I just live up to those expectations. Listen, I've worked as a hostess, a companion, a model, an actress; I've done everything but sell my body. So don't tell me I don't know what excites men."

Fumio had no reply to this, and the television sounded loud in the sudden silence. Mayumi returned to painting her toenails. When she was finished with them she continued on to her fingernails, holding out her hands occasionally, turning them this way and that, admiring the finish. She blew on them to dry them, her lips a kissy O. She shook her hair. Suddenly she looked straight at Fumio. "You know what? I think you're a homo."

Fumio felt the blood drain from his face. In a flash, he wondered how much Tatsuya had told her about him. It was quite possible that he'd at least hinted about it and that she'd been playing with him all along, knowing it.

"It's true, isn't it?" she insisted.

"Did Tatsuya say anything?"

She rolled back onto her elbows and let out a full, throaty laugh. "So it's true, it's true." She kicked her heels in glee.

Fumio flushed hotly. "So what if I am?"

She gazed at him wonderingly. "You? A homo? I don't believe it." She looked him up and down. Apparently she had all the misconceptions of homosexuality fostered by the Japanese media. Fumio had seen those romantic comics depicting gay love, so laughably out of touch with reality that he'd felt mocked by them. People seemed to want a beautified, sanitized version of homosexuality, preferably a romantic love story of two young boys — always beautiful, but in an ephebic, non-sexual way, wraiths almost — who grow out of their wayward passion as they get older. It had to be a phase, a beautiful phase, granted, but temporary. No one wanted to imagine that middle-aged men could be gay, that most were not attractive, that few had their loves requited, that many sought out their furtive pleasures in public restrooms, host clubs, or all-night porno theaters. There were no flowers, no sweet kisses exchanged under a cherry tree, no linked pinkies and pledges of eternal love — despite what one saw in certain comics.

Mayumi's lips curled back slightly. "I should have guessed it. There's something about you that's not normal. I just couldn't put my finger on it till now. No wonder Tatsuya never worries about us two being alone together. In fact, it should be me who's worried when you two are alone together." She laughed, finding the idea delicious in a perverse way. "But he hates homos. He would never let you touch him." She looked at him for confirmation. Fumio said softly, "He's *nonke.* That is, he's not homo." He realized now that Tatsuya had never told Mayumi about him for the simple reason that Fumio would be able to reveal where Tatsuya worked. It was an unspoken trade-off: he wouldn't expose Fumio as long as Fumio didn't expose him.

Hardly able to keep her fingers from trembling, Mayumi tapped out a cigarette from her pack on the table and lit it. She leaned closer to him, fascinated in spite of herself. "What made you decide to turn homo?"

"I didn't decide to be homo." Fumio always resented this sort of question when he heard it asked on TV. It was a common misconception shared by all the media that a gay man had had a choice in the matter, that he'd chosen it as an alternative to 'normal' sex. Still, Fumio couldn't blame her; even he himself had thought so in the beginning. Until quite recently, he'd believed that he'd come into 'this world' from choice, out of curiosity. He knew now he'd only been fulfilling a deep-rooted need all along. It was Tatsuya who'd opened his eyes to the truth, and perhaps if he hadn't met Tatsuya, he would never have known the joys and the agony of it all. "No one chooses to be any such thing," he said. "In fact, if most homos had a choice, they'd probably wish they were non-homo."

"Then why don't you try to have a girlfriend? It might put you on the right track. I'm sure you'd like it. Your body would, anyway." She sounded sincere, as if she were actually trying to be helpful.

"I've had plenty of girls, thank you. And they did nothing for me."

"But have you ever slept with a woman?"

"Yes. That's what I'm telling you."

"And didn't you like it?" She was flabbergasted.

"I was just going through the motions. There was no emotional fulfillment in it for me."

"And there is with a man?"

"Yes. There's no comparison."

"How is it different?"

"Everything about it. My deepest feelings are involved with a man. With a girl, it's only physical. They're not the same experience at all; one is play-acting, the other is real."

"You just haven't found the right woman. If you found one who knew what she was doing, you'd never go back to your little boys."

"I already know what I want, and what I'll always want. But there seems to be no use trying to explain it to you; we're talking in two different languages. I don't know if you can understand me, even if you tried."

She made a slight grimace of disgust, but then her features suddenly became more animated. "Tell me," she said, a prurient curiosity lighting up her face, "how do you do it? What do you do with each other? Are you the boy or the girl? I'll bet you're the girl. You like to have the other do it to you." She all but clapped her hands in glee. "Does it feel good? How awful. It must be something like constipation."

"You understand nothing, so it's useless to talk to you." Fumio felt his face turn red, but knew he mustn't show any weakness before this girl.

"Or do you use your mouth?" she went on. "I know some girls who do. But you probably do it better because you know what boys like." She picked up her beer and took a deep drink, then set it down with a bang, lasciviously licking her lips. She wasn't afraid of him now. The fact that she knew he was gay had weakened him somehow, as if that knowledge had drained him of all masculine impulses. Mayumi tapped her cigarette on the ashtray and watched the ashes flutter down. "I wish you'd tell me all about homosexuality. I think it's fascinating."

"This isn't a talk show. I don't have to tell you anything."

"Don't be so stingy. Come on. Do you people have favorite types the way women do? And if so, what's your type? The muscle man? The pretty boy? Does penis size matter?" She gave a high, trilling laugh. It was all a joke to her. Suddenly she seemed delighted by a new idea. "Don't you wish you were a girl so you could get what you really want? I know! How about if you dress up as one? You might be able to fool someone on a dark night."

Fumio knew it was futile to explain that he didn't want to be a girl-substitute. In fact, he suspected that men who went after transvestites were not really homosexual at all, but represented a branch of the mainstream called heterosexuality.

"I'm not one of those," he said in a tired voice. "I have no desire to play at being a girl."

"You might find you like it. Come on, I'll even help you out, give you make-up tips, help you select the right dress for your figure.

Maybe we can both go out and pick up some boys. We'll get them so drunk they won't know the difference. It might be fun."

Fumio felt a weariness suffuse his body. In the course of the last few minutes, he'd seen himself turned from a figure of hatred into one of scorn, then into a figure of fun — the fate of many gays. For Mayumi, as for most Japanese, gays were merely aberrations, clowns or freaks who could safely be laughed at, if not bullied or even pitied. The general feeling was that there was something wrong with gays for the simple reason that they were different — supremely different, as different as a person could be. Yet, this humiliation at her hands was cleansing in a way. Fumio felt as if all of Japan were interrogating him, bullying him. He'd thought it would be a lot worse, but now he found the idea of being known as gay wasn't so bad. After being put through this torture, this initiation, the other side would feel better. He could take anything after that.

He wondered, indeed, whether he were enjoying this grilling at her hands. After all, he could choose to get up and walk out if he wanted to. Perhaps it was because he was finally telling the truth about himself to someone, callous and unsympathetic as she was, and the act of giving voice to his identity was a validation of it, an affirmation. Indeed, Mayumi was merely holding up a mirror to him, showing him his own face, albeit in a cruel and hurtful light. And she was a link — however tenuous — to Tatsuya. To alienate her was to alienate Tatsuya. That was something he didn't want to do. He would put up with anything for Tatsuya.

"Have you had enough fun with me yet?" he said in a small voice. She tapped out another cigarette and slipped it between her lips, fumbling for the lighter with her fingers splayed out. Fumio picked it up and lit it for her.

"Thanks." She shook her hair free from her forehead. "Listen, I still say you should try to find a girlfriend, even if you can't feel anything very deep for her. You can at least just go through the motions."

"But that would be unfair to her. And not much fun for me, either. Let me put it this way: how would you feel if you had to sleep with another woman?"

"That's different. A woman's body is sensual, desirable. The idea of two women making love is much more acceptable to me. I've never done it, but I'd rather sleep with another woman than with a man I didn't care for. I just can't imagine a man desiring another male body. Ugh!"

"You don't find men sexy?"

"Of course I do. But only if I love him will I feel anything physical for him. If the love isn't there, the man — any man — is disgusting. That's the way women are made. For us, love comes first. Then sex."

"What makes you think a man can't love another man?"

"Don't be ridiculous. It's not natural."

"Well, nature has made many men who love other men. They didn't choose their inclinations; they were just born that way. So I'd have to say that 'unnatural' is not the right word for it."

"You hate me, don't you?" she said suddenly.

"Hate you? Why should I hate you?"

"Because you envy me. Gay men must hate all women because we get to do openly what they can only dream of doing. I can make love any time with — "

Fumio felt the blood drain from his face and, simultaneously, Mayumi stopped in mid-sentence, her face frozen as if she'd just been struck by a new thought. Slowly, visibly, her shoulders began drooping under its weight.

"So that's it," she said weakly. "That's why you live here with us. That's why you put up with me. You're in love with Tatsuya, aren't you?" And now Fumio couldn't stop a flush from spreading over his face, down his neck and his shoulders. "It's true, then, isn't it? It's true!" Then more slowly, thoughtfully: "It's true. You love him." A look of loathing twisted her face momentarily. "No, you couldn't possibly know what it feels like to love someone, would you? How can you understand how normal people feel about each other?"

Fumio got up to go, but she gripped him by his t-shirt. Her face was distorted with fury. "You'd better not touch Tatsuya in that way. If he doesn't kill you, I will. Or I'll find someone who will. I don't want him tainted in any way by your homo hands."

It was on the tip of Fumio's tongue to tell her the numbers of men Tatsuya had been with. But he knew he wouldn't, and it was torture. He could not hurt the boy he adored — even to pain this girl. He felt he was the shield protecting his friend against darts and arrows, and he didn't mind being sacrificed for that purpose. In fact, he got a very joy out of the act — for when Tatsuya learned that his secret had not been divulged, it would make him see how much Fumio cared for him. Much more than this shallow, insensitive girl.

"I wish I were a man so I could beat the crap out of you, homo. You're worse than a woman. You're like a rotten version of a woman."

In a weak, broken voice, Fumio said, "What's wrong if I love him? Am I doing you any harm by it? He'll never look at me the way he looks at you. You have no idea of the depth of my feelings. For you, it's a joke, but I probably love him more deeply than you ever will, no matter how your feelings change."

"What do you mean, how my feelings change?"

"You don't love him. You're just playing with him, using him like a toy."

"You're wrong. You just don't know how wrong you are." From the stricken look on her face, Fumio wondered if he'd actually hurt her. In a more gentle tone, he asked, "Can you tell me from your heart that you love him?"

"Yes, I love him. Maybe not in the way girls' comics portray love. I need him in my own way. And he's been good to me. For your information, because you'll never find out, Tatsuya is a wonderful lover. He's the only man who's ever given me any real satisfaction."

"Why don't you marry him, then? You know he loves you."

"Do you think marriage is the only way of validating love between two people? You sound like one of those gossip columnists for women's magazines. Ugh." She flipped back her hair and violently stubbed out her cigarette. "Besides, I have to keep my options open. So does he. We both agreed to it and he understands. That's the kind of relationship we have. It's something you would never understand."

Fumio had always wondered if it was because of her unconcerned attitude toward Tatsuya that she retained her hold over him. Most of the other girls in Tatsuya's life had been frantic to keep him, and this very fact had put Tatsuya off. He'd even said as much. But Mayumi acted as if she didn't care about her lover's feelings. That, no doubt, was what drew him to her — because he wasn't needed, he had to be the one who clung. Fumio wondered if every love affair didn't have this element in it — the beloved who was cruel and scornful, and the lover who pined after the other.

The mood had turned calm after the outburst. Mayumi drained what was left of her beer and sighed. "Would you mind getting another can for me, please?"

Fumio went to the kitchen to get it. When he returned, she'd gotten up to the sofa and was lying down on her side with her eyes closed. He picked up the remote control to turn off the TV.

"Leave it on. I'm watching it with my eyes closed."

Fumio set the beer on the table. She opened her eyes wearily and turned to him. Noticing something on his t-shirt, she half-sat up.

"Looks like I got some fingernail polish on it. Sorry."

He peered down and saw what looked like sprinkles of dried blood spotting the hem of his t-shirt. "It's all right."

"I have some nail polish remover in my bedroom."

"I said it's all right."

She reached for the can of beer and popped off its tab. The beer hissed and foamed out of the hole so rapidly that she had to jerk the can up to her mouth to suck up the overflow.

19

IF ANYTHING, this summer was even hotter than last. Fumio could picture Tatsuya and Mayumi at the beach right now, either on the Shonan coast or at Kujukuri on the Pacific coast of Chiba prefecture, their two bodies bronzing side by side under the hot sun like a scene from a soft drink commercial on TV. It was a distinct contrast to the picture he probably presented, lying here in his t-shirt and shorts, sweating in a cramped apartment, a small electric fan blowing hot air into his face. There was a certain irony in the fact that, after all that had happened, he was back again in a one-room six-mat apartment not very different from the one he'd lived in before all his adventures had started. He'd been here for about two months now, ever since Tatsuya had apologetically asked him to leave the condominium they shared. Fumio knew that Mayumi had put him up to it, but rather than fight for his rights, he'd volunteered to move out. With the secret of his feelings for Tatsuya out in the open, it would have been difficult to stay there. The condo was much too small for three people and one open secret.

Since moving into this apartment, a dark thought had begun to haunt him: the possibility that Mayumi and Tatsuya had planned it all together from the start, so that they could have the condo to themselves. Mayumi would not be above such machinations, nor, for that matter, would Tatsuya. Strangely enough, the thought that Tatsuya might have betrayed him like this didn't pain him at all. If anything, it only made Tatsuya that much more attractive to him. The cruel callousness with which he'd been dropped once his usefulness was gone only reaffirmed the egotistical nature of beauty. Fumio knew that a handsome boy's selfishness was natural — for beauty only looked at itself. He would leap at the chance to be betrayed again by Tatsuya. It would be almost as good as being loved by him. A kind and gentle Tatsuya would have disappointed him, perhaps even earned his disgust. And Mayumi's callow narcissism was a perfect match for Tatsuya's selfishness; the two of them formed a beautiful pair of partners in evil, statues carved out of exquisite teakwood. Now that he could look at them from a distance, as it were, he could almost appreciate the aesthetic perfection of their compatibility.

A train roared by, rattling the glass in the sliding veranda door, making the whole apartment shake as if an earthquake were in progress. Through the white gauzy curtains fluttering at the window, Fumio could watch the train go by just a dozen meters from his apartment, and even see the individual faces of some of the passengers. He knew they couldn't see him because the room was too dark by contrast with the sunlight outside. It gave him a certain pleasure to know that people outside couldn't see him at all, though he could watch them. It was like being invisible, wrapped in a storybook sensation of invulnerability. He liked to heighten this feeling sometimes by taking all his clothes off, the breeze shifting the curtains dangerously, almost allowing outsiders a glimpse of his nudity.

Summertime brought out the most erotic feelings in him. He sat up and pulled his t-shirt over his head, then wriggled out of his shorts. The heat was much more bearable like this, with the breeze licking at his exposed skin. He reached for one of the magazines in the hollow box under his television set. There was a stack of magazines there — *Barazoku, Adon, Sabu,* and even *Samson* — all gay-oriented, which he now bought without any fear. The thought of how he'd tremblingly paid for his first *Barazoku* brought a smile to his lips. He felt no self-consciousness about buying them anymore, provided the bookstore was a little-frequented one. And though he did glance around to make sure there was no one he knew, he no longer bought other magazines to camouflage what he really wanted. On the other hand, he hadn't yet lost the little thrill he felt each time he purchased a gay magazine. He liked to think there was still an element of danger involved in the act, a defiantly illicit rebellion. Whereas his earliest purchases had been exploratory in nature, his growing collection of magazines now had but one purpose: to find a boy who looked like Tatsuya. It didn't matter how fleeting the resemblance was; anything that distantly reminded Fumio of his friend gave him a thrill. If he sought diligently enough, there were always boys who could be found to serve as models for the original — this one had legs like his, another had his back. And there were even a couple who — when viewed through the charitable prism of memory — even had his face. It was as if only Tatsuya — and the memory of him — could interest Fumio anymore. The fact that he could only have him through pictures merely added to the poignancy of his worship. And the daily lengthening distance of time which separated them served to make his yearning for him that much more potent.

He lay face-down on the tatami mat, the magazine open before him. It was pleasing to feel the coolness of the tatami against his naked belly as the warm air raked over his back, his sweat already a thin, oily film. Idly, he flipped through the magazine, noting the many letters from men looking for friends and lovers. He himself didn't feel the least interest in finding a replacement for Tatsuya. Indeed, no one could ever replace him. In that respect, there would always remain a huge gap in his life which could never be filled. Until this enforced separation, he hadn't realized how deep his feelings for Tatsuya had been. It had transformed everything in his life — the way he thought of himself, the way he looked at the world. Now that he could no longer meet him, there was a pall over everything; sunlight wasn't as bright, colors weren't as vivid.

Impatiently he glanced at the models in the photographs. The first boy was too young and much too thin — Fumio could count the ribs on him. The second boy looked Filipino — not bad looking, but no substitute for the pure Japanese beauty Tatsuya exemplified. Putting aside the magazine, he reached for a cigarette, lit it up and turned onto his side so he could face the open window. For a while he smoked meditatively, thinking about nothing. The afternoon was quiet; there was no one out on the streets below. Again, a train came barrelling past his window, shaking the whole apartment. A keen feeling of loss filled him. He suddenly knew with a sense of finality that he would never get his friend out of his mind, for the rest of his life, no matter how long he lived. All other boys would be compared to his perfection, with that dreamlike face and body, and the all-too-seductive cruelty.

Strangely, it was the cruelty he missed most; the cruelty had at least formed a bond between them, even though it might have been the obverse side of love and affection. A boy as beautiful as Tatsuya could only be cruel, and use his beauty to manipulate others for his own ends. Perhaps his affair with Mayumi was nothing more than a means to another end.

At the thought of Mayumi's smug self-satisfaction, Fumio could not stifle the almost furious jealousy which enveloped him. It had seemed so easy for her to secure Tatsuya's affections. Perhaps even now she was lying with him, revelling in his caresses, those expert caresses polished by a hundred lovers. Fumio's only satisfaction lay in the hope that perhaps someday she, too, would be discarded by Tatsuya after he'd had his use of her. Then she might understand what he felt now. But somehow he doubted it. Her shallowness wouldn't allow her to even guess at the depth of his own feelings; only another gay boy could.

The absolutely hopeless pathos of a gay boy loving a *nonke* was something no one should be allowed to experience. And yet it was his unique lot, it made his life shine with a solitary mellow light in the darkness, like the steady glow of a candle on a Buddhist altar. The suffering he cherished for Tatsuya would never fade away simply for the reason that it would never have a chance to become used up — it would always be alive, an ever-present memory, eternal and unchanging in his heart.

From down in the street came the happy banter of a young couple in love. "Give it back! It's mine!" "You'll have to get it back from me." Fumio pictured a young man holding up something he'd snatched from the girl, and she — with a play-acted angry look on her face — pummelling him with her fists, both of them all but glowing from the first happy blossoming of their love. It was the sort of scene Fumio himself would never take part in, though he could indulgently forgive these two now from his lonely height, a solitary, forsaken homo in a world of happy heteros.

He wondered where Tatsuya was right at this moment. What was he doing? What was he wearing? Was he thinking about Fumio? Did he ever think about Fumio at all? Surely they'd been more than just friends? He stubbed out his cigarette and reached to pull out another magazine from the box under the TV. With the assurance bred of familiarity, Fumio turned to a certain well-known page and opened it out before him. There was a photo of a boy facing away from the camera, standing with his weight on one foot, emphasizing the seductive curves of his buttocks. A shallow groove ran up his smoothly tapered back. It was almost the exact pose Tatsuya had assumed on that hot summer afternoon when Fumio had first put his eye to the peephole. He noted again the clean roundness of the buttocks, so smooth-looking and firm that they should have belonged to a statue. Pale white, they seemed to float below the deeply tanned back, encased in the phantom outline of a swimsuit once worn, a bikini so tight that nothing was hidden, not even the clean dark cleft separating two globes of perfect symmetry.

Fumio ringed his fingers to form a peephole and brought it up to his eye. Gazing down at the boy's body, he imagined himself back in his old apartment, pressed close to the wall, looking for the first time upon his unknown neighbor, a boy of supernatural beauty. Nothing had changed since then. Fumio felt once again all the excited thrill of illicit trespass, the fresh wonder of discovery, and the unflowered bud of nascent hope still dreaming tightly in his heart, waiting to unfurl, to blossom, and to die. The buttocks were lovely. Lovely beyond words.

Book Two: Dances Sacred and Profane

1

WITH A sickening screech and a gut-wrenching lurch, the airplane found firm ground beneath it once again. Outside the plane's window, the frieze of distant trees shot past level and smooth like an unrolling scroll. Fumio was glad to be back on Japanese soil. The honeymoon in Hawaii had been a success but he couldn't suppress a secret relief at returning to Narita, Tokyo's international airport. The faintly gray-blue sky over the distant metropolis in the west gave him a pang of joy; after days of pure blue tropical skies, even the smog of Tokyo was a welcome sight.

The plane taxied toward the distant terminal building, and even before the stewardess announced that seat belts could now be unfastened, many impatient passengers had gotten out of their seats and were busy unloading their luggage from the overhead compartments. As a first-time air traveller, Fumio had dutifully waited for the announcement, but by then the aisle was filled with passengers jockeying for access to the exits.

At last the plane arrived at the terminal and the exit doors were opened, disgorging the restless passengers. It looked like nothing so much as Shinjuku Station at rush hour. They were back in Japan.

Fumio and Seiko joined the milling crowd of homecoming tourists going through the process of re-entering Japan, having their passports stamped, picking out their suitcases at the baggage carousel, and joining the tail end of one of the many long lines before the counters of the customs inspectors. Patiently they waited their turn. Seiko, with her usual practical sense, had made sure to pack their suitcases so that everything could be seen at a glance when opened. As they waited, Fumio glanced at the young woman who was now his wife, and as often happened, experienced a feeling of disbelief. Sometimes it seemed like some horrible joke that he was actually married to her. It wasn't that Seiko was unattractive; on the contrary, Fumio was quite aware of the admiring looks other men cast at her. On the beaches of Hawaii, when they walked side by side, he'd felt proud to be seen with her. And her personality was compatible with his; they shared the same tastes in music and movies. She wasn't at all the immature party-girl type of woman he'd come to loathe. Despite her youth — she was only twenty-three, a year younger than Fumio — she was level-headed and could take care of practical matters. She was strangely mature for her age, almost a throwback to the traditional Japanese woman who did everything for her husband, leaving him free to concentrate on his work. In short, she was the perfect wife. The only problem was that he didn't love her.

Once they were through customs, the tinted automatic doors beyond opened onto the busy lobby, crowded with returning tourists, departing passengers, airport employees, gawkers, greeting committees... the whole frenetic, fast-paced atmosphere of Tokyo in a sudden burst. Standing in the midst of it, Fumio realized that he'd almost forgotten how hectic the life they'd left behind in Japan had been. But he knew the seeming chaos around him was ordered by a purposeful efficiency; the Narita limousine bus left the terminal for Tokyo station every twenty minutes with a punctuality that Fumio now looked upon as uniquely Japanese. They bought their tickets and had their luggage loaded, then boarded. It was a ninety-minute ride into Tokyo, but today, as usual, the traffic was so heavy that delays pushed the time back about forty minutes.

On the bus, both suddenly felt their accumulated tiredness hit them as if it had been held at bay by the excitement of travel. Seiko shut her eyes and was almost immediately asleep, her head leaning against the glass of the window. Fumio had taken the aisle seat, from where he gazed out the window at the passing scenery. The expressway leading into the heart of Tokyo was as featureless as all such roads, with turfed banks dotted with shrubs. The ugly urban sprawl of Tokyo wouldn't become visible until the bus hit the heavy traffic in the approaches to the Shuto Expressway. He looked forward to it as to the familiar face of an old friend who was not quite handsome.

He closed his eyes and thought back on their ten-day stay in Hawaii. Already it was assuming the features of a dream. Despite Australia's recent popularity, Hawaii still had not quite lost its status as the most favored destination for honeymoon couples. Fumio himself would have preferred a less traveled spot, but Seiko had insisted upon Hawaii for some reason, and he'd given in to her pleading. Upon arriving in Honolulu Fumio had immediately felt culture shock, though not because of the language or the people. In fact, he'd been surprised by the number of Japanese there... so many that it hadn't seemed like a foreign country at all. "This is no different from

Harajuku," he'd told his wife. From all the Japanese tourists everywhere snapping away with their cameras, it was easy to fall under the delusion that the whole island had been developed as a recreation facility for overworked Japanese. Indeed, there was a feeling among some that Hawaii was a sort of Japanese outpost, planned by ingenious resort developers back in Tokyo. Rich Japanese owned lovely houses and condominiums along the coast, and familiar businesses and services from back home had set themselves up to serve the many Japanese visitors. What was especially embarrassing to Fumio was the sight of provincial tour groups following their flag-carrying guides. He couldn't help but wince when he saw the local people's reactions to these excursionists, and was glad that Seiko had insisted on avoiding the obvious tourist traps. They themselves had come here as part of a packaged tour but recently these tours had become flexible to the point where one was pretty much free to pursue his own interests.

Seiko had been to Hawaii before, so it was familiar territory to her. Like many young women her age, she was much more well-traveled than most of her male counterparts. In fact, as Fumio noticed, the vast majority of Japanese tourists in Hawaii consisted of young girls who'd come here with groups of friends. The few Japanese men to be seen — neatly dressed, with a certain naive expression on their faces — were, like Fumio, obviously here with their newlywed wives.

Their first day in Honolulu was spent buying souvenir gifts for everyone back home. In the duty-free shops where all the clerks spoke Japanese, Seiko consulted the list of people who'd attended their wedding, each name followed by the amount of money the guest had given the young couple. Buying the appropriate return gift was real work, a continuation of their gruelling wedding work, but after it was done, they were free to enjoy the rest of their trip. On the second day, they had more time to explore the island on their own. Seiko wanted to rent a car and drive around the whole island of Oahu. She had gotten an international driver's license in anticipation of this, and Fumio was glad to let her do the driving. In fact he was resigned to letting her make all the decisions while they were in Hawaii. This was her third time here and she seemed to be in her element. The language presented no problems; she had been taking English conversation classes for four years now and was quite confident speaking it. Fumio himself had begun studying English conversation in anticipation of the trip, but was relieved that he hardly had to use it.

They found a relatively secluded beach, a quiet one on a little-visited corner of the island. The few people there were almost all Americans, probably tourists from the mainland. Unlike Japanese, who generally stayed in the fashionable Waikiki area where their resort hotels were, Americans seemed to seek out the quieter places. Fumio and Seiko changed into their bathing suits in the car — they'd been wearing them under their t-shirts and shorts — and got out. Seiko had chosen a skimpy white high-leg swimsuit which she would never have dared wear back home. In her dark sunglasses she looked very attractive, and Fumio noted the way the men's heads turned to follow her walk. He himself was wearing a tiny black bikini in which he would have been too embarrassed to be seen on the beaches of Japan. However, just being away from home had seemed to fill him with a new boldness. He delighted in the play of his youthful muscles as he strode on the warm sand. It felt as if the sun's rays were caressing him, seductively polishing his golden skin to a sexy sheen. A flirtatiousness completely alien to him possessed his body with a freedom which felt quite natural in these surroundings.

They found a secluded spot in the shade of some palm trees, and spread out their beach towels. Fumio still couldn't get over the blueness of the water. Somehow he had assumed that the real thing wouldn't live up to the promises of the travel brochures and TV ads. But now, as he gazed at the sea before him, the aquamarine, turquoise and indigo shades of blue had an unreal, almost hallucinatory quality. He felt slightly detached from the scenery, as if he were viewing it all from a theater seat in the dark. The Americans didn't appear to be interested at all in the beauty of the sea. For the most part they lay on their towels soaking up the sun, reading paperback books, rubbing sun-tan oil onto their pale white skin now baking a brick red. Many of the men were overweight and out of shape, but quite a few of them were strikingly well-built. Despite himself, Fumio found his gaze wandering longingly to some of them. With the secrecy guaranteed by his dark sunglasses, he was free to admire their bulging hard muscles, their massive chests and shoulders.

Normally he wasn't one of those who went for foreigners. He didn't like their hairiness, for one thing. Some Japanese boys claimed to be attracted by just this attribute, but Fumio was among the majority of Japanese who preferred clean, smooth skin. He thought the color of the Americans' skin too pink to be sexy — it reminded him of bath soap or wax dolls. And blond hair against tanned skin just didn't seem right somehow, as if the image were being seen in negative film; hair should be black. Still, he couldn't help but admire some of the physiques displayed on the beach. He himself was considered well-built back in Japan, but he knew he couldn't compare with the beauties he saw here. Their chests and shoulders were broader, their legs longer, and their overall musculature more defined. Perhaps it was their greater physical power that gave them such arrogant stances, for they seemed to walk around as if they were born to be dominant.

Far from being put off by this, however, he found himself getting aroused — for the first time in a long while. Since becoming engaged to Seiko, he'd tried to keep his true desires under control — suppress them, if possible. But somehow, this only succeeded in making them that much more intense, as if a fire were confined in a small space, making it burn white hot, then blue hot.

He had never played around behind Seiko's back. Women didn't interest him in the least, of course, and as for men, there was only one man for him and that man was out of reach. His feelings for Tatsuya had not changed at all. A constant, vague pining in his heart had become an enduring condition. He felt like an invalid forced to live with a permanent disability. So, since his love was forever unrequitable, he'd done what many men (and women) have done in similar circumstances since time immemorial: gotten married. Though nowadays twenty-four was quite young for a man to 'settle down', he'd done it because it was the thing to do, even for gay men. It was what all Japanese men did at some point between the ages of twenty-five and thirty — the marriageable age. Since life held no more pleasures for him, he felt he might as well get it over with as soon as possible. And he had seen the practical advantages of a union with Seiko.

He had no doubt that he had made the right decision. He'd long wanted to settle down and get on with the business of living as an adult member of society. Also a part of him still believed that a wife would straighten him out, make him forget about these forbidden urges he felt toward men. Actually, the decision to marry had come quite suddenly. During their courtship one day, Seiko had said suddenly, "I'm thinking of having an operation."

"What kind of operation?"

"On my eyes."

Seiko had been born with a single fold over each eyelid, giving her a very oriental look. But like many young women, she wanted double folds so she would look more like the western models on TV and in magazines... eyes that looked bigger, more alluring. The magazines she read were full of advertisements for hospitals and fashionable clinics which specialized in the operation. Readers who couldn't afford the expensive surgery were offered all sorts of alternatives for producing the desired double fold, everything from make-up tricks to a sort of stick-um which temporarily created the effect.

"Fumio-san, what do you think of people who get the operation?"

He'd thought for a moment, then given his truthful answer. "I see nothing wrong with it. But you look fine the way you are."

"Don't you think women with double folds are more attractive?"

"I think it depends on the woman. Some women look better with single-fold eyelids." He named a popular actress.

"Oh, her. She's special. I'm talking about normal women. Most people would agree with me that women with single-fold eyes have a stern look. They're not as friendly or approachable as women with bigger eyes. After all, I know from experience that the girls who get the most dates are those with double-folds."

"Hmm... "

"And anyway, if the operation gives a woman the feeling that she's more beautiful, that can only be a plus for her. It will give her increased self-confidence and social acceptance because this world is made for beautiful people. And there's really no physical danger in it. It's quite a simple operation. Almost everyone's doing it now. Even young girls in elementary school go to the clinics, accompanied by their mothers. I saw it on TV."

"You've obviously made up your mind about it already."

"It's something I've wanted to do ever since junior high school. If I go through with it, will you stick up for me in front of Father? Being the hidebound traditional Japanese man he is, he's dead set against it."

"Well, I wouldn't want to go against your father's wishes... "

"But he listens to everything you say. If you ask it of him, I'm sure he'll say yes. He won't even listen to me, even though I'm his own daughter. He dotes on you, though, and you know it."

"Of course I'll stick up for you if it comes to that. But why do you want to do it? You look fine enough as it is."

"I want to look my best for the wedding photographs." That was when Fumio realized that they'd passed the dating stage and that their engagement had become formal. They'd met through a *miai*—an arranged meeting with a view to marriage. Like most such affairs, it had all been rather formal. The first meeting was held at an expensive traditional Japanese restaurant in Akasaka. At one side of the table sat Seiko and her parents; facing them on the opposite side were Fumio, his mother and his brother. At the head of the table were the traditional go-betweens, in this case Fumio's department head in college, and his wife. There was the usual stilted talk at first, and Fumio could feel his mother's and brother's tension; they were much more ill at ease that he himself was.

After the dinner and more small talk, the older people discreetly excused themselves in a stylized manner. The young couple were finally left alone and Fumio relaxed for the first time. Seiko, too, seemed to be relieved after all the formalities were done with. "Do you mind if I relax my posture?" she asked politely, a little deferentially.

"Go right ahead."

She had been sitting up stiffly with her legs folded under her in the formal posture which most young women today were not used to. He himself loosened his tie and grinned. "I could really use a beer."

Seiko nodded and pushed the button to summon the waitress. After that they began talking as any normal young man or woman would talk. She had just graduated from Seijo University, a college well known as a sort of finishing school for young ladies from good families. But, to Fumio's secret relief, she didn't fit the usual stereotype of the Seijo coed. At first she was not very talkative and Fumio found himself doing most of the talking. But with the help of the alcohol, she gradually warmed to his feeble jokes. They got along quite well for a couple meeting for the first time.

Fumio had heard from friends that there was an unwritten law of etiquette which required that the man ask his *miai* partner out at least three times after the initial meeting — usually for dinner dates. If there were no more dates forthcoming after the three, then it was understood by all the parties concerned that one of the partners had found the arrangement unsatisfactory. In fact, though, no one really knew the actual 'rules' for a *miai* nowadays. Since the traditional arrangements had been relaxed, people were free to do as they liked, and when Fumio had asked around, he'd found that different people gave different advice. Nevertheless, the 'three date' rule seemed to have the authority of tradition behind it and he went along with it.

They dated the requisite three times, each time becoming more comfortable with each other. On the evening of the third date, they'd found themselves — quite by accident — in the area north of Shinjuku called Kabuki-cho where love hotels abounded. More out of obligation than anything else, Fumio had halted his steps before the entrance of one. They'd dated three times, after all, and he wanted to signal to her that she was not unattractive as a woman.

Seiko didn't show any surprise. She merely looked down at the ground and said nothing. Fumio read this as an assent. He stepped inside the entrance to make his intentions even more obvious, and there wasn't the slightest protest. In silence, without a word to each other, they entered, got their key from the clerk, and took the elevator up to their room.

After that night, their dates became regular. Fumio began to like Seiko as a person. They enjoyed the same kinds of music, movies, and food. He came to feel that marriage to Seiko might be possible — and after the operation on her eyes, it was a foregone conclusion. Her father had finally given in to her — and Fumio's — wishes in this regard.

In most other things, however, Seiko was a traditional, dutiful daughter to her parents. She still observed many of the accepted customs. Though the young couple, as was customary, began living together virtually as husband and wife after the formal announcement of their engagement, Seiko spent the last night before the wedding at her parents' home, according to tradition. There, she made her formal bow of thanks to her parents for all they'd done for her, and despite her secret feeling that it was all an empty gesture, she later told Fumio that she'd been somewhat moved. Though she didn't have the courage to look either of her parents in the face, she knew there were tears in her father's eyes, and she could hear her mother off to the side sobbing.

The wedding was held at a wedding palace in Higashi-Nakano. They were one of a long line of couples waiting to get married. The ceremony itself was brief, in the Christian style which was so popular now; Seiko had always dreamed of wearing a white wedding gown. The reception afterwards was held in one of the many banquet rooms in the same building. Fumio and Seiko sat separately from the assembled guests, at the table of honor on a raised dais. They felt like spectators at an event to which they were vaguely attached. The important personages gave their usual boring speeches, filled with the usual mild double entendres suitable for the occasion, and the guests laughed politely at all the right places. Then the cake-cutting followed, along with the candle-lighting ceremony and the reading of the letter of thanks from the bride to her parents. The crying and the applause were all in their proper places. Both Fumio and Seiko had attended enough weddings to know the whole procedure. For their 'first night', they merely took the elevator up to one of the bridal suites on the top floor, from where they had a wonderful view of the city. Neither was in much of a mood for the sights, however; they ordered food from room service, and when it arrived, wolfed it down like starved animals. Because of the frantic activity, and the custom dictating the blushing bride to make a show of her meekness and humility, Seiko hadn't had a decent bite to eat all day.

After eating, they went to bed but neither felt up to making love. Besides, they would need all their energy for the honeymoon flight to Hawaii the next morning. They watched a video movie on TV until Seiko fell asleep.

Fumio gazed at the sleeping face of his wife now, the deep tan of her skin looking out of place in the gray light from outside the bus windows. Such a tan could only go well with the white sand beaches of Hawaii, the unreal blueness of the water stretching all the way out to a horizon which vanished into a tropical haze of dreams. He thought back again to that afternoon on the beach, away from all the Japanese tourists. Among the American men on the beach, one in particular had struck his fancy, a well-built, dark-haired Caucasian about thirty years old sitting on a beach towel in the shade reading a book. Fumio noticed him glancing up every now and then, seemingly in his direction. Though the distance made it hard to tell, it seemed the man was smiling at him. Fumio turned over onto his stomach and Seiko began rubbing sun-tan lotion onto his back. Its seductive coconut scent filled the air. The sound of the waves added a soothing background to his sensual thoughts, blending well with the outdated surfing music from someone's radio nearby. It was all like a scene from an American movie.

"I'd like to eat a hamburger," said Seiko. She was looking in the direction of a palm-thatched hut on the beach. A line of people stood before its counter, waiting to buy hamburgers and hot dogs.

"Sure." He got up, and together they strolled over to the hamburger stand. Fumio had been waiting in line for about a minute when he became aware of someone standing behind him — the man he'd noticed earlier. Seiko was completely unaware of Fumio's secret agitation. When her turn came to order, she stepped up to the window, and the man took this opportunity to mutter something in an undertone to Fumio. Unable to understand English, Fumio could only stare back at him. The other repeated his statement, but by the time he finished it, realized that Seiko had also overheard it. She was standing there with an indignant epression on her face.

Fumio turned to her for a translation. "What did he say?"

Ignoring his question, she spoke a few words in English directly to the man, who shrugged with a weak grin and walked away.

"What did he say?" repeated Fumio.

"Nothing." The man had turned around once again, and Fumio stared at him, trying to interpret his inscrutable gaze. "I'm not hungry anymore," said Seiko. "Let's go back to the hotel."

Something inside Fumio was pleased at her displeasure. Inside the car as they drove back she explained. "Do you know what that man did? He made a pass at you. Right in front of me. Don't they have any sense of propriety?"

"You mean he was a homo?" he asked innocently.

"Yes. You have to be careful. Foreign countries are full of them."

"Really?"

"When I was travelling through England with Yuka, we met up with a Japanese boy who was traveling alone. We decided to travel together, the three of us, for the remaining week. And would you believe it? Everywhere we went, the English men would make passes at the boy. Right in front of us, too! Only once did they ever make a pass at us girls. We concluded that all English men are gay. There do seem to be many more gay men abroad than at home... "

Fumio smiled to himself. True, to the untrained eye, that might seem to be the case. But only because most Japanese people had no idea of the extent of the gay underground in Tokyo. Homosexuality was probably just as widespread in Japan as anywhere else, only it was kept well hidden, both by those in the rose world, and those outside it. From reading *Barazoku,* Fumio knew that the gay lifestyle in America was quite different. Sometimes he couldn't believe some of the things he read about: men kissing each other in public, holding mock marriages, marching openly in gay parades. He knew that such things would never be tolerated in Japan. There was an aspect of the Japanese character which wished to keep unsightly things concealed. And a part of him felt that homosexuality should be hidden. Perhaps its clandestine nature in Japan was what made it so exciting for him. Still, he wondered what would have happened if he'd been traveling alone in Hawaii. The experiences he might have had... But it was all wishful thinking. Now that he was a married man, employed as an instructor at a *juku,* he couldn't risk the carefree lifestyle he'd once enjoyed as a college student. The gay scene was most definitely out.

2

THE BUS was finally pulling off the Shuto Expressway, the elevated maze of roadways in the heart of Tokyo, and they were approaching the end of their ride, Tokyo City Air Terminal. A short taxi ride from there would take them to Tokyo Station, where they would board the Chuo Line train bound for the western suburbs of the metropolis. The sky above was gray and the air blurred by fumes from motor vehicles. Seiko, as if someone had prodded her awake, abruptly opened her eyes and looked out the window. She seemed a little surprised at finding herself all the way back in Tokyo after her own dreams of Hawaii.

It was nearly seven-thirty by the time they arrived at their home in Kokubunji. Behind the clouds the sun was lowering in the west but the air was still sultry. Laden down with luggage and souvenirs, they got out of the taxi. "We're home," called out Seiko, sliding open the front door. From the darkness at the end of the hallway, her mother approached, hurrying toward them, wiping her hands on a kitchen towel. "Welcome back," she said. "You must be tired."

"Where's Father?" asked Seiko.

"He had to attend a meeting. He said he'd be a little late." Fumio thought he detected a note of relief on Seiko's face. He himself didn't quite feel up to facing the older man tonight.

"Come on in." Seiko's mother helped them with their luggage, leading the way to the living room. Fumio sank down onto the tatami with a feeling of exhaustion. Now that the honeymoon was over, his new life would begin. From tonight, he and Seiko would be living permanently with her parents. The brief life they'd shared in his old apartment was now a thing of the past.

The sliding doors were open onto the garden and a cool evening breeze played through the room. The house was an old-fashioned Japanese-style home in a quiet residential area about five minutes' drive from Kunitachi Station. Most of the homes here had stubbornly kept their Japanese character, with walled-in gardens and hedges. From where he sat, Fumio relished the leafy *ume*-plum tree in the garden, as well as the gingko tree next door. The orderliness of nature in Japanese life was something he'd taken for granted until now. It was good to go overseas every now and then, if only to learn to see his own country with new eyes.

Seiko came out of the kitchen with a tray and two glasses of ice-cold barley tea. "Would you like to take a bath first, to relax before dinner?"

"No, I think I'll take one afterwards."

"Mother has cooked dinner for us tonight. Japanese food."

"Oh, good."

The older woman began bringing out the dinner, and wouldn't think of Fumio's helping her. At the same time, Seiko began setting out the souvenirs they'd bought in Hawaii, checking the items against a list she had in her hand. From time to time she consulted her mother as to which gift would be appropriate for whom. Seeing her at this task, Fumio realized that their wedding work wasn't over yet. He felt a renewed gratefulness at the disciplined way Seiko took care of things. She would be a valuable marriage partner. Only after she had organized their gifts did she herself sit down to table.

When everything was set out, the young couple began eating as the older woman sat by serving them. After ten days of American food, they were glad to have Japanese fare again. "I wouldn't be able to survive for long without *miso* or *natto*," said Seiko. She was fond of going to foreign countries, but only on visits. As far as she was concerned, Japan was the safest country in the world, the only place to live.

"As for me," said Fumio, his mouth full of food, "I don't think I can live without a Japanese bath. I don't feel as if I've put a finish to the day unless I've soaked up to my neck in piping hot water."

"Your bath is already prepared for you," said Seiko's mother.

"Wonderful."

"Seiko, watch your manners." The way Seiko held her chopsticks was a bit childlike: they crossed awkwardly like half-opened scissors, and her mother was always apologizing to Fumio whenever she noted this lapse in her daughter. "We spoiled her," she said. "This child is strongheaded and willful, and she will have her own way. I hope you will bring her in line, Fumio-san."

Seiko put on a pout. "Mother, we are not living in the Meiji period. A husband does not bring his 'bride' in line anymore."

Fumio laughed. "It's true, Mother," he said. "If a man these days tried to tell his wife what to do, she'd divorce him just like that. No, I'll let her spread her wings. An independent woman is an asset to any marriage."

"You indulge her," said the older woman, though with a smile. "Seiko, not many men would be as kind. You make sure you hold onto him. You're not likely to find someone as kind as Fumio-san."

"I'm quite happy with him, thank you."

Fumio felt as if he'd landed in a home drama of the type his mother used to watch. He wondered if this was what happiness was. So often, the word 'marriage' was used as a synonym for happiness: that a woman had 'found happiness' was a euphemism meaning she'd met her marriage partner. Likewise for a man, marriage was considered a major benchmark in his life. Only after he was married was he accepted as a full-fledged member of society. Until then, he was merely 'playing' at life.

As soon as Seiko finished eating, she excused herself and went upstairs. The younger couple's rooms were on the second floor. Though the house had originally been a single-storey building, another floor had been added since Fumio and Seiko had become engaged. The second floor consisted of a bedroom for the young couple, a study for Fumio, plus another room for the children to come. In addition, there was a small, western-style toilet. But for bathing, they still had to use the bath downstairs. Also, because there was only the one kitchen on the first floor, Seiko would have to cook downstairs. Meals were taken in the old family dining room next to the kitchen, though the younger couple usually ate late at night after the older couple had gone to bed. There were no outside stairs as Seiko had desired, so the younger couple still had to use the old front entrance to get to the the stairs built by the carpenter at the end of the hallway.

Fumio stayed on chatting with his mother-in-law. Though she didn't drink, she accepted the glass of beer he poured out for her and merely held onto it for form as he drank his. The weariness of travel began to make him feel drowsy. He could hear Seiko upstairs laying out the futon. "Fumio-san, you're going to have quite a handful with our selfish daughter. I only hope marriage will make her more responsible."

"On the contrary, it is I who will constantly be in her debt. In Hawaii, she did all the work for both of us. Because her English is so good, I was relying on her for everything. She can certainly take care of things, even a good-for-nothing like me."

"My, you are the newly-wed. But of course, you're at the happiest period right now, aren't you?"

"I guess so." Fumio hated this remark. It always sounded like an ominous warning of things going downhill after this. But everyone said it to him; it was the standard greeting for a couple in their first year of marriage. What he resented most about it was the responsibility it thrust upon him: of looking and acting as if he were deliriously happy. As a hidden homosexual, the newly-wed husband's burden was doubly odious to him.

"Why don't you take your bath now?"

"What time is Father coming home?"

"Don't worry about him. He'll probably go out drinking with his cronies as usual. He was very lonely with you two away, so he's been going out much more than usual. I expect he'll be coming home as soon as he can get away tonight, though."

Fumio went down the hallway to the bathing room, slipped out of his clothes and got into the tub. As he sank down into the piping hot water, he told himself he was glad to be born Japanese. Only Japanese could understand and appreciate the aesthetic pleasures of a hot bath. In other countries, bathing played merely a utilitarian function in a person's daily life. Here, however, it was a pleasure to be appreciated and enjoyed alongside good food, music, or art. What added to his pleasure was that the bath tub in this house was made of hinoki wood, and its fragrance, brought out by the hot water, filled the tiny dark bathroom. The little window was open halfway, allowing a bare glimpse of the darkening sky. The leaves of the ginkgo tree next door were silhouetted against the frosted glass of the window like a shimmering lace curtain.

Seiko knocked on the door and slid it open, placing his *yukata* in the bamboo wickerwork basket. He finished bathing, dried himself off and slipped into the light summer kimono. Already feeling relaxed after the fatigue of travel, he went into the kitchen, poured himself a glass of beer and settled down in an armchair on the veranda.

Seiko had gone to take her bath, and her mother had retired to her room. Left alone for a few minutes, Fumio gazed blankly out into the garden, idly following the progress of the wisp of smoke from the mosquito coil at his feet. In a little while Seiko came out to join him, wearing her striped pajamas. She, too, had a glass of beer in her hand. "Well, we're finally back, aren't we?"

"Mm." The beer he'd drunk had gone to his head rather quickly, and now he felt drowsy. They chatted for a few minutes, but Seiko could see that Fumio could barely keep his eyes open.

"If you're tired, why don't you turn in? Don't worry about Father."

"All right." He went upstairs. As soon as he opened the door, he saw that the bedding had been laid out. Instinctively his glance went to the pillow at the head of Seiko's futon. The green side was up. Originally it had been a pillow which read YES in English on one side and NO on the other, a sort of marital aid for the benefit of shy couples; depending on how the wife felt that night she placed the YES or NO side facing up. It was a gentle, modest communication between spouses which saved a lot of hurt feelings, and was also a face-saving way for the woman to state her sexual desire. Fumio wondered how many couples used such a system. Given to them by a friend as an engagement present, the yes-no pillow had been a sort of joke at first. They had laughingly used it in the early days of their courtship but before they knew it, it had become an established part of their life. When the original pillowcase wore out, Seiko replaced it with another pillowcase which she'd sewn herself, colored green on one side and red on the other — the colors replacing the words.

Now the sight of the green side up sent a wave of uneasiness through Fumio. In Hawaii they'd been too excited by the travel and sightseeing to work up any romantic feeling, but now that they were home again, Seiko probably felt relaxed enough for it. And because this would be their first night at the home where they would live from now on, perhaps it was her way of inaugurating the occasion. He wondered how he could get out of it. Not that she was too demanding sexually; far from it. She turned the pillow to the YES side only once a week at most. But even this amount had gradually become a burden to Fumio. He sometimes felt like a gigolo again, a host performing for a paying partner. He hadn't expected it to become such a task. And when he thought that it might continue for the rest of his life, he had serious doubts about whether he would be able to continue his role.

Sometimes he didn't respond at all to her hint, ready with the excuse that he was tired from work. But of course, Seiko never said anything at such times. Indeed, their sex life was an unmentioned part of their existence, a necessary but hidden aspect of their everyday lives. As with most couples, their year-long engagement had virtually been a marriage already. Seiko was allowed by her parents to spend the night over at Fumio's apartment as often as she wished. And whenever he stayed overnight here, it was assumed that Seiko would share his room. Since they were officially engaged, it was only a matter of registering their union at the city office to make it legal. The wedding ceremony itself was but a formal ritual, a social announcement of the fact that they were man and wife.

So their sex life had lost its initial novelty and become quite routine. Fumio knew that Seiko didn't expect married sex to be as exciting as anything she might have experienced before. Yes, he'd known from the start that she wasn't a virgin when they met — not many Japanese girls were, past the age of twenty. But, like most experienced husbands-to-be, he hadn't made any inquiries about her past life. This wasn't done out of any feelings of tact or respect. He merely wished to forestall any sort of questioning on her part about his own past. It was true she'd asked in a perfunctory way about his previous girlfriends, and he'd made up a suitable story, but luckily, she hadn't pursued it. She wasn't the jealous type, thankfully.

As he sat there smoking his cigarette and wondering what to do, he heard the front door opening downstairs. It seemed his father-in-law was back. His relief at this interruption was tempered by the fact that he would have to go down to greet him. By the time Fumio got to the living room, the older man had already changed into the *yukata* he preferred for at-home wear. His wife was putting away his suit. Seiko was in the kitchen preparing his after-work drink and the snacks to go with it.

"Ah, Fumio-kun. You're back. How was Hawaii?"

"Wonderful, sir, thanks to you. We both enjoyed ourselves tremendously."

"That's fine. Why don't you sit down?" He indicated a place at the table as he himself sat down cross-legged on a seating cushion. Fumio sat down opposite the older man and looked at him. Professor Akiyoshi hadn't changed very much since their first meeting. But Fumio had never seen him look so relaxed and happy as he'd been these past six months. All during the engagement, it had almost seemed as if the older man were the happy fiancé. As his wife brought out the drinks Seiko had prepared, the professor was tapping out a cigarette from his pack. Then, suddenly he sat up formally and made a bow. "Welcome to the house. From now on, you are truly a member of the family."

Taken aback, Fumio also found himself sitting up formally and returning the bow. "I hope I won't be a trouble to you... " His mother-in-law stood in the doorway of the kitchen looking on until this formality was over, then she, too, took her place at Akiyoshi's side and made her greetings. Fumio felt a heavy responsibility descend upon his shoulders, an almost palpable weight. He hadn't thought very deeply about what he'd been doing all this time, but these bows seemed to have all the finality of a sealed pact.

The professor's wife began pouring out the drinks for the men. They sat with the television on before them, talking about the things the younger couple had seen in Hawaii. The professor himself had been there many times, and was quite familiar with the islands. Though Fumio found himself talking glibly about the honeymoon trip, he was actually thinking of something quite different. His life was sure to become more complicated now that he was moving permanently into the same house as the professor. But there seemed to be nothing he could do about it; for the past two years, things had proceeded like clockwork, as if according to some preconceived plan of intricate complexity.

3

IT HAD all started with a telephone call. Fumio had been sitting in his apartment one afternoon when the phone rang. With half his attention on the textbook he was studying, he answered it. To his surprise, he found himself listening to the familiar voice of Professor Akiyoshi. It seemed the older man had discovered Fumio's phone number through a detective agency. Indeed, he had had Fumio continuously monitored ever since their break-up. It was true that once or twice there had been strange incidents which made Fumio suspect he was being watched by detectives. But he'd thought it was the *yakuza* who were after him, angry that he'd betrayed a cardinal rule of the water trade: never compromise the customers. Had Akiyoshi complained to Genji's management despite his promise not to pursue the matter? Or was it merely paranoia on Fumio's part, a paranoia fueled by guilt and regret? Whichever it was, the nightmares which resulted kept him continually on edge. So when he learned that the older man had merely had him monitored out of frustrated love, he felt so relieved that he was ready to forgive him for anything.

Akiyoshi, still abjectly in love, begged the younger man for a reconciliation, and Fumio relented, amazed that he was forgiven so easily for his part in the blackmail. And partly because he felt so bleak about his future. After his own unrequited longings for Tatsuya, he could understand the depth of the older man's passion. So, partly out of pity, partly out of self-interest, he began seeing Akiyoshi from time to time afterwards, though without anything sexual in their relations. However, the older man seemed completely happy just to be with his young protégé, treating him to extravagant dinners and taking him out to see plays, movies, concerts. Fumio had wondered if the professor had passed the age at which he was still bothered by sexual desire. For the physical side of it didn't seem as important to him any more as the emotional side. It was love which had forced him to return to Fumio. Perhaps Fumio's betrayal had even deepened the older man's infatuation, the raw hurt hardening into a scar forming an unbreakable bond between them, sealing and sanctifying their attachment. At any rate, the betrayal was never mentioned again.

After a time, the professor asked Fumio to work as a teacher in one of his *jukus.* With his background as a private tutor and the college degree he would shortly obtain, Fumio had all the necessary qualifications for the job. As for the professor, it was a way of bringing the younger man closer to his own world. For Fumio's part, he saw no point in half-heartedly studying for a vague future. With graduation coming up, he would have to think seriously about a career. The job the professor offered would open up all sorts of other possibilities, what with Akiyoshi's many connections in the academic world.

Fumio accepted. Even before graduation, he started training for the job at one of the downtown branches. He'd been teaching for almost a year at the Kichijoji branch when, one day, during a lunch date with the professor, the older man had abruptly brought up the subject of marriage. When Fumio told him he had no prospects in mind, Akiyoshi timidly suggested having a *miai* with his own daughter. If he could have Fumio as a son-in-law, he said, his happiness would be complete. And, as the ultimate show of his love, he promised to leave everything to Fumio upon his death. Because Seiko was his only daughter, and he had no son to will his inheritance to, having Fumio marry Seiko would be the best way to make it legally and socially acceptable. Akiyoshi owned the house in Kokubunji as well as a summer villa in Kamakura inherited from his own father, a university administrator and, later, a politician. Ownership of the *jukus* would also pass to Fumio eventually.

Fumio felt as if he were the penniless beggar boy in *The Arabian Nights* suddenly being offered fabulous wealth. Struggling to keep the joy from showing on his face, he'd agreed to the *miai.* Though it wouldn't have mattered one way or the other to him personally, he was delighted to discover that he and Seiko turned out to be mutually compatible.

There was no problem with the marriage on Fumio's side. His mother, awed by the prominence of the professor's rank and prestige, had meekly agreed to letting her son live in Tokyo with his wife's family. Being only a second son, Fumio was free to choose his own household; his older brother and wife would take care of their mother in old age. But she did evince a little opposition at first to Fumio's petition to become a *muko yoshi,* an adopted son-in-law. Because the Akiyoshis had no son, Fumio could, according to custom, be adopted into the family and legally take on the family name.

This was the professor's desire. For Fumio himself, the change of name was hard to take, so he could understand his mother's feelings. But compared with the benefits offered by the professor, it was a loss he could very well suffer. He talked his mother into seeing it his way. In the end, she was happier for his sake than sad at the loss of the name.

The living arrangements of the Akiyoshi household were the usual in such cases: the younger couple lived upstairs so that the older people wouldn't have the inconvenience of having to climb the stairs. The separation of the generations also ensured a reasonable harmony within the household. Luckily, Seiko's mother doted on Fumio as much as her father did — to the extent that Seiko had once complained to Fumio: "My parents treat you much better than I've ever been treated..." To all outward appearances, the Akiyoshi household was a model of harmonious unity.

The women of the house had already retired, and the two men were drinking and talking by themselves. Professor Akiyoshi was quite drunk by now. His face was flushed and his eyes had an unfocussed look to them. Fumio was familiar with the older man's moods, and the way alcohol affected him. Obviously he'd been drinking quite a bit tonight before coming home, and the added beers had further intoxicated him. As they talked, Fumio sat back against the dresser behind him, fanning himself with a paper fan, his yukata becoming a little disheveled.

He had taken to wearing a *yukata* in the evenings to satisfy his father-in-law's whim. Underneath the light summer kimono, instead of a pair of shorts, he wore an old-fashioned Japanese loincloth, the type so often glimpsed by the older man on the bodies of youths at festivals. Fumio's *yukata* had now come almost undone in front, allowing generous glimpses of the pure white cotton of his loincloth. Though he didn't look in his father-in-law's direction, he knew the other was glancing at the generous amounts of flesh he was exposing. He got a furtive pleasure from this little game of allowing glimpses — and glimpses only. For he knew the cruelty and humiliation of it was thrilling the older man. It was the least he could do, a bone thrown to a dog — and a bone gnawed clean beforehand — in return for all that the professor had done for him.

Their past relationship was a secret between them, unmentioned even when they were alone together. That was the promise. And the secret was guaranteed to remain intact because the very dynamics of the situation ensured a stand-off; while Fumio held the threat of destroying the professor's career with a scandal, it would be at the cost of throwing away his own financial security and future happiness. That was not likely. Yet the professor actually seemed to enjoy the threat — or perceived threat — hanging over him. No doubt the possibility that his whole world could suddenly come tumbling down around him imparted a delicious tension to everyday existence.

For Fumio, too, the tension of living with a permanent secret in this household was not without its perils. But he didn't mind. Strangely, he felt only a contented joy... as if nothing could go wrong from now on. He took another sip of beer and threw back his head to laugh — ostensibly at a joke on TV. Glancing at his father-in-law, he noted the older man's head nodding heavily. He yawned, stretched, got up. "If you'll excuse me, I have to use the toilet."

The professor seemed not to have heard him. Fumio stepped out into the darkened hallway and walked down to the urinal room just next to the toilet. As he closed the door behind him and stood there loosening his loincloth, he heard a slight noise out in the hallway. "Is that you, Seiko?" he asked.

The door slowly creaked open. "It's me," whispered the voice of the professor. He tiptoed in.

"What are you doing here?" hissed Fumio. "What if someone should come? Don't be a fool!"

"Don't worry. They're both asleep."

"You promised not to do anything."

"I know. I just want to stand here. That's all." The tone of his voice was pleading, like a little boy's asking his mother for candy. Fumio could hear the clock ticking loudly in the other room. Suddenly the professor reached his arms around Fumio's shoulders. Instinctively, Fumio pushed him away with his elbow. The older man tumbled backwards, hitting the door with a loud bang and rolling out into the hallway.

A commotion was heard from the direction of the older couple's bedroom. "What's the matter?" called the voice of the professor's wife.

"Nothing. It's quite all right," Akiyoshi called back in a calm voice. "I just had a little slip on the wooden flooring. A little too much to drink tonight, perhaps. I'm no longer as young as I once was."

The sound of slippers shuffling along the floor indicated the approach of the professor's wife. Her voice sounded concerned, though a little tired. "Be careful, Father. Here, take my arm."

"It's all right," said the professor in an exasperated tone, a bit petulant. "Fumio-kun will give me his shoulder. Won't you?"

"Of course, Father." He had put his *yukata* in order and stepped out into the hallway before the light was switched on. The older man got to his feet, leaning heavily on the young man's shoulder. As they made their way to the older couple's bedroom just before the front entrance, Fumio could feel the warmth of the older man's body through the cotton material of their summer kimonos. It was all he could do to repress a shudder.

4

AFTER HIS two-week honeymoon vacation, Fumio was back at work. He rather liked his job as a *juku* teacher. It allowed him to enjoy the authority and respect of being a teacher without being hampered by the regulations and extra duties which were usually thrust upon public school teachers. He had, indeed, once contemplated becoming a public school teacher because he liked being around young people so much — their energy and enthusiasm seemed to rub off onto him, bringing back his own youth. He was one of two mathematics teachers at the Kunitachi branch, a short bicycle ride away from his home in Kokubunji. Out of a total of seven full-time teachers here, two taught Japanese, two taught math, and the others covered English. In addition, there was Mr. Kameya, the *juku* head (a former student of Akiyoshi's), and three young women who took care of administrative duties.

Fumio's first class started at four o'clock in the afternoon, and his last class usually ended at about ten at night. Each class was two hours long, with a ten-minute break in-between. On Mondays, Wednesdays, and Fridays, he tutored groups of sixth-graders studying for entrance exams to private junior high schools. On Tuesdays, Thursdays, and Saturdays he taught junior and senior high school children hoping to enter prestigious high schools and universities.

Now he watched the faces of his students as they struggled intently with the problems he'd just assigned them. They were, for the most part, children who liked to study, who wanted to enter the school of their choice, and their dedication showed. Because they were free to concentrate on their studies, *juku* students had a much better relationship with their teachers than elsewhere. Hence, *jukus* had none of the disciplinary problems usually encountered at normal schools. The quality of teachers at *jukus* was usually quite high, too; the high salary attracted the best ones, whereas public school teachers received the standard wages of all public officials. *Jukus* could afford the very best teachers because they were so enormously profitable in education-mad Tokyo. Children went to them after school for study in classes intensely geared toward entrance exam preparation. *Juku* cram schools had originally sprung up to fill a crucial gap; the curricula of most public schools didn't cover the materials needed to prepare students for the tough entrance exams given by good universities.

The Kunitachi branch had been established a mere three years ago. Professor Akiyoshi had rented the whole second floor of a newly-constructed office building near the station. There was enough space there for a large administration room, a waiting lounge for parents, and four classrooms, clean and spacious, well lit by large windows. The floor just below was a convenience store where, naturally enough, the students went to buy snacks during their breaks. Of the teachers at this *juku*, three of them like Fumio were young first-timers just out of university. The other four were veterans who had been lured away from other *jukus*.

Having Fumio on the teaching staff was a natural choice on the part of the school. After all, since he had successfully passed the entrance exam for one of the top universities in Tokyo, he obviously had the qualifications. Still, Fumio's mother had initially been opposed to his becoming a *juku* teacher. In her eyes, it would have been far better for him to join a large corporation which would guarantee a lifetime's security. With his university degree, it shouldn't have been difficult at all to join a large firm... or failing that, to at least get a respectable job as a public school teacher. Like most people in the provinces, she had a higher image of public officials than people in the metropolis did. What she didn't know was that, though Fumio was a lowly freshman teacher now, Akiyoshi fully intended his young protégé to head the *juku* someday, before eventually taking over the whole chain.

Mr. Kameya, Fumio's boss, had in fact been instructed to gradually break Fumio into the running of the school. After a certain number of years had passed, hopefully when the *juku* was running under its own steam, Fumio would step in as the natural successor. So, though on the surface there was no hint that the whole thing was a family operation, it was indeed just that. Nominally, the funding for the school came from several sources, the majority in the name of Yoshiko, Akiyoshi's wife. Akiyoshi himself, as an active professor at a national university, had no legal right to run an education-oriented business, and was listed as a member of the advisory board.

From where he stood now in front of the blackboard, Fumio

could see the orange cars of the Chuo Line trains passing by, packed with salarymen returning home from work. He felt at one with the commuters, a fully responsible member of the work force, married, clean-living, hard-working. In his conservative gray suit, he felt there was no trace in him now of the insecure, innocent young student from the provinces he once had been. He was now a part of this thriving, bustling metropolis, the most exciting city in the world.

A yawn forced its way to his mouth and he glanced at his watch. It was already past ten o'clock. No wonder he was feeling tired. He shut his textbook and several children looked up. "Time up, everyone. Finish up those problems at home and show them to me next class."

The children began putting away their books and saying goodbye to each other. As always, there were one or two students who acted as if they wanted to stay even longer, to study until their eyes could no longer stay open. Fumio went to his desk in the administration room and put his teaching materials away. A couple of the other teachers were still working at their desks. They nodded their goodbyes to him as he headed toward the door. When he got home he rang the door bell and Seiko came down the stairs to greet him at the front door. It was just like the dramas he'd watched on television, and a part of him felt as if he were acting a part. Still, he felt happy that it was the part of a normal, happily-married man. The professor hadn't come home yet. Yoshiko was in front of the TV in the living room waiting up for him. The younger couple went upstairs where Fumio changed out of his suit as Seiko stood by with the yukata in her hands, ready to hand it to him.Then Fumio went downstairs for his bath, while Seiko went to the kitchen to have dinner ready for him when he came out.

She had prepared a Japanese meal tonight, and though she had already eaten, joined him at the table to serve it to him. Until the professor came back, Fumio was the man of the house and his wife and her mother literally waited on him hand and foot, with a solicitude matching that of his own mother back home. Tonight, Seiko's mother had joined them at the table. She had switched off the TV set in the living room, but Seiko now turned on the small one in the dining room, on the cooking counter. Her mother gently chided Seiko for this. "When I was young, a wife would never watch television while her husband was eating. She would have been roundly scolded."

"Mother, when you were young, there was no television — at least not in every household."

"Well, the radio, then. Anyway, how can you pay enough attention to Fumio-san's needs with one eye on the TV screen? A wife should always anticipate her husband's needs, take his rice bowl to refill it without his even asking. Heaven help me if I had acted toward your father as you do now. He would certainly have lost no time putting me in my place."

"I'm surprised," said Fumio, his mouth full. "Sensei always seems so gentle and kind all the time."

"Oh, you don't know the half of it," said Seiko. "Father seems so happy now that you're in the house. But he wasn't always like this. He's changed. To me, he was always the strict disciplinarian. Wasn't he, Mother?"

The older woman merely smiled without answering.

"Father dotes on you," Seiko went on, to Fumio. "He does everything you say. Take the car he bought us. Supposedly it was a wedding gift for both of us, but I know that you happened to mention one day how much you liked the design of the new Volvo. And what happens? He goes to the Volvo dealer the very next day and picks one out in your favorite color."

Fumio had been at pains to have the professor tone down his outward signs of affection for him, but apparently to no effect. "You seem to like the car, too," he said weakly.

"Oh, I do. But I also know that if I had asked him on my own, I would never have gotten it."

"Seiko," her mother remonstrated.

"But it's true!" She turned to Fumio. "Take my eyes, for instance. The operation. If it hadn't been for you, Father would never have allowed me to have it. But he listened to you and relented."

Fumio knew she was only voicing a long-held grudge, but he couldn't remember seeing her this worked up over it before. "Sensei might seem a little gruff sometimes, but that's a parent's prerogative, isn't it? All in all, I find him a kind man."

"To you, maybe. But then he always wanted a son. I sensed it even when I was a little girl. I was a disappointment to him, I know. Maybe that's why I was so rebellious."

Fumio smiled. "You were rebellious? I find that hard to believe."

"But I was. And I was punished for the least little thing, too. One time he even used his belt on me. Father was always so old-fashioned in everything he did. For instance, I couldn't even date boys till I was in college. My friends all laughed at me. They were a little afraid to come over because of his constant scolding. I was so ashamed."

In his mind, Fumio was contrasting Seiko's picture of the stern patriarch with the fawning, humiliation-loving masochist he knew.

"Seiko," said Yoshiko. "Your father comes from an old-fashioned family. They were very Japanese, traditionalists to the core. But you'll find, as you get older, that that is the best way. The old ways, tried and proven, are always the best in the end."

"I don't know about that." She thrust out her lower lip in a pout. Yoshiko went on a little more gently. "Fathers must be strict with daughters. That's the way things are. Daughters must make good wives, otherwise it will reflect badly on your upbringing. Parents always think: what will her future husband say if she turns out to be willful? But sons are different. Boys must be allowed all the freedom they can, because someday they will be the breadwinners and have to support their families. It's not an easy life for men. In any case, you'll find out when you have children of your own that it's not an easy thing to raise them."

"If we have a child, I want a girl. And only girls. And I'm giving them all the freedom they want."

"How about you, Fumio-san? Do you prefer boys or girls?"

He scratched his head. "Either is all right with me."

The mention of children depressed him. Ever since his engagement, people had been asking him how many children he wanted, whether he wanted a boy or a girl for the first child, and so forth. He hadn't even been married before he was being saddled with the responsibility of children. It seemed that everything conspired to trap him in society's mesh — marriage, a wife, children, a job, responsibility... Already he was being made to conform, to fit the mold designed for all young men. He couldn't help but fear the step-by-step process by which everyone was pressed into his ordained role.

Marriage had been but the first step. At first he had welcomed the process. When he'd been so acutely aware of his own difference from others, he had wanted to be like all the rest... to blend in, to be unnoticed, to camouflage among them. The process of becoming a responsible member of society was a sort of discipline, no different from the training a soldier undergoes to prepare his body to meet the demands of combat. Fumio's business suit had been his warrior's armor. But now that he thought back on the freedoms he'd enjoyed as a college student, he felt like an adventurer sitting at home, dreaming of past exploits which no one believed in, least of all the children who gathered around to hear his stories.

Who would have imagined, as they saw him sitting at the dining table now with his wife and mother-in-law, the very picture of contented bliss, that he'd once been paid to have sex with middle-aged men, that he'd been in love with a heartless, handsome youth? His experiences in the gay underworld of Tokyo seemed like a distant dream.

The television had been on all this time, though no one was paying attention to it. As a cosmetics commercial came on, however, Seiko suddenly perked up. "I like this commercial." They watched an attractive young woman sitting beside a swimming pool, obviously basking in the regard of a Western man sitting across the patio. She lifted her dark sunglasses as if casually taking in more sun, and when she opened her eyes, Fumio recognized with a jolt, Mayumi, Tatsuya's girlfriend. There could be no doubt. She looked much prettier and more sophisticated than when he'd known her as a roommate, but her eyes and slightly parted lips were unquestionably those of the same vain young woman.

As a deep male voice intoned the name of the lipstick, he felt a curiously sharp pang in his chest, and for a second, Tatsuya's face came before him, vividly. He recalled the time they'd driven out onto the expressway in the Porsche early that morning, the first time he had gone to work at Genji. The way the clouds had rolled down the mountainside in the gray of dawn... Suddenly he felt like the heroine of a housewife's romance, the young woman who has had to marry against her wishes a man chosen by her family, though in her heart burns an illicit love for the young master...

"You don't look so well, Fumio-san."

He realized with a start that he'd been gazing blankly at the TV screen all this time.

"No, Mother, I'm fine. I guess I'm just a little tired from work."

"Why don't you go upstairs and lie down?"

"I think I will."

"Seiko, what are you dawdling for? Are the futons set out?"

"Yes, Mother." Her reply, though dutiful, had just the slightest tinge of daughterly sarcasm in it.

5

FUMIO AND Seiko were up in their room on the second floor when they heard the professor come home. It was about 11:30. Some twenty minutes later, after he'd had a quick bath and changed into his *yukata*, they heard his steady tread coming up the stairs. He knocked once and entered their room, and immediately Fumio as well as Seiko got up to the formal sitting position. When he saw them, the professor said, "No, no, you should relax. After all, it's your own room."

He sat down on the cushion Fumio provided for him, and Seiko got up to get him something to drink. "A beer," he called after her. She disappeared down the stairs. "Fumio, how was your first day back at work?"

"Fine. It felt good to be back in the classroom."

"Good. I'm glad you like teaching. Someday you'll be running that *juku* and I want you to learn the business from the bottom. The way our education system is in Japan, there's no limit to what you can do in the education business. It's really one of the most profitable things you can get into. And once you're running the *juku*, all you have to do is let the others do the work and take in the profits. Your name on the organization roster will be all that matters."

Fumio did, indeed, look forward to the day when he would be running things. He had many ideas of his own he wanted to implement; from the start he had looked things over and imagined how improvements could be made.

Seiko, too, had told Fumio that she looked forward to his coming into his own. She didn't see herself as the wife of a teacher for the rest of her life. She wanted to enjoy the good life — join a private sports club where she could go swimming during the day, play tennis, take aerobics lessons. But most of all, she wanted her own house, to live away from her parents. Her best friend, Yuka, had married quite well, to an elite businessman in a large corporation, and lived in a fancy apartment in Tama Center, a bed-town recently developed after the model of American suburbs.

The professor said to Fumio in a low voice, "What's this talk I hear about your wanting children?"

"I said nothing of the kind, sir. It was just something Seiko-san and her mother were foolishly tossing about."

"Listen, I think it's a good idea for you to have children. Yoshiko is all in favor of it. And I gather Seiko isn't against it. What do you think?"

"Yes," said Fumio uncertainly. "But we do want some time to ourselves before we have our first child."

"Nonsense. The sooner you have them the better. Seiko is probably bored to death playing housewife. In her heart she wants a child, like all women. It's what they're made for."

Seiko heard the remark as she came up the stairs. "So I'm nothing more than a machine for producing children, am I?"

"Biologically, yes. And your hormones work in such a way that you feel happiest when nursing and raising children. Your mother was like that and you're probably no different."

"I resent that," she said, but her tone of voice indicated that she didn't really hold it against him. She set the tray down on the table and opened a bottle of beer. As she poured it out for her father, he said to her more gently: "I just want to see my grandchild before I die. Is that too much to ask?"

She laughed. "You're hardly on your deathbed, Father. In fact, I've never seen you look so healthy and happy. Since we moved in here, you're younger than ever."

"It's the presence of you young people that revitalizes me." He looked at Fumio. "To have a young man in the home, so full of energy and life... "

To change the subject, Fumio asked Seiko, "Lately you seem more open to the idea of having children. Didn't you used to say you wanted some time together before being saddled with that responsibility?"

"I did. But in the last few months, it seems all my girl friends are having babies. And two of them are pregnant now. They all seem so happy."

Fumio had noticed that Seiko always did what her girl friends did, especially her best friend, Yuka. In fact, he suspected that one of the main reasons she'd married him in the first place was because her girl friend had married. "You make it all sound like a race or something. First, to get married, then to have babies."

"Well, it's true that if you want to stay friends, you have to be at the same level. When the first friend gets married, it's not so bad. But as gradually more and more of your friends are married and you're still single, you find yourself with less and less in common to talk about. You lose touch. Married women tend to seek other married women as friends. The same thing is even more true when your friends start having babies. That puts a further distance between you. A woman who has borne a child can't relate to a woman who hasn't. And likewise, a woman who has never had a child doesn't understand the concerns of one who does. So, I don't want to be left behind. I would feel as if I were missing out on the things I should be doing. You see, I want to live my life to the fullest... and to do that, I have to go through what everyone else does."

"And here I thought you were so independent," laughed Fumio.

"Independence is good while you're single. But when you're married, you can't afford the luxury of independence; you're no longer on your own. There are other people to think about, more responsibilities. I'm a grown-up member of society now, too, you know. Like you."

"Yes. Like me." Fumio was just pouring the last of the bottle into the professor's glass.

"More beer here, Seiko," said her father.

"All right."

After she'd gone downstairs to get another bottle, Akiyoshi whispered, "Fumio, please have children. Give me a son. You must have a boy. You realize, in effect it will be our boy — I mean yours and mine. To my mind, you and I are married. When you had a *miai* with Seiko and married her, you married into this house, you married me. Anyway, that's the way I feel in my heart. And how much closer can we get? You share my name, you sleep with my daughter, we live under the same roof. I always think of you. Your son will be our baby, Fumio — yours and mine. Complete my happiness."

The older man looked almost apoplectic as he said this in a furious whisper. Listening to the cheerful sound of Seiko talking with her mother downstairs, Fumio tried to keep the repugnance from his face. He found himself secretly wishing the old man would die soon. Then he would be free. The smell of the other's breath was so sour that he almost wrinkled his nose at it.

"Sensei, what happens happens. I'm going to let nature take its course."

"No, you must try." He cut off his impassioned whisper when he heard Seiko's tread on the steps.

Seiko came in smiling. "What are you two looking so serious about?"

"Nothing. Just business talk about the future of the *juku.*" The professor accepted the beer she poured out for him with a smile.

Later, after he'd left, Seiko was sitting in front of her make-up table rubbing cold cream onto her face. She turned around to look at Fumio lying on his side. "Father's taken to dropping in here almost every night. I wish he'd leave us alone. I hope it won't be like this all the time."

"Why? It doesn't bother me so much."

"Well it bothers me. It doesn't feel like we're living our own lives. Why does he do it? He never came into my room to talk with me when I was living here alone, and he never visited us at your apartment, either. It's just as I said — he dotes on you. You're the son he always wanted. You have a lot of influence over him. Why don't you hint that we need some time together, by ourselves?"

"He's an old man used to having his own way here."

"He's selfish. A typical old-fashioned Japanese male. The tyrant in his own home. How can we even have the privacy to make babies with him always barging in? I feel him between us, even when we're in bed. He leaves his smell behind, an old man's smell."

Secretly, Fumio had to agree — the professor's presence was almost palpable in the room, and it wasn't only the smell.

"I wish we didn't have to live here with him," Seiko muttered, bringing up her old grudge.

"But he went to all the trouble and expense to add this new floor to the house. If we were starting out on our own in Tokyo, do you realize how expensive it would be? How much do you think a half-way decent condo costs? We wouldn't be able to afford it on my salary. Here we pay no rent, and we're living in a good location. Remember what it was like at my old apartment? And that cost 60,000 yen."

It was true. She'd complained about the cramped space, the noises she could hear from the neighbors, the sound of the train going by at night. At the time, she'd felt she could never live away from this comfortable suburban bed-town where she'd grown up and where all her friends were. That had been the source of their rare arguments.

"And it makes your mother happy to have you near," he went on. "Your father must have taken all that into account. And remember: someday we'll come into this property, too."

"In the meantime he has his say over everything we do here. He keeps us chained here — so he can keep his eyes on us always."

Again, Fumio secretly agreed with her: it was as if the professor had trapped him in this house so he wouldn't ever escape again... trapped him with the ties of matrimony, job, responsibility. But when he thought of what the future had in store for him, he felt he could put up with it. In time, he would become more independent — someday, completely independent — and the owner of this land and house, to say nothing of the Kamakura property and the *jukus*. For a young man in his twenties, the vision was intoxicating. Living under the same roof as the professor was just a small price to pay, and a temporary one.

To change the subject, he said, "What do you really think about having babies?"

"I'm all for it. I wasn't before. But when I saw how cute Yuka's baby is, something inside me cried out for one just like it. Besides, having a baby will at least give me something to do, an occupation.

Right now, I'm bored just being a housewife, waiting for you to come home. I want to get out of the house. I had no idea it would be this dull."

"That must be the man reason why most couples have babies."

Fumio was thinking that if they did have a baby, Seiko would be so taken up with raising it that he himself would be left more or less alone. He'd been with her now for a whole year, and a part of him wanted a vacation from her, to taste a little of the old freedom once again. With a baby, Seiko's time would be taken up fulltime with child care, leaving him freer. But once again, he heard the echo of his father-in-law's words: "The baby will be our baby, yours and mine. We are married to each other now."

Impatiently, he stubbed out his cigarette. Seiko was consulting a small desk calendar on her make-up table. She mused silently to herself, counting with her fingers.

6

IT WAS well past midnight and the party was getting to its wild stage. Every year's end, most companies, large or small, held an annual party designed to let people forget about all the hardships and troubles of the closing year. They were literally known as 'forget-the-year' parties. A junior member of the company, usually a freshman, was designated the special activities coordinator, and he would set up the location and make all the necessary arrangements.

In the case of Fumio's *juku*, the coordinator was a young teacher who'd just been hired in the past spring. He had rented a traditional-style party room in Shinjuku, complete with sliding paper doors and tatami floors, and waitresses in kimono-like uniforms. The last person had just made his contribution to the party's entertainment, and a slight lull had fallen over the group. Everyone was expected to have at least one specialty with which to enliven the party. One teacher had done impersonations of famous television personalities, while another had performed some shop-worn magician's tricks. The idea was to throw away one's reservations and dignity, at least for the evening; it was a good way to blow off stress and get rid of some pent-up frustrations.

Fumio's specialty was something he'd learned in his host club days. He'd stripped his torso bare and applied cosmetics to make it look like a face, then with his abdominal muscles made the face go through various expressions. This had raised a big laugh, especially as it was done by Fumio, an otherwise rather quiet person. Now the *juku* head, Mr. Kameya, stood up and began urging some younger members to play a classic party game, a risqué version of the children's paper-scissors-rock competition. Two people, to the accompaniment of the assembly's singing and hand-claps, would dance and cavort, climaxing their performance with paper-scissors-rock. The loser had to strip off one item of clothing. Then the singing and dancing were repeated for another round as the game continued. The object was to get down to where one of the players was too embarrassed to remove anything more, whereupon the other was declared the winner. The two youngest members of the staff, a young English teacher named Kojima, and Miss Toda of the administration staff, were singled out to play the first bout. Reluctantly, they got to their feet and stood before the revellers. To the rhythm of hand-claps and the whole party singing a nonsense song, they danced. At the climax, they thrust out their hands, Kojima's hand clenched in the rock position (with the fist closed), and Miss Toda's hand in the scissors position (her two fingers thrust out). The men expressed their delight with a shout; Miss Toda had lost. Laughingly, she undid an earring, and dropped it to her feet.

The game continued. At the climax of the next round, Kojima put out his hand in the rock position again, but this time Miss Toda had hers in the paper position (an open palm). She jumped up and clapped in delight. Kojima began unbuttoning his shirt. As the game progressed, the situation began to assume a slapstick quality. After a certain point, no doubt befuddled by the alcohol, Kojima began losing continuously. He seemed to be unaware that he was always putting out a paper to Miss Toda's scissors. The men groaned loudly at his obtuseness. Miss Toda delightedly clapped her hands as he stripped off his left sock. Now he was down to his t-shirt and shorts. Miss Toda herself still had on everything but her earrings, stockings, and bracelet.

"Kojima," said Mr. Kameya with mock seriousness, "if you don't win the next round, it's going to have serious consequences for your future in this *juku*."

"I'm trying my hardest," he said helplessly. The game recommenced. He lost again. Now with his t-shirt stripped off, he had nothing more to take off than his briefs. "Well, it looks like the game is over," he said sheepishly. "I lost."

"Nonsense," said Mr. Kameya. "You're not a man if you stop at this point."

"What!" The party laughed and clapped.

"But I have nothing more than my briefs on."

"That's all right. Give it one more try. Look at Miss Toda. You haven't even got her past her blouse."

"All right," said Kojima. "But I can't be held responsible for the conclusion of this game."

"Just concentrate on winning."

They began another round of singing, and at the climax there was a terrific groan from the men: he'd lost again. He sank down to the floor in a comic faint. "Take it off! Take it off!" All of them were chanting and clapping in rhythm, even the women. Kojima, buoyed by this drunken hilarity, put his hands on the elastic waistband of his briefs and, coyly imitating the movements of a professional stripper, eased them down. Some remnant of modesty, however, kept him from pulling them off completely.

"Off with them!" shouted a co-worker next to Fumio. Everyone took up this cry, including Fumio. He was thoroughly enjoying himself. Kojima turned his back on the group and began pulling his briefs down.

"Not fair!" shouted Fumio. "Turn around and face the music!"

"Hear! Hear!" When Kojima turned around, the women in the company covered their eyes, feigning fright. One of them gave a little shriek. Fumio felt his face burn. He himself was unable to turn his eyes away from the sight of this suddenly revealed treasure.

It was two-thirty when the party finally broke up. By now the trains had stopped running and the only way for most of them to get home was by taxi. Some planned to stay in capsule hotels and sleep off their intoxication until next morning. Fumio had already called home at about one o'clock, letting Seiko know he wouldn't be coming home tonight. Like some of the others, he, too, planned to stay in a capsule hotel and go home in the morning.

As he said goodnight to a couple of co-workers stumbling off toward the taxi stands, however, the thought of having to spend the night in a capsule hotel began to lose its appeal. Though accommodation was cheap enough there, these hotels were like nothing so much as enormous beehives. Their sleeping spaces were literally capsules just large enough to hold one person lying down. Inside were a reading light, cooling and heating vents, and a tiny ledge for personal belongings. Changing rooms, lockers, television rooms, saunas, and baths were communal. Fumio had a vision of all the men sleeping in these vast hives as ants or bees, part of an enormous army of such insects which, in the morning, would curl out of their niches and go back to work, marching on, mindlessly, until they died.

Suddenly depressed, he found himself turning his steps toward a long unvisited part of Shinjuku, the 2-chome gay district. Ever since his engagement to Seiko, he'd made sure not to backslide into his old ways. Not that, like some gay men, he dreamed that marriage was a way to cure himself of his 'bad habits', that once he had a wife homosexual desires would fade away like an old dream. Or that he wanted to keep the wedding vows he'd made. Such illusions didn't have any influence on his actions. However, his true reason was just as quixotic and unreasonable. After losing Tatsuya, he'd avoided all the places which brought back memories of him. He went to no gay places. A part of him still believed that his break-up with Tatsuya had been caused by his own homosexuality. If he could somehow purge this 'defect', or tear this aspect of his personality out of his system, he might be worthy of Tatsuya's friendship again. Fumio still wanted to keep Tatsuya as a secret romantic ideal in his heart. He knew most people did something similar; not everyone could have the partner of their choice.

But now, perhaps fired by the sight of the young instructor's nude body earlier, he found himself yearning to do something illicit, something secret from Seiko. A feeble flame inside him had been stirred which he'd thought long dead. Suddenly quite clear-headed, though still feeling the euphoria of the alcohol, he headed purposefully toward a gay bookshop he knew which was open all night. At this time of night, there were few people about, but he noted men here and there walking alone or in discreet pairs. Feeling a little self-conscious despite his determination, he entered the vestibule of an entertainment emporium and walked up the narrow stairs to the second-floor bookstore.

Nothing had changed. There were the usual displays of magazines and videos, sex toys and fancy briefs. A stack of *Barazoku* and other popular gay magazines was beside the counter. He picked up a copy of *Barazoku* and began flipping through it. It was the first time in more than a year he'd seen the magazine. Since becoming engaged to Seiko, he'd thrown away all his old copies, fearing she might come across them while cleaning up. Among the advertisements in the back pages was one for a 'touch room' called Mirror Man. Intrigued, Fumio read the copy. Apparently, a touch room was nothing more than a private video viewing room, but one which was somehow modified so that the man in the next cubicle could be observed. "Enjoy the thrill of watching... and the thrill of being watched!" was Mirror Man's slogan.

Fumio wondered how such a thing could occur. Touch rooms

hadn't been around back in the days when he was exploring the gay scene. He checked the accompanying map and discovered that Mirror Man was located nearby. And it was open all night. He glanced at his watch. It would certainly be a better way to pass the time than listening to the snores of other sleepers in a capsule hotel. After verifying its location, he put the magazine back and headed out the door. A ten-minute walk brought him to a quiet area of Shinjuku away from the usual neon lights. The building he was looking for was in an otherwise nondescript commercial area. A small sign in the foyer read 'Mirror Man, 2F' without giving any indication what sort of place it was. No one who wasn't in the know would even guess. It could be anything. Still, feeling a little nervous about being seen — after all, a teacher was a respected member of society, and required to live a stricter life than most people — he stepped into the foyer and walked up the stairs to the second floor.

The entrance to Mirror Man was an automatic door made of translucent plastic tinted purple, with a hand-written sign taped onto it which read 'Members Only'. As he approached it, the door slid open, revealing a darkened interior. He stepped in. An attractive young man with the body of a weight-lifter greeted him. "Good evening."

"Uh, this is my first time here," said Fumio.

"I see. You came for the videos?" Fumio nodded. He knew they also had massage services. "Right this way, please." The young man's manner was so pleasant that Fumio felt immediately at ease. Against one wall were about eight cubicles made of a durable alloy which looked solid and air-tight, like the compartments inside a cargo ship. Fumio could hear the sounds of video monitors in operation; he guessed that at least a couple of other men were in. He was led down a narrow aisle to the left, to the cubicle at the far end. Just before the row of cubicles was a tiny waiting room with a small sofa and a side table. On the side table were several copies of popular gay magazines.

The young man opened the door and allowed Fumio to enter. Immediately, Fumio was reminded of the private rooms in Genji. Inside was a tiny space just large enough to hold a single video player, a large TV monitor, a couch against the wall, and next to it, a side table. On the table was a box of tissues. The young man handed Fumio a plastic binder filled with a listing of the various videos available. The titles were very much like the teasing-ridiculous ones he had become familiar with from the videos he'd seen before. The accompanying photos and brief descriptions only indicated the types of action: 'young boy with middle-aged man'; 'rough worker with delicate boy'; 'tattooed *yakuza* with college boy', etc. Most of them seemed to be SM in orientation. Fumio wasn't attracted to any of the rough-looking actors who looked like construction workers. Instead his eye was caught by the attractive young man starring in 'College Boxer', who had the well-trained body of an athlete. This video was described as 'a young man alone'.

"I'll take this one." After the employee had left, Fumio looked around. On the walls were pin-up photos of attractive men, along with several original drawings, including a signed pencil sketch of an erect penis. Otherwise, the place seemed no different from an ordinary video room. Then he noted that the wall on the right side didn't extend all the way to the end. A tiny gap was left, perhaps twenty-five centimeters wide. And in that gap was a mirror whose angled reflection allowed him to see the couch in the next cubicle. There was no one there now, but he could tell that anyone sitting there would be exposing the lower half of his body. By the same token, the other would no doubt have a clear view of the same portion of Fumio's body. He understood now the advertisement's line about 'the thrill of watching... and the thrill of being watched'.

The employee returned in a couple of minutes with the video, along with a cup of warm oolong tea. Fumio accepted the tea and watched as the other slid the video into the player, pressed the play button saying, "Have a good time," and stepped out, closing the door behind him. The compartment was completely private once the door was shut. Fumio locked the door and lay back on the couch. Though there was no one in the next compartment yet, he glanced a little worriedly at the mirror in the gap. Once the next room was occupied, the real show would obviously be in the mirror, but until then, he had only the video.

He settled back to watch it. It had been so long since he'd last enjoyed a porno video. Occasionally, with Seiko, he'd watched an adult video borrowed from the neighborhood rental shop as a prelude to their intimacies, but like most such videos, it usually concentrated on showing the woman's body, never the man's. That problem wouldn't exist with this one. A very good-looking young man in a t-shirt and boxing trunks was in a gym going through the usual routine of a boxer in training: jumping rope, shadow boxing, hitting a punching bag. After a few minutes of this, he had worked up quite a sweat. A trainer helped him unlace the gloves. He took them off and continued to shadow box with his taped hands until his t-shirt was drenched. Then he peeled off his t-shirt and began skipping rope again. Tiny drops of sweat leaped off his wet hair... the muscles in his chest twitched in time to his jumping.

When he tired of this, he put aside the rope, gathered up his things and went into the locker room. There, he stuffed his t-shirt into his canvas bag and stepped out of his trunks. He was wearing a jock strap whose gleaming whiteness contrasted sexily with his bronzed body. He sat down on the bench and began wiping the sweat off his body with a towel. Then he applied the towel to his hair, drying it briskly and leaving it slightly tousled. He went to a full-length mirror and gazed at his reflection, running his hand through his hair. He stood there gazing a little critically at his own muscles, touching them and rubbing them as if to test their tone. He ran his hand over the solid muscles of his chest, in massaging motions at first, but gradually making his caresses more and more sensual in nature. His eyes closed. Dropping the towel to the floor, he hooked his thumb under the elastic strap of his jock strap and pulled down.

As the pouch slipped off the genitals, the sudden appearance of the mosaic-like censor's patch hid everything about them except for their pink color. The boy began fondling himself, but because nothing was visible, Fumio had to use his imagination to fill the gap. The slightly vacant expression on the young boxer's face gave no indication of any pleasure he might be feeling. The censor's patch danced with lewd enticement. By now the motion of the boy's wrist had become a steady, smooth pumping. Fumio glanced nervously at the box of tissues beside the couch, then at the closed, locked door. He knew he had complete privacy in here, and that no one would care what he did.

Before he could do anything, however, a noise distracted him. Someone was entering the cubicle net door. He sat up and waited. In the mirror, he saw that a young man had sat on the couch and was leafing through the video menu the employee had handed him. There was no way Fumio could see his face, and his own anonymity was similarly guaranteed, but he could tell the other was quite tall, perhaps 180 centimeters in height. And he seemed to be a young man, a college boy or even a high school boy, judging from the blue jeans and white sneakers he wore.

After a while the employee left to get the video the boy had chosen; he returned shortly, inserted the video into the player, turned it on, then left again. When Fumio noticed in the mirror that the boy had lain back on the couch to watch the video, he did the same. From this position, he had a good view of the lower half of the boy's body... and knew he was giving the other boy the same view of his own. It was a little disconcerting not knowing if the other were looking in the mirror or not, but the detached anonymity of the situation was somehow deliciously thrilling.

Briefly, he wondered how the other looked... then decided that it didn't matter. The only thing that did matter was that on the other side of the partition was a young homosexual man who had the same kinds of desires he did... who dreamed the same dreams and wished the same forbidden wishes. Fumio found all his attention focussed on the mirror now; as exciting as the video would normally have been (the young boxer was on his knees, and seen from the back, his buttocks muscles were clenched tight, his pumping wrist a frenzied blur), it had now become a mere distraction. For the boy in the mirror had begun to touch himself lightly on the crotch.

Not daring to breathe, Fumio continued to gaze into the mirror, still not believing that he was allowed to watch another boy at this so private act. It felt strangely unreal, as if the other were communicating with him through means of gestures across a great space. The mingled sounds from both their video monitors formed an unnoticed background accompaniment. Suddenly Fumio half-raised himself. The fingers in the mirror were tracing the outline of what was underneath the boy's jeans, a lengthened hardness in bold diagonal relief. His own inhibitions immediately vanishing, Fumio felt his right hand, almost of its own volition, reach down to the front of his pants and give a soft squeeze.

The hand in the mirror replied by tugging seductively at the zipper, but without pulling it down. Fumio swallowed hard. He was aching to see more. His own excitement had blossomed, and the knowledge that the other could probably see it plainly beneath the soft cloth of his slacks was strangely liberating. And then time seemed to stand still. In the mirror, Fumio saw the hands slowly drawing down the zipper, then begin to undo the fly. Stopping his own caresses, he gazed transfixed as, with a brazenness like something seen in a dream, the jeans were pulled down, exposing gleaming white briefs. These in turn were pulled down, allowing an uncensored, fully exposed penis to pop out.

Fumio felt as if a film had glazed over his eyes, yet everything was still so nakedly sharp-focussed. There, perfectly framed by the mirror, was the incontrovertible visual proof of another boy's excitement. The penis, and almost nothing else, was visible. This was the naked, glorious truth which had lain hidden behind all those censors' mosaic patches. It was a sight he had long dreamed of being able to watch to his heart's content, without any fear. Hungrily he gazed, feeling his mouth go dry. Again, the thought came to him that he was assured of complete anonymity... as was the boy himself in the next cubicle so brazenly exposing himself.

What added to Fumio's pleasure in watching was the knowledge that the unknown boy was probably enjoying putting on this show. And then the hands began toying with the genitals, lifting, pulling, squeezing, fondling, rubbing. Watching the hands at their work — so obviously playing to Fumio's rapt attention, playing for an audience of him alone, Fumio felt himself unable anymore to withhold response to the other's unspoken urging. Leaning back on his elbows, he lifted his hips off the couch and pulled down his own pants and briefs. As his naked erection emerged, his heart hammered crazily in his chest, and when his pants were bunched down around his ankles, he lay there for a long moment revelling in what he'd done.

The mirror, of course, was angled so that his own genitals were fully visible to his neighbor. As the hands in the mirror paused in their activity, he could almost feel the other boy's gaze drinking in the sight he offered. It felt liberating to know that he was being watched, perhaps with an avidity that matched his own. He hadn't been this aroused in a long time. And he knew the feeling was mutual... for the erection he saw in the mirror twitched once or twice, as if involuntarily. And then the boy's right hand closed over the stiff shaft, gripping it tightly. It began a stroking motion in a slow, sensual rhythm.

Fumio lost no time in responding. With his eyes on the mirror, he timed his motions to the other's. Masturbation had always given him his greatest pleasures, but until now it had been a solitary enjoyment. Sharing it with another like this somehow added to his own pleasure, deepening it... as if a single line of melody had gained accompanying chords and harmonies. It was difficult to escape the illusion that his own touches were giving a direct stimulus to his partner, and vice versa: that the mirrored hand's stroking was stirring up his own arousal. Could heterosexual men ever get this much pleasure?

Watching the kneading, teasing motions of the hand in the mirror, Fumio sensed something intrinsically gay in the sight... an insouciance, a dare, a challenge, perhaps even a defiance. There was something raw, meaty, and masculine in this. No woman could ever give him pleasure of this intensity. What he was enjoying now was something only a man — and a gay man, at that — could appreciate.

This was his first homosexual experience of any sort in more than three years, and he realized now how much he missed this world. It wasn't something he could just wash out of his system and wish away. It was a permanent part of him, perhaps the most precious part. Marriage to Seiko hadn't vanquished it nor diminished it in any way. This experience, sordid as it might appear, was giving him more pleasure than anything he'd ever gotten from the straight life. Behind Seiko's back he was getting the pleasure he was denied in the marriage bed. What perhaps gave him the most excitement was the fact that he was a newly-wed husband, supposedly at the peak of his happiness, with a young wife, a promising career, and a good home in Tokyo. If he were to be discovered in Mirror Man, the ensuing scandal would completely wreck his marriage, his career, his life... but that thought only heightened the intensity of this experience. His re-entry into the gay underworld had the delicious fear of exposure as its spice, its intensifier. In the mirror, the fist's up-and-down jogging had picked up speed. Fumio, with his free left hand, pulled the box of tissues closer...

7

ON SATURDAYS, Fumio only taught three classes in the afternoon, and was usually home by seven. He and Seiko had agreed that she didn't have to cook evening meals on weekends, so tonight he'd stopped in at a Chinese restaurant on the way home. The winter wind felt chilly against his back as he pedalled his bicycle up the slope toward home, but by the time he'd reached the top, pumping as hard as he could all the way up, the exertion had warmed him up. The ten-minute bicycle ride between home and work was virtually the only exercise he got these days, so he tried to make the most of it.

His house was a short distance from the top of the slope, in a quiet block of homes near the Chuo Line's pedestrian overpass. He swung off the saddle and pushed open the front gate, wheeling his bike toward the vinyl shed beside the house. From somewhere in the neighborhood came the sound of a young child practicing the piano. It had been a busy day today, what with the entrance exams coming up so soon, and he was a little tired. He rang the doorbell expecting Seiko to answer it, but her mother opened the door instead.

"Welcome home."

"Where's Seiko-san?"

"You have a visitor upstairs."

"A visitor?" For the first time, Fumio noticed an unfamiliar pair of men's shoes on the floor, turned around so the wearer could slip into them when he left. And he could hear voices coming down from upstairs. He wondered who it could be. Seiko's girl friends occasionally dropped by to visit during the day when he was working, but there had never been any visitors this late in the evening. As he climbed the stairs he heard laughter — the sound of a man's voice mingled with Seiko's. When he slid the door open and stepped into the room, he saw a handsome young man sitting at the table with a glass of beer in his hand, and Seiko pouring it out for him from the bottle. They both turned to look at him, and the young man half-rose in greeting. It was Tatsuya.

Seiko got to her feet. "Oh, Fumio-san, Mr. Aoki came to visit at about five o'clock. I thought you wouldn't mind... "

"No, of course not. How are you, Tatsuya?"

Tatsuya re-folded his legs under him again into the formal sitting posture and bowed slightly. "I've been a bother here," he said politely.

"Oh no, not at all. Please make yourself comfortable."

"Forgive me for dropping in unannounced like this. I happened to be in the neighborhood and couldn't resist the chance to see how you were doing."

"It's been a long time." Fumio sat down and loosened his tie, handing his suit jacket to Seiko. "So you've been drinking beer. Here, let me pour for you." Fumio couldn't believe he was so blithely mouthing these usual trivial greetings when his whole being was vibrating with joy at seeing Tatsuya again. Yet it was this formal manner he had forced himself to adopt which allowed him to restrain all his wild emotions.

"Mr. Aoki says you're old friends from college," said Seiko.

"That's right," said Fumio. "We got into a lot of trouble together." As Seiko went downstairs to get him a glass, Fumio gazed at his friend. Tatsuya looked the same as ever. Perhaps there was something subtly more mature, more self-assured about his manner. But he still had the smooth, almost supernaturally beautiful face, with the same cleanly shaped eyebrows and dark fringe of eyelashes. Every hair on his head was neatly combed into place. And he was obviously still making good money: he wore an attractive, expensive-looking suit.

For Fumio, this thrilling privilege of being able to look upon his friend's face once again was like an unasked-for dream — but a dream slightly shadowed by a nascent fear. Why had Tatsuya come back into his life after all this time, when everything was going so smoothly for him, when he'd finally resigned himself to not seeing Tatsuya for the rest of his life? "How did you find me here?" he asked, hoping his anxiety didn't show.

"Through the college alumnus listing. They send out a newsletter every year bringing us up to date on what's happening to everyone."

"I don't keep up with those things." Fumio remembered clearly that he'd looked for Tatsuya's name on the listing but had been unable to find it.

"You should. It's quite interesting to see what our classmates are doing now. How they've succeeded... or failed, as the case may be."

"Do you still work at the old place?"

"Oh no, I quit that sort of thing long ago." Tatsuya laughed lightly. "I've finally gotten a foot in the door of the entertainment business."

"That's wonderful." The word 'entertainment' had suddenly triggered a whole throng of painful memories for Fumio.

"I was with a modelling agency for a while till I met up with a man in J Productions. The head of the company seems to have taken a liking to me, so I'm taking acting lessons now. Who knows where it'll lead to? Basically, I'm just waiting around now for a good role to come along."

"I saw Mayumi on television the other night."

"Yes, she's on quite a bit. Her stage name is Yasuda Manami. I was just talking about her with your wife. Seiko-san seems quite interested in the entertainment world."

"Oh yes. When we happened to see some famous people in Hawaii, she was as giddy as a schoolgirl. I don't go for that sort of thing myself. Are you still living with Mayumi?"

"Oh, no. We broke up ages ago. It seems my presence would have compromised her reputation as an up-and-coming actress."

"I see."

"Her agency gave me a hefty sum as a sort of consolation fee. I didn't mind — as long as she didn't. Things were coming to a head anyway, so it was only a sweetener."

An irrational hope suddenly sprang up in Fumio's heart: Tatsuya had been spurned by Mayumi, so he'd come back to Fumio to try to pick up where they'd left off... Two loving friends, completely platonic in their affections. Even for Fumio it was too saccharine a dream... but that didn't stop him from clutching it to his heart like any schoolgirl.

Seiko came back with the beer and two glasses on a tray, along with some more snacks. "I hope you don't mind if I join in."

"Of course not," said Fumio, hiding his irritation. He would have preferred to be alone with Tatsuya; there were so many things he still wanted to find out about this sudden reunion. But despite his anger, Seiko's presence was — at the same time — somehow reassuring, as if she were his secret confederate.

After they'd touched glasses and taken a drink, Tatsuya asked him with a friendly smile, "How's married life?"

"Oh, it's all right. Your life becomes much more orderly. You eat on time. But there are some things I miss."

"Such as — ?"

"Oh, you know... " He was hoping that Tatsuya would get the hint. A sudden recollection of the time they'd worked together at Genji brought back such a sharp pang of longing that a cool, gnawing sensation began to eat away at the pit of his stomach. It suddenly seemed as if he'd last seen Tatsuya just days ago instead of years.

"The old freedom from responsibility, huh? You shouldn't glamorize those old days so much. You look much happier now than you did back then."

"Do I?"

"Yes. You're very lucky to have found a wife like Seiko-san. She's very nice. And she obviously dotes on you. I envy you."

Seiko brought her hands up to her face in a girlish gesture indicating a blush, and Fumio felt a pang of annoyance.

"Being married becomes her. She told me she was never the type that glamorized marriage, but since we've been together, she's turned into a model housewife. Unbeknown to herself, she was after all just a marriage waiting to happen."

Seiko laughed. "Maybe it's true."

Tatsuya looked at Fumio. "But I didn't think you were the type to get married so young."

Fumio felt a chill go through him. The ugly bud that had been dormant in the back of his mind now burst into full bloom: Tatsuya had come to blackmail him after all. Fear threatened to ruin his joy in their reunion. But Fumio's fond hope that Tatsuya had come back out of remorse, out of a desire to renew their friendship, was so strong that he managed to suppress it.

Seiko poured out beer for both the men, then for herself. "Fumio-san has told me about the way you two used to go disco-hopping. I imagine it was quite a surprise to you when you learned that he'd settled down."

"It was. Quite a surprise. Especially as you didn't even let me know of it."

"We didn't know where to send the invitation," said Seiko smoothly. Fumio felt grateful at how quickly she'd covered up for him, protected him.

"And moreover," went on Tatsuya, "to learn that he is now the son-in-law of the famous Professor Akiyoshi." He turned to Seiko. "One sees a lot of your father on TV these days."

"You can be sure he's quite vain about it, too," she laughed. "He's so puffed up, he thinks himself quite the star."

"If he's not careful, he may find himself in the pages of *Friday* or *Focus*."

"Coming out of a hotel with a young actress?" She shook her head, incredulous. "Oh no. He comes home quite punctually now. Since Fumio-san and I moved in here, Father says he has something to look forward to."

"Oh?" Tatsuya looked from one to the other, a crooked smile on his lips. Unable to meet that look, Fumio picked up his glass of beer and downed it in one gulp. Seiko had picked up the beer bottle even before he'd replaced his glass on the table. As she poured out more beer for him, she giggled.

"And how about you, Mr. Aoki? Are you still disco-hopping? Finding it hard to give up your wild lifestyle?"

"I go occasionally," he said, with a self-deprecating gesture.

"I'll bet you have lots of girlfriends."

"Well... "

"I'll bet you make lots of girls cry... "

Fumio was surprised to see how animated Seiko's features were. There was a glow in her eyes that made them look bigger, darker, more alluring. It was obvious she'd fallen under Tatsuya's spell. Tatsuya had the power to charm any girl, but Fumio knew that Seiko would be especially susceptible to any attentions, as their night-time intimacies had been a little neglected recently. Still, it irritated him to think how easily his wife had fallen for Tatsuya.

"We're running out of snacks to go with the beer," he said.

"Let me go downstairs and rustle something up," said Seiko. She excused herself and left. Fumio knew she was probably going to make some of the dishes which were her specialty. Under the tutelage of her mother, she'd become particularly adept at making those light snacks which went so well with a late-night drink.

Only after he heard her busying herself downstairs in the kitchen did Fumio feel free to talk openly, for the first time. "Why did you come here, Tatsuya, after all this time? I thought I'd never see you again."

Tatsuya sincerely seemed puzzled by the question. "Why not? We're friends, after all. Are you still mad at me for kicking you out of the apartment?"

"Well, no. I realized you needed privacy with Mayumi. It was hard for me, too, living as part of a threesome."

"But now you obviously have no more worries about finding a place to stay, right? I mean, you're not really hard up for cash now, are you? You look set up for life."

Again, Fumio wondered if Tatsuya's motive in coming here was blackmail. It wasn't unthinkable. "How did you and the professor reconcile?" asked Tatsuya, pulling out a pack of cigarettes. He still smoked the same Egyptian imports.

"Well, when he indicated that he was ready to forgive me, I felt I had nothing to lose: I went back to him."

"But... marry his daughter? That's going beyond mere reconciliation."

"Actually, it was the professor who introduced us."

"He asked you to marry his daughter?" Tatsuya paused in the act of pulling a lighter out of his jacket pocket.

"Yes."

"I see. This is beginning to get interesting. So you and the professor, behind her back — ?"

"No. There's none of that. That was the deal we made. I'm through with that sort of thing, and he understands. He's happy just to have me in his family, living under the same roof with him."

"How romantic." Tatsuya tapped his cigarette against the tabletop before lighting it. Fumio noticed he still had all the graceful, studied motions for everything he did — as if he'd learned all his moves from watching movies... the copied performance of a very skillful, and sexy, actor. "I can see things would get very sticky if it were otherwise. A very dangerous situation."

Fumio didn't want to tell him how he had to put up with the older man's secret pleading sometimes. The less Tatsuya knew about the true nature of things, the better.

"So you're out of all that now... " mused Tatsuya, exhaling a plume of gray smoke.

Fumio resisted the urge to light up himself. "Of course. It's the straight road for me now. I feel like I'm breathing fresh air after a very long time in a dirty, airless cave." He felt his throat constrict as he added, "I don't know why I did some of the things I did back then... "

Tatsuya looked at him, and for a moment Fumio felt a stab of panic. But then, to his relief, the other merely laughed. "At that age we all do foolish things, Fumio. We act impulsively, do things we later regret. It's something that happens to a lot of guys. You'd be surprised at how many. Maybe it's a part of growing up. Anyway, it's obvious you're not 'like that.' Your wife is a very attractive woman."

"Seiko?" Fumio was surprised. He knew men were attracted to her, but to earn this compliment from someone of Tatsuya's caliber was unexpected. True, since her eyelid operation, she did have a more seductive look. But for him, her present look was a mirage thinly superimposed over his memory of her in the pre-operation days when she still had single-fold eyelids. It seemed like only yesterday she'd lain in his apartment with the bandages over her eyes as she recuperated from the operation, hiding from her friends until all the scars had healed.

"Looks like you're on easy street now, Fumio. You really pulled a sharp one. I envy you. Married, with a home, and a business coming to you: every host's dream."

"I really don't think of myself as a host anymore."

"They never do, after they've become successful," laughed Tatsuya, then added in a more serious tone, "I guess I shouldn't have talked you into doing... what we did to him."

Fumio flushed. At the mention of the blackmailing, he felt a thrill go through him.

"No," he wanted to say, "on the contrary... " But he didn't dare reveal that their extortion of money from the professor remained, for him, the peak moment of glory in his youth. The planning of it, the perpetration of it, and the aftermath had been the climax of his friendship with Tatsuya, when he'd felt the closest to his hero, indeed almost at one with him. And this secret still lay between them... would always lie between them, linking them, branding them as co-conspirators. They'd committed a crime together, and that was a bond stronger than marriage, a bond almost as strong as love itself.

"Where is the professor, by the way?"

"Sensei? He's on a research trip. He won't be home until next Tuesday."

"I see."

"He's always busy. We hardly ever see him around here anymore. As you mentioned earlier, he's becoming quite well known now." Fumio mentioned a television program which was very popular at the moment, a political round-table discussion which employed scholars, critics, as well as well-known television personalities debating current topics, whether it was trade with the US or political corruption in the Japanese government. It was the first program in Japan to really come out with hard-hitting criticisms of the government, and had been an immediate hit with the viewing audience, even though it was broadcast so late at night. "Sensei is one of the semi-regulars on the panel now."

"I know," said Tatsuya a little listlessly.

Fumio suddenly realized there might be another explanation for Tatsuya's visit tonight. Because Professor Akiyoshi now appeared on television with greater frequency (there seemed to be a boom for those intellectuals who could talk glibly about international affairs), Tatsuya might be under the assumption that the older man could act as a connection for furthering his own ambitions in the entertainment world. That would fit in with the mercenary, self-seeking aspect of Tatsuya's personality. After all, Fumio himself had once been a victim of it, used and discarded without a thought. Yet he couldn't feel any anger at the memory; somehow, it was this very vulgarity that added to Tatsuya's attraction.

Seiko's footsteps were heard coming up the stairs. She had the tray in her hands with the snacks she'd made. Fumio could tell at a glance that she'd gone to a lot of trouble to make them as tasty as possible. "Thank you, Seiko," he said, adding gently, "you must be tired. We can look after ourselves. You can go to bed anytime. It looks like we'll be talking over old times for a little while longer."

"Oh no, it's quite all right. I'm not tired tonight. I might even have a few more drinks myself."

Fumio groaned inwardly, chagrined that she hadn't gotten his hint. There was something a bit frisky about her tonight. Usually she was only too glad to find an excuse to go to bed. As she sat down at the table and joined their conversation, Fumio felt an unexpectedly sharp resentment at being unable to have Tatsuya to himself. In fact, from the way Seiko was hanging on tonight, it almost seemed as if she suspected the former relationship between the two young men, and was jealously coming between them to prevent its recurrence. No matter how many times Fumio hinted to her that she could go to sleep, she never went. And to his anger, Tatsuya seemed intent on keeping her here with his talk. His stores of gossip about the entertainment world fascinated Seiko.

It was a torture for Fumio to be here in the same room as Tatsuya, breathing the same air as him, yet unable to ask him the questions he was dying to ask. He excused himself to go to the toilet, and when he returned, Seiko and Tatsuya were laughing away.

"What's so funny?" he asked.

Tatsuya answered: "We were talking about the singing abilities of some of these so-called talents. Listen, are you doing anything next Friday night?"

"Not really."

"How about going out for some singing at a karaoke box? Just like we did in the old days. Do you feel up to it?"

"Sure." Fumio recalled the golden days of their special friendship.

"Am I invited, too?" asked Seiko.

"Of course. I wouldn't dream of passing up a chance to hear your impersonations of Nakamori Akina."

She laughed, and Fumio suddenly knew that his wife and Tatsuya had probably been having a good time even before he'd returned tonight. Indeed it would have been difficult for any woman to resist the charming attentions Tatsuya was capable of. Fumio felt a twinge of jealousy, but he didn't know for whom, Tatsuya or Seiko.

He glanced at his watch and saw that it was past 11:30. Not without a hint of malice, he forced himself to yawn. "It's getting a little late. Maybe we should call it a night."

Seiko seemed disappointed when Tatsuya agreed. "I guess I should be going," he said, looking at his own watch.

"Why don't you spend the night?" said Seiko suddenly.

To his surprise, Fumio found himself seconding the suggestion. "Yes, why not?"

Tatsuya looked uncertain. "I don't know... "

Seiko got up. "I'll lay out the futon in the extra room. It's no trouble at all."

"No, please... " said Tatsuya.

"It's really no trouble," said Fumio. "You can wear an extra pair of my pajamas. I think we wear the same size. Come on, why don't you stay over? Seiko doesn't seem to mind. We rarely have company here, what with my job. And she was enjoying herself this evening listening to your talk." Still, Tatsuya demurred. "Or do you have a girl waiting for you back at your place?" needled Fumio somewhat maliciously.

"It's not that... " Tatsuya glanced at Seiko in a boyishly embarrassed manner. Fumio regretted his own impetuous joke; now he would torture himself with the picture of Tatsuya in the arms of a woman. Somewhat more gently, he said, "It's so late now that you'll really have to rush to catch the last train. Why not take it easy?"

"Well, as a matter of fact, I have my car parked down the road. In a side street which is really no parking."

"Why didn't you say so?" said Fumio, a little more heartily than he'd intended. "So that's it." He felt inexplicably relieved.

"Oh... " Seiko looked clearly downcast.

Tatsuya got to his feet and gave a slight bow. "Well, I've really enjoyed myself here this evening."

"So did we. We're looking forward to seeing you here again, Tatsuya. Now that you've been introduced to Seiko, feel free to drop by anytime."

"All right."

After they'd seen Tatsuya off at the front door, the young couple checked on Seiko's mother. They apologized to her for the noise they'd been making, but she told them she hadn't been bothered at all, that she was glad to see they had company. They went back upstairs, where Seiko began cleaning up the table and putting it away. While Fumio changed into his *yukata*, Seiko drew out the futon bedding from the closet and spread it out. When she was done, she sat in front of her make-up mirror preparing for bed. She was humming a tune. Fumio knew she was thinking of Tatsuya, and this irritated him. "What time did you say he came?" he asked casually.

"Oh, about five. I was surprised, believe me. But he seemed nice enough, so I let him in. He said he was willing to wait. You're not angry, are you?"

"No, of course not. But what were you doing all that time?"

"Talking."

"About what?"

"All kinds of things. He knows so much, about so many things."

"Yes, I know."

"Are you jealous?"

"About Tatsuya? Don't be ridiculous. He was one of my closest friends."

Perhaps she noticed his dark look in the mirror, for she said playfully, "Do you really think he has a girlfriend waiting for him back at his apartment?"

"I wouldn't be surprised."

"Why do you think he hasn't married yet? Does he want to play around all his life?"

"He's only twenty-five. I'm sure there's a lot more things he wants to do before he gives it all up and settles down."

"Do you think marriage means giving up on life? Some people

think of it as the beginning of 'real life'... "

"I wouldn't know yet," he said a little more softly. Then, as if in apology: "I only know I didn't give anything up when I married." He thought ruefully to himself that if he hadn't given up anything, it was only because he'd had nothing to give up.

"I'm going down to take a bath." Seiko gathered her bathing gear together and left. It was only after she'd gone downstairs that Fumio noticed her pillow was red-side up. Obviously she wanted to keep her thoughts on Tatsuya tonight... He slipped into his own futon, wondering if the annoyance he felt was jealousy or not. He only knew he wanted to punish her for some reason. Her behavior had been strange all night.

When he heard her coming up the stairs after twenty minutes, he closed his eyes. The door slid open. No doubt thinking her husband asleep, Seiko turned off the lights and came to bed. She lay silent in her futon for a long time. Fumio could hear her breathing in the dark. He imagined her thinking about Tatsuya's beauty, and perhaps indulging in some innocent fantasies. With all the perverse delight of sullying a pure innocence, he pulled off his cover and slid over to her futon to claim his husband's prerogatives. She didn't resist. Silently she moved over, making room for him, and he felt the warmth where her body had been lying. In the dark, he only knew where she was by the slight sound of her breathing, and her warmth. He half-raised himself and pushed his knee through the opening in the front of his *yukata*, feeling it slip away from the lower half of his body. As he moved over onto her, he felt her arms come up around his back. The aroma of the shampoo she used seemed to grow more pungent. Usually their sex was perfunctory: Seiko just waited for him to do everything, never demanding anything or complaining afterwards. It was as if she were merely a receptacle for his desires. Fumio knew from talking to his co-workers that for most of them, sleeping with a woman was no different from an act of self-pleasure. He could never forget the cynical words of Mr. Kameya who had drawn him aside during the party given for him as a send-off to the wedding: "Don't give her anything fancy. If you do, she'll expect it every time. Just do it simply and quickly, and that's what she'll accept as normal. Believe me, that's what it'll end up after a while. It's for your own happiness — and hers — not to work yourself too hard. Just give it to her straight and simple and she'll be satisfied with that all the time."

Fumio had followed that advice, more out of his own inclinations than anything else. He knew that Seiko — unlike some of the girls he'd met in Roppongi during his host club days — had never experienced an orgasm with him, and he doubted if she even wanted to. And that was fine with him.

He turned his thoughts back to Tatsuya. Usually, it was Tatsuya whom he relied upon at such times. Although the moments of true intimacy with him had been few, they'd proved to be enough; replays of them had played hundreds of times in Fumio's mind, night upon night, to enrich the barrenness of an increasingly routine act. What Seiko didn't know wouldn't hurt her. Indeed she was the beneficiary of these fantasies which sparked an ardor she herself would never have been able to. And tonight, the recent proximity of the original made the image in Fumio's mind so much more vivid than usual that he was in danger of calling out his name.

"Oh... " The moan had come from Seiko. As if only now realizing that he was making love with her, Fumio opened his eyes and looked down at her. Normally she was silent, or moaned softly enough not to be heard downstairs. But tonight she was surprisingly ardorous in her responses. Maybe it was all the alcohol she'd drunk which emboldened her so. He felt a little embarrassed at her loss of decorum. To his dismay, her face was twisting into a familiar mask — the one all girls donned in moments of passion, which made them all look the same. Her lips were curled back, exposing her teeth, and her eyes were wildly unfocussed, gazing off into another dimension, glowing with something he'd never seen in them before. It took him a moment to realize that he knew its cause. Like him, she too was making love with Tatsuya.

8

SEIKO HAD always been known among her friends as a good singer. There had even been a time when she'd seriously considered becoming a singing idol. But that dream now found its only outlet in occasional visits to Do-Re-Mi-Land, a karaoke box in Kunitachi. Tonight she seemed even more energetic than usual; with the microphone in her right hand she was belting out a Nakamori Akina song as if she were on stage before thousands of people. On the video monitor above her head were a pair of lovers acting out a melodramatic scene which had nothing to do with the words to the song which appeared as subtitles at the bottom of the screen. Tatsuya was flipping through the menu of songs available in a thick, photo-album-sized binder while Fumio drank his beer and shouted encouragements at his wife.

The karaoke box they were in was actually nothing more than a tiny soundproof room with a sofa and table. A karaoke set with remote-control selection buttons and a huge video monitor took up almost all the rest of the space. There was barely enough room for the singer to stand up and dance the song's choreographed steps. The glass-windowed door allowed anyone to peer inside (perhaps to ensure that no under-aged patrons had smuggled in any alcohol), and the room in general had a musty, tobacco smell.

Seiko was a regular customer here, and had used her member's card to get them a discount tonight. "How much time do we have left?" she asked as she finished her song.

Fumio peered at his watch. "About five minutes." The two-hour session they'd paid for was already nearly over.

"Just enough time for one more song," said Tatsuya. "And I know just the one." He picked up the remote control and, checking the number codes in the menu, punched in his selection. In a little while the song's introduction flooded the room and Fumio groaned as he recognized the tune, a hackneyed lovers' duet.

"Just the thing for a young married couple like you," said Tatsuya, picking up the other mike and handing it to Fumio.

"No thank you. My voice is still hoarse from singing that last one." At Tatsuya's request he had sung a Sakai Noriko tune, duplicating the girl idol's voice by singing falsetto, an act which had always brought laughs whenever he sang it in the old days.

"But we have to have something romantic to close out the night," Tatsuya insisted.

"Then why don't you take it?"

"If you insist." Not needed to be asked twice, Tatsuya — who loved karaoke — took back the mike and gazed at the words to the song flashing on the screen. The first verse was for the man, with the woman's reply coming in the second verse. Tatsuya and Seiko, each holding a separate mike, sang the sentimental duet in a campily exaggerated fashion, but when their voices blended together on the choruses, it was difficult to suppress a shiver of true melancholy. These songs of unrequited love or parting were usually used by shy suitors to approach the person they liked, and as Fumio watched his wife singing with Tatsuya, he had mixed emotions. Certainly it wasn't jealousy, he told himself. On the other hand, ever since that night she'd 'betrayed' him with Tatsuya, he'd been loath to touch her body.

As the song came to its climactic ending, the two singers gazed into each other's eyes. Fumio applauded them loudly, and Seiko, her face looking a little flushed, smiled awkwardly at him.

"We'd better be going if I'm to catch the last train home." Tatsuya had come by train tonight. They walked him to the station, a five-minute walk, then headed home themselves on foot. The night was warm for this time of year and Fumio felt exhilarated. The beer he'd drunk had left him in a pleasant mood, but more than that, it was the excitement of singing which now buoyed his spirits up. Unlike his wife, he wasn't a good singer, but a visit to a karaoke box always helped him release the pent-up stresses and frustrations accumulated from his teaching job.

The uphill street narrowed as it approached the foot of a steep hill and became a footpath winding up behind some homes, then climbed the embankment along the Chuo Line tracks. Almost no one else was about.

"I haven't had so much fun since I can't remember when," said Seiko.

"You certainly looked like you were enjoying yourself. Especially that last song with Tatsuya. You really sang well together."

"He has a good voice."

"So do you, Seiko."

"You know," she said after a pause, "wouldn't it be nice if we could set Tatsuya up with one of my unmarried girl friends?"

"Hm." Fumio looked at her sideways, thinking of the expression on her face as she'd sung the duet with Tatsuya. "Are you sure you don't want him for yourself? After all, extramarital affairs are all the rage now."

"Silly... " She hit him hard in the ribs with her elbow, then walked ahead of him a few paces so he couldn't see the expression on her face. As she passed under a street lamp, she suddenly called back over her shoulder with a saucy look: "If I didn't know any better, I'd say you actually sounded jealous just now."

"Jealous? Who wouldn't be?" The memory of her 'betrayal' abruptly returned, sparking something sadistic in him. What he'd intended as a joke began turning, with no volition on his part, into a spiteful teasing which gave him a strangely perverse satisfaction. "You were practically making love with him with your eyes."

"I was not!"

"You were, too. And I wouldn't be surprised if he had it up hard for you."

"How indecent." She seemed genuinely hurt by his cruelty, and Fumio regretted what he'd done. In what he hoped sounded more like his usual sense of humor, he said, "Seiko, if you ever have an affair, just don't let me find out about it. What I don't know won't hurt me."

"That's what wives are supposed to say to husbands." She slowed her steps to allow him to catch up, but when he did, he sensed that her mood had already passed from playfulness to something more serious. In silence they approached the pedestrian bridge to their left. At this point, the Chuo Line was far below, and the bridge passed high over it. Few trains were running this late; the houses on the other side were all dark and quiet, an occasional lit window suggesting a student up late doing homework, or cramming for entrance exams.

Seiko turned onto the bridge but stopped in the middle, leaning over the railing to gaze down at the tracks on the Tokyo-bound side. "Are you really so afraid that I might have an affair?" she asked him with a hurt look on her face.

"Of course not. I was only joking about it because I know you never can."

"Is there something about me that indicates I might play around, or cheat on you?" She looked so worried that Fumio hastened to reassure her: "No, Seiko, no. As I said, it's all a joke."

"Fumio-san, if anyone, it's you who are so cold recently."

"Me?"

She turned her face away to look down over the side of the bridge. "I realize it can't always be a honeymoon, but... once or twice a month? I wonder if you're seeing someone else...." This last was intended to be said in a playful manner, but Fumio could tell there was real concern deep down. He tried to laugh it off, thinking of the half-dozen times he'd managed to visit Mirror Man in secret.

"How can I cheat on you?" he said. "I'm too busy at work. And you know women don't go for me. I'm not a good-looking fellow like Tatsuya."

She continued to gaze down at the tracks, seeming to contemplate their shiny parallel gleams, glowing faintly in the dark, stretching all the way into the vanishing distance. To Fumio's surprise he noted the flash of a tear in her eye. "What's the matter?" he asked, alarmed. The tear dropped down onto the tracks below. Fumio felt a stab of guilt. He wished he'd been able to love her more — he wished he were normal. But it was too late to change anything now. A homosexual man married to a woman had to accept the fact that his life could never be anything other than a sham, otherwise he could go crazy feeling foolish regrets.

"Do you think it would make a difference if we had a baby?" he asked shyly. "I know that's the stereotypical gossip columnist's solution to any marriage on the rocks, but still... "

"Is our marriage on the rocks?"

"I mean — "

"I, too, thought having a baby might be the best way to bring us together more. But I'm beginning to wonder if the reason I want a baby so badly has another reason."

"Another reason?"

She was silent for a long time, and when she spoke again, it was as if she'd taken another tack. "Maybe it's my fault. I haven't tried hard enough."

"What do you mean? You've been trying hard. It's — well, maybe it's me."

"No," she said. "If anyone is at fault, it's me."

He stared at her. "What are you talking about?"

"Fumio-san, is this what you expected marriage to be like?"

"Huh?" The sudden question had caught him unawares. She didn't wait for an answer, but just shook her head gently back and forth, almost regretfully. "I don't know about you, but as for myself, it — it just doesn't feel like I'm married. There's no big change in my life, no shifting of gears. It isn't at all what I pictured it to be. Do you know what I mean?"

"I think so. But that's probably what everyone thinks at this stage."

"True. My girl friends also say the same thing. After the engagement, the planning for the wedding, the honeymoon... after all the excitement dies down, there's sort of a feeling of letdown. I think: is this all there is? Maybe it's all been built up too much. We're told that marriage is happiness — I mean, the words 'marriage' and 'happiness' are virtually interchangeable for most young women."

"Seiko, aren't you... aren't you happy?" He was afraid of the answer.

Still unable to look at him, she whispered in a voice so faint that he had to lean toward her to catch it. "Fumio-san, I'm sorry. There's something I haven't told you." Faintly, the sound of a railroad crossing bell came to their ears. Clang! clang! clang! It had to be far away because there was no crossing in sight, none, at least, between here and the station. Fumio didn't dare speak. She began in a small voice. "Fumio-san, do you want to know why I agreed to the *miai*?" She took a deep breath and it all came out in a rush. "I was seeing a man while I was still a student at Seijo. He was an assistant professor, married and with two children. But I didn't care. I loved him. I would have done anything for him."

Fumio felt his heart go faint. He felt detached from it all. He didn't want to hear anymore, but felt helpless to stop it. Seiko's voice went on and on like the soundtrack of a movie he'd ceased to watch. "I was acting foolishly, I know. I got pregnant with his child. And I had to have an abortion. Mother guessed that something was wrong with me — I wasn't myself for weeks. She got the truth out of me. Soon after that, Father found out about it and forced me to break off with the man. He told me I had to marry as quickly as possible before I got into any more trouble. Before there was a scandal. That's why I was more or less forced into having a *miai*."

Fumio still said nothing. He didn't have the least desire to find out any more about the affair. It was all over. He didn't know if he felt relieved, hurt, jealous, or angry. It was very much like being in the position of having to make a speech at a wedding. Anything he had to say would be superfluous and would only be listened to out of form.

Someone rode by on a bicycle, its light generator making a buzzing sound interrupted brokenly by clicks. The train finally came into sight, its twin yellow headlamps like a pair of close-set eyes, and with a roar passed directly beneath them, the wheels of its ten cars clickety-clicking, clickety-clicking, gradually fading away in the direction of Tokyo.

Finally he spoke. "So you married me because of that?"

She shook her head. "I was fond of you. Attracted to you. If it hadn't been you, I wouldn't have agreed to the marriage." Listening to the recitation in her even voice, it was easy for Fumio to imagine it was all happening to someone else. He knew she hadn't been a virgin when he first met her — that was too much to expect in this day and age in Japan — but she had seemed inexperienced and naive. If she'd been seeing a married man before their marriage, though, she had to have been putting on an act all along.

The sounds of the night sounded strangely distorted, as if heard through a rolled-up tube. A single motorcycle with an altered muffler buzzed loudly by on a nearby street. He realized Seiko was crying silently into her handkerchief. He didn't want her to cry — it was all so useless. Though their marriage had been a sham from the start — on his part as well as hers — somehow it was a relief to know he wasn't the only one who'd been unhappy. At the same time, he had mixed feelings about having been deceived by her act.

"There's nothing more to say, Seiko. Let's go home." The sound of the train finally died away in the distance. They resumed their walk home.

The new knowledge sank in slowly. Out of the welter of Fumio's emotions, one fact emerged clearly: he was now free. He could come home late at night now... he could even stay out all night. Seiko wouldn't hold anything against him. She would interpret it as his disgust at knowing she'd been touched by another man. But he didn't feel glad. After all, she could have kept silent about her past. The fact that she'd confessed at all meant she was openly declaring her unhappiness in the marriage. A woman who intended to seek happiness with her husband would have kept it secret. There were plenty of women who played around before marriage but who became happy, faithful wives. Perhaps she still loved the other man, hence her unresponsiveness in bed. Despite his hurt pride, Fumio knew it had cost her a lot to make the confession. Yet what had sparked it off? Had it come on the spur of the moment, from a carelessness fueled by alcohol, or had it come out of a deep unhappiness? Had she planned to confess from way back and was only looking for the right chance? Or had it been done out of remorse, knowing of Fumio's own unhappiness? In any case, her deep sense of honesty wouldn't have allowed her to keep it secret for very much longer. Their marriage had been a sham from start to finish, and the fault was just as much Fumio's as it was hers. He had agreed to the professor's proposal out of self-seeking motives. For that matter, the professor himself might be blamed for his part in it. And a further case could be made that it was all the result of circumstances, the play of cruel fate.

Fumio knew he could go crazy trying to apportion blame for the failure of the marriage. But the truth was, deep down in his heart, he didn't care. He'd never really loved her, indeed, was incapable of it. He even felt grateful that it had come out into the open at last.

Seiko spoke in a soft voice. "Still, I imagine a lot of men play around before they marry." Fumio could still hear the sound of that now far-off motorcycle buzzing in the night like a bothersome mosquito. He pictured the young rider, and thought of Tatsuya as a young man of eighteen blasting around the rice paddies of his hometown in a friend's sports car. There was no moonlight tonight, and the shadows were especially deep. Fumio felt as if he were suffocating. Something seemed to be growing inside him, ready to come out. He realized with a faint shock that it was a desire to make a confession of his own. But was that possible? Were such things done?

He turned his steps toward a small park beside the road. It was dark and empty. He sat on a swing and Seiko took the swing next to him. The rusty chains supporting the seats creaked loudly in the dark. "Seiko, I, too, have a confession to make."

"A confession?"

In the dark he couldn't tell what her expression was, but he pressed on. "It's very, very difficult to talk about."

"I think I know what it's about," she said resolutely. She turned her swing to face him, and as if forcing her resolve, said bravely, halting once or twice in her speech, "Does it have to do with another woman? If so, I'd rather not hear the sordid details."

Fumio was a little surprised at the calmness with which she was taking it. Seiko, mistaking his hesitation as a confirmation of her guess, went on: "I thought as much. A woman knows things like that. When you hold me, your mind is far away. I know."

Fumio was tempted to laugh. "If only it were so simple, Seiko." And he had a vision of all the couples in Japan who at one time or another were forced to confront the issue of the husband's deception. Yet how laughably commonplace and simple their problem was. He would give anything to be in their shoes at this moment.

"I don't understand," she said. "You'll have to explain."

"I'll try. It isn't the usual sort of thing." Fumio couldn't look at her face. "I am not like other men."

"What do you mean?"

Still looking down, Fumio went on: "Somewhere along the line, I discovered that I am not attracted to women in the same way other men are."

"You're homo?"

He didn't answer. She repeated her question, the second time not sounding so incredulous as the first time, but more as an echoing confirmation.

Fumio nodded. "I have homosexual feelings."

"So what? Many men probably do. It's a passing thing. I, too, have been attracted to other women. In high school I had a crush for a whole year on an upper-classman girl."

"No, this isn't like that at all." He looked at her for the first time since the start of his confession, and saw that she was looking down at the ground, defeated-looking. He wondered if he was making his own confession as a sort of revenge, to get back at her for the pain her confession had caused him. But at the same time, the feeling of catharsis he felt as he divulged his secret was undeniable.

"I believe you're telling the truth," she said. "This isn't something one lies about."

"I suppose not."

"But how did it happen?" Inevitably, perhaps, she shared the misconception that homosexuality was a slip, an error into which some men just accidentally fell.

"It isn't something that 'happens', Seiko. Rather, it's a gradual process of self-awareness. I was a normal boy in junior high school, and all through high school. That is, I thought I was. Because I got the usual crushes on girls. But when I came to Tokyo, things seemed to change inside me. Maybe it was the freedom, being away from home for the first time. But for some reason, I started getting curious about the homosexual world. It all started from a chance thing..."

Seiko's eyes were glowing in the dark, but there was no revulsion in them. Fumio felt as if he were one of her girl friends in high school disclosing her first experience with a boy, telling them all how she lost her virginity, what it was like the first time. A part of him was even a little disappointed at her lack of revulsion. He had expected an outburst, and this anti-climactic reaction caught him unawares.

"I didn't feel homosexual," he went on. "I thought I was just playing around. But before I knew it, I was hooked. No, I take it back. I guess I was acting on my true instincts all along when I became curious about that world. After all, plenty of normal men never become fascinated by it as I did."

Seiko was listening intently, interested. "I always thought homos were obvious. You know, the way they walk and talk — just like women. But you're so normal."

"You have the image of homos as raving queens, which some are. But that's only a small percentage. Most look quite normal. But because they have to hide their true identities, so many of them assume the most potent disguise of all: the boringly normal married man."

"Like you?"

"Yes, like me. You'd be surprised how many others are like me, posing as normal. They're all around you — businessmen, salarymen, doctors, government officials, policemen, sportsmen."

"What do you feel when you hold me?" She seemed sincerely curious about this aspect of him, not at all vindictive or spiteful.

"What I always feel with a woman — that if only she were a man, I would enjoy it so much more. I'm sorry. It has nothing to do with you personally. You are very attractive, and sexy. It's just the way I'm made."

"Why did you marry me?" she asked suddenly. "Did you think marriage would change you?"

Fumio was taken aback. "No, I'm not that naive — though

there are many men who are. I guess I thought marriage would somehow be good for me. Because I was getting quite morbid for a while. And there were also the other pressures — the kind everyone has — to marry at the marriageable age. Please don't misunderstand me. I like and respect you as a person. You are a good wife — far better than most. Any man would envy me."

She was gazing at the far-off lights on the other side of the tracks. "Then you married me for Father's money."

"No, Seiko, it isn't that at all. Your father's a very nice man, and he likes me... treats me well. I have nothing to complain of."

She suddenly laughed, sounding harsh, and shook her head. "It's all a farce. Marriage is all a farce. It has no meaning. No meaning at all."

Fumio merely bowed his head, feeling weary from the labor of his confession. "So what happens now?"

"I don't know," she said.

Fumio was silent for a long time before speaking. "One of the reasons I'm confessing all this is that maybe we should seriously think about our marriage. Are we happy?"

She said nothing.

"Do you want a divorce?" he asked her point blank.

"No." She looked at him, unblinking. "There are worse marriages."

"But any marriage which doesn't have at least the pretense of happiness has no hope for survival."

"Why do you say that? We can still make it work. Build a home for ourselves, have a family."

"With someone like me for a husband?"

"Listen. Most of my friends are married, so I hear stories. They don't all have ideal marriages, either."

"Sure, but — "

"At least you don't beat me. And you don't neglect me. You don't gamble, play pachinko, drink excessively, or stay away for days without telling me. You don't keep other women. I don't have to live with a domineering and spiteful mother-in-law. From all these points of view, I have a good marriage. My friends envy me. They said Seiko-chan was the one who ran off with the golden prize, just as I won the school prize for best composition when everyone thought it would go to someone else. They said you don't need to be a beauty to win happiness — the beauties all become unhappy..."

"Stop it. I don't want to hear anymore."

"But I mean it. All things considered, I am not unhappy. Most marriages, after the first year, are not sexually happy, I know. So what if our sex life isn't ideal?"

"But can you stay married, knowing your husband is homo?"

"Of course. Why should anyone else find out about it? It'll be a secret just between us two. As long as you don't do anything that would scandalize us, keep your habits private and don't bother anyone, we can get along just fine."

"That would be a strange sort of marriage."

"I'm sure there've been stranger ones."

"I can't believe we're actually saying these things. It's like a dream or something."

"We're not living in the Meiji period anymore. And we're both open-minded people. So, why not?"

"But if I'm allowed to play around, you should be just as free."

"Me?" She looked surprised, and Fumio blushed.

"Yes. I mean, if your assistant professor still — "

"Oh no. It's all over between that man and me. I'm through with all that."

"But you're still so young. With your whole life ahead of you."

She shook her head.

"Listen, Seiko. If — " He started again. "If you ever feel you want to seek companionship outside the marriage, you should feel perfectly free to do so. I know you might get lonely... "

She didn't answer, merely looked straight ahead. But Fumio thought he detected a shiver go through her.

"I really mean it, Seiko."

She turned to look at him. "This really is a strange marriage. I'll bet there's no other couple in the world who have said the things we said to each other tonight."

"Maybe not."

"Above all, we mustn't let Father find out about this."

"Right."

"He's very, very old-fashioned and wouldn't understand the first thing about it."

"Yes, I know. The Japanese gentleman of the old school."

She hugged herself, making the swing's chains creak. "This feels like something in a novel, or out of a ladies' comic."

Fumio felt as if he were at the end of a long night's session of cramming for a test. His head ached slightly, and his eyeballs felt raw. He shut his eyes. There was a haunting, yearning ache in his soul now which he suddenly recognized as déja vu. He knew with a supreme certainty what Seiko would say next. He waited and waited for her to say it, for, as soon as she said it, it would be exactly as he'd expected. But she said nothing.

9

FUMIO PULLED the car into the shadows under the overhanging branches of a huge zelkova tree. The tree itself was on the other side of the wire fence against which he'd parked. It was about ten o'clock at night, and all was quiet.

"This is the park I was talking about," said Fumio, indicating the wide-open space beyond the fence.

"How do we get in?" asked Seiko.

"Follow me." He got out of the car and waited for Seiko to shut her door before locking up. Then they began walking up the narrow street which skirted the wire fence. About fifty meters on was a large thoroughfare, where they turned left and followed the line of the fence until it approached a pedestrian overpass.

"I know this place," said Seiko. "We're near a high school, aren't we?"

"Yes. The park entrance is just up ahead."

As they passed under the pedestrian overpass which linked the park to a high school across the street, Seiko glanced up and noticed some dark shadows huddled on the overpass. "Who are they?" she asked.

Fumio squinted in the direction she pointed. He could make out a couple of young men squatting beside tripods on which were mounted cameras aimed at a particularly dark section of the park. Attached to each camera was a huge zoom lens.

"Ah, they're stationed at their usual posts. Those are so-called photo snipers, with infra-red lenses attached to their zooms so they can photograph in the dark. They get their voyeuristic thrills by taking pictures of kissing couples, petting couples, even couples having sex. Later on, they can sell their sniper photos to magazines which specialize in these real-life peep shots."

"That's disgusting."

"I know." Fumio had often seen them creeping about in parks, sometimes quite openly, cradling their expensive cameras, eaten by the hunger to look, look, look, becoming one big eye in the darkness. For camera buffs, it was the handiest way to make some extra money; they didn't even need a model. And the more natural-looking their shots were, the more the voyeur-readers enjoyed them.

"Don't the couples know they're being watched?"

"Anyone who plans to use the park for sex had better assume that they'll be spied on. Some people might even get a thrill out of knowing they're being watched."

"Yuck!"

"Well, at least they know their privacy is assured — if their photos ever appear in a magazine, at least their eyes will be covered with a strip of black so that they won't be identified."

Fumio led her past the knee-high concrete barricades at the entrance to the park and took her arm as they stepped onto a paved bicycle path. A lone jogger, an older man wearing a sweatsuit, passed them from behind; just in front of them was a young girl walking her dog. All was quiet.

The path continued along the outfield perimeter of a baseball field now all lit up by floodlights. In contrast to the brightness of the field, the trees surrounding it were plunged into utter darkness. Scattered among the trees were some benches, toward which Fumio led Seiko. Arm-in-arm they walked beneath the trees. The darker shadows in the gloom were boys and girls, sitting on benches or standing up against the trees, locked in embraces. Some were kissing.

"Snuggle closer to me so they won't feel intimidated," Fumio whispered. He felt his wife's warm body press closer to him. When the kissing couples saw they were only another man and woman, they resumed what they were doing. If a lone walker, or a couple of males, had entered this grove, they probably would have broken apart at their approach. As it was, Seiko was able to get a thrill out of watching the unhidden intimacy of other couples. Fumio felt her excitement through their linked arms.

They found an untaken bench, and as they sat down, Seiko instinctively laid her head on Fumio's shoulder. Though it might appear she was snuggling contentedly against her lover, in fact she was avidly observing the surrounding scene.

"Oh, look at *them*," she whispered, barely able to keep the excitement from her voice. Fumio glanced at the spot indicated by her chin. A particularly lascivious-looking couple were leaning against a tree trunk, entwined in each other's arms. Their lips were glued tightly together, and they were gently gyrating their heads to make the kiss more stimulating. The boy's hand was up under the girl's sweater, and moving provocatively around. Seiko was barely able to suppress her embarrassed giggles. "It's just like an American movie."

Indeed the young couples out here tonight seemed to have lost their Japanese inhibitions, and were acting out everything they'd seen in foreign movies. One might not have guessed — because the darkness hid them — that they were Japanese at all. Fumio felt Seiko shiver with excitement. She put her lips close to his ear and whispered, "How can they be so openly passionate, in front of all these other people?"

"Well, for one thing, they expect the others to be too busy to notice."

"They're getting a thrill out of putting on a show, the exhibitionists. Come on, let's go. This is embarrassing."

"Don't you mean, rather, that you're getting horny from watching them?" She pinched him playfully, and he jumped up, pulling her after him. Soon they were out in the open again, walking along the bicycle path. Ahead of them, around a gentle bend, was the soccer field.

"It's a relief to get away from those steamy scenes," said Seiko, a little too heartily. "It doesn't seem right somehow, that they should get their pleasure from showing off, and we get ours from watching."

"What's wrong with that? There is an excitement in watching which is related to, but different from, the pleasure of actually doing it yourself."

"But it can get out of hand. I've even heard that there are many young men now who get more pleasure out of watching erotic videos than from having actual sex. I hope it's not true. It's a depressing thought for women."

Fumio wondered if voyeurism were an innately Japanese pleasure. Though he knew it was a universal trait, he was convinced that no other nation had refined it to as esoteric an art as Japan had. Perhaps it was the cramped closeness of Japanese living quarters, whose lack of privacy willy-nilly forced neighbors to become eavesdroppers or eye-witnesses to others' pleasures. So when the chance came to sneak away from other eyes, Japanese couples made the most of it. And because outward signs of affection such as public kissing were frowned upon, the least show of intimacy in the darkness of a park was enough to excite anyone watching. Perhaps when any sign of affection was hidden away and considered indecent, one wanted to peek, if only to confirm one's neighbor's humanity.

He thought of something Seiko had once told him. In Japan, whenever she took a bath in public, she always worried in the back of her mind about a man somewhere spying on her. Yet when she was in Hawaii, she'd worn the skimpiest bikini she could find. And in Europe, she'd seen Japanese women actually going topless on the beaches, simply because the European men didn't seem to get excited at seeing a woman's breasts. She'd been disgusted by the sight of Japanese businessmen there, in their sweaty business suits, ogling and taking pictures.

They had arrived at the area south of the soccer field where the trees were most thickly clustered. A little ways off the path was a public restroom, and in the darkness behind it, a tiny stone bench. Peering into the dark, Fumio descried the form of a young man sitting there alone. After they'd walked on a bit, he whispered to Seiko, "There was a young guy sitting on that bench behind the restroom. Did you see him?"

"I didn't even notice the restroom."

Fumio realized how different a gay man's eyes might be from other people's. He could see, eerily hovering in the protective shadows of the trees to their left, the furtive figures of some more men. "The next time we go around, make sure to look. This is the area I was telling you about, the gay cruising ground."

"This is exciting." It was Seiko who had asked Fumio to show her this place tonight. He'd been telling her about the gay scene in Tokyo, and she'd become fascinated by what she heard, especially about the promiscuity of the cruising scene. In fact, she became so intrigued that she begged him to take her to one so as to have firsthand evidence that such places actually existed. When they got to the end of the path they turned around and began slowly retracing their steps. This time Seiko looked more carefully, though without making it obvious. "I see him," she whispered. "What's he doing just sitting there?"

"He's waiting for someone to approach him."

"But who? I don't see anyone else around."

"No? Look carefully among those trees."

She turned her head and caught her breath. "I see them." Apparently her eyes were gradually adjusting to the dark, and coached by Fumio, she was learning where to look. "They're everywhere," she whispered. "I can't believe there are so many. And it's all so silent."

"As I told you, no words are exchanged. One of them will pretend to urinate against a tree, and another will approach him and pretend to do the same. They will examine each other in the faint light and if they are attracted to each other, one of them will walk away with a glance over his shoulder as a sign for the other to follow."

"Where do they go?"

"There are plenty of hidden dark places here in the park where they can have complete privacy. You'd be surprised."

"I can't believe it. Right here in this park. I've been here many times during the day. When I was in high school, we had track meets here, held by that high school across the park. Do people know what happens here?"

"Not many of them. There's plenty of graffiti in the men's room, so anyone who uses that restroom will know that gays come here at night. But most straight men are scared away by it. They probably feel threatened, as if they'll be attacked or something. That seems to be the straight man's biggest nightmare — being approached by a gay man. So the only men who come to this section of the park at night are gay men. Shh."

A couple of young men came walking side by side along the bicycle path from the opposite direction. As they passed, snatches of their conversation could be heard. It sounded innocuous enough. Seiko glanced over her shoulder at them. "Are those two boys gay?"

"No doubt about it."

"But they were discussing baseball."

"Only because we were near. As soon as we're out of earshot, they'll resume what they were discussing."

They were approaching the area near the baseball field again, where the heterosexual couples were. Fumio looked around and seeing no one about, quickly led her through a gap in the hedge which came alongside the path at this point. "This way."

The trees grew more sparsely here, but clusters of mulberry bushes planted especially thickly near the perimeter fence gave them plenty of protection. Just beyond the wire fence could be seen the homes surrounding the park. The windows of some of these were open, and lights could be seen inside, the steady cold white of fluorescent lamps, and the faint bluish flicker of television sets. At a particularly thick cluster of bushes, Fumio had Seiko kneel down. They were both wearing jeans so it was no problem to sit on the grass which was quite dry. "If anyone approaches us, we're a couple making out," he whispered.

"All right." Her voice sounded excited, and was trembling from her shivering.

"Can you see that narrow alleyway formed by the space between the wooden fence of the baseball field and the surrounding hedge?" He pointed.

"Yes."

"Sometimes men use that area. You can see everything that happens there from here."

"You've obviously been here before."

"Yes. But just to observe. The cruising scene is not for me. I'm squeamish about getting too intimate with a stranger."

"I see."

"I don't want you to think that I got my kicks as a voyeur. I just liked to come here to relax. You don't know what it's like to keep your true self hidden all the time; I think it builds up a lot of tension and stress in your system. Coming here at night, if only to know I was among other gays, relaxed a lot of that tension. At least I didn't feel I was all alone in the world."

"What sort of men come here? Why don't they go to the gay bars and pick up partners there?"

"Many reasons, I guess. Some don't want their identities known. In gay bars, you have to be pretty open. I imagine for some men, this is the only way they'll feel safe about having gay encounters — in the dark where their identity is never an issue. And others like the thrill of doing it out here, meeting unknown men, having quick sex, then going home to a wife and kids who have no idea where they've just been. There are no words exchanged, just a glance, a touch, a fondle, and then the real thing. It's usually over very quickly."

"How unromantic. I'm glad I — "

They froze at the sound of a twig cracking. It had come from behind them, about twenty meters off. Fumio put his finger to his lips. "Shh." He pulled Seiko closer to him and leaned in toward her as if kissing her. "Anyone watching us thinks we're a couple making out so passionately that we don't notice a thing around us. Can you see anything?"

"I think so. Yes, I can."

"What do you see?"

"A middle-aged man skulking among the bushes there."

"Good. Keep watching."

As Fumio slowly turned around so he could also see, he spotted a man who suddenly froze at the sight of them. There was a tension-filled moment before the man whirled around and walked rapidly off in the opposite direction. Seiko gripped Fumio's arm. "I'm scared. Who was that?"

"I don't know. But there's no need to be afraid. He might have just been a voyeur. Or he might have been a gay cruiser. In any case, he won't come this way again — he's more scared than we are."

"Let's go home."

"Wait."

They waited another ten minutes or so. Then Fumio said, "In any case, we should go back to the car and wait a little longer before trying again."

"All right. But I think I've seen enough to know you were telling me the truth."

They got to their feet, brushed the grass stems from their jeans and headed back to the bicycle path. Now that they were out in the open, Seiko seemed much more relaxed.

"Fumio-san... if you want to, you can go back there and watch... or whatever. I'll wait for you in the car."

Fumio looked at her and grinned. "No. As I told you, it's not my thing." He laughed aloud. "Since time began, there surely has never been another married couple like us."

"I'm sure there hasn't." Seiko laughed with him. "But I'm glad we're not like most people. They live such boringly normal lives. And their marriages are all lies. Most couples keep things from each other. At least we're honest."

"Not many women would put up with having a homo for a husband."

"Well, it might easily have been the other way around. What if I had been a lesbian?"

"Have you ever had lesbian feelings?"

"Well, when I was in high school I guess I had a crush on an older girl in school. But that's something a lot of girls go through before they become interested in boys."

"Who was she?"

"An upper-classman, a third-grader. She was a real athlete, a hundred-meter specialist on the track team. And fast — she even made it to the Metropolitan finals. When she lost, I cried my heart out."

"Was she very attractive?"

"Her hair was cut very short, like a boy's, and she had a very handsome face. It wasn't the kind of face most boys would like. But in an all-girl school like mine, girls like that are the recipients of crushes — you know, love letters and presents put in their shoe lockers. I sent an anonymous letter once but she never found out who sent it. I think she was sweet on another classmate of mine — but I'm sure it was all innocent, idealized and romantic. They even exchanged diaries and wore each other's rings."

"Oh, you'd be surprised. I think a lot of those so-called tender romances might have been real love. And some of them might have been requited."

"Maybe so. Things like kissing and hand-holding went on all the time. Now that I've grown up and can look back on those days

I suppose there was a strong undercurrent of sexuality in some of the friendships. Most girls my age at that time were actually afraid of boys and men — they seemed so dirty, hairy, and smelly. Like our fathers. We idealized the sexless, pretty boys, or the neuter girls."

"Do you ever fantasize about what might have happened if that *sempai* had returned your feelings?"

"I don't know. I might have been scared off."

"Or you might have been introduced to a whole wonderful new world."

"Oh no. I'm boringly heterosexual. I'm sure of it. For me, nothing can take the place of a man."

They'd reached the car. There was a soft drink machine nearby, from which they bought a can of coffee each. Sitting in the car, they took sips and gazed out at the darkness of the park.

"What sort of man was he?" asked Fumio suddenly. "The man whose child you conceived?"

For a moment Seiko appeared unwilling to answer. She continued gazing out toward the park. Finally she spoke. "He was an assistant professor at my university, a very intelligent and enthusiastic teacher. He wasn't what you'd call extremely handsome, but he had a voice I loved to listen to. I think I was mostly attracted to his intelligence, and his devotion to learning. He taught sociology. I found myself going more and more to his office to ask questions, first with my girl friends, and later, by myself. One time he asked me out for a cup of coffee afterwards, and things went deeper and deeper from there."

"Was he the first man in your life?"

"No." She hesitated. Then, laughing, she said, "This feels so strange... as if I'm talking with one of my girl friends, not my husband."

"You're right. If you don't want to tell me about it — "

"No, it's not that at all. It just seems odd that I would be talking like this to my husband. I feel as if I can tell you everything. I'm sure there's no other couple in Japan which talks as we are doing now."

"Probably not."

"In answer to your question, no, I was not a virgin when I met my sociology teacher."

"Then how did you lose your virginity?"

"It was when I was in high school. My friends and I used to go out to Shinjuku and Shibuya a lot. One time we met up with a group of boys with whom we took to going out regularly, all as a group thing. There was one boy in the group I particularly liked, and he sensed it. We continued to meet each other as part of the group, but gradually he started calling me at home a lot. One day we planned to meet each other in secret from the others, and that led to regular private dates. On our third date we ended up going to a love hotel in Kichijoji."

"Weren't you worried about what was going to happen?"

"No. I was desperate to lose my virginity. Among the girls in my group, it was almost a race to see who would lose hers first. A girl named Reiko was the first, and she told us all about it. After that, I suspected one or two of the others also lost theirs, but were hiding it for some reason. When I lost mine, I didn't tell anyone, either."

"How was it?"

"The first time? Oh, miserable, as I suspect most girls' first time is. He was completely inexperienced, and it was awful. He acted so unfeeling about it, only wanting to get it over with as quickly as possible."

"Most boys that age are just as desperate to lose their virginity as you were."

"Anyway, the experience soured me on sex for a long time. I didn't go out with him after that, though we continued to meet publicly as before."

"And then came the professor?"

"No. Next was my second experience, with a girl friend's older brother. This was when I was a freshman in college. I used to go over to her house quite often, and her brother would sometimes chat with us. He was so good-looking that I gradually came to look forward more to seeing him than his sister."

"What sort of boy was he?"

"He was tall, about 180 centimeters, with an athlete's build. He was on the university basketball team."

"Tell me more about his body — his chest, his shoulders, his back."

Seiko laughed. "Are you falling in love with him, Fumio-san? His chest was big and broad, and his back was well-muscled. His legs were long, and his hips slender."

"I like the way you describe him. He seems my type. Go on."

"We started seeing each other in secret. It was strange, because for some reason, he didn't want his sister to know we were going out together. And I, too, didn't want her to know. I don't know why. It seemed almost incestuous somehow for us to be meeting behind her back. But of course that only added to the thrill of our relationship. Whenever we met in their house, we had to act as if we were idle acquaintances... when in fact, we were already sexually intimate."

"It sounds like you were having fun. What went wrong?"

"Well, he wasn't what you'd call the sensitive type. When we started going out together, I quickly found out he was only interested in my body; the whole date was a prelude to the only thing he really wanted — the trip to the love hotel. After he got his pleasure, that was it."

"A typical college boy. You can't blame him, though — that's the way boys are at that age."

"True. It wasn't till I went out with an older man that I realized a woman could also enjoy sex."

"The assistant professor... "

"Yes. He was so much more relaxed and sensitive to my feelings than the others. Of course he'd had a lot more experience than them. It was he who opened everything up for me."

"He 'lit your fire', as they say in those trendy dramas."

Seiko lowered her face in embarrassment. Fumio cleared his throat. "What do you mean by 'sensitive to your feelings'?"

"The way he — well, I don't know if I should say this — "

"Go ahead. We're both adults here. And we're married, remember?"

"He used his hands to warm me up to it for a long time before the actual act. And the way he used his mouth. I didn't know such things could be done, but when he did it, it just seemed so natural a part of love-making."

"And how was the actual act?"

"Wonderful. The others — they lasted only a short time, going for their quick finish. He made it last."

"And how well was he... endowed?"

Seiko stifled a nervous giggle, then held her two index fingers apart before her.

"I see. So everything would have been perfect if only he hadn't been married."

"Yes."

"How did it feel, having an affair with a married man?"

"Not as thrilling as the trendy dramas make it appear. The only thing I really wanted was to be able to see him openly. You see, he promised me all along that he would eventually divorce his wife and marry me. In fact, though, as I now know, he was stringing me along all the time. He had no intention of separating from his wife. I found out later that his wife conceived another child during the time we were seeing each other. I took that as proof that he was only playing around with me."

"It's the old story. A married man is dealing from a position of strength in any affair like yours."

"I know. My friends told me the same thing from the start. But they didn't realize how much in love with him I was. In fact, I was truly in love for the first time in my life. And happy in every way, mentally as well as physically. I couldn't break it off if I tried, even though I knew it wouldn't end well, that I would only be hurt. It was like a drug. And I guess the fact that he was married gave him a taboo status that increased his desirability. You know, playing with fire and all that."

"But you had to break up when your parents found out about the abortion. Did you regret it afterwards? Did you want to see him again?"

"Well, I did see him again. Even — forgive me — after we were engaged. But we didn't get intimate. He said he wanted to continue seeing me. In fact he was begging. But I must have been tiring of him, because I could tell him coldly that it was all over. I think he took it much harder than me."

"And has he tried to contact you since we've married?"

"Yes, he's tried. But I refuse to see him."

"I think he's in love with you. If he wasn't before, he is now. Maybe the break-up increased your desirability in his eyes."

"I'm sure it has. Well, I'm a married woman now, in any case."

"Yes, but married on paper only. Remember... you always have my permission to — "

"I am not interested in seeing him anymore. That's all past now."

"But you're still so young and attractive. Don't you long for someone who can take his place — I mean, now that you know I can't?"

"Not especially."

"Isn't there anyone you're interested in at the moment? Even casually?"

"No."

"Well, as I said, you're always free to find someone. I'm sure there will be plenty of men attracted to you."

"It almost seems as if you're hoping I have an affair."

"Well, you told me I was free to pursue my pleasures outside our marriage. The same goes for you. If you like, you can even find another partner, as long as no one finds out about it."

"Anyone I like?"

"Of course. Though I'd be happy if he were someone I could approve of."

"You sound like my father about my boyfriends."

"I'm serious. When the time comes, please let me know. I'll let you know if I approve or disapprove of him."

She laughed. "Why don't you choose the man, so that we'll both be satisfied with the choice?"

"All right," mused Fumio, wondering how far to take it as a joke or a real suggestion. However, Seiko seemed to take it lightly enough. "Won't that be grand? I only ask that he be handsome."

"Don't worry. I wouldn't want you to have an affair with a man who wasn't. Somehow it would give me a bad taste. As a point of aesthetics, I myself would get more satisfaction from knowing you were in the arms of a handsome man."

"If he's too handsome, you might want him for yourself, though."

"If I choose him for you, I'll only pick someone that I couldn't have for myself."

"Just as long as we don't end up fighting over the same man. We have to be ethical about this. Fair play says you don't take my man, and I don't take yours."

"Deal."

Seiko laughed again. "You know, anyone listening to us would think we were deranged or something."

"Maybe we are," Fumio replied. "But if so, then that's the way I like it." He started up the car—it sounded loud in the silence. "Let's see. What movie is it we're supposed to have watched? So I can talk a little about it just in case your parents ask."

"Oh, they won't, don't worry. I know my parents. And Father will only hog you to himself so you can drink a nightcap together."

"He probably will."

As he steered toward the main thoroughfare, the road made a little turn so that the car's headlights swept smoothly through the park like vigilant searchlights. The trunks of the ranked trees looked like gray stone columns in an underwater grotto.

10

THAT NIGHT Fumio rushed straight home from work without stopping by the pub for his usual drink. He got back at 10:30, and from the cooking sounds coming from the kitchen, knew that Seiko was already home.

"I'm back," he called out.

"Welcome home." Wiping her hands on her apron, Seiko came straight from the kitchen to take his briefcase, then his suit jacket. "You're home early today," she said, with a touch of the artificial in her voice.

"How did everything go?" he asked her softly, searching her face for clues.

"Fine."

"What time did you get back?"

"Oh, about ten." She went upstairs to put away the jacket and briefcase as Fumio sat down at the kitchen table. Seiko's mother came in from the living room and opened the refrigerator to get him his beer.

"Oh, Mother, please. I'll do that."

"You just sit and relax. You must be tired."

Seiko came down again and went back to her cooking.

"What time did the concert end?" Fumio asked her, pulling off his tie.

"About nine. Afterwards, we went to have a cup of tea at a classical tea room nearby."

"You could have stayed longer, you know, Seiko. It isn't often you get a chance to go out with your girl friends since you got married."

"What are you talking about, Fumio-san?" said Yoshiko. "She already has too much freedom as it is. Look at her — preparing dinner for her husband at this time of night. Is that any way for a wife to act?"

"Mother... " he protested weakly.

"Someday she will have to bear the responsibility of raising a child. If you spoil her before the child is born, she'll never make a good wife and mother."

"That's just it, Mother. I want her to have as much freedom as possible before all the pressures and worries of raising a child."

"You're too kind to her, Fumio-san. But young people today are very different from when I was a young woman."

"Thank heaven I wasn't born back then," said Seiko, bringing the dinner to the table. Her mother was already pouring out the beer for Fumio.

After the meal, as Seiko went upstairs to prepare the bedding, Fumio went to take his bath. In the solitude of the bathroom, he was finally able to let his guard down. All through the meal he'd felt the pressure of having to put on an act before Seiko's mother,when he was dying to get Seiko alone to ask her about this evening. In the *juku* classroom his mind had been so far away that even his sixth-grade students had sensed it. Indeed, he couldn't keep his eyes off the clock. At seven o'clock the concert would start. Since the concert hall was a few minutes' walk from Nakano station, Seiko would probably be in front of the station by six forty-five. What was she wearing tonight? What was she feeling as she waited?

The students detected his uneasiness and were particularly unresponsive to his lesson tonight. Fumio gave them an assignment that would keep them busy so he would be free to pursue his thoughts. It was hard to believe that the phone call had come a mere three days ago; it loomed so largely in his imagination that it seemed a whole year had passed since then. He and Seiko had been getting ready for bed, and Seiko, sitting in front of her make-up mirror, had said casually, "Oh, you got a telephone call from Tatsuya-san today."

"Tatsuya? What time?"

"Eight o'clock in the evening."

"That's strange. He knows I work during the evening. Why would he call when he knows I'm at work?"

"I told him you were at work, and asked if he wanted to leave a message for you. One thing led to another, and we ended up talking for an hour. I hope you don't mind."

"Of course not. Why should I? And what did he want?"

"Well, he didn't have anything in particular to say. I think he just wanted to talk to you. He seemed a little upset at first, though he calmed down as we talked. He said he'd like to go out drinking with you again sometime."

"What did you two talk about?"

"Mostly music. He started out talking about that time we went to the karaoke box together. Then we started talking about various singers and entertainers. Oh, did you know he was once friends with Yasuda Manami?"

"Yes. Of course. I met her once or twice myself."

"Why didn't you tell me? Anyway, we got to talking about Manami. He knows so much about her that no one else does. The image she projects on TV is really so different from her real self... " The animated look on Seiko's face made her look like a young schoolgirl. It was difficult to believe she was a married woman of twenty-three.

"Does he still see her?" he asked, in what he hoped was a casual manner.

"No. But he is still friendly enough with her to be able to get free tickets to her concerts."

"I don't go for those cute-girl pop songs."

"I know. But I do. And Tatsuya-san... "

"Yes?"

"Well, he sort of invited me to go with him to a concert."

"Just the two of you?"

"I told him no, of course," she added hastily.

Fumio looked at her carefully before voicing his thought. "Doesn't it have all the elements of a secret tryst?"

"That's why I felt I should tell you." She looked at him worriedly.

"So what did you tell him? You declined his invitation?"

"Well, actually, I told him I didn't know. He urged me to think about it, and that if I felt it was wrong, not to go against my principles. For his part, he said there were really no underhand designs behind his invitation."

"I see."

"There's another thing." She blushed.

"What is it?"

"Well, he asked me if I was going to tell you about the invitation. I told him of course. Then I said, 'Shouldn't I?' And he said, 'Of course... but it's up to you.'"

"Meaning, of course, that you shouldn't."

"That's why I told him I'd think about it." She looked down.

A flicker of excitement rippled through Fumio. He thought: Tatsuya works fast. He's only met Seiko twice and already he has the confidence of having made a conquest... which he might have, at that. Fumio had given Seiko permission to see other men with just this hope in mind: that she and Tatsuya would become friendly with each other.

"Do you want to go?" he asked.

"Well, if you let me. He's your best friend, after all."

Before Fumio's mind's eye, a scenario of unbelievable depravity suddenly unfolded: he imagined Seiko in Tatsuya's arms... and found he liked it.

"Tatsuya was a real ladies' man back then," he said absently. "He made a lot of girls cry. It's dangerous for me to let you go. You realize that. If you agree to see him, you're virtually giving him the go-ahead to try his luck with you. And he's very good at what he does."

"If that's all he's after, maybe I should turn him down."

"Do you find him attractive?"

She looked down and didn't answer. Fumio knew the answer already from the way her eyes sought something to focus on.

"He's your type, isn't he?" he said quietly. "I know you like those wickedly handsome smooth talkers. Come on, tell me the truth. You can tell me."

She looked up. "Yes. I think he's very attractive."

Fumio had known it all along. It was just a confirmation of what he'd felt in his heart from the first. And he wondered if he'd subconsciously hatched the scenario from the first, too. His ability to create evil frightened him. He looked at her. "Go ahead and tell him yes."

He thought he detected a shiver go through her body. If so, it was a twin to the one racing through his own. "And tell him you didn't ask me about it."

She looked startled. "You mean to say — "

"If you're going to have an affair, it may as well be with someone I know. And I approve of Tatsuya."

She stared at him for a long time. "How can you be so calm about it?"

"Because I think maybe things would have turned out like this anyway, eventually. From the first time I saw you two together, I could tell you felt something for him."

She looked abashed, so he quickly added:

"Go ahead and see the concert. Have a good time. And if things turn out that way, let them. If not, there's nothing lost. But I know Tatsuya, and I know he was attracted to you."

"But I'm a married woman. And there are so many single women out there who would gladly go out with him."

"He has a taste for forbidden fruit. The usual things bore him. He told me himself that a married woman is the tastiest treat — there's the least danger of her pushing for a deeper commitment. A married woman who plays around is usually only doing it for pleasure. And you'd be surprised how many wives play around."

"What made him think I'm that type?"

"You're an attractive woman and he fell for you... that's all there is to it. Tatsuya is used to getting what he wants. But let me warn you, he doesn't stay with one woman long. He's a promiscuous sort. For all I know, he has several other women looking after him. Don't lose your heart to him — accept it as playing around... for fun... not a serious thing. That way you won't get too hurt when the break-up comes."

"That makes it all the easier for me to treat it lightly as an affair."

"That's the spirit. Don't let your emotions get the upper hand."

"Aren't you jealous, Fumio?"

"Of course not. As I told you before, you're free to play around. It's only fair."

"No, I mean the other way. I suspect Tatsuya-san is your type."

He looked at her, stunned. It took a moment for him to find his voice. "You're right," he whispered weakly. "He is."

"The athlete type with a handsome face. Tanned..." He and Seiko had been browsing through some gay magazines just the evening before, making comments about the pin-up boys' faces and bodies, and comparing favorites, when Seiko had suddenly asked him:

"What type of men interest you, Fumio-san?"

"Young men. Athletes. Well built."

"Isn't that what all gay men desire?"

"Actually, no. You'd be surprised. Most gay men have only certain types they're after. Some like older men, father figures. Others want a younger brother, an effeminate Johnny's Club type. And believe it or not, there are some who prefer fat men. There's even a magazine aimed at their tastes, *Samson.* They probably got their first sexual urges watching sumo wrestlers on TV."

"I can understand that. Some of the sumo *rikishi* are incredibly good-looking, well built and sexy."

"I agree. As for me, I didn't recognize that I was attracted to men until very late, but thinking back on my schooldays, I can see now that I was excited by seeing virile athletes at their sports, men who gave off a strong smell of masculinity."

Now Seiko was repeating softly, "Just your type... I think I begin to see the picture. Fumio-san, what were your feelings about Tatsuya-san? I suspect they weren't what most boys would feel for a friend."

For a moment Fumio had felt an instinctive panic at being discovered. But this was soon overshadowed by the feeling of trust engendered by his many recent disclosures to Seiko. Indeed, he was beginning to feel more and more that there was nothing he needed to hide from her anymore. "You're right. I was completely infatuated with him. Head over heels in love."

She looked at him in sympathy. "That must have been terribly awkward for you. Did he ever suspect your true feelings?"

Here, Fumio balked at telling the whole truth. He thought of his humiliating confession to Mayumi and what it had cost him, and felt he had to draw the line somewhere. "No. He didn't have the faintest idea, as far as I know."

"I see." A faraway look came into Seiko's eyes. "So in effect, I'm an emissary sent to make love with Tatsuya, in your place. To make up for the impossibility of ever having him for yourself."

"If you want to view it like that, fine. Because I will get a vicarious pleasure out of knowing he held you in his arms. The vision is most definitely enticing. So you needn't feel any qualms in that regard. You will have my utmost blessing in this enterprise."

"It feels strange to be actually urged by your own husband to have an affair. And with his best friend. My friends would never believe me if I told them this was happening. They'd think it was something out of an erotic novel. Something they could only fantasize about. And yet it's really happening to me."

"Just call it love in modern Tokyo."

She laughed...

Now, as he sat soaking in the tub, Fumio began calculating. If Seiko and Tatsuya had actually gone to the concert, there would have been no time for them to do anything afterwards. But, if Tatsuya had arrived with an excuse — that the tickets had not come through, for instance — anything could have happened in the three hours they'd been together. From the look on his wife's face this evening, it didn't appear that she was hiding anything. But he knew she was capable of the most complete discretion. In any case, he would know in a few minutes how everything had gone.

Suddenly, he heard the glass door of the bathroom slide open slowly.

"Is that you, Seiko?"

"It's me," whispered the voice of the professor. He tiptoed in wearing his *yukata.*

"Welcome home, sir. You're home a little early tonight." Fumio had been so engrossed in his thoughts that he hadn't even heard the professor come home.

"The radio talk show was canceled because of a damned baseball game. Would you like me to wash your back?"

"Of course, sir. I'd be honored."

Fumio got out of the tub and sat on the pink plastic bath stool, as the older man hiked his *yukata* up around his hips and squatted down, dipping a washcloth into a water-filled basin and scrubbing soap onto it. With a slight grunt, Akiyoshi began vigorously scrubbing his son-in-law's back.

"How does that feel, Fumio-kun?"

"Wonderful, sir."

"Are you and Seiko getting along quite well?"

"Couldn't be better."

"I'm glad to hear that. She seems happy enough. It's clear that you two get along so well together. You're making my fondest dreams come true."

"Seiko-san is the perfect wife for me. I doubt if I would have met anyone who is more understanding."

"So... might we expect our child soon, then?"

"I'm leaving that up to the gods, sir. Whatever happens will happen."

"You're so old-fashioned in some ways, Fumi-chan."

"Perhaps so."

"I trust you are the man of the house when you two are alone. If you know what I mean... "

Fumio flushed. Pretending to misunderstand the older man's insinuation, he stated blankly, "We don't have those old-fashioned ideas about male superiority. In fact, we see each other as equals."

The professor tisked. "Young women nowadays... how can a man put up with them?" His scrubbing slowed to a halt. In a conspiratorial whisper, he asked, "You aren't finding any pleasures outside the marriage bed, I trust?"

"Of course not."

"Good. Because if you were, I might be very jealous... "

Fumio didn't like the course the talk was taking, so he fell silent. But when he felt the touch of a bare hand on his chest, he lightly slapped it away. Without a word, the older man went on scrubbing and scrubbing the younger man's smooth muscled back as if nothing had happened.

Shortly afterwards, Fumio was sitting upstairs alone watching TV, waiting for Seiko to finish up with the dishes and join him. But when he heard her coming up the stairs, then slide open the door, he didn't have the courage to look her in the face. He pretended to be absorbed in the baseball game. As if nothing were out of the ordinary, she sat before her make-up mirror and began preparing for bed.

"How was the bath?" she asked.

"Wonderful. Sensei was kind enough to wash my back for me."

"Oh?" She began rubbing cold cream onto her face, spreading it out in an even film, then briskly massaging her facial muscles with circular motions of her fingertips. She went about it all with such a practiced, absorbed air that Fumio found the performance quite fascinating to watch. He was surprised that she didn't want to tell him immediately about what had happened tonight with Tatsuya. Though he was dying to ask her, he somehow felt it would be unseemly for him to betray his eagerness to hear all the details. After all, even though he had virtually pushed her into it, it was her private affair. And he did have his own pride to think of. A small part of him — the traditional part — told him that his wife's betrayal of him constituted a desecration of his masculine rights. But still another part delighted in his symbolic emasculation. For if a wife was a man's castle, a man's property, then Tatsuya's free use of Seiko constituted an invasion of Fumio's most sacrosanct rights. It meant nothing less than that Fumio himself had been violated.

He felt a weakness in the pit of his stomach, the same feeling of vulnerability he'd experienced that night in the apartment when Tatsuya had gently but firmly pushed apart his thighs...

Unable to restrain himself anymore, he asked as casually as he could: "Well? How did everything turn out?"

She stopped massaging her face and picked up a cotton swab from the box beside her. After dabbing at her face a little, she paused to look straight at him in the mirror's reflection. "He was a gentleman, you may rest assured. We just saw the concert and had a cup of tea afterwards, as I said. He said he was busy today. But he did ask me to see him again sometime."

"And what did you tell him?"

"I said it might be possible."

"Don't be too discouraging. He has plenty of other girls he can turn to if you play hard to get."

She giggled. "Honestly, you sound just like one of my girl friends. Don't worry. He sincerely seemed to want to see me again."

"Just don't get overconfident. He's broken many girls' hearts in his time."

She laughed aloud this time. "Actually, I was relieved that it all turned out to be so innocent. My heart was pounding like crazy at the thought of what might happen. But after the concert started, it began to seem as if all the things you and I were saying the other night were nonsense. Maybe he did just want to see the concert with someone who liked the same kind of music."

Fumio felt irritated at her carefree attitude. "Didn't he make any suggestive remarks, any hints that he was interested in you as a woman?"

"No, silly. It was all above board. Anyone seeing us might have thought we were a couple of college classmates."

"What were you wearing? Did you make yourself up attractively?"

"Only my usual going-out fashion. I'm not going to make myself look like a vamp or something — how would that look? Do you want him to think I'm throwing myself at him?"

"No, of course not."

Seiko continued dabbing at her face with the cotton swab. "He was with his friend's wife, after all. It wasn't as if I were an OL or a schoolgirl he picked up. But I could sense the vibrations there. We women know these things. We might have been gabbing about pop music, but the tension was there just the same."

"Still, I'm a little surprised that he's playing it so carefully. He's usually not so subtle. This isn't like him — he usually goes for the jugular on the first date. It shows he's playing it carefully. Or that he really likes you. But you can be sure that he'll be a little bolder on the next date."

Seiko tossed away the swab and picked up her hairbrush. As she began brushing out her hair, she mused absently, "How can he be so bold about dating his best friend's wife behind his back? I mean, it's as if he feels no fear at all, no bad conscience about violating the most sacred rules. What gives him the gall? Do you think he has such a low opinion of my chastity? Do I look like such an easy conquest?"

Fumio felt a sudden remorse at his wife's innocent self-reproach. For he knew the true reason behind Tatsuya's cocksure attitude. "Seiko... it's not that he has such a low opinion of your faithfulness. It's something else." He took a deep breath before going on. "Seiko... he knows."

"Knows what?"

"He knows I'm a homo."

She turned around to stare at him. "He does?"

"Yes. That's why he's so bold in his pursuit of you. He must know you get no sexual satisfaction at home."

"But how did he find out about you?"

"Well, after all, we were room-mates. It's hard to hide something like that when you're living together."

"And that's why your friendship broke up?"

"Yes. Like most straight men, he's not comfortable being around a gay man. He just disappeared from my life until that night I came home to find him here."

"But why did he return, then?"

"I don't know. I'm still trying to figure it out myself. The charitable thing is to suggest that he forgives me, or that he came to realize how unjust his condemnation of me was. But to tell you the truth, he's not the type to be charitable. My hunch is that he wants the connections Father is able to get for him in the entertainment world. After all, he still hasn't given up his dream of becoming a star. I think that's also another reason why he wants to have an affair with you. Maybe he wants to make doubly sure of his access to the professor."

"Maybe he wants to steal me away from you — cause our break-up, then marry me afterwards."

Fumio felt a chill go through him. He knew Tatsuya would not be above doing such a thing. "Anything's possible. Or it might be something completely different. Who knows? Maybe he's after a lot more than we think."

"This is scary. I don't know if we should be playing with fire like this. It could get a lot more dangerous. Maybe we should stop it before it's too late."

For Fumio, it was just this dangerous aspect of their game which made it so seductive... like the lure of taking the plunge into bottomless depths when one is inching closer and closer to the edge of the cliff. The closer to danger he was pushed, the more he liked it. "As for me," he said, "whatever his reasons, I'm just happy that he even returned to my life. And though he might only be using our friendship to get what he wants, still I'm happy that I can see him every now and then."

"He is attractive, isn't he? Almost irresistible."

"Yes. And since I can't have him, I want you to."

She put away her make-up gear and started gathering her bathing things together. "So you want me to pursue this affair?"

"Of course. As long as no one finds out about it. As long as I'm supposedly in the dark about it."

"It might be more difficult from now on. Mother was just telling me that I shouldn't be going out so much on my own. She says it doesn't look good for you."

"Don't worry about Mother, I'll take care of her. I'll tell her about cases where dissatisfied women separated from their husbands because of their lack of freedom. I don't care if she sees me as the milksop. Whatever works for us."

Fumio felt the delicious thrill of being a co-conspirator once again. He watched as Seiko put her hair up in back and secured it with a dark blue plastic barrette. The nape of her neck looked so slender and white, and so seductive, that he felt he could understand why any man would find her desirable.

11

AS USUAL, Sunday night's television fare was quite meager. Seiko's mother eagerly looked forward each week to the regular historical drama on NHK, and the younger couple usually watched it along with her, good-naturedly laughing at the professor's acrid comments about the inaccuracies in the production. Tonight, however, only Fumio and his mother-in-law were watching TV. Fumio had never been interested in Japanese history, so he couldn't understand the popularity of this program. Normally he let his mind go pleasantly blank, only keeping alert enough to make the appropriate comments to any remarks which might be made. Tonight, Yoshiko herself didn't seem to be able to lose herself in the drama. She was taking nervous sips from her tea and glancing up at the clock.

"I wonder how Father's dinner is going," she said.

"I'm sure everything is going fine," replied Fumio soothingly. He, too, had noticed that the professor was beginning to spend more and more of his evenings out. Guiltily, he wondered if the older man had returned to his familiar haunts in Shinjuku's 2-chome, driven there by Fumio's coldness. It was true that Akiyoshi had promised not to press Fumio for intimacies, claiming that he didn't need them anymore, but one couldn't help but wonder if the older man hadn't been putting on a brave front, hiding his true feelings for his son-in-law's sake. This must have been how things were here when the professor was spending so much time in gay host clubs, and later, at the apartment he'd obtained for his young protégé.

"Sensei is quite busy, and getting busier. He told me that the producers of a new talk show on Fuji TV are sending out feelers in his direction."

"It must be nice to feel so wanted." She focussed her attention again on the drama. The scene showing political intrigues in the Shogun's court had given way to a private chamber in the castle where the romantic moments of the hero were usually centered.

The telephone rang, and Fumio jumped. He'd been waiting all evening for it. Being the one nearer to the phone, he picked it up.

"Hello."

"Hello? Fumio-san? This is Seiko."

"Oh. How's it going?" He nodded to his mother-in-law to indicate the call was for him.

"Wonderful. It looks like I might be a little late coming home tonight, though. Etsuko drank a little too much and is feeling the effects of the alcohol, but she still insists she wants to attend the second party. We're going to a karaoke pub. It looks like I'll be able to sing finally."

"That's fine. Have a good time and be careful coming home. And say hello to your friends."

"I will. Bye."

He hung up the phone, his heart pounding.

"Was it Seiko?"

"Yes. She says she's going to be a little late tonight. They're going to a disco and maybe later to a karaoke pub."

It was understood that Seiko was celebrating her girl friend Etsuko's birthday tonight with some other friends from college, with a second party afterwards at a disco.

"Fumio-san, you're really spoiling Seiko. She should be treated more severely, the old-fashioned way. I can't believe you don't mind her not making your dinner every night."

"Well, she doesn't get much chance to go out since we married, and I feel it's only fair. I was afraid she'd be bored in the role of a housewife. Besides, it's her friend's birthday. Etsuko-san hasn't been able to meet Seiko since we got married. They were best friends in college."

"And you don't mind her going out like this?"

"No, not at all. She already told me about it, Mother. I gave her my permission already."

"Well, if it's all right with you... " she said, yielding but looking a little disgruntled about it.

He went back to watching TV but was too excited to concentrate at all. *It looks like I might be able to sing...* That had been their secret signal indicating that the clandestine couple were going to a hotel. He glanced at the clock. She'd probably called from the disco just after Tatsuya had made the suggestion. Fumio had heard the music in the background. Everything was going as planned. Tatsuya had invited her over the phone a couple days ago to go out dancing with him. When Seiko had said it might be difficult to get permission to do so, he'd said, "Tell him some girl friends invited you out." She'd known then that he intended to make his move on this second date. From the moment Fumio had been told about it, he prayed feverishly for the tryst to succeed. Together, they planned out the strategy for the night...

Fumio now felt like a playwright who has written a masterful drama, but has to stay home on opening night. He only wished he could be kept informed about it every little step of the way. All through dinner he'd imagined the attractive young couple dancing with each other. Seiko had worn a relatively demure dress when she'd left the house, but Fumio had made sure she'd had a more daring skin-tight body-conscious dress secreted in her handbag. She could always change into it — as many girls did, who were too modest to be seen on the trains in the sexy clothes they wore on the dance floor — in a public restroom near the disco or in the stairwell of an adjacent building.

The thought of his wife dancing opposite the young man he loved had made him a little feverish. Now, as he imagined the couple leaving the disco — perhaps arm in arm — he had to put his hand over his eyes. Perhaps he really did have a temperature. At the mental picture of Seiko walking along in her sexy disco dress and high heels, Fumio experienced the curious desire to be merged into her body. He estimated how long it would take to get to the hotel. Was it within walking distance, or were they getting into Tatsuya's car?

Vaguely he listened to his mother-in-law complaining about Seiko's selfishness: "Ever since she was a young girl, she's had her way. When she was in kindergarten she was the only one who... "

The nearest love hotel. Fumio pictured them entering, checking in, getting the key, taking the elevator up to their room. Once in the room, Seiko would feel so nervous that she would try to hide it by her chatter. Or perhaps there was no chatter at all; as soon as they were in the door, Tatsuya had drawn Seiko to him, blotting out any thoughts from her mind with the warmth of his kiss. Once they kissed, everything else would follow predictably. He imagined Tatsuya would invite Seiko to take a shower first, then wait in bed as she took it. He might even undress as soon as she was in the bathroom. He would be waiting confidently under the sheets, perhaps smoking one of his Egyptian cigarettes held languidly in his fingers, so sexy, so assured of himself. And Seiko would come out of the shower, her hair wet, the hotel towel around her middle, with Tatsuya watching her with those eyes of his slightly lowered.

Would Seiko play shy, as some girls did, or would she boldly romp over to the bed? After she was sitting on the bed and had been talking with him for a while, he'd casually put his hand to her hair, stroke it, tell her how beautiful she was. Fumio could feel Seiko's excitement at the sound of his voice...

On TV, the historical drama had ended with the thundering sound of horses' hooves pounding toward a gathering battle. 'TO BE CONTINUED' flashed on the screen, and the previews for next week's showing came on, followed by the news and a weather report. Yoshiko rattled the newspaper as she searched the television program schedule on the back page.

"There's really nothing good on tonight," she murmured, peering through her thick-lensed reading glasses. As she looked up at Fumio, they slipped down the bridge of her nose to rest comically low. "Is there anything in particular you wish to see?"

"Is the movie any good?"

"It sounds like an American action movie. A police story."

"I'll pass on that. How about a music program?"

"There's a pop song show on." She picked up the remote control and pressed the channel button. The screen blinked to a colorful backdrop before which pop stars, as each was introduced, came running down a sort of ramp. For a moment, Fumio thought he recognized Yasuda Manami in the line-up, but a closer look proved he was mistaken. The pop singers all looked the same these days, with their over-done hairstyles and exotic, ethnic costumes. It would have been too much to have to watch Mayumi just as Seiko was making love with Tatsuya. He'd seen her several times on TV and had never failed to be amazed at the contrast between what he saw and the memories he'd had of her. Before the cameras, she was quiet, and rarely spoke, giving off a shy, demure image — nothing like the brash, confident, talkative girl he'd known. No doubt her production company had drilled her not to speak, as an inadvertent slip might make her seem more interesting than the bland cute-girl image they'd manufactured for her. She was known for her beautiful smile more than anything else.

"That isn't the singer whose concert Seiko went to the other day, is it?"

"No, Mother."

Yoshiko had made the same mistake. "Well, they all look the same to me... "

As the first singer began singing, Fumio let his mind return to the hotel room. He wondered if Seiko would have the courage to go through with it tonight. Her voice had sounded a little nervous over the phone. What if she changed her mind and declined Tatsuya's invitation at the last minute? Or, even if she was persuaded to go to the hotel, was unable to take the final step? As excited as she'd been when they'd planned it all, Fumio knew it would be difficult for her to actually allow herself to do it. Tatsuya might think she was playing shy, or 'hard to get'. As he drew her to him, she would begin to shiver from real nervousness and cling to him for support. His hand would reach for the zipper and slowly pull it down, the material of the dress sliding apart to reveal her warm flesh beneath... the smooth skin his fingers lightly began to caress...

Tatsuya, of course, was an expert at undressing women. He'd told Fumio many times of the techniques he used... and of how the woman's resistance dissolved at the gradual disrobing. Seiko would prove no different from the dozens of other women who had succumbed to Tatsuya's charms. And as for Tatsuya, Fumio knew his tastes: he would not be disappointed at what he saw beneath Seiko's dress. Perhaps he would be undressing himself at the same time to calm her nervousness, to melt her modesty. Fumio could almost see his body as it was gradually disclosed to Seiko's eyes: the upper torso as the t-shirt was pulled away, exposing the well-muscled chest and shoulders, the barley-colored skin tanned a deep tone, the nipples a darker brown, the underarm hairs peeping out black from the armpit. And as the briefs were pulled down, the strip of white about the hips where the sun had been unable to tan him...

"Fumio-san, are you all right?"

"Yes, Mother. I'm fine. Just a little tired, maybe."

"Should I get you something to drink?"

"No, really, it's quite all right."

She got up anyway, and bustled about in the kitchen, coming back in a moment with a glass of cold oolong tea.

"Thank you."

She looked at him a little worriedly before returning her attention to the TV show. A boy singing group from Johnny's Club was on, and the screams of the teenaged girls sounded like the whining of a jet coming in for a landing. Fumio glanced at the clock again. At this exact moment, his wife was in a hotel room with Tatsuya, perhaps being held in his arms. They might even be naked atop the crisp white sheets, he pressing his body against hers, making her feel the warmth of it, the hardness of his muscles, and smell his cologne, exactly as Fumio remembered it from that one night he'd slept with him. And once again Fumio was overcome by the confident masculinity of Tatsuya, the ease with which he made all his moves... and he could all but see the abandoned cigarette smoking in the ashtray, feel the salty taste of his lips on hers.

Fumio felt dizzy. "Maybe I do have a little headache... "

"Are you all right?"

"I'll be fine. Maybe if I go upstairs and lie down."

Worriedly, she watched him get to his feet. "Take care, Fumio-san."

"I will. If you'll excuse me, Mother."

He went upstairs feeling like a thief and slid the door shut behind him. For a long moment he just stood there in the dark, waiting for his excitement to die down. He couldn't help but picture how Seiko's face always looked during sex — and contrasting it with how Tatsuya's looked then: cool, calm, unemotional. With fingers that trembled, he undid the sash of his *yukata*, shrugged his way out of the kimono, and felt it slip down his body to the floor. As he closed his eyes, the better to enter the dark cavern of his imagination, he slowly dropped down to his knees like a penitent before some holy shrine.

From his futon Fumio heard the sound of a taxi cab pulling up before the house. He turned his head to read the clock. It was 2:30. All was quiet outside. Though he knew he must have drifted asleep, in fact it felt as if he hadn't slept at all. His mind was still feverish and his stomach all cramped up, as if nervous about a coming sexual encounter. The sound of the front door opening downstairs was stealthy — but not quiet enough to escape the ears of Seiko's mother, who had apparently gotten up and met her daughter at the door. Fumio could hear the sounds of their low voices but not what was said.

Finally Seiko's footsteps came up the stairs and the door slid open. The lights were out except for a small night lamp beside Fumio's pillow. He stirred, pretending to be awakened.

"I'm sorry to wake you," she whispered.

"It's all right."

"Mother said you felt unwell."

"It's nothing. Just tired."

Now that the moment had come, he didn't know how he should play it: the worldly husband blasé about their open marriage, the solicitous partner anxious not to hurt her delicate feelings, or the lascivious lecher eager to hear the juicy details.

Seiko clicked on the room light, went straight to the make-up table and began taking off her earrings and necklace. Before the mirror she always became self-absorbed, even with Fumio in the room. It was her one place of communion, of solitude, where she could successfully shut out the whole world as her eyes gazed at the image of the woman she presented to the world.

Fumio waited. She slipped off her blouse and began applying cold cream to her face to take off the make-up. The pale pink of her bra straps glowed in stark contrast to the dark tan she'd gotten on the beaches of Hawaii, on their honeymoon. Fumio couldn't wait anymore. "How did everything go?" he whispered hoarsely.

"All right." She didn't seem to want to talk about it.

"You went to the disco?"

"Yes."

"And afterwards?"

"A hotel."

"I see." He waited for her to talk. She continued taking off her make-up with vigorous wipes of the tissues. Faint wafts of her perfume came his way. She was always at her most attractive and seductive before the make-up mirror. When all her make-up was off, her face looked so much younger; she could have passed for a high school girl.

Noticing his continuing regard, she made a gesture of girlish modesty. "Don't stare at me so." He turned his back to her and heard her undressing behind him. She'd sometimes evinced a shyness about undressing before him, even after long intimacy, but tonight's modesty seemed somehow different. As if, because she'd been held by another man, Fumio had necessarily relinquished some of his husband's rights. He was no longer allowed to gaze upon her nudity. For Fumio, this humiliation was tinged with erotic submission: after all, it was Tatsuya who had forced him into this subservient crouch.

He heard her put on her nightgown and slip into her futon. Apparently she didn't intend to talk about what had happened tonight. Fumio thought of the long night he'd spent imagining her every move: now she's undressing... now she's in his arms... and now they're.... He'd been with them in spirit — had even shared their ecstasy.

"Seiko," he said, his voice trembling. "Tell me what happened, please." He was still looking away from her.

She sighed lightly before speaking. "We went to a love hotel. We had sex."

The casual way she said it made the bottom drop out of Fumio's stomach. "And was it good?"

"Yes. He is a good lover. An experienced lover."

"Better than your assistant professor?"

"Tatsuya was the best. Ever."

Fumio felt a thrill go through him. It excited him to hear his friend's name on his wife's lips, those lips still fresh from kissing the boy he loved. He turned to her eagerly.

"And has he kept his body in shape?"

Seiko was gazing up at the ceiling as if still seeing Tatsuya's face and body. In a far-off voice she said, "He lifted me easily in his arms."

"How romantic," he said, without irony.

She shook her head. "He wasn't what I'd call a tender lover. He's too assured of his own prowess. He seems to think that the woman should be grateful at his condescending to sleep with her. And I'll bet many women actually *are* grateful."

This observation gave Fumio untold satisfaction. He liked to think of his beloved as a cold-hearted, selfish beast in bed. "He's had countless women," he said, as if bragging about a coddled son. "So many that I don't think he even remembers most of them. I remember walking with him in Shibuya, and during an hour's time, three different women greeted him on the street — and he confessed to me later that he couldn't remember where he'd met any of them."

She laughed. "The typical playboy. I can see why they fall for him, though. If he had been my first lover, I would have been head over heels in love with him. But I don't think he's the kind of man I'd want as a lover. For someone to play with, he's ideal. After he's had his fun with me, though, he'll go to another woman, I know. He isn't the kind to stay with one woman for long. I feel sorry for the girl who falls in love with him. She's in for a heartache."

This sort of talk excited Fumio. Just talking about his hero was enough to make him happy. And hearing him described from a woman's point of view — seeing Tatsuya through different eyes — was stimulating. He had once wanted to become a woman just so he could approach his hero. Now, in a manner of speaking, that dream had come true. During the hours he'd waited for Seiko tonight, he'd become Seiko, had accepted Tatsuya's caresses and kisses.

"I know his type," she went on. "Always looking to pick up a new girl — new blood. Why are some men like that? As if they need constant new stimulation, new challenges..."

"Maybe you'll be the one to put a stop to all that."

"Oh no. In fact he was quite blunt about his view of me. He didn't come on with any of that romantic patter about loving me forever. He said he saw me as a sexy woman and wanted my body from the moment he first set eyes on it. He says when he is attracted to a woman, he needs to know how her body looks under her clothes — her breasts, her hips, her sex. And how she reacts to his caresses. He says every woman feels different on his skin — in temperature, texture, and tactility."

"And what did he say about you?"

She giggled. "He called me a thoroughbred. I had to keep myself from laughing, though I admit I was secretly pleased. I think my desirability for him is enhanced by knowing that my father is famous."

"You would be attractive no matter who your father was," Fumio said sincerely. Never before had his wife looked so attractive as she did at this moment. For the first time since he'd met her, he felt a powerful desire for her. He was glad of the futon covering him. The thought came to him that she was his wife — that it would be natural for him to slip into her futon and satisfy his desire. But he knew that this desire had been aroused by Tatsuya. He only wanted her because she was now filled with Tatsuya's essence. If he were to touch Seiko's skin, he'd be touching skin that had touched Tatsuya's. She might have showered after the sex, but something secret would still remain. He ached to reach out and touch her softly, if only to brush this magical essence. But something prevented him. For if he were to touch her, that talismanic medium would be destroyed in an instant. He had to preserve her inviolability as the sacred vessel in which Tatsuya's being was preserved, as a living urn.

With a start, he realized that his thinking was gradually becoming more primitive. He had regressed to the point where he actually accepted the belief that a human body was very much more than mere bones, tissue, and blood... was, indeed, the embodiment of certain natural forces hitherto reserved only for the gods.

"I feel like a spy," said Seiko, "a sexual spy. He has no idea that you know about this affair — that you engineered it, even. When I was in bed with him, I kept imagining you there, watching over us, gloating... And it made my pleasure that much more intense. I've never gotten that aroused before — never. The illicitness of it all was too much for me. I think he was surprised at my response."

"Oh?" Fumio's throat felt dry.

"I felt like a woman for the first time. Not a girl, but a woman. An actress, even. I really felt as if I were doing it before an audience. I did things I've never done before. Afterwards, I felt ashamed, even."

"Ashamed?"

As if the word had cast a sudden shadow over her previous excitement, Seiko now spoke in a more serious voice. "Fumio-san, I don't know if what we're doing is right. While it was happening, I didn't stop to think about it. But on the taxi ride home, I started to have my doubts. Should we be doing this?"

"Why not? You shouldn't feel guilty about it. You have my permission, my blessing even. I want you to enjoy it. Why shouldn't there be marriages like ours? Both partners in a marriage should be able to decide what kind of relationship they will have."

"I know, but — "

"Maybe you feel bad because it was so pleasurable. You're trained to think that any pleasure must be paid for. Take it as it comes. We might all be dead tomorrow. Why live with regrets?"

"How about you, Fumio-san? Why should I be the only one to get something out of it?"

"I am. I get pleasure from hearing about it." A sudden thought flashed through him. Here he was getting vicarious pleasure again from viewing others at their pleasure. Things hadn't changed at all from the time he was a poor student peeping in on Tatsuya next door. Was that his lot in life, to be the envious spectator, always on the outside looking in?

"Seiko, you know I'm in love with Tatsuya. And I feel if I can't have him, then the next best thing is to let you have him. I get a pleasure, too, knowing you're in his arms. I wouldn't want any other woman in his arms but you."

"Still — "

"Don't you see, Seiko? Your pleasure is my pleasure."

She opened her mouth to answer, but nothing came out. She tried again and failed, then finished weakly, "As long as it's all right with you..."

"And did he make another date with you?"

"Yes. He said he wanted to see me again, though he didn't set a date. He said he'd call me." She sounded almost bitter as she said this.

"Don't worry. That's his way of keeping you on a string. He'll call back. I know it."

"Do you think so?"

"I know it." He felt like a woman reassuring her girl friend about an errant lover... a lover they had in common.

12

FUMIO WOKE up first. From his futon he glanced over at Seiko's sleeping face. She looked so peaceful that he didn't feel like waking her. Stealthily, he slipped out of bed and crept out of the room, re-tying his *yukata* sash. Downstairs, Seiko's mother was already up, busy in the kitchen.

"Good morning, Mother."

"Good morning. Are you feeling better?"

"Much better, thanks."

She gave him a curious look and went to the refrigerator. "There's some fresh salmon I just bought yesterday."

"Mother, please don't bother. I'm just going to make myself some coffee and Seiko-san will make me something later."

"It's no bother at all." The older woman seemed intent on making his breakfast so he refrained from challenging her will. She had a frown on her face as she worked, and her movements were a little stiff and mechanical. Yoshiko brought him his miso soup and rice. The cucumber pickles were already set out on the table.

A little nervous, Fumio sat down and unfolded the newspaper. An earthquake in Indonesia had caused massive damage, leaving dozens of people dead and thousands homeless. Poor construction standards were blamed for the disaster.

The glass door slid open and Seiko came in, rubbing her eyes, her hair a little dishevelled. "Good morning, everyone. Father still hasn't come home yet?" She looked at the clock.

"He'll be back in the afternoon."

"Mother, I'll make that." She went over to where her mother was setting out the salmon, and took over. Yoshiko gave up her place at the counter, coming over to the table and picking up her cup of green tea. She took a loud sip and set the cup down with a little bang.

"Seiko," she said, her voice trembling a little. "Do you realize what time you came in last night?"

"I tried to be as quiet as possible. I'm sorry I woke you."

"Two or three o'clock in the morning. Is that any time for a married woman to come home?"

"Mother — " interrupted Fumio, but he was brushed aside.

"You keep out of this, Fumio-san. This is between Seiko and me." She turned back to her daughter. "I didn't want to say so last night because it was late, but it's my duty as your mother to say it now. Anyway it's partly my fault that you are the way you are."

Seiko had stopped preparing the fish and was standing against the counter looking downward, pulling nervously at her hair. Her mother was sitting at the table with her hand clutched around the tea cup, the reading glasses she wore magnifying the stern pupils of her eyes.

"Seiko, do you know that Fumio-san was so upset last night after he received your phone call that he went straight up to bed with an anguished look on his face?"

Fumio was startled. The real reason had been so different; she'd read his excitement as its opposite... Fumio looked at Seiko hoping she'd realize the misunderstanding — he was sure she did, though it was difficult to tell from her shocked expression.

"Yes," the older woman went on. "You should have seen him. He looked positively ill with worry. He couldn't concentrate on watching television at all. I'm sure Fumio-san was worried to death about where you were."

"Mother," he interrupted again. "I gave her my permission to stay out late with her friends. It was Etsuko-san's birthday."

"It doesn't matter. Such things just aren't done. A woman's who's married must stay at home to look after her husband at all times." She turned back to Seiko. "How do you think we feel before Fumio-san? I, as your mother, am ashamed. I don't have the confidence to face your husband. What must he think?"

"Mother," repeated Fumio weakly.

But Yoshiko was not to be swayed in her anger. "Seiko, you're so lucky. Most women have to live with their husband's mothers, and that's not easy, no matter how nice she is. There is always friction. And here you are, living with your own family where you've grown up and been sheltered. How many other women can say that? You're so lucky Fumio-san consented to become a *muko-yoshi*. Not many young men his age would have."

Seiko hung her head and Fumio felt sorry for her. He sensed a little envy in the older woman's voice. He knew she'd had a hard time in the early days of her own marriage, having to live with the professor's late mother, a strict authoritarian of the old school. Seiko, who had been a grandmother's child, coddled by the senior woman of the house, had told him of the countless humiliating ways in which her mother had been scolded and bullied by the old lady. Fumio had felt quite sorry for Yoshiko.

Having vented her initial anger, Yoshiko now calmed down somewhat, taking a loud sip of tea. "We gave you too much freedom as a child. I can see that now. But because you were an only child we showered all our love on you. It's no wonder you turned out the way you did."

Seiko had tears in her eyes. "You used to be so much more open-minded before. But it seems the older you get, the more conservative you become. Or maybe it's only since I got married. You expect me to be the perfect Japanese wife just because that's what you were. But you had no choice in the matter. Things are much different now, in case you didn't realize it. Fumio-san understands. Fumio-san is much more understanding than you. In fact, he's the most understanding person I've ever met. He cherishes me much more than my own family ever did."

"Seiko," he protested.

"It's true." She turned to her mother again. "You say you gave me too much freedom. It wasn't freedom you gave me, it was indifference. You let me have my way because you didn't care what I did, so long as our precious name was not tarnished. And when I did tarnish it —"

"Seiko!" Her mother looked horrified at what she was about to say.

Seiko, realizing that Fumio wasn't supposed to know, calmed down. "Even now, Father treats Fumio-san like a beloved son, while he barely notices my presence. You ask me why I go out all the time, well, I'll tell you. It's because I can't stand living in this house. I can't take the stifling atmosphere of this place. And as soon as we can afford it, Fumio-san and I are moving out of here."

"Wait!" Fumio called out. Seiko had rushed out of the kitchen and dashed upstairs.

As he got up to follow her, his mother-in-law stopped him. "Don't worry, Fumio-san. She always gets like this when she's scolded. Just let her have a good cry and she'll be back down, contrite as a kitten."

But Fumio was already on his way up. "If you'll excuse me, Mother."

Upstairs, he found Seiko sitting blankly before the bedroom TV set. A morning housewives' show was on, but the sound was turned down. The remote control lay limply in her right hand.

Fumio sat down near her and for a long time didn't say anything. Outside the veranda window, he could see wispy white clouds etched like scratches on the deep blue sky. Spring was definitely in the air, though there were still traces of coolness.

"Seiko, you shouldn't lose your temper like that. Your mother might suspect something was wrong."

"I know. But I couldn't help it. I guess I had a lot of resentment stored up inside me. And it all came out at once. I'm sure it's because of my nervousness about last night. I couldn't sleep all last night thinking over what I'd done."

Fumio had likewise spent a restless night, but for different reasons. He'd felt the spooky presence of Tatsuya in their room, an eerie illusion which he hadn't been able to shake all night. Even now he could almost smell the cologne his friend liked to use, though he knew it had to be his imagination. Seiko was sure to have showered after her tryst.

They were looking at each other, he imploringly, and she with her lower lip thrust defiantly out. She looked so appealingly artless in her rebellious pose that he was tempted to draw her to him. But there was something else between them now, since last night: Tatsuya's presence. He had held her last night, and Fumio had no right to come between them. This is Tatsuya's woman, Fumio told himself with some pride, suppressing a shiver of delight. Her infidelity last night with his hero had magnified her worth in his eyes, increased it out of all proportion to prosaic reality. She was now an emissary to a god, and he felt unable to intrude upon her inviolability.

Seiko turned off the TV with an impatient flick of her wrist. "Maybe we should stop playing this dangerous game. Before we realize it, we may get in over our heads. If Mother or Father were to find out what we're doing, they would be revolted."

Fumio didn't want to lose the magical connection he had to Tatsuya. Even talking with Seiko like this was like being with him. Seiko herself had been subtly transformed by the night, emanating a heightened glamour; a new excitement had entered their marriage, and Fumio knew he wasn't the only one who felt it.

"Do you really want to back out of it?" He looked closely at her face and saw by the look in her eyes that she, too, was thrilled by the dangerously unconventional relationship they had. "If you're that afraid of your mother, there are other ways. You can arrange to meet him during the day. Go back to taking your English conversation lessons at that language school. You can use them as an excuse for leaving the house in the afternoon. How about that? Your mother can't get mad at you then."

She gave a half-hearted laugh. "I suppose I could brush up on my English."

"And it'll enable you to help me pick up men when we travel overseas."

She, too, seemed to recall the episode on the Hawaiian beach. "Oh yes. You'll probably have a lot more luck than me... "

Fumio laughed, then getting serious, said, "Do you really want to move out of here?"

"Yes. I think we should. That way we can live our own lives."

For a moment Fumio pictured a home of their own, and the freedom it would allow. To his own shame, he thought mostly of the erotic possibilities — the ease with which Seiko could invite Tatsuya over to spend the evening. Might not a time come when they could open up about the secret behind the relationship, to let Tatsuya in on it? Then the things they could do would satisfy even the wildest of Fumio's imaginings... Trying to keep the excitement from his voice, he said, "Let's think about it. We would have to consult your father about it, of course."

"Why? I would prefer it if we just left on our own."

"Your father is a much more understanding man than you give him credit for, Seiko. In fact, I think you'd be surprised at just how liberal his leanings are." But in his heart he knew the professor would never consent to letting him go. At least, not while he still loved him.

13

FUMIO WAS not able to speak with the professor alone until the following Sunday, when Seiko and her mother were out of the house. Seiko had gone downtown for some shopping, while Yoshiko was visiting her sports club with some friends.

The two men were in the old wing of the house, with its eight-mat Japanese-style room. The day was overcast with a hint of rain in the low clouds. Because of the strong wind outside, the glass doors of the veranda remained shut. Their panes rattled slightly with each gust.

The professor seemed particularly expansive this morning. He'd poured out the tea for both of them, and now sat back on his floor recliner, with one knee up. The sedate pattern on his at-home kimono contrasted with the fresh, youthful look he wore. His skin had never looked so healthy and alive.

Fumio, having just come in earlier from his weekly morning jog, was still in his sweatsuit.

The professor cleared his throat. "How is this year's new batch of students?"

"Just fine. I have a couple of bright students in my late class who look like good prospects for the best colleges. One has indicated that he wants to go to Waseda, and two tell me they want to try for Keio."

"And do they have a chance?"

"Every prospect of it. If they keep up the good work. It gives me something to strive for — makes me feel my time isn't completely wasted."

"And of course it'll look good on the *juku*'s achievement record. At your branch, there are already two students who made it into Tokyo University, and several who made it to Waseda. Get a few more into the good schools and we can raise the tuition. The standards of your students will rise, too, so you won't have to worry so much about the dullards."

"There are already a couple of boys who know more than me about some of the newer math. I'm going to be hard put to keep up with them."

"You'll do fine. In a couple of years, you'll be behind the desk in the head office, anyway. Just keep plunging on till then. After that you won't have to worry about any kind of studying — just keep an eye on the account books and take home your salary envelope every month."

"Seiko-san will be glad about the extra money."

"Yes, I'm sure. Fumio, what's this I hear about your wanting to move out?"

"Oh, that. It's a whim of Seiko-san's. She keeps harping about wanting more freedom."

"It seems to me she has more than enough freedom as it is. We went through a lot of expense to add on the second floor for you two. Moving out now is out of the question."

"Yes, sir, I realize that. It's just that... what can I give her as a reason?"

"You don't have to give her a reason. Just put your foot down. You're the man of the house, aren't you?"

"Well... "

"Fumio-kun, you should really put a stronger rein on Seiko. If you let her have her way too much, she'll run your life, do exactly as she wishes. That's not a good way to start out your marriage. You have to let her know you're in charge. A man must do that, otherwise the relationship will lack the necessary center, the required discipline."

"Yes."

"And her mother was telling me that she came in at two-thirty in the morning the other night. That is unthinkable. You mustn't let her go out at all hours."

"Maybe it's just the difference in thinking between our generations, but I think she should have some freedom. Because as soon as a baby is born, she'll be completely occupied by her duties as a mother. And the duties of raising a child last a long time. If she doesn't have time to do what she wants now, she never will."

"Don't worry about Seiko's welfare, Fumio. Just think of yourself. Let her take care of herself."

"Father, I really think you should be less hard on her. She truly feels unloved. The other night she told her mother how you cherish me more than you do the daughter of your own flesh and blood. That's a hard thing for a child to state. It hurts me, too. That's why

I give her her freedom."

"But it's true, Fumi-chan. I do love you more than I love her. I can't help it. I've always wanted a son, and was terribly disappointed when our baby turned out to be a girl. As things turned out, we were never able to have another child, so I looked forward ever since Seiko was a child to the bridegroom she would someday bring into this male-less house. I wanted her husband to be someone I myself could love and cherish. And in you I found the perfect person."

"But you mustn't let it show so obviously. She'll suspect something. And you promised that once I moved in here, you would do nothing that would arouse the suspicions of Seiko-san or her mother."

"But it's so hard, Fumi-chan, you don't know how hard it is for me. I've tried — believe me, I've tried." His tone of voice had become wheedling, and Fumio noted with alarm that the older man had reverted to the familiar diminutive form of his name. "I lie down here at night just below your bedroom, and hear you two walking around up there. But the hardest part for me is when it gets quiet upstairs. I imagine what you're doing in the silent dark. Sometimes I hear a gentle creaking sound, ugly in its suggestive furtiveness. I don't want to be jealous of my own daughter but I can't help it. You know I've always loved you in the same way, Fumi-chan. I always will. You're in my mind always."

"Father, you promised... "

The older man slid forward on his knees until they were almost touching the younger man's. Fumio felt distinctly uncomfortable. He looked around. The family altar was directly behind him, its wood blackened from age and its portals open to disclose the memorial tablets of the professor's parents. Every morning the professor's wife struck the tiny devotional bell at exactly eight o'clock, pressing her palms together in prayer — Fumio could hear it from the room above. Even now the odor of the incense sticks still lingered in the air of the room, subtly cloying, lending an aromatic depth to the slight gloom.

He himself had always felt uncomfortable before the altar back home. His father's memorial tablet had rested solidly on its ledge, a stern, commanding presence even in death. Fumio had been unable to think impure thoughts in its presence, feeling that his soul was stripped bare before his father's watchful spirit.

The family altar here was much more dominating, and the professor's genealogy so much more respectable than his own. He envisioned behind the black wooden box whose interior was burnished with a dull gold color, all the ancestors gathered en masse, like a silent, mournful army, voiceless and forbidding.

"Fumio, don't treat me so cruelly. You're so cold. I recall the old days when you were so much nicer to me."

"I thought you liked me to be cruel. You get your pleasure from humiliation, don't you? Why shouldn't I continue to withhold what you want? I'm only treating you like the grovelling homo that you are."

He hoped this kind of talk would satisfy the older man's craving, but from the way the professor crept toward him on his knees, it was obvious that it was having the opposite effect, inflaming his lust further.

"I like it when you humiliate me so cruelly. But I need it physically, too."

"Get back." Fumio found himself sliding backwards. "How can you even think of it, before your ancestors? What would they think of you?"

"Why should I try to deceive them? They know how I am, I can't hide it. This is something I just can't give up until I die. I don't care if I get condemned to all the fires of hell for it. I'll take that risk."

"Father, you should be ashamed."

"Fumi-chan. Don't make me beg so pitifully." He reached out to touch his son-in-law's chest.

"Will you... will you stop treating Seiko-san so harshly, then? If you promise to let her live her life as she wishes, as any young woman of today wishes, then I will. But only if you promise."

"I promise. I have no choice. I won't say anything from now on, no matter what she does."

"You promised, sir. Before your ancestors. And I'll hold you to your word."

He let the older man run the zipper down his sweatsuit and pull it apart at the collar, exposing his bare chest. Fumio felt his nipples tense from the sudden chill, and the heat from his own chest against his face. The eyes of the older man were pinpoints of focussed desire. His mouth was slightly open and working as if chewing on a soft piece of meat. Mastering his disgust, Fumio turned his face aside as he felt the other's fingers and palms flatten against his breast.

He leaned back against the wooden pillar beside the family altar. The professor was in a posture of supplication — as if grovelling before the tablets of his parents, of all the watching ancestors. The ticking of the old-fashioned clock was loud.

Fumio stared at the photograph decorating the calendar on the opposite wall. Since this room was so rarely entered, the calendar hadn't been changed since last autumn. The picture for October showed a Japanese maple in full ruddy splendor, its tiny splayed leaves crimson against a pale turquoise sky. A temple garden was visible, and one corner of the temple itself. Fumio counted off the months on his fingers. Already, it had been almost nine months since he'd first moved in here. There were two more weeks till Golden Week, but the *juku* would operate as normal during the holidays. Seiko could now see Tatsuya as often as she wanted to, though she should try to space out the assignations. Fumio felt all the joy his wife would feel meeting the handsome young man who was her lover... The sky outside had lightened somewhat, though the clouds still hung gloomily beyond the trees in the garden. The harsh breathing of the older man filled the room; because he was a heavy smoker, his breath had a rancid odor.

Fumio wondered how often the old man would press him like this. He'd been counting on the fact that the professor's sexual desires would lessen as time went on, allowing Fumio some freedom; but apparently they were still very much alive. Within that decrepit body of his, erotic yearning writhed and squirmed like some unholy, ever-youthful parasite.

To sweeten this bitter medicine Fumio thought of Seiko with Tatsuya... and how the young man's healthy, hard body must have pressed down from above with all the overpowering supremacy inherent in masculine muscle and sweat. Fumio had once experienced it, and now they both had. It was a secret bond between husband and wife, a subterranean link which no one else could share.

There was a sound from the front door. The professor pulled away and quickly sat up, putting his kimono into order. Fumio, in a flash, had pulled up the zipper of his sweatsuit.

The footsteps went upstairs. Seiko was calling for him.

"I'm down here," he said, a little breathlessly.

The footsteps came pounding down. The glass door to the hallway slid open with a loud bang. "Fumio-san, what are you doing here? And in the dark?"

A cough.

"Father? Is that you?" She switched on the light.

"Fumio-kun and I were just having a little talk. About you." The professor was wiping his mouth with a handkerchief, and to Fumio's eyes he looked like the guiltiest little schoolboy caught in a prank. "He asked me to give you more freedom. Maybe I've been a little too harsh on you. It must be the pressures of work; I've been so busy lately."

Seiko's eyes were big. She looked toward her husband.

Fumio was feeling an enormous relief which manifested itself as a delicate trembling throughout his body. He couldn't believe his luck. If she'd come back a few minutes later, all would have been lost. "You finished your shopping a little early, didn't you?"

"Yes. So I took care of some other business while I was there." She looked a little out of breath herself.

"Oh?"

"I enrolled in that English conversation class we were talking about."

"That's nice. Now you can indulge yourself to your heart's content. That is, with your father's permission." He turned to the older man, who blustered heartily:

"Yes, by all means. Fulfill your dreams. And enjoy yourself at it."

The young couple glanced at each other with a secret look of complicity, all but smiling in their private joy.

14

KICHIJOJI WAS at its most sensual in the late evening. Everywhere one looked, there were young couples arm-in-arm, perhaps bound for the cloaking darkness of Inogashira Park to the south of the station. If their intentions were more intimate, they could seek the shelter of any number of love hotels which nested around the park; north of the station were many more, their gaudy neon signs lining the length of an entire block, including one whose roof was adorned with a miniature Statue of Liberty.

Strolling the streets on his way to his destination, Fumio felt all the excitement of a man bound for a secret extramarital assignation. In contrast, the young lovers walking all about seemed so innocent to him in their simple, pure happiness.

The pub was located in the basement of a four-story building which also housed an Italian restaurant and a beauty parlor. He took the four steps down and pushed his way through the door into a darkness alive with the sounds of lively chatter against the background of small-combo jazz. After a moment to orient himself, he peered about in the smoky haze and spotted a hand waving to him from a booth in the back. It was Tatsuya.

Earlier at work Fumio had received a phone call from him, and they'd talked briefly before making a drinking date for tonight after work. Fumio had called home to let Seiko know he'd probably be late tonight, but for some reason had hesitated to tell her who he was going out with. He told himself he planned to tell her all about it afterwards anyway.

"Hello, Fumio. It's been a while."

"Yes, it has. Since that time we went to the karaoke box, in fact."

This was the first time they'd met since the start of Seiko's affair with Tatsuya, and much of Fumio's excitement at meeting his friend now was generated by the fact that Tatsuya was completely unaware that Fumio knew all about his wife's infidelities.

"Have a seat, Fumio. I've already started in on my beers, as you can see."

Tatsuya looked better than ever. Perhaps his affair with Seiko had even added an extra luster to his beauty, giving him an evil patina which made him yet more irresistible. At any rate, the secret knowledge Fumio possessed couldn't help but color his view of his friend. He wondered if perhaps Tatsuya got a thrill almost sexual — even more than sexual — from meeting the innocent husband like this. As for Fumio himself, he loved being the sacrificial foil for this beautiful young man's cruelty. If this was supposed to be psychological torture, then torture was simply another name for love.

As Fumio set his briefcase on the seat beside him, Tatsuya was eyeing it with a wry expression. "Well, you look quite the young instructor."

Fumio gave a little embarrassed laugh. "I've become the respectable member of society I thought I'd never be."

"That's good. At least one of us has settled down to the straight and narrow."

Fumio peered at his friend closely to see if the statement held an intentional irony, but the open, honest look on Tatsuya's face immediately allayed his suspicion. Apparently it had been a guileless quip.

A waiter, at Tatsuya's signal, had brought over another glass mug. Tatsuya took up the half-filled pitcher on the table. "Come on, I'll pour for you."

Fumio wondered if he could keep his secret knowledge from showing on his face. Since the start of Seiko's affair, he had received intimate reports from her after each tryst, giving explicit details about what the couple did with each other. It was almost as if he'd watched them on video. Now it felt odd to see his hero clothed in the garb of innocence, laughing at his jokes, for all the world like an old college chum. Fumio imagined himself as a spy — the reverse of Seiko — pretending innocence while knowing the truth all along. He took a long drink from his mug and let out a contented sigh. "It's been quite a while since I've been out on the town like this with a friend. Drinking with co-workers just isn't the same thing — nothing more than an extension of work, really."

"Do you usually go straight home after work?"

"Yes."

"Quite the faithful husband, aren't you?"

Again, Fumio looked at Tatsuya, wondering about any hidden barbs in his statement. But, as before, there didn't seem to be any malice intended. He wondered if he wasn't being overly sensitive on account of his own deception.

"How is Seiko-san, by the way?" asked Tatsuya.

Despite the innocent look on Tatsuya's face, Fumio felt an electric shock go through him at the mention of his wife's name. He himself had planned to introduce the topic of Seiko as a way of getting a secret thrill from appraising Tatsuya's reactions to it. But he'd been beaten to the punch.

"Oh, fine. She's taking up her English conversation lessons again. I think she should get out of the house more often. The atmosphere between her and her parents is getting a bit strained."

"Maybe you should take her out sometimes, Fumio. She might be feeling cramped as a stay-at-home housewife. Women need attention; they like to be pampered."

"Take her out? But I'm too busy. And anyway she has her girlfriends to keep her company. The other day, she came in at two or three in the morning after one of their birthday parties. Women these days are really independent. I think she enjoys being with her friends more than staying at home."

Tatsuya laughed. "Maybe so. You'd better be careful she isn't seeing another man."

Fumio's heart almost stopped. "Don't worry. I trust her. She would never deceive me like that." He wondered why Tatsuya was being so bold. It scared him. Perhaps Tatsuya was preparing to break with Seiko already, after having tasted all the thrills he wanted from her. He was perfectly capable of dropping her to move on to his next sexual challenge. Or was he prepared to confess tonight, having set up the whole thing solely for the purpose of devastating Fumio with a well-timed confession? That, too, was something he wouldn't be above.

"I'm just joking with you, Fumio."

"She seems happy enough with married life, I'm glad to say."

"How about you, Fumio?"

"Me? Of course I am, too."

"You've changed."

Fumio wondered whether Tatsuya was secretly referring to their past adventures together. Briefly, the thought crossed his mind that Tatsuya might be jealous of his own happiness. The fact that Fumio had once been infatuated with him but had now found happiness with another might be galling to someone who was so confident of his own power over others. His affair with Seiko might be nothing more than revenge for this.

"How have I changed, Tatsuya?" Fumio felt a flush creep over his face. "Are you trying to imply something?"

"Imply — ?" Tatsuya looked surprised. "No. What do you mean?"

He stared at Fumio for a moment, and seeing a guilty look in his friend's eyes, suddenly seemed to understand.

"Oh, that." Tatsuya actually looked as if he just remembered it. He laughed. "Are you still worried about that? You're a lot more innocent than I thought. The things you're thinking of — I don't even give them a thought anymore. We were drunk at the time. And young."

Fumio, feeling a relief not unmixed with a lingering suspicion, took another long pull at his beer. "How is Mayumi, by the way?"

"Mayumi? I don't see her very much these days. Her success or failure has nothing to do with me anymore. Once she started appearing on television, I was just in her way."

In the latest weekly magazines, there had been a lot of space devoted to her. After a hugely successful co-starring role in a popular trendy drama, Mayumi was scheduled to appear in her first feature-length movie in the coming winter. There was a lot of gossip about a relationship between her and her new co-star. Fumio felt a slightly malicious delight in recalling the articles. More as a way of gauging Tatsuya's feelings for his former girlfriend than to learn anything new, he said, "She's in the entertainment news a lot these days."

"You mean about her and the new boy wonder?"

"Right."

To Fumio's surprise, Tatsuya seemed quite blasé about the whole thing. "That little guy is a homo. The whole thing is a publicity stunt for the upcoming movie. It was all staged, with the magazine photographers 'secretly' informed beforehand about their date. The truth is, Mayumi is practically living with the producer of the movie, in secret from his wife. The whole entertainment scene is disgusting, if you ask me. But there's a fortune to be made in it if you play your cards right."

"Don't tell my wife about that actor being homo. She's a fan of his from way back."

"Oh, he's famous enough in 2-chome, you can trust me."

"So what are you up to, as far as work? Are you still with that production company?"

"Only on paper. I'm working on another angle now. There's more than one way to get into the entertainment business. You'd be surprised."

"What are you doing in the meantime, to keep body and soul together?"

Tatsuya's reply was almost a mumble. "I'm back at the clubs."

"The host clubs?"

"Yes."

"Genji?"

Tatsuya nodded, unable to look Fumio in the face. Fumio felt his face flush again, and took a quick drink to hide his surprise. He'd thought Tatsuya was long out of that world. "And you're not working tonight?"

"I thought I'd take a couple of nights off — I've been a little busy lately."

"I see."

Fumio's mouth had gone dry at learning that Tatsuya was back in the gay world; he almost didn't dare ask his next question.

"And your love life? How has that been?"

"I don't have a steady girlfriend, if that's what you mean."

"So you're playing around again, is that it?"

"Mm-hm."

Fumio thought he detected an uneasiness in Tatsuya's attitude at this line of questioning, so he eagerly pursued it. "With your looks you'll never lack for women, don't worry. I envy your freedom."

"Oh? I'm surprised to hear that from you, the newly-wed husband."

"Settling down with one woman isn't all it's cracked up to be."

"You seem happy enough."

"Well... "

"I guess you're the type that's made to be tied down, domesticated. In fact, you're the very picture of the contented suburban husband. Next will come the children to cement the marriage — "

"Everyone's telling me I should have children."

"Are you trying for it?"

"Well... "

"Why shouldn't you? Women seem to be programmed to be mothers. There are women I know in their late thirties who used to tell me they wouldn't dream of giving up their careers for a life of domestic drudgery. Now that the biological clock is ticking down, though, they're beginning to panic; they all want a baby before it's too late. It's in their genes, deny it though they may."

"Oh?"

"Sure. And for married women, it's even more of a biological imperative. Plus the fact that it's supposedly good for the stability of the marriage: once a child comes along, the wife will settle down and stop playing around."

Fumio felt a jolt. "Don't you mean 'husband'?"

"Huh? Did I say 'wife'?"

"Yes."

Again, Fumio wondered at Tatsuya's reason for inviting him here tonight. "You almost make it sound as if Seiko herself is — "

"What are you talking about? I meant no such thing."

"Well, then stop making such slips of the tongue."

"You are really over-sensitive tonight, Fumio. Is something wrong?"

Fumio felt his head swim. An abyss had opened up before him, luring him to its very edge. He wondered if he was bold enough to go to that edge and peer over. The thrill of the bottomless depths was so enticing that he couldn't resist.

"As a matter of fact... " he began.

"Yes?"

"If you promise not to tell anyone..."

"I won't tell."

"I do have my worries about Seiko."

"Worries? What kind of worries?"

"Well, I want to trust her. And I'm sure she's telling the truth when she says she goes out with her girl friends. But sometimes I wonder... "

"You think she might be seeing another man?" The expression of concern onTatsuya's face was strangely mixed with a look of expectancy.

"Yes."

"Don't be ridiculous. I'm sure a lot of young husbands worry themselves with that fear. In fact, they probably get an erotic thrill out of imagining their wives having adventures."

"You're probably right."

"Do you have any reason to suspect her?"

"No. It's just a feeling. She hasn't called out another man's name while making love, or anything like that."

"That's good. I wouldn't want to wish an experience like that on my worst enemy." Tatsuya suddenly seemed to be taking it all lightly, in the vein of casual chatter. "Fumio, speaking as man to man... are you keeping her satisfied?"

"What do you mean?"

"I mean, in bed. That's really important for a woman."

"I don't need you to tell me that."

"I know. I'm just making sure. If you could hear some of the stories women tell me, you wouldn't be quite so complacent."

"I know I'm not the great lover you are — "

"Now, now."

"A woman would never want to leave you. In fact, if I were a woman — "

"But you're not." Tatsuya seemed to be getting uncomfortable again.

"Do you remember the times we swapped girls? They all wanted to go back to you."

"Well, it's disgusting that they would just come out and tell you like that."

"But I wormed it out of them. I wanted to know."

"Oh?"

"And the thing is, I understood their feeling. I know I can't compare to you when it comes to looks, personality, everything. You are the very image of a girl's dream lover." Fumio knew Tatsuya's discomfort was becoming acute, and he himself felt an inverse joy directly proportional to it. The sight of tiny beads of sweat breaking out on his friend's forehead sent a shiver of delight through him.

Tatsuya shifted uneasily in his seat. "Let's change the subject. You're embarrassing me with all this praise. It's taking the taste out of my drink."

"All right."

"How has Professor Akiyoshi been?"

"Oh, fine, I guess." Now it was Fumio's turn to be uncomfortable. He hadn't expected this sudden shift.

"Does he bother you at all with his attentions?"

"Sometimes." Fumio signalled to the waiter for another pitcher and poured Tatsuya and himself what remained. "I wonder how old a man has to be before he gets tired of all that nonsense."

"You should know yourself that some keep it going until they die. There are various ways they can be satisfied, even when their steam runs out."

"I know." Fumio flashed back to certain customers he'd had at Genji. "In Sensei's case, he's still pretty infatuated with me, but it's gone beyond the physical. He wants Seiko and me to have a baby so he can dote upon it."

"I see the picture. Because he can't have you himself, he's having you vicariously through his daughter. That takes a load off you, I'll bet. But I'm sure he gets a certain level of satisfaction out of it even so. He probably enjoys listening in on you two."

"Stop it."

"He probably creeps up the stairs at night after his wife is asleep..."

"That's disgusting."

"I'm just joking."

"I know. Really, he seems quite contented with life. He said he always wanted a son, and now he has one: it seems I fit the bill perfectly."

"I'm sure you stand to inherit quite a bit when he's gone, eh?"

"I don't think about it that much."

"Really? If I were in your shoes, that's all I would be thinking about, night and day. I might even be thinking of ways to quicken the process."

"Stop it. This is starting to sound like Tuesday Night Suspense Theater."

They laughed. The new pitcher came and they drained their mugs and refilled them. The music had stopped playing, and the customers' attention was centered upon the far end of the pub where an upright piano stood against the wall. A young woman sitting before it now played a brief arpeggio to loosen her fingers, and when the noise in the pub had died down, she launched into a moody jazz piece.

Fumio, who normally didn't listen to jazz, felt himself drawn into the music, with its suggestions of melancholy ennui. It was the whole ambience of the pub, really, with its cigarette smoke and dark interior, which put him in the mood of a romantic hero. He glanced occasionally at Tatsuya, but his friend seemed a little bored, even irritated. Once or twice their knees brushed, and though Fumio felt a sensual jolt each time, Tatsuya didn't even seem to notice.

The music ended, and scattered applause sounded. The pianist went into her next piece.

Tatsuya looked at his watch. "Hadn't you better phone your

wife and tell her you'll be late?"

"Don't worry. You make it sound as if she had me around her finger. I'm not quite the milksop you seem to think I am."

"I'm just thinking about your domestic harmony."

"Right." Fumio felt a thrill at the cruel casualness with which Tatsuya was playing the situation. He wondered if he also toyed with Seiko's feelings like this on their clandestine dates. Perhaps the two lovers had visited this very pub, and Tatsuya was serenely enjoying the aesthetic juxtaposition. Fumio wished Tatsuya would talk about Seiko again. He wanted to hear her name on his lips. Curiously, it was almost as if he could feel her body pressing against his side, her knees wedged between those of the two men in her life. He knew he was getting drunk. He found himself applauding automatically when the music ended, but without recalling having heard it at all.

Seiko had said about Tatsuya, "He's always the recipient of caresses, never the giver. He wants to be the beloved, not the lover."

Fumio felt a thrill go through him as he recalled something else Seiko had said that night: "He likes to have his women get down on their knees... "

He glanced at his watch. "It's getting late. Almost time for the last train. Do you have any plans for tonight?"

"Not especially."

"How about coming home with me and spending the night over? That way we can continue drinking at my house."

It was a common enough invitation, but for Fumio it held a double-edged meaning. With the three of them in the same house, the air would be freighted with explosive possibility. The sexual tension between Tatsuya and Seiko, sleeping under the same roof, might reach ignition point. Why not make some excuse so they could all sleep in the same room? And Fumio, lying between them, secretly intoxicated by the proximity of the two guilty lovers, could feign a drunken sleep so deep that the lovers would be able to consummate their desire in the very presence of the sleeping husband...

He felt faint. If Tatsuya suspected anything behind the invitation, he didn't show it. "No, I don't think so. Perhaps some other time."

"Then what about a hotel?"

"A hotel?" Tatsuya's puzzled look brought back to Fumio what he'd just said on the spur of the moment, fired by the lascivious pictures in his head.

"Yes, a hotel," Fumio repeated, surprising himself with his calm confidence. "It's too far to walk back to your home in Meguro, and the last train — " he looked at his watch " — just left a couple of minutes ago."

"No, I don't think so."

"Where are you going to stay, then?"

"I'll catch a taxi home, as I always do."

"But it's such a long way to Meguro. You'll end up paying more for cab fare than you would for a hotel."

"I can afford it."

"How about if we go to my house, and I drive you home in my car? That's just as out of the way as Meguro. Then we can — "

"Boy, you are persistent. You sound just like some customers I know."

With a jolt, Fumio remembered that Tatsuya was working at Genji again. He felt his insides glow with a new excitement. Trying to master his emotions, he murmured, "Well, it's obvious you intend to run out on me tonight unless — "

"Unless?"

"Unless we consider it an outside date."

To Fumio's relief, Tatsuya didn't seem surprised at all by the suggestion. In fact, he was taking it all in stride — and a part of Fumio withered a little at his humiliating new status... as the unattractive 'client' who has to pay for the companionship of a beautiful boy.

"Sure," said Tatsuya. "Call it an outside date."

"And the main office needn't know," added Fumio eagerly.

"Right."

"The prices haven't changed that much, have they?"

"For an old friend, no. Of course not."

"Good. There are plenty of hotels nearby." At the thought of becoming a paying customer for the first time, Fumio felt a vast freedom open up before him, a vista of endless possibilities. Once he'd crossed the invisible line at the border, the scenario was his to direct as he liked. He was so eager to finish his drink that he couldn't swallow it down smoothly. "And the beers are on me."

"Right."

The pub had begun to empty out but there were still quite a few customers left. The pianist was taking a break, sitting at the counter and talking with the bartender. The two young men stepped outside. The night for Fumio had changed; it was now charged with an electric immediacy which sent shivers up and down his body. He thought of his wife at home, and his shivering became more intense. This new twist to their relationship with Tatsuya was bound to intrigue Seiko, and he thought of what her reaction would be when he told her all about it in the morning. But as he began to consider the situation, he realized that both the thought of telling her, and the thought of keeping it secret, were equally exciting. The difference had become inconsequential. For tonight he would become Seiko, and experience the very pleasures she had experienced. It would be like entering her body and seeing the world through her eyes. Never before this moment had he felt so close to his wife.

As he led the way to the street of love hotels, it was all he could do to keep from stumbling in his imagined, unaccustomed high heels.

15

THE DRIZZLE had gradually turned into a regular shower, and now it was a steady downpour. Fumio was driving very carefully because, despite the furious pace at which the windshield wipers were working, the front glass still looked frosted and wavy. Luckily the traffic was light.

"Be careful," said Seiko. "This is a tricky intersection."

"I know." He felt a sudden irritation at his wife's solicitousness. She had been strangely silent during the whole ride, and Fumio had been too preoccupied with his own thoughts to pay much attention to her. He had not, after all, told Seiko about his night with Tatsuya, and he wasn't sure why. A residue of guilt now soured his mood, along with another emotion. Ever since sleeping with Tatsuya again, his feelings about his wife's affair with him had suddenly undergone a change. He now felt an edge of bitterness, perhaps even jealousy toward her. He'd come home early that morning by taxi, and Seiko had immediately known by his mood that something had happened. Indeed, there was no way he could hide it. To her questioning, he'd answered that, yes, he had been with another man, though he hadn't divulged his partner's name. She'd even felt happy for him...

The fact that he now had a secret from his wife added another layer to his complex of feelings about Tatsuya. He and Seiko were both playing out the extra-marital trysts of popular fantasy, only their lovers were one and the same, a god who accepted the embraces of men and women alike, a being elevated so far above common morality that he shone with a particularly cruel and evil blaze, seductive beyond words. And Fumio was worshipping in secret at the shrine, side by side with his wife, though outwardly acting only as the handmaiden to Seiko's ritual devotions.

"Well, it looks like we may easily find parking, at least. That's one good thing about a rainy day." They were on their way to do some shopping at Kinokuniya supermarket before Fumio went to work later in the afternoon.

Seiko nodded, barely listening to him.

"What's the matter?" he asked.

She didn't reply.

"You're thinking of him, aren't you?" asked Fumio, with a sudden prescience.

There was no response, and in that silence dwelt an affirmation.

"I understand," he said softly. Fumio's jealousy flared up again, laced with the temptation to divulge the secret of his tryst with Tatsuya. One reason he had been loathe to mention it earlier was that he suspected, and had suspected for some time, that she was falling in love with Tatsuya. As careful as she'd been to keep her emotions dry and detached, to treat the whole affair as a playful game, she'd fallen victim to her emotions. Fumio knew this even if she herself didn't, for he'd been noticing how much care she took to look her best for her dates... and the secret glow which came into her eyes whenever she knew she would be seeing her lover again.

"About Tatsuya — " she said, a little bashfully.

"Yes?"

"Maybe I've been playing it a little too aloof."

"What do you mean?"

"I think he's beginning to cool toward me. Maybe I've outlived the excitement I gave him initially."

"What makes you say that?" Fumio was alarmed.

"I suspect he has another lover."

"What?"

"Perhaps my aloofness was too realistic. He's turned to someone else. I just know it."

"Do you have any proof?"

"Only my woman's instinct."

Fumio saw tears in her eyes despite her struggle not to let them show. "You're in love with him." He stated it flatly, trying to hide any emotion of his own from showing.

She nodded. "I couldn't help it. I tried to avert it as long as possible, but how could I? I'm afraid my feelings for him were much deeper than I myself suspected. What shall I do?"

Fumio was assaulted by a flurry of contradicting emotions. A part of him was gloating: it was entirely possible that the 'other lover' she suspected was none other than himself. At the same time, he shared her worry that Tatsuya was cooling toward her. If Seiko lost her appeal to Tatsuya, then Fumio's own appeal would surely pale along with it. His own value in Tatsuya's eyes lay in the fact that he was the unknowing, betrayed husband — one of a matched, double set of pieces on Tatsuya's game board. Again, he felt glad that Seiko was having doubts about Tatsuya; if she'd been too happy, it wouldn't have been fair. Her happiness would have been at his expense: after all, she was betraying him with his own lover.

"If you're that worried about him," he said finally, "why don't you call him? It might put your mind at rest."

"Is it all right?"

"Of course."

"I've wanted to call him so much, but I didn't want to do anything behind your back... after all you've permitted me."

"Don't worry." He pulled the car into Kinokuniya's parking lot, and they both stepped outside, opening their umbrellas. The rain was coming down in sheets now, lending an oppressive atmosphere to the afternoon. Seiko led the way to a phone booth on the main street. No one was using it; she stepped inside and held the door open for her husband. Accepting the invitation to get in out of the rain, Fumio joined her, drawing the door shut behind him. Huddled against Seiko in the cramped space, feeling her wet umbrella against his leg, Fumio shivered. He didn't know if he felt excited or jealous at being able to listen to his wife's conversation with her lover.

"Do you know his number?" he asked. He was ready to pull out his memo book.

She nodded and reached for the phone, but hesitated before dialling.

"Go ahead," he said. "Dial." She began dialling the number with a facility which showed she'd memorized it. As she waited for the line to connect, Fumio watched the expression on her face, noting with envy the subdued radiance of a young woman about to speak with the man she loves. Her hand was at the throat of her sweater, pulling it together. Almost hidden by the tumble of her hair about her shoulders was the faint pulse of a tiny vein on her neck. And her face, cast in a half-shadow by the overhanging boughs of the tree beside the phone booth, looked infinitely fragile. He turned his face away and leaned his head against the cool glass of the booth window.

"Hello? Tatsuya? I didn't wake you, did I?"

Fumio imagined Tatsuya's reply at the other end.

"No, you don't sound sleepy," laughed Seiko, as if in relief. "It's just that you took so long to answer. What were you thinking about when I called?" she asked coquettishly. The rain was sliding down the glass of the phone booth in straight drips.

"Me? Oh, I was thinking about you, of course. Hm? I'm in a phone booth." She looked at Fumio. "I was a little worried about calling from home. My mother might suspect something from the tone of my voice. Right. Fumio? He's at home, too, preparing his lessons. He has to work late tonight again."

There was a long pause as Tatsuya said something at the other end. Seiko looked straight at Fumio to indicate that he was the subject of their conversation. She laughed. "Oh, no, of course not. I trust him. Though there is a young woman at the *juku* who seems to have caught his fancy." She made a conspiratorial moue at Fumio.

Fumio brought his ear close to the receiver, and Seiko let him listen in, pulling it just enough away from her ear for them both to hear. Fumio heard Tatsuya's familiar voice sounding tinny and remote. "What if he decides he wants to get a little more intimate with that girl?"

"He would never do such a thing."

"Don't count on it. The straightest-looking men are often the most dirty-minded. How do you know he doesn't have fantasies and tastes which you can't satisfy?"

Fumio's heart raced as he thought of the night he'd spent with Tatsuya, enjoying a satisfaction which no woman could ever give him. At the same time he couldn't suppress a twinge of fear; Tatsuya was treading awfully close to revealing their secret.

Seiko exchanged a knowing look with her husband. "I don't care about what he does outside the house as long as he doesn't bring trouble home."

"You're quite broad-minded. If he had paid more attention to you, there would have been no need for you to... "

"I wish we could meet more often."

"Come on. Don't go into that again. You know I want to see you more often, but if we did it too much, he would begin to suspect. And if he were to find out, I don't know how I would be able to live with myself. He is one of my best friends, after all."

"I think maybe it's just because you're his best friend that I don't feel so guilty about it all. As if he wouldn't mind it so much..."

Tatsuya gave his mellow laugh. "Don't be ridiculous. You have no idea how a man feels about his wife betraying him — it doesn't matter with whom."

"Still, I just wish I could spend some more time with you. Without the need to hide or be secretive. I don't like these quick, furtive encounters we have. I want some time when we can just relax and be with each other."

Seiko looked at Fumio, and instinctively, he reached out his hand and clasped hers. He was giving her his approval. But Tatsuya was laughing. "That's impossible. Besides, isn't it just this danger about our relationship which gives us the greatest thrill? I love the guilty expression you get on your face each time I mention your beloved husband's name."

Seiko flushed, but Fumio squeezed her hand to reassure her. He wanted to hear more. Despite his thrill at listening in on this intimate lovers' conversation, he was a little puzzled by the coldness on Tatsuya's part. He had expected a little more warmth and affection, even if it was play-acted.

"Tatsuya." Seiko had suddenly stiffened and was straining her ear, almost pushing Fumio away. "Is there someone else there?"

"Here? Of course not. I'm all alone. Who else would be here?"

"I don't know. You tell me."

"You're acting paranoid. After all the dangers I risked in seeing you, and all the ways I've shown you what you mean to me, to be accused like that... I'm sorry to say you're acting out the stereotypical jealous married woman."

"You'd know about that, wouldn't you?"

He sighed audibly. "You know, you disappoint me. You were so worldly at the start that I was pleasantly surprised. I thought: this is the woman for me. But now it looks like you're changing into just another woman having her little affair. A normal woman after all..."

Fumio saw tears in his wife's eyes. He put his finger to his lips, begging her with his eyes to calm down. She did.

"I'm sorry. Maybe it was just my imagination."

Fumio couldn't hear the rest of the conversation as he pulled away in fear that Tatsuya might suspect his own presence here. He gazed out vacantly at the cars passing along the wide boulevard. After Seiko hung up, he asked, "Why did you ask him that?"

"I don't know. Just my woman's instinct. I just sensed some other presence there at the other end. And another thing: he never once mentioned my name over the line. I notice things like that."

"It seems like pretty flimsy evidence to me. Besides, if there was a woman at the other end, she would have known from what he said that he was talking with a lover."

"True... " She still didn't seem convinced, however.

Fumio shook his head. "Maybe he's right; you *are* paranoid.

You're letting your feelings run away from you. You're so infatuated with him that you're starting to imagine things."

"I'm sure that's it." She had turned her face away. "I'm just so worried. The things you told me about him. His promiscuity. There's no guarantee that I can keep his interest for very much longer. What do I have to offer? There are so many other women out there, who would be only too glad to take my place."

Fumio had nothing to say to this, yet the despair he felt for his wife was strangely tinged with a kind of expectation. "After all," she went on, "as you told me before, he's only after thrills in his relationships with women."

"True." Fumio had often told her — whether from a desire to hurt her, or to warn her — about the games Tatsuya used to make out of sexual conquest. Now he recalled something he'd told her quite recently: "When we were in college, he bragged about it all the time. The more difficult and out of reach a girl was, the more he tried to have her. And he almost always succeeded. With his looks, who could resist him? He was especially proud if he got them in pairs: two sisters, a couple of close friends who vied for his affections, a mother and daughter... Social taboos meant nothing to him. Engaged women, newly-wed brides, virgins, lesbians, even deformed women... those were his challenges. For him, sexual conquest was taken for granted. He just needed something to spice it up. Only by such added thrills was there any sort of excitement in it for him."

And now, Fumio thought, a husband and wife combination. We are only a couple of trophies to be added to his numerous others. He thought of Tatsuya, coolly playing with the deepest emotions of a husband and wife, making a mockery out of the marriage bonds, toying with the most sacred of human commitments. Yet, ironically, at the same time, Tatsuya was acting as a link between Fumio and Seiko, binding them together in a way nothing else could. With his body, he was uniting a husband and wife who felt no love for each other. Both husband and wife loved this cruel, callous youth whose beauty was potent enough to destroy any human happiness... and even more than potent enough to create it.

The branches over their heads swayed slightly from a gust of wind, interrupting the steady, monotonous drip-drip-drip sound which had accompanied their conversation. Rainwater accumulated on the leaves abruptly pattered down in scattered droplets. Fumio's heart felt heavy. "Tatsuya is a cold man," he said. "He has no feelings for the people he's conquered. For him it's all a game."

"But the thing is, I don't mind it. He may hurt me and treat me like dirt, but I go back for more."

"I feel the same way. What is it about him? What kind of magnetism draws us to him? I think it's his very cruelty which attracts us."

"Maybe so. For me, one small act of kindness on his part is worth more than a thousand like it from another man. I can live for a week on one smile from him."

Their body heat had fogged the glass of the windows. The outside world was no longer visible. Fumio felt as if they were in a snug cave, muffled from all outside concerns. He looked at his wife again. She was staring straight ahead with a blank expression. When she turned to look at him, her eyes were dead, almost unseeing.

"Fumio-san, I'm afraid of losing him. That's what I feel most afraid of now. I know it's terrible to say it to you, and you must think I'm horrible, but I can't hide it from you. I'm so much in love with him that I would give anything to keep him. If he is with another woman now, it would kill me."

"I understand. Don't forget, if there were another woman in his life, I'd be just as upset as you. As if I, too, were being betrayed. I can forgive his seeing you, but not anyone else."

She lowered her face in shame and went on: "I just know I'll try everything to keep him. If he were to leave me, I'd probably be willing to throw everything away just to get him back, and I'm worried. This all started out as an amusing game, but I've gotten in beyond my depths. Things are now much more serious than we ever bargained for. Please believe me."

"I suppose we were wrong to think we could remain untouched by the power he has over people."

She fell silent. Then, with a look of agony on her face, she turned to him and said in dead tones: "Fumio-san, please help me win him back."

Fumio stared at his wife. She was serious. Her feelings for Tatsuya had put her in a region where logic and common sense had no meaning. She was asking her husband's help in regaining the feelings of a straying lover. Only Tatsuya could do this, he thought.

"Don't worry, Seiko. I'm sure things will turn out all right." He hoped he sounded more confident than he felt. "Listen, if it'll give you any comfort, we can find out where he lives, and I'll drive you over there today. I can call in sick to the *juku*."

She shook her head.

"Well... " He wondered what he could say to comfort her. The look of hopelessness on her face pained him. He cleared his throat.

"If worse comes to worst you can always... "

She stared at him blankly. With a nervous laugh he went on: "Well, there's more than one way... He's — Tatsuya is a host, a professional gigolo. Someone you pay money to enjoy. I know of at least one person who has actually paid money to spend the night with him, after being dropped by him. Even if you don't go so far... even if only to have some time with him, to... "

"Fumio-san!"

He couldn't bear to face her look of disgust mingled with hurt. "But Tatsuya is the sort of man whose affections you can buy with money. I wouldn't think any the less of you for it. In fact, I would even — "

"I haven't fallen *that* low. I still have *some* pride, you know."

But Fumio couldn't stop himself, as if, in humiliating her, he was exorcising the deepest, most inaccessible pains within himself, producing an anesthetized numbness which was dangerously close to pleasure: "If you like, I'll pay for it myself." He closed his eyes so he wouldn't have to see her face, and wallowed, obscenely, in the delicious luxury of self-pity.

16

FUMIO WAS totally unfamiliar with this part of Tokyo. On either side of the narrow street he was walking on were towering walls which allowed only the barest glimpses of the imposing homes barricaded behind them. There was a quietness to the whole area despite the presence of a major traffic artery just a few blocks away — as if the silence itself had been bought with money. Once again, by the light of a street lamp, he checked the map hand-drawn for him by a kind policeman back at the *koban.* The apartment he was looking for was a little ways further on, up a cul-de-sac next to a tiny park. He thought he could see some trees up ahead.

Fumio had taken the train out here tonight without Seiko's knowledge. In order not to arouse her suspicions, he'd called home after work, telling her he was going out drinking with some fellow teachers. As the street began climbing a slope, the homes on either side of him became more modest in size; here and there could be seen one-room condos of the kind rented by the more well-to-do class of students. He felt like a police detective tracking down a suspect. Though he and Seiko had both gotten Tatsuya's telephone number from him, they had never been told where he lived, only been given a general idea of the area. And on none of his clandestine dates with Seiko had Tatsuya ever taken her home; they'd always ended up in a love hotel, or in his parked car. So when Fumio decided to find out on his own if Tatsuya was cheating on Seiko, he had to do a little extra footwork.

Checking the telephone directories was no help. Tatsuya's number was not listed. Very few hosts or hostesses ever listed their numbers for fear of being tracked down by an over-zealous admirer. Calling the host club where he worked was also useless. No employer of such a business would ever dream of divulging private information about an employee, except to the police. That left only one way. The next time Seiko had a date with Tatsuya, Fumio secretly staked out the station plaza which was their rendezvous place. When Tatsuya came driving up in his new Porsche to pick her up, Fumio — sitting by the window of a coffeeshop facing the plaza — carefully noted down the car's license plate number. Armed with this information, he'd made a trip to the land office where the car was registered. There, it was merely a matter of filling out an application and paying a small fee for a copy of the vehicle's official registry. The officials asked no questions; for all they knew, he was a friend buying the car from Tatsuya and needed the document to transfer registry of the vehicle. Naturally, the document listed Tatsuya's home address.

As he came to the park he slowed his steps. There was a wire fence surrounding it, with its only opening facing the narrow street down the slope to the left. This street had cars parked all down its length, with just enough space for a vehicle to squeeze through, and ended in a cul-de-sac. At its terminus were clustered several two-storey buildings. One of them was Tatsuya's.

There seemed to be no one about, so, as casually as he could, he started up the street, peering furtively at the nameplates of the buildings on either side. Urban Heights... Edel Higashi.... He found Green Highland Mansion on the right, just next to the park. As he approached it, he turned into its entryway, quickly checking the rows of mailboxes within to verify if Tatsuya lived in room 201. But though almost all the mailboxes had hand-written slips of paper in their respective name slots, there was none in 201's.

The wire fence which surrounded the park in the next lot blocked off the far end of the passageway. Fumio turned back and came out onto the street again. A quick glance at the row of parked cars ensured him that Tatsuya's red Porsche was there. He retraced his steps until he came to the entrance of the park. A pair of tall shrubs flanked the entrance, the one on the left all but hiding a vending machine. Fumio bought a can of cold coffee and made his way toward the swings. It was one of those tiny parks found throughout the city, minuscule open spaces where a mother might take her child to play in the afternoon. Only two cherry trees gave any shade from the sun in summer, and the restroom was one of those portable facilities found at construction sites.

Moving the swing slightly back and forth, Fumio popped open the can and took a sip before setting it down on the ground. He reached into his jacket for his pack of cigarettes and tapped one out, lighting it up and blowing out a stream of smoke. He felt absurdly calm now that he'd finally learned where Tatsuya lived. The earlier excitement of the hunt had given way to something else: the satisfaction of having found the solution to a puzzle. He thought of his reason for coming here and smiled. Though Seiko had no idea of what he'd done, still, it was almost as if she'd hired him as a detective to catch her lover in the act of betraying her. But even without her interests in mind, Fumio knew he would have come here anyway; he had to confirm, for reasons of his own, if Tatsuya was seeing another woman.

Just as Tatsuya had been the first man to awaken a woman's ultimate pleasure in Seiko (Fumio thought of the mixture of awe and pride with which she'd shyly described to him her first orgasm), so he had been the one to acquaint Fumio with his own sleeping homosexual longings. He could well understand Seiko's almost feverish desire not to let Tatsuya go. But in Seiko's case, this desire had lately modulated into something quite different... so gradually that Fumio almost hadn't noticed it for a long time. Helplessly he had watched it turn into a sexual jealousy which grew alongside her burgeoning love like a monstrous tumor, a companion growth which could not exist without the other. And now it had all but consumed her, was ready to destroy her. She cried into her pillow every night, trying not to let Fumio hear — and he, not daring to acknowledge being a witness to her shame, lay awake in the dark, unable to console her in her misery — a misery brought on by himself.

He crushed out his cigarette and gulped down the rest of the coffee. From where he sat, he could see the light on in Tatsuya's room; it was obvious from the layout of the building that room 201 could only be the one on the upper right corner. Getting up from the swing, he walked around to where he had a more direct view of the veranda. There was a small light on, indicating that Tatsuya wasn't asleep yet; he usually put out all the lights when he went to bed. This could mean that he was up watching television, but Fumio couldn't see the telltale flicker of a television screen lighting up the room. In a one-room apartment, it would be unmistakable. If Tatsuya was up doing something, the larger light would be on.

Fumio knew from experience that Tatsuya liked to keep the small bedside lamp on while making love. It was quite possible that he had a visitor with him now. Any one of the cars parked out on the street now could be the girl's. He was tempted to sneak up to Tatsuya's door to see if he could get a better clue. But he knew there would be no way of knowing, from the outside, if there was anyone else within. That left the veranda. If he were to climb the wire fence and stand on the nearest metal post, he might, by leaning to his left, be able to catch a glimpse through the window. But that would be too dangerous. Someone seeing him might phone the police.

The thought that Tatsuya might be in bed with a girl at this very moment made Fumio's knees go weak. And he wasn't able to say whether he would have been angered, saddened, or even glad to have Seiko's suspicions confirmed. To see another woman leaving Tatsuya's room, to know that Tatsuya had betrayed Seiko, left Fumio with two choices: he could disclose it to her and break her heart... or he could live with the terrible secret. The responsibility he held over Seiko's happiness gave him such a feeling of power that he felt a sudden kinship with Tatsuya himself: together, they were the perverse custodians of Seiko's welfare. Fumio found himself almost wishing there was another woman in there, a woman who was younger and more beautiful than Seiko. And at the same time, he didn't want to know if there was anyone up there or not. He had a sudden intuition that what he found out tonight might be enough to destroy his own happiness. Indeed, he found himself hoping that nothing happened tonight. For now that he knew where Tatsuya lived, he could always come back again anytime, even if only to sit here knowing where the man he loved was. He needed to color the empty spaces in his imagination — spaces which could only be filled out by his dreams.

The sky was clouded over and no stars were visible. Fumio tapped out another cigarette and nervously lit it. The girl might spend the whole night in Tatsuya's room. He was prepared to wait as long as possible — until the last train for home, anyway. He looked at his watch. There was still time for about three more cigarettes. The smoke curling up from the cigarette in his fingers was like the ghostly wisp of a fog.

He looked up again at the light in the window. It was still on.

He thought wryly of the desperate consultations Seiko had had with him the other night. After the lights were out and they were in their futons, she'd begun questioning him eagerly on the secrets of keeping a man. "There are no secrets," he'd laughed. "If there are, I'd like to know them myself."

"I'm afraid I might not be giving Tatsuya as much pleasure as other women might... more experienced women."

"Nonsense."

"Well, he's had so many women before me. I—I might not have enough sexual expertise to satisfy a man that worldly."

"Seiko, if anything, it's your innocence which probably appeals to him."

"But he seems so unresponsive sometimes."

"True, he's not much of one for giving outward signs of his pleasure. Believe me, I know from my own experiences with him. But that doesn't mean he's not satisfied physically."

"As a woman, it's so hard for me to know what gives a man true pleasure... "

"Why are you so worried about the physical side of your relationship? There's more to it than that."

"I know. But I'm so worried about losing him." Shamefacedly, she confessed to her desperate hope of ensnaring Tatsuya through sexual techniques. Having no one she could consult about a problem so intimate, she'd come to her husband for advice. As for Fumio, he felt he couldn't honestly disabuse her of her notion, for it was one with which he could completely sympathize. "All right," he said. "Go down to the kitchen and get a sausage. And don't let Mother see you... " It was the strangest tutoring Fumio had ever given. But Seiko proved an eager student. A little shy at first, she watched his initial demonstration wide-eyed, but gradually warmed to his lesson, even asking pointed questions. Giggling nervously, she expressed her amazement at his considerable expertise. He wiped the sausage before handing it to her. "Now you try it... "

He almost hadn't noticed the sound at first. A door had just closed softly, its sound carrying far in the quiet night. Quickly he put out his cigarette and stationed himself beside the bushes at the entrance of the park. Someone was coming down the stairs. He was surprised at his own excitement. Sweat had broken out all over his body at the sound of the door, and his knees felt sickeningly weak. At this rate, he would never make a good detective; he felt guilty about spying on someone like this.

The footsteps were quiet. Apparently she was alone; Fumio

couldn't hear Tatsuya's footsteps accompanying hers. Though there was no need for him to hide — the girl had no idea who he was, after all — he crouched down in the shade of the bushes. The girl reached the bottom of the stairs and turned onto the road. As she emerged from behind the screening fence, Fumio caught his breath. It wasn't a woman after all. In fact, it wasn't even Tatsuya's visitor, but a next-door neighbor or someone, for it was a middle-aged man. But something made Fumio look more carefully... and he suddenly knew that it had been Tatsuya's visitor... for it was Professor Akiyoshi.

He almost called out "Father," but caught himself just in time. He thought of the cars he'd seen parked in the nearby street and realized that there had been a gray Mercedes-Benz among them. But he hadn't even thought of checking the license number. His head spun. Shakily, he returned to the swing and sat down. What was the professor doing with Tatsuya? He felt his face flush. For a long moment his mind was blank, refusing to function. Vaguely he heard the sound of a car starting up, driving away...

He pulled out another cigarette and tried to marshall his thoughts. Only after he'd taken a long pull at his cigarette and exhaled the smoke did he feel himself capable again of rational judgement. It was as if the pieces of a complex puzzle were coming slowly together in his mind. Or at least into a reasonable picture. It was apparent that Tatsuya's numbers game had not only included husband and wife, but father-in-law as well. But for what purpose? It was possible that Tatsuya had gotten a sensual pleasure, even an aesthetic satisfaction, out of playing all the members of the family off one another. Viewed by an outsider, the whole complicated picture might take on the aspect of a crazy work of art: the husband ignorant about his wife's affair, the wife ignorant about her husband's affair, and both of them ignorant about their parent's affair — all with the same man. It only needed the mother-in-law's participation to complete a masterpiece of perverse lust, a supreme parody of the happy family in the suburbs. But it was difficult to believe that even Tatsuya would erect such a complicated structure for the sheer pleasure of a twisted numbers game. It wasn't like him. There had to be a more lucrative reward behind it all.

Fumio closed his eyes, swinging gently back and forth. And then it came to him. In his mind he suddenly saw it all: Tatsuya had erected an elaborate triple blackmail scheme. Played right, timed right, he stood to gain from it, as each party to the affair paid in secret from the others, unwilling to let his own secret be known. Perhaps Tatsuya had planned it like this from the very beginning, setting up the reunion just so he could milk the family separately, unknowingly, for money over a long period. Such an arrangement, necessarily kept secret within the family, could have gone on forever. Viewed in such a light, it was a masterpiece of evil. And Tatsuya, as the plan's mastermind, acquired an even more seductive glow — but a glow tinged with the shadow of its own imminent decay.

Fumio wondered if such a beautifully evil picture could be real. Wasn't there a simpler explanation for all this? A part of him still desperately wanted to believe that Tatsuya had been attracted to him all along, at least a little, and that his secret affair with Seiko was a way of sublimating that attraction. Maybe the affair with the professor was the same thing. Fumio couldn't believe that a man who supposedly despised homosexuals would come back again and again to a gay man who he knew adored him, worshipped him, loved him with a devotion just short of religiosity...

Fumio looked up at the window again and saw the light still on. Tatsuya was there at this very moment, alone. Unknowing. It had been several weeks since Fumio had last seen him. A sweet ache filled out his chest. He found himself getting to his feet and walking toward the building. Going up the stairs, he felt a momentary qualm. He would be losing any advantage he had over Tatsuya by revealing that he'd tracked him down to his lair. But it didn't seem to matter anymore. Nothing mattered to him anymore except for his aching need to see Tatsuya once again, and to be in his presence... to learn the truth. The meeting so suddenly approaching loomed with all the inevitability of eternity, sweet and seductive as a martyr's violent death.

He rang the doorbell. His hand was shaking. There was a long pause, and he wondered if he should ring again. A nagging fear began to haunt him. The professor's presence here might have been a coincidence. And Tatsuya might not even live here; he might have moved since registering his car — or used a false address. Just as he was turning to go, the door opened. It was Tatsuya, looking a little tired. He didn't seem surprised at all to see Fumio at his door; only a momentary puzzled look flitted through his eyes as if he were trying to remember if he'd given Fumio his address.

"Fumio? What brings you here?" He was wearing an elegant bathrobe open at the neck to reveal his silk pajamas underneath.

"Can I come in?"

"Of course." Tatsuya stepped back so Fumio could enter. "Sorry the place is a mess. I was just getting ready to take a bath." Fumio gazed around at the single room. The floor was of bare wood and the walls were white. The furnishings were minimal: a large double bed, a night table topped by a simple lamp with a frosted white shade, a canvas director's chair, and a huge 32-inch television set. The only light came from the lamp, casting the whole room into a mysterious gloom. Instinctively, he found himself looking around for telltale signs of the professor's visit.

"I'll make you some coffee or something." Tatsuya went off to the kitchen. Fumio didn't even have the presence of mind to refuse it. He sat down on the only chair and waited as Tatsuya made the coffee. A very tasteful painting hung on the wall to his left, a harbor scene done in soft pastels. He found himself longing for the peace reflected in its cool waters. Tatsuya came back with a coffee mug in his hand. "It's instant — I hope you don't mind."

"Of course not. I like instant."

"Some people don't, you know."

"I know." He took a sip. The coffee was scalding hot.

"Sorry. I should have warned you: I like my coffee hot." Tatsuya had sat down on the bed.

"That's okay. By the way, what was Sensei doing here?"

"Sensei?"

"I saw him leave just a few minutes ago."

"I see."

"The professor was here with you, wasn't he?"

Tatsuya crossed one leg over the other and bobbed his foot up and down. "I suppose you saw him leave, so it would be foolish to deny it. Yes, he was here." The only sign of his nervousness was an impulsive reaching for a pack of cigarettes on the side table. With his usual smooth gestures, he tapped one out and offered it to Fumio.

Fumio shook his head. "Since when were you and the professor friends?"

"Does it seem so odd that we should be friends?"

"Maybe 'friend' is the wrong word to use. Perhaps we should say 'customer'... or 'outside date'. You'd never give it away free to an old man like him."

"You put it so crudely. You're letting your emotions run away with you. He came to me of his own accord."

"Because you pandered to his weaknesses."

"I like to feel I did it as a personal favor. He is a very lonely man, you know."

"Stop trying to make excuses."

"You don't get it, do you, Fumio? The professor is in love with you. Hopelessly in love. Can't you feel any pity for him? Day after day he sees you, yet you treat him like dirt. He's a man, too, you know — a man with feelings, with desires. And he's tortured by the thought that he can't have you. He's a regular now on the 2-chome scene, picking up boys who remind him of you. He came to Genji once, and recognized me. He knows we're friends. So I stood in as a substitute for you, that's all. I felt sorry for him."

"Liar! You're a liar!" He wished he hadn't come... wished he'd never met and fallen in love with the cruellest boy in Japan.

"His feelings for you are so deep. He told me he wants to be buried with you in the family vault. With your bones next to his... forever."

Fumio felt a chill go through him and he couldn't suppress a visible shudder. For a young man like himself, in the prime of life, the thought of his own bones resting alongside those of his father-in-law was grotesquely morbid. He knew older couples sometimes pledged their love in this fashion, but he couldn't picture himself dead, no matter how hard he tried. A love which went beyond the grave was obscene, a selfish display of vanity, not true love. For him, love was an emotion rooted in the physical, the prerogative of healthy young bodies. For an older man to feign it was a travesty of nature, a cruel joke. Fumio closed his eyes and caught an imaginary whiff of incense just by picturing his father-in-law's scrawny body.

The telephone rang. "Excuse me." Tatsuya reached over to the night table to pick it up. "Hello?" He glanced briefly at Fumio and continued: "No. I'm not busy." Fumio took another sip from his coffee and pretended he couldn't hear a thing. The coffee was less hot now. Tatsuya sat back on the bed and brought his legs up, resting his head against the headboard. "Just getting ready to take a bath. What are you doing?" Tatsuya glanced at his watch with a look of impatience. Fumio pretended not to see. "Oh? All alone? At this time of night?" There was a subtle desperation in Tatsuya's expression which Fumio found himself relishing. A glow like that which suffuses the body after a good meal warmed him from inside. "No, there's no one here with me." Again, Tatsuya looked at Fumio. "I told you before and I'm telling you now that I'm all alone. Who else would be here at this time of night?"

The person on the other end spoke for a long time after this, and Fumio watched the shades of troubled anxiety which passed across Tatsuya's face in succession.

"Listen. You probably don't know how foolish you're making yourself look. If you keep up with this sort of accusation, you can only succeed in putting me off. No one likes to be suspected of — "

Fumio finished off his coffee and set the cup on the floor. Tatsuya shifted the phone to his other ear. "You sound a little distraught tonight. Listen, I'll call you back when you're in a better mood. Goodbye." He hung up and made a wry expression at Fumio. "Women... "

"You were quite abrupt with her."

"You have to be like that with them sometimes. They let their emotions carry them away, they lose their grip on reason. That's the one thing I can't stand about them."

"You sound like you're ready to break up with her."

"Maybe I am."

"Poor Seiko... "

The look Tatsuya gave him was delicious beyond words; it made everything worthwhile. For Fumio, the whole thing came down to this single moment. A little shakily, Tatsuya retrieved the cigarettes he'd laid aside and pulled one out, lit it with a gold lighter. "So you know." Smoke curled out from between his lips as he said it. Fumio had never seen Tatsuya looked so cowed, and he felt a little sad at his hero's disgrace. Yet the brazen coolness with which Tatsuya had carried on the intimate conversation with Seiko had snapped something inside him — perhaps the desire not to be outdone, to be made a complete fool of. At any rate, he'd blurted it out before he could stop himself.

Tatsuya took a long drag at his cigarette, then exhaled loudly. "Well, it looks like the secret is out. I suppose I've acted like an idiot, playing around with my friend's wife." He spoke the words as if he were reciting lines that had been scripted for this moment.

"Don't be regretful on that account. You know I'm gay. She gets nothing out of our marriage; it's a farce."

"Does she know you're gay?"

Fumio nodded. "I told her."

"This is amazing. I don't know what to say. Do you mean to say you didn't mind being betrayed by her, that you didn't track me down here because of — "

"I do feel as if I've been betrayed. But not by her."

Tatsuya stared at him. Fumio went on, trying to keep his voice from sounding shrill: "I thought you cared for me. Even a little."

"Why? Because I consented to spend the night with you the other night? Don't be foolish. I was only doing a job."

"It was only a job for you? There was never any more feeling for me than that?"

"Fumio, I don't like men in that way. You know that. I like you as a friend. But anything beyond that is impossible for me. I can only love women."

"Then love Seiko."

"What?"

"She's infatuated with you. She'd do anything for you. Stay with her. You have my permission."

"What are you talking about, Fumio?"

"If it's money you're after, don't worry about it. There are ways. There are always ways. I can get it for you without her even finding out. The *juku* can pay for it. I can always tell the professor that it's going to a mistress. He'll understand, even condone it, provided I stay married to Seiko."

"This is impossible."

"If you don't want to continue it as an affair, that's all right. At your word, Seiko will elope with you. She'll throw away our marriage at your slightest command. She'll do anything you say. Instead of this playing around, we could come open, let Seiko choose to be with the man she loves, free her from the bondage of being married to a homosexual who can never give her love or happiness. She can divorce me and marry you. Then you can have everything I have, everything I look forward to getting: the house, the land, the *juku*, the money. As for me, I'm willing to throw everything away if you just give the word: my marriage, my career, my pride... everything!"

An ecstatic look had transfigured Fumio's face. He wore the expression of someone who has seen a vision: nothing less than a glimpse of his ultimate purpose in life. For he had a sudden foretaste of the joys he would experience in the role of the betrayed husband, wallowing in the most shameful humiliation a man could experience. But for him, it would be the source of his greatest delight, because he knew that Tatsuya would forever be in his debt: he would owe everything — his entire happiness — to Fumio... and what greater gift could one give to the man he loved? Fumio could now fulfill the tragic heroine's dream and enjoy, for the rest of his life, a masturbatory contemplation of the sacrifice he'd made of it.

"But why?" There was a horrified look on Tatsuya's face.

"Don't you know? You're the only one I've ever cared about, and will ever care about. Everything I have now is a joke, a meaningless joke, without you. Just give me the word, Tatsuya. Your happiness is all that matters to me, and I'll do anything for it. You're the only one I'll ever love."

Tatsuya had gotten to his feet. "I think you should leave now, Fumio."

"But I haven't had your answer yet. I've just started talking to you."

"I've heard enough. Go." Tatsuya was now advancing threateningly upon him.

Fumio reached for his wallet. "Listen. I've got money. I can pay for your time. Consider it a short-time. I just want to talk." He clutched a handful of 10,000-yen bills and held them out. Tatsuya knocked them out of his hands, and when the bills had fluttered to the floor, grabbed them up and flung them back in Fumio's face.

"Get out before I call the police."

"Good. I'll tell them all about how you planned to blackmail us all. Wasn't that your scheme from the start?" Fumio found himself shoved back, slammed against the edge of the opened door, then outside in the chill of night. The door slammed in his face, and he heard the lock click into place. He closed his eyes and lowered his head until his forehead touched the cold steel of the door. He could hear nothing. Tatsuya seemed a thousand kilometers away, at the farthest end of the earth. And nothing in the world would now get Fumio past this door. It was closed forever.

17

"AKIYOSHI SEIKO-SAN," announced the nurse at the window in an official-sounding voice, even though Fumio and Seiko were obviously the only ones in the waiting room.

"Yes." Seiko got up and handed Fumio the magazine she'd been reading. "I'll be right back."

"All right." He watched his wife go off down the narrow corridor beside the counter toward the examination room in the back. The nurse at the window left her post to help the doctor attend to Seiko. Left all alone in the waiting room, Fumio felt a keen craving for a smoke, but managed to suppress it. Instead, he began flipping through the magazine he'd been handed, a women's weekly full of travel articles, cooking hints, and gossip. Seiko had been engrossed in an article about Yasuda Manami, and he now began reading it.

As always, whenever he came across Manami in the media, Fumio peered closely at her photograph to try to discover any resemblance between the glamorous actress in dark sunglasses and the young girl he'd known as Mayumi. There was none. Back when they'd been room-mates, he had often seen her without any make-up, her hair up in curlers, her feet on the table, picking her nose. But the actress in the photograph was an elevated being who had nothing in common with his own world. She was the reigning commercial queen on TV, the biggest-selling commodity this year, whose advertising spots for a brand of canned coffee, a travel agency, a car maker, and a cup-noodle company had made her face instantly recognizable to the public. In reading the article about her, Fumio was merely becoming one more of the millions who were following her exploits in the press. In the entertainment media, she had for some reason — perhaps as part of the image created for her by her production company — been endowed with a cloak of purity, immune even to charges that she'd been having an affair with the director of her latest movie. The public loved her and she could do no wrong. The critics even sided with her against the estranged wife of the director, making the latter out to be a conniving shrew who had made life hell for her husband.

But apparently that scandal was now destined to fade into obscurity, if the title of the article, 'Happy Ending', was any indication. "Wedding bells seem to be in the offing for Yasuda Manami (24), the star of such smash hits as *Faraway Island* and *Strawberry Kiss,* and the singer of numerous Top Ten singles. The reigning commercial queen is finally on the verge of 'goal-in'. The man she's been in love with all along, who has waited patiently through all the months of her fame, can at last claim his deserved prize. Our intrepid photographer succeeded in snapping this pic of the true man in Manami's life, an up-and-coming young actor named Shimazaki Ken."

Fumio felt a sharp pang as he examined the photo of Tatsuya with his new name underneath it. Actors who'd had no credited roles yet, or entrepreneurs whose businesses weren't disclosed, were a staple of entertainment news; one always learned of them first in an article about the suddenly-announced marriage of an actress or songstress. Fumio knew that Mayumi's production company had probably engineered the whole thing in order to clean up her image in the eyes of the public, who always delighted in a 'true love' angle. Once she was rehabilitated as a member of straight, married society, she could get on with her lucrative career.

As for Tatsuya, he was sure to get some exposure at first, if for nothing else than the fact that he was Yasuda Manami's husband. The press conference after the wedding should be enough to cement his image in the public's mind. The production company probably wouldn't go all out in an extravagant televised wedding; Manami wasn't quite that big yet, and her recent scandal had cast a slight shadow over the proceedings. Still, Tatsuya was sure to get a firm foot into the entertainment world. Perhaps this was all the result of careful planning on Tatsuya's part, too, the culmination of a carefully constructed strategy. And yet Fumio was still haunted by the thought that, in her heart of hearts, Mayumi might indeed cherish some feeling for Tatsuya. She might even love him, in her own fashion.

Tatsuya, too, might have endured true agony during the months away from her. He was always one to make light of the things which really mattered to him. Fumio felt the familiar flames of jealousy lick through him. The moments he'd spent with Tatsuya now seemed a distant dream, unreachable except through memory. For Tatsuya had now entered the ultimate world of illusion: the entertainment industry. The only contact Fumio could have with him henceforth was through the television screen, CD covers, or weekly magazines...

The other side of the apartment wall had become public domain, and Fumio had been joined at the peephole by the whole world.

"Sorry to have kept you waiting." Seiko had just returned to the waiting room. Fumio stood up, thrusting the magazine aside. He paid the nurse at the window, and together with Seiko, bowed his thanks.

"Please take care of yourself," intoned the nurse mechanically as the young couple left the clinic. Their car was parked just outside. As soon as they were safely inside it, Fumio turned to Seiko.

"Well?"

She nodded, a little solemnly.

Fumio felt relief and joy flood him. "Everything all right?"

"Everything is fine."

"That's good." A radiant tenderness replaced the steady feeling of dread which had been bothering him all morning. "That's wonderful. We'll have to notify Sensei immediately."

"No, not just yet." Seiko's serious expression could hardly mask the joy she felt. "Let's keep it to ourselves for a little while longer before breaking it to anyone else. I want to bask in this joy without interference, and savor it, at least for the rest of the afternoon."

"All right." Without feeling any self-consciousness, he reached over and let his hand come to rest on her belly. She allowed it to rest there for a few moments before gently placing her own hand over his. To all outward appearances, they were a young couple deeply in love, basking in the first flush of married happiness.

"I hope it turns out to be a boy," said Fumio, like any newly-informed father.

"Me, too. In fact, I'm sure it will. Somehow I just know it."

"Do you think he'll resemble — ?"

"I'm sure of it. I do hope so."

They smiled at each other for a moment, and Seiko went on: "I'm glad you're taking it like this. I admit I was a little afraid that you might become jealous at the critical moment, even though we were both prepared for it."

"Don't be silly. Why should I? You're carrying the baby I could never bear. You are my closest link to him."

"It's funny — this child will have two fathers."

"And two mothers. I want to mother him, too, you know."

Fumio felt happy at the thought that they would both be able to watch over Tatsuya's son, to cherish and nurture this living souvenir of the man they both still loved... a solid symbol of their combined love, one who would never again run away from them.

Fumio grinned. "I wonder what Father's reaction will be when he notices the boy's looks."

"Oh, he won't even notice. He'll be such a doting grandfather that he won't even wonder about any lack of resemblance. But it's Mother I'm more worried about. Sometimes I think she knows a lot more than she lets on, as if she can see through every illusion or lie."

"Something tells me she wouldn't mind — even if she knew the true story. As long as our family is together, and happy, what does a little thing like that matter?"

"What, indeed?"

Fumio had started up the car and was pulling out into the narrow street in front of the clinic. The university campus across the street was a quiet, wooded sanctuary with all the calm repose of a temple's grounds. The sky above was slightly overcast; the weather report this morning had indicated a slight chance of rain.

"I'm hungry," said Seiko. "Why don't we go to a family restaurant for lunch? I don't feel like cooking. And I'd like to have a filling meal."

"Sure," said Fumio. "There's a Skylark Restaurant just down the street. Does a hamburger steak sound inviting?"

"Yes!"

"After all, you have to eat for two now, not just yourself."

"Silly," smiled Seiko. "You sound just like Mother now." She settled back contentedly against the seat cushions and languidly squirmed her back muscles.

— THE END —